"THERE SHE IS," HE SAID. "THERE'S MY WILD CHILD."

Morgan dropped her eyes. She liked him—liked his heat, wanted it to stay there, close to her, warming her, but her eyes kept returning to her brother and his pizza-slinging girlfriend. The couple looked so—disgusting, Morgan managed to think before she swerved back to him.

"Shut up and kiss me," she said, even though Moth hadn't been saying anything.

"Wait." He placed his head close to her ear and whispered. "I have something to tell you." He tugged at her earlobe with his teeth and she shivered. "Do you want to know about the Ring of Fire?"

Morgan felt her body soften to the handsome boy.

"Is that . . . the party? Around the—"

"Solstice," Moth instructed. "Your birthday." Moth's breath smelled like sugar and . . . more sugar.

"My—" Morgan was confused. Her birthday wasn't until September.

"Sshh." Moth's hiss was wet against her ear. "It's a secret. Secret solstice, secret day." He cupped her chin, turned her head until their eyes met. "Shhh." He placed a finger on his lips. "Don't worry. You'll know when the time comes."

BETWIXT

TARA BRAY SMITH

poppy

LITTLE, BROWN AND COMPANY
New York   Boston

Poppy

Hachette Book Group
237 Park Avenue, New York, NY 10017
For more of your favorite series, go to www.pickapoppy.com

Poppy is an imprint of Little, Brown Books for Young Readers.
The Poppy name and logo are trademarks of Hachette Book Group, Inc

First Paperback Edition: January 2009
First published in hardcover in October 2007 by Little, Brown and Company

Library of Congress Cataloging-in-Publication Data

Smith, Tara Bray.
  Betwixt / Tara Bray Smith. — 1st ed.
    p. cm.
  Summary: Three alienated teenagers are drawn to a strange outdoor concert in the woods outside of Seattle, where they discover that they possess magical powers and that their destinies are intertwined.
  ISBN 978-0-316-10693-1 (paperback) / ISBN 978-0-316-06033-2 (hardcover)
  [1. Supernatural—Fiction. 2. Seattle (Wash.)—Fiction.] I. Title.
  PZ7.S659435Be 2007
  [Fic]—dc22

                                                              2007026924

10 9 8 7 6 5 4 3 2

RRD-C

Printed in the United States of America

Book design by Tracy Shaw

For anyone who has wandered.

So quick bright things come to confusion.

—William Shakespeare,
A Midsummer Night's Dream

I

MOTH TO A FLAME

Chapter 1

ONDINE MASON HATED BUTTERFLIES. That wasn't true. She just hated orange butterflies. No, that wasn't true either. What she really hated were the orange butterflies painted on her blue ceiling, the ones she was staring at as she tried to wake up.

They seemed to move. One moved. Ondine could swear one moved. One had a woman's head. It looked at her. Not cruelly, just *coolly*. As if it were studying her. It crawled off the ceiling and flew away.

"Ondine!"

That would be Ralph.

She pressed her fingers to her eyelids. Everything that had been orange turned blue, and all that was blue, orange. The effect was called the afterimage. She had learned about it in Raphael Inman's summer art class. The afterimage appeared after you stared at something for a long time then shut your eyes, proving Ondine's long-held feeling that what was real was part in the world and part in her head. A butterfly, after all, had just flown out of a painting.

This didn't happen in the real world. But part of Ondine knew that it didn't really matter what happened in the real world. What mattered was what she saw. There was a real world in the afterimage, too, just a different one, intense but momentary.

She kept her fingers there until the stars came and her eyes began to hurt.

The butterflies looked like orange eggs stacked on each other, split by cigars. They were awkward and childish and they made Ondine feel embarrassed. She and her mother, Trish, had painted them a long time ago, when she was eight and Trish, an architect, had just finished renovating the house on Northeast Schuyler. Her father, Ralph, had set up a scaffold and she and her mother painted lying down on their backs, as Ondine imagined Michelangelo had in the Sistine Chapel. They wore head scarves so they wouldn't get paint in their hair, and they transformed the whole ceiling into a jungle set against windless blue. In it they placed a panther, a bald eagle, a monkey, and a tiny white mouse hidden in the corner — she felt the panther needed company — all interspersed with bright bursts of orange butterflies set among green leaves.

"Très Rousseau," her mother had said. Ondine didn't know what it meant, but it sounded good. She had loved butterflies then.

4

"Ondine, get your butt out of bed and come down and help your mother!"

She looked at the clock. Ten-twelve. In exactly three minutes, fifteen minutes after Ralph Mason had told his only daughter he wanted her downstairs to go over last-minute details of the move (the Masons were supposed to be on the road by noon), he would be pissed. Though *pissed* was a relative term with Ralph. Ondine's father was a mild-mannered man, more scientist (which is what he was) than domineering dad. When Ralph got pissed, he set things down in an aggressive way, like his cup of coffee. Ondine could just see him now, really placing that mug down like he *meant it, young lady.*

She was going to miss him.

She was also going to miss Trish. Even Max she'd miss, though she wouldn't miss taking Max's mangy terrier, Ivy, to the park every day while her precious little brother had his cello lessons.

This was because Trish and Ralph and Max were moving to Chicago.

Ondine was not.

And this made her hate butterflies even more.

Ten-fourteen. She yanked on a pair of her father's old scrubs and headed down the stairs.

∽ ∽ ∽

"So, Ellen and Mark are just next door, and you know you can always call the Harrises, and your first trip to Chicago is in just a month. Honey, are you sure you want to do this?"

Trish Mason was not looking at her daughter when she spoke. She was looking out the dining room window at the Japanese maple, whose new leaves were shooting pinky-red arrows toward a mercury-colored midmorning sky.

Her mother, Ondine knew, was crying. Trish always cried. Ondine, never. It wasn't that she didn't feel sad. She just couldn't seem to get the tear ducts working when they should. Her throat would swell, her cheeks flush, she'd feel awful, but nothing would come out. When she was younger she'd practice with Visine, just to see what it felt like to have tears cascading down her cheeks, but since she wasn't much of a pretender and carrying around Visine made her look like a twelve-year-old pothead, Ondine became known as the girl who didn't cry. It made her popular on her soccer team — and scared in private. She told no one and allowed people to chalk it up to her naturally stoic nature.

Her mother flexed her fingers and put a hand to her eyes.

"We're going to miss you, you know."

"I know," Ondine replied, and reached across the dining room table.

Here is what Trish was crying about: The Masons had decided to go to Chicago for a year. Dr. Mason, an obstetrician turned in vitro pioneer turned geneticist, had gotten a yearlong research grant at the Chicago office of Xelix Labs, the genetics think tank based in Portland. The family — Trish and Max, that is — had decided to go with him. Trish, originally from the Midwest, wanted a change of scenery and had clients in Chicago. Max, a cellist, wanted to study at Spenser Conservatory. Ondine had asked to stay, to the surprise of her parents, though they were used to their only daughter being headstrong. She wanted to finish high school with her friends, she said. She also wanted to study with Raphael Inman, the legendary Portland art star who had returned from New York and was now teaching at Reed. That was usually how it went, Ondine going in the opposite direction from her family. She didn't know why; it just did.

She squeezed her mother's left hand, and Trish's wedding ring of twenty years — three years older than Ondine — glowed in the sun.

"Are you sure *you* want to do this?"

Trish sighed. "No. But it would really help if you wouldn't be so pigheaded and come."

Ondine twisted in her wooden chair. "I told you. I'm not going to some whack-ass suburban school in — what's it called? Glencoe? — for my senior year." She could hear her own childishness. She was normally calmer, but now . . . now she had to act like a brat. It would help them leave. "I'm not the one who decided to take the sabbatical in Chicago — Dad did. And you

7

and Max wanted to go with him. But my life is here, Mom." She looked at her mother. "You decided to go. Remember? We all sat around this table" — she tapped the dark wood and it sounded in the open room — "and we voted, and Dad wanted to get the grant, and Max said he wanted to be in a city with a better symphony, and you wanted to be closer to Nana, and Vita is in Chicago, and you liked that stuffy Glencoe with all of its antique shops —"

Trish, used to her daughter's bossiness, laughed and covered her long, narrowish face with her hands. Tall and slender, her mother could pass for thirty-five, Ondine thought, though she was almost fifty. Only recently had she begun to go gray, and the white strands traced her mother's black hair like snow on dark branches.

"Evanston, Ondine. We're in Evanston. Not the same thing."

"Ooh, I know what's gonna happen," Ondine went on. "When I come you're gonna be wearing a fur coat, and we're gonna have a butler in our mansion in Glenkillyoursoul —"

Trish stood and kissed her daughter on the crown of her head and then pinched the back of her neck.

"I'm getting another cup of coffee, and that one's from Max. You're going to miss him, Miss I-Don't-Need-No-One."

"Huh." Ondine blinked.

"You want one?"

"You know I don't drink Starbucks."

"No, you just eat the ice cream."

"Not fair!"

Trish called back from the kitchen. "No, baby, that's your problem."

Ondine looked out the dining room window at the maple in the backyard. Her parents had planted it a few days after they brought Ondine home from the hospital. They called it their baby tree. Now it was full grown.

It had started to sprinkle — early summer was often rainy in Portland — and the branches were black and slick. The tree's leaves were sprouting; the spears that emerged from the crooked branches hinted at the fullness of the summer tree. There was an awkwardness about the tree, though. Dwarf Japanese maples were small and packed, as if there were too much activity for the spindly limbs to handle. Like Ondine herself: petite and delicate — peaked caramel-colored face, bright mouth, pointy limbs — in a family of stately pines.

And her eyes, violet, like the sky before a storm. Ralph and Trish had brown eyes. Max's were hazel. But Ondine. No, Ondine's eyes had to be *purple,* wide set, and heavily lashed. Beyoncé and Yoda's love child. Dr. Mason couldn't even try to explain that one.

"Sweetheart." Ralph kissed his daughter on the top of her head and placed a mug of coffee in front of her. His face was paler from winter and she loved the way the freckles splashed across it like mud on a Portland sidewalk. "Everything's pretty much packed, doll."

"Thanks, Dad."

Though her father knew she didn't drink Starbucks, he was absentminded and anyway, it smelled so good this morning. Ondine thought of all the mornings ahead when Ralph wouldn't be making coffee, and though she had told herself she wouldn't, her throat swelled. She took a sip to quell it and looked up. A key ring looped around his bony fingers.

"Here are the keys — car, house, garage. Jesus. I just can't believe you're not coming. What's your mother going to do?"

He took his daughter's hand. "Are you sure about this?"

Her sadness just made her more certain.

"The class at Reed this summer is the most important thing I can do for my art. Raphael Inman is teaching. He *never* teaches. I told you there was no way I could miss it. And next year's senior year. I can't switch schools for my senior year."

She stopped, swallowing the rush of words that she knew probably sounded more like justification than anything else. Still, Ralph and Trish bought it. Most people did. Ondine could convince almost anyone to do almost anything.

Her father matched her silence. He was an affectionate man, and always told Ondine that he loved her, but living in a house with two strong women made him quiet at times. He looked into his daughter's eyes as if he would be able to locate what made her so stubborn.

"We're going to miss you."

She pressed her hands into her knees and rubbed them.

"Dad —," she managed to respond. "Don't make me change my mind."

"Then don't do this, honey. There are lots of good programs in Chicago. The best school in the country is at the Art Institute —"

How many times had Ralph Mason looked at her in just this way, trying to read what was behind her velvety eyes? He couldn't. Ondine was a normal young woman, a budding painter, a bratty sister (at times), a good daughter, a great friend to the people she chose to trust. And though he had been there at her birth — delivered her, in fact — there was something untouchable about the girl that even her own father could not get at.

She traced circles on the dining room table, where the Mason family had set their coffee mugs so many times before.

"Dad, I —"

She couldn't tell him about the dreams she'd been having: the butterflies, the strange women. She couldn't tell him about the way the things she painted sometimes, if they were good enough, true enough, had a way of lifting off the canvas and floating away.

"Nice bed head."

Max Mason walked in the back door with Ivy. He was a solidly built thirteen-year-old — Ondine thought a little pudgy, though he seemed to have slimmed down in recent months — and he was wearing his typical weekend outfit of a white hazardous waste–removal suit. He had begged his father to get him one from Xelix, and Ralph, perplexed yet strangely moved by his son's oddity, had.

"Yo, Pop! I'm ready!" Max's round, wire-rimmed glasses had fogged up in the early June chill. That combined with his leftover preadolescent tummy and his long arms and legs reminded Ondine of a jellyfish, all eyes and jiggling limbs. She watched her father's face lighten.

"All right, son."

"Max, honey, are you ready to go?" Trish came out with yet another cup of coffee for Ondine, looked at her son, and shook her head. "That suit's going to be uncomfortable in the car."

He shrugged and grinned, but he was staring at Ondine.

"What?" She tipped her chin and fingered a loosening braid.

"You're actually sad."

"Your dog stinks."

"You are," he retorted through a stuffed nose. "I can tell."

"Honey." Trish turned to Ralph. "Did you give her the folder?"

"Oh, right." Ralph got up from the table and picked up the

manila folder containing numbers his daughter would never call, insurance cards she would never use. Ondine had not visited a doctor since her childhood inoculations. She never had a sniffle, an ache or a pain, a bruise or a scratch. She took the folder and wondered whether her father — like she did — hoped that, just once, she would come up with a scraped knee, or would tell her parents her throat was sore and she didn't feel well enough for school today. Or would fall and break something: nose, collarbone, pinkie nail. Anything to prove she was indeed a creature of flesh, blood, and bone.

"Well —" Ralph put his cup down and twisted it so that the Xelix Labs logo squared with the edge of the table. Ondine knew it was her cue. It was time for the Masons to leave. She looked at her family gathered there in the half-light of morning, the maple behind them.

"Max, I will miss you," she began slowly, getting up from the table. "And I will miss you, Mom, and I will miss you, Dad." She pronounced the words carefully, formally. "But I'm staying here."

Her mother put her hand to her eyes again. Ralph looked out the window.

"Maybe you'll come at the end of summer?" Max asked.

Ondine nodded. She thought of her butterfly, lifting soundlessly off the ceiling. Of the pale gelatinous tentacles of Max the jellyfish, corkscrewing from an even whiter canvas.

"I'll visit."

Ralph cleared his throat. "Well, I guess we'd better get on the road then. Max, you ready?"

"Yeah, Dad. I'm all set."

Ondine embraced her father, hugged her mother and kissed her neck — she smelled like wood and flowers — and felt she would melt the whole time. She went over to her brother and put her arm around him even though he was bigger than she was. The shiny white polyester of his silly suit crinkled in her grasp.

"Yeah, I'm sad, Max. I am actually sad. I'm human, aren't I?"

∽ ∽ ∽

FOR TWENTY MINUTES SHE LAY ON HER BED. There was movement downstairs — voices, footsteps, doors opening and closing — but she had said her good-byes. Ondine was like that. Once a decision had been made, she tended not to look back, and her family knew her well enough to respect that. Till then she liked to take time with her thoughts — like waking out of a dream is how they seemed to her. Ideas appeared as if by paint-by-numbers. A bit here, a bit there. Then the whole thing would cohere and she'd have made up her mind. Until then it was all just shapes and colors.

Ralph and Trish wouldn't come up anymore. When she heard the garage door groan and the U-Haul back onto N.E.

Schuyler's quiet morning street, she knelt on her bed and watched her parents drive away.

A bird chirped. It had started to rain. Ondine lay down again, feeling weirdly calm. It was a Saturday in early June. School had ended a few weeks ago and she didn't quite know what she'd do now.

She picked up her cell and dialed a number she knew by heart.

"Hey," she began after a few moments. "Yeah, they just left."

The person on the other end said something and Ondine sighed. "I don't know, sad." She switched the phone to her other ear, leaning toward the window. "Yeah, maybe that is just the thing. Tonight though? So soon?"

She nodded. "All right. Call me at five. We'll figure out what to do then."

She lay back down underneath the butterflies and watched the pieces collect.

Chapter 2

J ACOB CLOWES WAS NOT AN UNFEELING MAN, but the eighteen-year-old punk holding the dishwasher's nozzle irked him. There he was now, thick black hair falling into his eyes, spraying a plate. He worked too slowly. He smoked when Jacob wasn't in the kitchen. Just then the room smelled of cigarettes. Dishwashers weren't supposed to care, he knew — Jacob had been a dishwasher once — but this one made his knees watery with anger.

That goddamned name. Nix. Who the hell had a name like that?

"Nix!" Jacob yelled over the din of the industrial machine. The boy pretended not to hear him. "Nix Saint-Michael!"

Nix looked up, then down again.

Punk. Jacob didn't like the way Nix worked, eyes half closed, almost asleep, yet walking and waking. Holding the nozzle with one hand, with the other — barely — a ceramic plate you'd think was heavy as plutonium.

"It's clean, Nix. The plate is clean."

Nothing.

In the beginning it had been that Nix was late. Now he was on time, but he moved so slowly that they were always running out of soda glasses. So now they were giving refills to save glasses, and Jacob didn't want to give refills. This wasn't a goddamned *Friday's,* for chrissakes. This was Jacob's Pizza. This was the oldest New York–style pizza establishment in once-groovily bohemian, now-gentrified Northwest Portland.

"Am I talking to myself? I believe there is a dishwasher here named Nix Saint-Michael, who I am trying to communicate with. Earth to Nix. We need some goddamned soda glasses!"

"Pop."

Nix spoke too softly for Jacob to hear him over the cranking hum and his thick black hair obscured his eyes, but Jacob could see what his mouth was saying and it pissed him off.

"Excuse me?"

"It's called pop here," Nix repeated under his breath. "Never mind. Just give me five, man."

"What do you think this is? A fucking old folks' home?" Jacob ignored the correction. "I don't have *five,* Nix. I don't even have *one.* I need those soda glasses *now.*"

Jacob Clowes was used to punks. He spoke the language, knew that Nix wouldn't respect him unless he was a bit of an asshole, so he played it that way. He had been a punk himself. A punk kid from Brooklyn who had moved out to Portland in the seventies. He had hated the rich yuppies once they started moving in during the eighties, but the businessman in him — the one whose daughter, Neve, now attended that liberal (but still freakishly expensive) private day school, *Penwick*, and whose wife, Amanda, a former experimental dancer/macrobiotic cook/Reiki healer who had discovered the joy of expensive wine — depended on Jacob's Pizza.

And tonight, like it or not, Jacob's Pizza depended on Nix.

Anyway, he kind of liked the kid. He knew Nix squatted up in the park. He knew there were dark scenes in the family, somewhere in Alaska. Nix wore long-sleeved black T-shirts, but Jacob could imagine the places where the boy cut himself. A lot of the kids he had hired over the years were into that kind of thing. He may not have been able to change them, but he helped them, gave them jobs, talked to them after their shifts, gave them rides home. Sometimes he and Amanda had them over for dinner, and some of the girls babysat for Neve a few times when she was a kid.

There were always the ones that fell through the cracks, though.

"Hey, punk. I told you to get those glasses through the washer ten fucking minutes ago. What are you doing?"

Nicholas Saint-Michael did not look up. It wasn't that he didn't want to. He liked Jacob. Jacob was, in fact, the best boss Nix had ever had since he first started hauling spruce chips for

18

Frank Shadwell back in Sitka when he was nine years old. That was another life, though, and in this one, he knew better.

Jacob repeated himself. "What the hell are you doing?"

Nix kept his eyes down. He couldn't look at Jacob. Physically couldn't. The man had a light around him so bright Nix had to keep his eyes closed or his back turned whenever his boss was in the room.

"What is going on?"

He set the plate down and let go of the handle of the spray nozzle.

"Man, I can't do this job anymore."

Even with his eyes half closed, Nix could see the light, blinding and painful as the sun, around the saggy sides of Jacob's faded black jeans.

"What did you say?"

"I said I can't do this anymore." He brought his hand to his brow to wipe back a slash of black hair, staring at the water and the soap swirling. Jacob's reflection shimmered in the sink, but the light wasn't in the reflection — they didn't show up there, he'd noticed — and so he spoke to Jacob's watery mirror image.

"Man, I just wash the dishes."

"Yeah?"

Nix felt the man come closer, reach over the pool of water, pull the nozzle out of his hand. He let him, though he shrunk back as Jacob's hand approached.

19

"No, Nix. You act like a dishwasher. You assume the pose of a dishwasher. But a dishwasher you are not. A dishwasher would wash the fucking dishes."

"Right." Nix's eyes stayed on the water. He wanted to meet Jacob's gaze, show him that he could do it, keep the job, make the owner happy. The dude had tried. Nix knew he had tried.

He forced himself to look up.

"I'm just messing you up."

"Messing *me* up?"

The man's face had hardened into a mask of disappointment. The wide mouth a ruddy dash; his dark, close-set eyes flat under frizzed black-brown eyebrows. And the fire all around him even brighter now, incinerating.

The closer they got the more they burned.

Nix looked away. "I can't stay."

"What did you say?"

"I said I can't stay. I'm bad for you."

Again Jacob moved closer and Nix watched a blazing hand approach his shoulder. He jerked away.

"What's going on?"

How could he explain something he himself could not understand?

"Jacob, man. I'm no good."

"Look, if you're hooked on dust, kid, we can work something —"

"Naw, naw. That's not it."

These cloaks of light, Nix had seen them before. Lately they had gotten bolder, more violent. That girl up at the squat who got her throat slit, dumped somewhere out toward Bend. The man Nix saw on the Burnside bus, killed in a holdup two weeks later. All those people on the road down from Alaska.

It had happened to Frank Shadwell before Nix's mother, Bettina, had done what she'd done. If Nix had stayed in Sitka, it would have happened to Bettina, too. Now the light devoured Jacob, and Nix couldn't look at him because he was afraid it was his own mind causing the fire.

He shook his head and spoke to the floor.

"I gotta go."

Jacob sighed. "Go take a break and smoke a cigarette or something and calm down. I'll cover for you while you're gone." He started to move behind the sink to take Nix's place.

"Man. I told you. I'm no good."

"Nix, take a friggin' break and come back and do your job."

"No." He let go of the nozzle. The fire diminished. It calmed him, made him more certain that he needed to leave. "I'm just fucking you up."

"What?" Jacob asked. "What are you talking about?"

Nix started to walk out of the kitchen, but stopped. He couldn't just leave. He owed it to the man. When he finally looked up, Jacob looked confused and sad.

"You tried, man. You tried."

"I don't know what you're talking about." Jacob shook his head. "But suit yourself, Nix."

"I think I will."

He had to say it. He had to make Jacob think he was a punk kid, an asshole with an attitude. A prick. A tweaker. Someone you didn't want around.

The slice he took on his way out of the kitchen—artichoke hearts and feta, Yuppie's Delight, Jacob called it—would get him through till tomorrow.

ↄ∽   ↄ∽   ↄ∽

IN SITKA IT HAD GONE THAT WAY, TOO.

Nix walked down the sidewalks of Northwest Portland toward the forest that crowned downtown like a shaggy head of hair, and he thought about Alaska. He hadn't let himself think about home often since he'd left, but in the last few weeks since Jacob had gotten the light, Nix had been thinking about his mother.

Bettina Saint-Michael had been the prettiest Indian to come out of Sitka's Mt. Edgecumbe High School since no one knew how long. Or that's what the white principal had said when he tried to pick her up at the grocery store she worked at after graduation. Bettina wasn't having any of it. She rang up Principal Harkin's mayonnaise; his cans of salmon (caught somewhere out in that water she looked at every afternoon while trying to picture what life was like across it); his white bread; his canned green beans; and the bottle of vodka Bettina knew was for Abby Harkin, his drunk wife; and ignored him when he said they should meet for lunch at Koloskov's Diner on her break to discuss college plans. Bettina knew what Principal Harkin was after and it had nothing to do with her fine Indian mind.

"Nicholas," Bettina had said to her only child many years later, "you treat women right, you respect them for what they know, and they will open up to you like flowers in springtime."

Bettina had laughed when she said that. She was undoing her hair from work at the cannery, and while she spoke, she ran her fingers through the soft dark-brown strands.

Nix loved to hear his mother laugh. She started like a bird, little pulses of high cool notes, and ended with her head thrown back, her hands holding her stomach. She would bang the table or the wall or whatever she happened to be next to and tickle her son and nuzzle and kiss him. She smelled like woodsmoke and fish and coffee.

That time so many years ago Bettina had laughed not because it was funny, but because she had to. Otherwise things would have been too sad. That winter was a long one. It was the first year she stopped putting in a summer garden, the year Daddy Saint-Michael had died and Bettina and Nix were left alone.

"Did you hear me, son? Treat a woman right and . . ." She trailed off, fingers still touching her hair.

Daddy Saint-Michael was Nix's grandfather, and he loved Bettina and her son more than anything in the world. Nothing was good enough for Bettina. Which somehow made Bettina think that she was not good enough for anything.

Nix, pudgy, saucer-eyed, was the son of a ghost who passed through Sitka on his way to somewhere else. Bettina didn't talk about him except to say that he had been her first love, and that he was smart and sad, and that he played Ann Peebles's "I Can't Stand the Rain" on Koloskov's jukebox the summer night they met.

He figured his father had worked for the mill or the fisheries, seasonal help like everyone else. Which would explain why Bettina always shimmered during the warm months, even in a town that slept for three quarters of the year. He figured he was Aleut, too, from somewhere farther west, because Nix himself was dark haired, dark eyed, full cheeked, and stockier than his mother, had thick hambone muscles when he was eight that he tried to hide under the parkas his mother was always buying him from hippie friends who had made their way to Sitka from California or wherever.

"Hello, little brother," they'd say with a straight face.

"You're not my brother," Nix once retorted. Bettina slapped him for that one.

By that time, the halos (he took to calling them, though only to himself — he never told anyone about the rings he saw) were already starting to appear. On strangers, blurry at first, as if he were losing his sight. Nix even asked Bettina for glasses. They started as a vibration, a slight fuzziness around the edges. He began to look at people, watch them. First the signs were subtle. How that old friend of Bettina's — his name was Jerry Klein but he went by Raven in Sitka — how Raven had turned silvery before Nix's eyes before he died of cancer. Then Mary Ives's little baby, turning blue in her crib. Mary so sad she didn't have another one and started to stand outside the bar down by the harbor, winter and summer both, bumming menthols, which turned to quarters, which turned to entreaties to take a pretty little Indian home.

Bettina and Nix moved into Frank Shadwell's house when Nix turned ten. Shadwell lived out near where the forests started, so Bettina didn't go into town as much as she used to. Nix worked for Shadwell at his mill; his mother cooked and watched satellite TV, and Shadwell peeled back the mask he had put on and turned into the mean drunk he'd always been.

He hit Bettina and called her a fat 'skimo whore only when he was drinking, but he was drunk often enough that Bettina didn't leave the house for fear of showing her old friends her face and neck. Nix's hatred of the man was clear and cold as a midwinter morning. He knew there was nothing he could do to Frank Shadwell, or for his mother, as long as Bettina stayed. All he could do was stare, his black eyes frozen, and wish his stepfather were gone. Sometimes, despite himself, Nix looked at his mother the same way.

That's when the light hit Shadwell. So fast and bright, Nix knew it wasn't a problem with his vision.

He tried to be good around the house, tried to calm things when Bettina and Shadwell started fighting, but every day the light around his stepfather gathered itself brighter. Then one day, Nix came home from school and Bettina was sitting in the kitchen, Shadwell bloody on the floor. She had shot him at close range, then sat there and waited for her son to come home from school. She said she didn't know what had made her do it. He wasn't drunk and hadn't even tried to hit her, but now he would never do it again. At least that's what she told the police.

Nix sat on a chair beside his mother and listened to her confess. He had wanted to scream that it was his fault. He had wanted to take the blame. He didn't. Nor did he take her hand and tell her that they should run away, like a good son should have, for when he looked at her, he saw the thinnest sliver of light outline his mother's slack shoulders, the ends of her soft fine hair.

He left town on a Greyhound the next day. He was fifteen

years old and had once been to Anchorage for the wedding of one of Bettina's high school friends, but other than that, hadn't been off the island where he was born.

Thousands of miles and Nix didn't know how many buses later he made it to Portland. He stopped in Vancouver; Canadian immigration hassled him and he had to leave. Seattle was too expensive, and he felt more alone there because of all the kids from U. Dub. He didn't know how to do anything besides work in a mill, but because of Shadwell he hated cutting down trees. Though he'd liked school and had been a pretty good student in Sitka, he was a runaway, and getting into the system would mean he'd be sent back up to Anchorage, where his uncles and aunts lived, to watch the people he loved die.

So he wandered. When he didn't know anyone, he didn't care what light they carried. He watched them on buses and in diners, in urinals and on the sides of roads. Bright ones, pale ones, lights strong as streetlamps and soft as match flame. Sometimes he stuck around so he could figure out how long it took for them to die — a few months, sometimes as little as a week or two. He learned to gauge the time based on the brightness and activity of the light. At first, when the light was thin, he thought it meant *maybe* — as in, maybe the wisecracking woman in the vintage mauve sundress and combat boots who worked at the Vancouver hostel had a curable kind of cancer, or maybe the old dude at Elliott Bay Book Company would quit smoking. But it only meant the end was further away; the cancer would take a year to metastasize; the debilitating — and fatal — stroke would come in many months. He'd memorize their faces or their names and then look in the paper for them. But even that made him love them in a way, so he'd leave.

He fell for a girl in Seattle. She worked at a flower stand, sold sweetpeas from her garden, and she never had the light around her, but someday Nix figured she would, so he stopped coming around. He moved and moved again, selling newspapers, dish washing, cleaning bathrooms and offices, delivering drugs — so many lights then — hawking fish, picking berries and apples, and, yes, cutting trees. He even drove an illegal migrant-worker van for a while. He didn't know where the visions came from, but he didn't question them either. Daddy Saint-Michael had once talked about people with the gift; Nix just figured he was one of them.

It felt more like a curse, anyway, but he was used to good things turning bad.

By the time he got to Portland he was tired. He'd been on the road for two years. He was seventeen and he had gotten taller, his wide cheeks sunken from scrounging for food day after day, and walking, always walking. He hadn't decided to stay, exactly; he was just too exhausted to leave.

There *was* something holding him in Portland. Something he didn't understand about the mountains that floated in the distance like faraway islands and the forests just at the edge of downtown, as if another world were on the other side of that blue-gray Oregon sky. He found a group of kids to sleep with in the park. They put up tents and moved around to avoid the cops. Things were clean — the people he was with were good — and no one had the light. No one close to him anyway. He got a job washing dishes at Jacob's: steady work, free food. He started to save money, even bought a book to study for the GED, which he read at night in his tent while the rest of the squat talked about politics and how they were going to hitchhike to Seattle or DC for the next protest. People played music and talked; Nix wrote letters to Bettina, knowing only his uncle in Anchorage would get them, but still feeling the need to let someone know he was alive. He even made a friend down at Jacob's, a straight dude, captain-of-the-soccer-team type who'd been delivering pizza there since he was in ninth grade. His name was K.A. D'Amici, and Nix hung out with him once or twice a week. He liked K.A.'s style, his honesty. He was planning to see him that night, the night he quit.

When the girl at the squat got her throat slit, and Jacob got marked, Nix had been in Portland a little under a year. He had just bought a SpongeBob sleeping bag from Goodwill and had started to feel something like safe. But then, a roll or two of dust every other week helped with that.

෴ ෴ ෴

Nix took a right past what he'd heard was the biggest Doug fir in PDX and down the trail marked with cross-country ski signs. At the split hemlock he veered right, careful to arrange the branches so as not to show the trail. Even a few pass-throughs would reveal where the squat was, and this one was so well hidden they'd already been there three weeks. Portland's cops weren't pigs — they fought crime on mountain bikes — but every so often they did their sweeps so that the Nike/Adidas/Intel nation up in Southwest could have something to talk about over their lattes.

"Yo, Nix! Help me with this radio, son."

Nix looked across the small clearing at the center of the tangle of bush a dozen or so people called home. A blond, skinny boy, about sixteen, with shoulder-length sun-bleached dreadlocks and trimmed Lincoln sideburns sat there in the dimming emerald afternoon. He balanced an old transistor radio on his lap. Finn Terwilliger was the squat's resident mad scientist. Usually he spent his time at the public library downtown, but during the day, when most of the kids were at jobs or hanging out downtown, Finn sometimes volunteered to stay behind at camp — watch the stuff while he worked on his inventions.

Nix had heard Finn's family were some kind of millionaires from down South but he'd never talked to him about it. All he knew was that the kid was cool—and smart. Lately Finn had been working on something he called a crystal radio, which he claimed would pull electricity out of the air. He said the area around Portland was a good place for it — lots of static on account of the mountains.

Nix stood over the boy, who hadn't yet looked up.

"Hey, bro." He clapped him on the back. "Bleek been by?"

Nix was talking about Tim Bleeker, one of Portland's busiest drug dealers. He kept his tone light, though he knew Finn hated the guy, since Bleek used to deal heroin to Finn's girlfriend, Evelyn. Nix also knew that Finn knew about his — habit. The thing for which he didn't have a better name.

Finn shook his head and hunched his shoulders. "Naw, man." He looked up. "Dust?" he asked, and then, almost inaudibly: "Already?"

Nix looked at his shoes. Nut-brown leather boots, twice patched. He'd worn them since Alaska.

"Nix, man, why are you messing with that shit?"

Shrugging, he looked off into the tangle of blackberry and nettle at the edge of his vision. Finn was straight, and even though dust was no stronger than Prozac, Nix knew the boy didn't agree with it — didn't agree with Prozac either, for that matter. Still, it helped Nix sleep and he liked the dreams it gave him. More like waking sleep: Bettina working in her garden; Daddy Saint-Michael and him on a boat, fishing. They were memories, he knew, but good ones, refined and scrubbed of everything that made real life so sad.

Jacob didn't wear the light in the dreams. His daughter, Neve, was grown up and Jacob was watching her get married. In the dream she looked like the girl from the squat who got murdered. She wore a white ribbon around her neck and carried a bouquet of pale blue sweetpeas.

"It helps me sleep, man. You know how hard it is for me to sleep."

Finn took a handkerchief out of his flannel pocket and blew his nose.

"You should try drinking chamomile tea."

Nix laughed.

"Naw, man, I'm serious. Dust is bad news, man. That shit's not strong, but now you got Bleek coming around here and Evelyn's starting to jones and this is a clean squat. We agreed at the beginning."

Nix shook his head. "Dude, dust is no stronger than Excedrin PM."

Though he wouldn't know. Dust didn't work on Nix the way people described it. No. It was much, much stronger. But he never let anyone know that. The closest he could come to describing it was that it was like everything slowed down but sped up at the same time. As if the world were bent. He didn't know how else to put it.

Still, it was a question. Why was he messing with that shit?

Hardly known, definitely controlled. Something kids on the West Coast had been passing around at parties for the last couple years, but not even big yet back East. The hype was predictable: *No, no, not angel dust, man. Totally different. Not addictive. Just mellows you out. Helps you study better. Awesome for fooling around. Girls love it. Like Ambien, but it doesn't make you go to sleep.* All the same stuff Nix had heard about everything else.

It did do one thing, though. It made the lights he saw seem natural. There, but not as harsh. Controllable somehow, though he wasn't doing anything to change them. He'd needed that, because his "gift" was coming back with a vengeance — as if to punish him for starting to relax.

Hardly a way to explain all of this to Finn.

The dreadlocked boy passed Nix two glass tubes, coughing. "Hold these." It had been a wet spring and most of the kids at the squat were sick, except Nix, who had never been sick in his life — or as long as he could remember. Sometimes he wondered if, when his time came, he'd be able to see the light around himself; or if his own death, at least, would be a mystery.

"All I'm saying is that you're bringing Bleek up here and soon the cops are going to get wise and we're going to have to find another squat. We've been here almost a month, man. We move now and we're gonna be moving all summer."

Nix rolled the tubes between his fingers and nodded.

"And berry season is coming, dude. You know how much I've been looking forward to berry season."

Nix laughed. "I hear you, man."

"I thought you would."

Just then the bushes moved behind them and a sandy-blond head appeared amidst the greenery.

"My brothers!"

Nix shrugged at Finn, who shook his head.

"Bleek," Nix said and offered a hand. Finn sat on the stump, staring at the muscular, clean-shaven kid who was now standing in khakis and a bright red fleece, his arms outstretched above him at the center of the clearing. Bleek's straight blond hair, already receding, was short and his beard was shaven. He sported tiny silver hoops in both ears.

"Ah, the great outdoors!"

"Keep it down, man." Finn hushed him from the stump. "This isn't Yosemite."

"Finn Terwilliger." Bleek arched a brow and showed a tight smile. "Always the sunny disposition. And how are you progressing with Evelyn? Off the tit yet?"

Finn narrowed his eyes but said nothing.

"I saw her at Krakatoa yesterday, and she seemed . . ." Bleek paused, looking up into the feathery branches. "Well, how shall I put it? She seemed very *moved* by seeing me. I think she's starting to like me. Not for what I offer her, like she used to, but for who I *am*." He smiled again and tilted his head, picking a few pine needles from the front of his fleece.

"She is lovely, that Evelyn." Bleek stopped. "Even with the track marks."

"Shut the fuck up," Nix growled.

"Of course." He laughed. "That was rude. It's just that Finn has a problem with me for some reason, and I can't seem to do anything about it."

Bleek took a step toward Finn, who kept his eyes on his radio.

"Finn, I am a lowly drug dealer. Some of us have to make a living so that we can pay our way through college. Some of us did not grow up with two last names followed by a number, Phineas Terwilliger the — what is it? Fourth? Fifth? Some of us weren't lucky enough to get kicked out of prep school after dropping sixty gees on our *edumacations*."

Finn looked at Nix and shook his head.

"See what I mean? This is what you've brought to this place now, and it's not going away."

"Calm down, brother. I'm leaving." Bleek took a rolled Ziploc from his fleece pocket and tossed it to Nix. "Here's your medicine, my friend. Doctor's fee will be thirty."

Nix eyed him. "Last week it was twenty."

"Supply has been down lately, bud."

He took a twenty out of his wallet and passed it to the dealer.

"I owe you ten. Next time I'll meet you downtown. You got to chill on Finn, man. He's not doing anything to you."

Bleek waved his hand. "Self-righteous hypocrites like Master Terwilliger bug me, Nix. It's really not your problem.

"Anyway," he continued, "I don't do IOUs." Bleek looked up and sighed. "But I'll tell you what you can do. You hear about the party that's happening in a few weeks? Around the solstice?"

Nix shrugged. He had heard there was something big happening around the 21st of June. A party somewhere around Portland where the Flame was supposed to play. He had heard the band only on other people's iPods. They didn't make albums — just bootlegs here and there — and there were only a few photos of them floating around on the Internet. Yet every kid in Portland knew every word to every song — which hadn't happened in the northwest since Nirvana, when Nix was still in utero. It would likely be the biggest gathering of freaks in the region all summer, but no one seemed to know where it would take place.

"Yeah, I heard something."

"When you get the four-one-one, you let me know and I'll call this transaction even, and throw in the next two rolls."

"Whatever, man. *Four-one-one.* I'm not going to help you deal to thirteen-year-olds in their daddies' BMWs."

Bleek smiled and sighed as if the idea pleased him. He nodded to Finn. "Ah, Evelyn. I remember her when she was just a wee thing."

Finn started. "Was it life that turned you into such a complete asshole, or were you born this way?"

"Born this way." Bleek smirked. "Just like you. Except with balls."

"Get the fuck out of here before I kick your ass."

"What are you going to do? Strangle me with your hairdo? You're pathetic, Terwilliger." He sniggered then turned to Nix. "Nothing like two fucked-up teenagers with nothing better to do with their time than harass hardworking men like myself! Fine. Deal's off."

"It's yours." Nix passed the roll back to the dealer.

Bleek parted the brush. "Nice talking to you, gentlemen."

"Uh, Bleek?"

When he turned and saw Nix's outstretched hand he smirked, then reached in his pocket for the twenty. He wadded it up and threw it at Nix, who caught it left-handed, never taking his eyes from Bleek's. The older boy's gaze fell first.

"Nix, buddy, you got to start hanging with some more motivated people."

Bleek let go of a branch and disappeared into the gathering darkness.

CHAPTER 3

IT HADN'T BEEN A PLAN EXACTLY. More like triage. Something to make Ondine feel better after her parents rolled out of the driveway; something to get her out from under her cornflower-and-cream-striped duvet before she convinced herself she'd made a huge mistake and called up Trish and Ralph and begged for a ticket to Glen-ho, Evanston, whatever. It was strange: just at the moment her "mirages" intensified — she didn't know what else to call the visions she'd had since she was little — she'd chosen to distance herself. Desperate to believe she'd made the right decision by staying, she'd come up with a distraction. Ergo (with impeccable teenaged logic), party. She'd been thinking of it for a while, a real grown-up affair with cocktails and hors d'oeuvres. Trish had left phyllo dough in the freezer and a few bottles of booze in the liquor cabinet. The Masons trusted their daughter, and why shouldn't they? Ondine was always trustworthy.

She supposed she should celebrate her newfound independence — isn't that what unsupervised kids her age did? — even if she didn't feel much like celebrating. Truth was, it was four in the afternoon and already she missed her family. She'd even made another cup of Starbucks just so that things wouldn't feel so empty. She'd taken a nap in Ralph and Trish's bed, pressing her head to where her mother slept. The pillow smelled like Trish's sandalwood-scented hair.

In her dreams, butterflies with women's heads flitted through red maple leaves. Max had turned into a huge white worm and was trying to climb onto a branch where Ondine and her father sat. Trish called to them from the house. Her voice sounded like bells ringing —

Ondine stumbled to her bedroom to pick up her cell.

"Hey," she mumbled. It had been drizzling most of the afternoon, but now the sun had broken through the clouds and was shining outside her window in greenish yellow beams. She rubbed her eyes then glanced at the clock. "Right on time."

At the other end of the line, Morgan D'Amici laughed.

"Yeah. I learned it in 'Nam. Jesus, Ondine, relax! It's a party we're throwing, not a tea for Laura Bush."

"Oh, right. You're right." Ondine giggled awkwardly. She didn't know her fellow senior very well, but one thing she did know was that Morgan D'Amici was funny, if a little pushy.

Flirtatious, Ondine was used to. Girls half hit on her all the time. But Morgan: the chick was beautiful all right, but *wow*. Intense.

The two girls had just started to be friends when they found out they'd both be taking Raphael Inman's painting class that summer at Reed. Ondine had always admired the girl from afar — student council; all APs; casually, indestructibly pretty — and had known her younger brother, K.A., since they were kids and played AYSO together. But she hadn't known Morgan as well. They'd hung in different crowds, Ondine gravitating toward the artsy kids and Morgan sticking with one or two quiet, admiring girls who'd rotate out every few months. She'd always been aware of the dark-haired girl, though, as someone would be aware of one's shadow.

Once they got to know each other, it turned out Trish Mason knew Morgan's mother, Yvonne D'Amici, from the hair salon Yvonne worked at, and Trish frequented. Trish invited the D'Amicis — without the father, whom Yvonne had divorced a few years before — to their last Christmas party. Over virgin eggnogs and complaints about little brothers, Morgan and Ondine got to know each other.

"So what time are we on for?" Morgan paused and her light, scratchy voice became serious. "And how are we going to get the booze?"

Ondine was again impressed by the other girl's initiative and laughed.

"Damn, Morgan. You're not joking about being ready for a party."

Morgan moaned. "I'm sorry — it's just the end of school was a few weeks ago and all the graduation parties sucked ass and I've been so *bored* lately. I want to make sure our class gets senior year started *right*."

"You're telling me."

"And I guess I'm just excited. You know — end of the year, Raphael's class." Her voice sweetened. "Our becoming friends . . ." Ondine smiled into the phone. She liked the girl's straight-forwardness, even if it was a little much. Half pushy, half plead-ing. "Right?" Morgan said now. *We're friends, right?*

"Totally."

A picture of Morgan flashed in Ondine's mind — except that it wasn't her, quite. It was Morgan's head — black-haired, doll-like — on a moth's body. Dark wings; dark breast; clinging to white satin, spattered with red. It was a tiny, odd vision, but it made Ondine's heart skip a beat. She took out a pen and a piece of paper from her bureau and shook her head. "All right. *Party*," she said, writing it down then crossing it out. "No. *Best — Party — of — the — Year*." On the other end of the line, Mor-gan *mm-hmm*ed. Ondine added *Ondine & Morgan presenting*.

"So what do we need?"

"Well . . ." Morgan contemplated. "Those little spinach squares my mom put in her purse during your last party. And frankfurters. We definitely need frankfurters. Cheez Whiz, three-layer bean dip. You know, all the really classy stuff." The girl's voice lowered to a sultry pitch. "Baby, all we need is *al-kee-hol*."

Ondine groaned. At five three and small boned — despite the fact that she was grown-up enough for her parents to trust her to live alone for a year — she looked very young. She always hated it — even the perks, like getting into movies on the cheap. Morgan, too, was small, five four and petite as a ballerina, although something about her demeanor seemed older. Not old enough to buy liquor without ID, however.

"You don't have a fake, do you?" Ondine asked.

"No." There was a pause. "But you know, I've bought before, at O'Brian's, out on Southeast Seventy-seventh. Even Tania Rabani bought there last week, and she looks about twelve. Except, of course, for those —"

Ondine dragged her pen across the page before her. An image flashed of Tania Rabani's twinkly-eyed baby face, perched above dauntingly ample cleavage.

"Ah, I'm beginning to understand."

Morgan laughed in a way that didn't sound quite happy.

"We just have to make sure it's a guy in the cashier's cage when we go."

"Preferably around fifty," Ondine added. "Trucker's hat, plumber's butt."

"Who just can't say no to a sweet li'l thing."

"You're bad."

"You don't know the half of it." Morgan's voice was low. "Some potential girl-on-girl action for him to chew on all night? It'll be cake, baby. Ho Hos."

Ondine wondered what it was that drew her to Morgan. She was so intense, her vision so focused. What was going on inside the chick's head?

"All right then. I'll pick you up at seven."

"Seven it is," Morgan replied.

Tossing her phone on her bed, Ondine smoothed her braids, and noticed her heart was beating — fast. She also noticed she'd drawn yet another butterfly below the list that so far had nothing but her made-up party name written on it. Nothing out of the ordinary, the doodling, but something about the last image haunted her. It was urgent, even deranged: insistent, thick lines and a wicked face peeping out of an insect's body. She tore off the first page and started again, continuing to work until the sun went down. She drew bodies with wings, trees, worms — all the things she remembered from her dreams. It was the way she felt normal, when she drew. Emptying out the well of her obsession, it allowed her to release her mind from its track. When she awoke, a world would have been created on the page. Not real, but something like it.

By the time six-thirty rolled around, she had a guest list and ideas for food she and Morgan could make in a few hours, both pages dotted with butterflies she couldn't quite remember drawing. Sighing, she put a curlicue doodle on one of them, which had taken on the face of one of the girls in her dreams. The face was peaked and pretty, black haired, with delicate dark eyebrows and a pointed chin. The eyes were light but focused, the mouth narrow. Not selfish, just small. A tooth, just the slightest bit sharp, stuck out from under a thin, puffy lip.

"Morgan!" she whispered to herself, and laughed as she headed for the shower.

∽ ∽ ∽

MORGAN D'AMICI APPROACHED HER FACE IN THE MIRROR as she might any problem. She studied it, sized it up, memorized its strengths and weaknesses, then set about making it better. It was not a bad face. Two sky-blue eyes (so innocent!) under whips of black brow. A sprinkling of freckles across the pert little nose. Her cheeks were a little full, her lips a slice too thin. Her hair was good. Thick and black — thanks, she imagined, to her Italian father, though he was blond. She figured it must have skipped a generation. She admired her neck, and her fine collarbones under luminescent skin, and the hollow where they met, like a sand dune. Morgan was a lovely almost-eighteen-year-old. A lot of people told her that.

A lot of people couldn't be trusted to tell the truth. Only she knew where the small imperfections were: the too-thin lips, the cowlick she hid behind a wash of thick bangs, the scar at the base of her pinkie finger. Morgan knew she was far from perfect. So she set about changing it. And here, in front of the mirror — the single place of solace in the vinyl-sided hell that some cosmic joke had made her home — was where she practiced.

Morgan picked at a small and fine eyebrow hair. She was having trouble grabbing it, though she'd spent half of last week's coffee-slinging tips — she was a barista at Krakatoa, Southeast Portland's busiest coffeehouse — on a year's supply of wax and a deluxe set of Tweezermans her mom got her at cost.

"Everything still where you left it, honey?" Yvonne D'Amici entered the frame. She hummed to herself, walking back and forth across the space between the laundry room and the bedroom that Morgan had occupied for her vanity. Yvonne was used to her daughter spending at least an hour every evening in front of the mirror, but still couldn't let it pass unremarked.

Morgan flicked her eyes back to the glass.

"I would think you would want me to look my best, Mom. You always said you wanted better for me than you had."

Yvonne set the white plastic basket atop the washing machine and looked out the window of the little house she and her daughter and son, K.A. — after Kevin Anthony, Yvonne's father — lived in. The sun was setting, a toxic orange blob sinking into the forest.

That was a cut, she knew. Yvonne had been pretty in her day. Not as pretty as Morgan, but enough to win her a place in the 1986 Rose Festival Queen competition and catch the eye of the — *jerk* — son of one of the judges, Phil D'Amici of D'Amici & Sons, Oregon's biggest grocery store chain. And she *had* wanted better for her kids. 14460 Steele Street was a crappy strip of tarmac laid down across a depressing swath of Portland's far southeast quadrant. They'd started there when Phil Jr. was still working as a stock boy, waiting for his legendarily miserly father to die.

Then, he'd said, things would be different. They had been. The new girlfriend's boobs, for example. The plugs for her ex's early-onset male-pattern baldness. And the convertible red BMW to show off both. By the time the elder D'Amici had his first heart attack, the bastard had already taken off. The divorce went final just two weeks before the old man died, which meant that Yvonne and the kids weren't entitled to a penny of it.

Most of the houses around them had wheels, but Yvonne paid her rent and she scrimped to send K.A. to soccer camp, and no matter what she said, Morgan *had* gone to France the summer after sophomore year. It wasn't easy after Phil Jr. took up with a Portland Blazers cheerleader a few years older than their daughter, making it clear that he'd pay the minimum in child support. He wanted his kids to work for what they had, he said, just like he had. *Right,* Yvonne thought, but she had made it. She loved and was proud of her kids. Morgan's insistence on perfection had made her a straight-A student and upcoming senior-class president, and K.A.'s talent had won him a slot on McKinley High's state-champion soccer team.

Still, there was something frightening about her daughter's will. It was just that Morgan was so — flawless.

Yvonne cleared her throat: "Morgan. Sweetie. You know I think you're beautiful."

Walking over to the vanity where her daughter sat straight backed, Yvonne rested her hands on Morgan's shoulders. She stiffened but let them stay.

"You just always did like the mirror a lot."

Morgan smiled and touched her mother's hand.

"And I think *you're* wonderful, Mother. Especially after what Dad's been doing —"

Yvonne cast her tired blue eyes to the ground.

"She's almost my age!" Morgan sighed and shook her head — though not, her mother couldn't help noticing, hard enough to mess up her hair. "Anyway, you know K.A. and I appreciate how hard you work for us."

Yvonne crossed her arms, shivering. "Are you cold? Feels like it's gotten cold in here."

Her daughter's smile, faked or real, disappeared. "Maybe it's menopause."

"Please, Morgan. Can't you be civil, just once? I'm not old enough for menopause. And anyway, menopause is hot —"

"Little mother-daughter bonding time?" K.A. D'Amici walked in and both women's eyes moved from the mirror to the tall, wavy-haired boy standing with a glass of orange juice in his hand.

"Speak of the devil!" Yvonne smiled and turned to her son.

"Well, if it isn't my brilliant brother," Morgan replied. "Kaka, did they let you dribble around the cones at soccer practice today? Or are they still waiting for you to be able to learn your right and left?"

K.A. grinned. Morgan could do no wrong in her sixteen-year-old brother's eyes. It was she who had come home from school and played with him when Yvonne was at the salon and Phil at the store; she who tucked him into bed when their parents were fighting, before the divorce; she who helped him with his homework.

"Nah." K.A. stood behind his sister. "We just braided each other's back hair." He picked up a tube of lipstick, opened it, and put some on. Then he rubbed his cherry-stained lips as his sister might have and lowered his face to meet hers. Though they looked nothing alike — K.A. was tall, softly blond, and baby faced; Morgan petite, dark haired, and rather pointy — something about their twin beauty cemented the fact that they were siblings.

He pursed his lips and vamped. "I think I'll wear this to Ondine's tonight." Turning the tube over to inspect the label, he asked, "What's it called? She-Devil? Perfect!"

Yvonne laughed. "K.A.!"

Morgan affected a yawn and nudged her brother out of the mirror.

"How did *you* find out about Ondine's? You don't actually think you're coming, do you? It's only for upperclassmen, you know."

"What's this? A party at the Masons'?"

"Just for kids, Mom. The Masons left for Chicago today."

"Yeah," K.A. chimed in. "We don't need any more replays of you being the last person to stay at their Christmas party."

"And the food! She wrapped up those spinach pies and put them in her purse!"

"Trish told me to!" Yvonne grimaced but laughed too. "All right, all right. I know when I'm not wanted." She tousled her son's hair and retreated into the kitchen.

Morgan had progressed to her eyeliner. Out of the corner of a black-lined lid, she shot her brother a death stare.

"I hope you don't think you're bringing that juvenile delinquent friend of yours."

K.A. smiled lazily. "Nix is cool. Anyway, what do you care? Ondine's not going to mind."

"He's a loser dropout, K.A." Morgan rolled her eyes. "Why are you wasting your time?"

He ignored her. "He quit today."

"Señor Stoney has a job?"

"I work with him. I told you that. Anyway, the word would be *had*. He walked out. Jacob said he thought there was something wrong with him."

"There is." Morgan tapped the side of her head. "It's called inbred IQ deficiency. It's in the water up there."

"Jesus, Morgan. Just because he didn't finish high school doesn't mean he's not smart."

She shrugged.

"Anyway, are you bringing Neve?"

She undid her hair and it fell to her shoulders. Her brother was referring to her new friend Neve Clowes, the latest in a string of cute, shy girls Morgan always trailed behind her. Neve — funny and tough — was different, and stood up to her a bit more. Morgan was beginning to tire of her.

"Neve is off-limits, little bro."

"Whatever."

"She's my *friend*, Kaka. I don't like mixing. There are about a hundred chicks at McKinley you could date. Why don't you pick one of them? Anyway, ever heard of not shitting where you eat? Clowes wouldn't be too pleased to have you dating his daughter."

Here K.A. had her. He smiled at his sister, his lips still red.

"Jacob Clowes *loves* me. I'm his *right-hand man*. I'm his *team leader*. He'd love it if I dated his daughter. Save her from all those *bad seeds* out there who just want to *you-know-what*."

Morgan closed her eyes and tightened her jaw. Neve's lacy blond hair, charmingly disheveled, pulsed behind her eyelids. That and her expensive clothes, the navel ring that poked from a stomach that stayed flat and hard no matter how much pizza Jacob Clowes fed her. The Cloweses were rich and spoiled Neve, though she never seemed to take anything too seriously.

"You always do this, K.A. You always get involved with one of my friends and then you break up with them." She turned in her chair. "Besides fucking over a number of very nice girls at McKinley, guess who else gets screwed?"

K.A. bent down and put his hand on her knee. A radio went on in the kitchen and the siblings could hear their mother humming along to Journey, washing the dishes. Both knew it would be another solitary night for Yvonne: *Will & Grace* reruns, a plate of leftovers, maybe a call to a girlfriend or a visit to her younger boyfriend at the bar he worked at down the road. Then sleep, and the whole thing would start over again the next day.

Morgan's head fell. K.A. moved his hand to her shoulder.

"I'm not going to leave you alone, Morgue. I would never do that."

"How can you say what you will and won't do? You don't know. *He* didn't know."

"Dad's an ass." K.A. held his sister's chin and kissed her on the forehead. "And I'm not him."

Morgan looked up.

"Yeah." He nodded again, smiling his She-Devil smile. "Who loves you?"

"You do."

"I do."

She nodded and whispered, almost too quietly for her brother to hear: "I do."

CHAPTER 4

T WASN'T HIS FAULT. It wasn't his fault. It wasn't his fault. With every step of his holey brown boots back through the forest toward downtown Nix repeated the mantra to himself: *Not my fault!* He said it so many times he started to halfway believe it. Still, Nix knew he'd blown it — big time. Finn Terwilliger had kicked him out of the squat soon after Tim Bleeker left. He hadn't said much — just got up from his stump, gave Nix a hug, and walked away. It meant Nix had to go. Theirs was a clean squat. Finn had told him that from the beginning.

Evelyn couldn't be around Tim Bleeker when she was still so fragilely sober. So why had Nix brought the dealer there? He'd known it would mean getting kicked out and he'd done it anyway. Everything he had been working on in Portland for the last year was falling apart. And despite his mantra, Nix knew it was his own damn fault.

He made it to a grassy clearing and sat on a bench. All of Portland spread out before him — the silver snake of the

Willamette River, the little houses as far as he could see, and the dome of Mount Hood in the distance, so much like an active volcano that he almost expected a wisp of smoke to swirl from its pointed peak. He ached for his mother, for his uncles and aunts, for Daddy Saint-Michael, for the cousins he'd left behind in Sitka, and for the island itself — the fish and the trees and the wind and the ocean.

The mountains before him stretched all the way home. He thought of his grandfather, pointing to them, then pointing to Nix. Trying to get him to understand something. What was it? What was in those mountains? What was under them, waiting to come out?

A few families sprawled on the grass picnicking; a couple of kids Nix's age played Frisbee. A boy kicked a Hacky Sack around. They seemed so carefree, so happy. Nix wondered what separated him from them. He thought again about his dreams, and dust, the lights he saw around people, the mess he'd made of his life. There was something wrong with him — something broken. Was he crazy? Like the bums he saw on the Burnside bus, talking to themselves, reading their Bibles in the hopes that a key to their madness would be hidden there? He felt like a pariah. A marked man hunted by a vision of light that didn't make sense, that was so awful and cruel that it must mean he was crazy.

Yet he didn't feel crazy. What he did feel was old.

The sun dipped lower in the west. Out there was the ocean.

Ninety miles away: bays and shoals and beaches and cliffs and the wide-open sea. Nix had heard there were tunnels under Portland that led out to that ocean. Evelyn had told him about them late one night at the squat. Shanghai Tunnels, they were called: underground passages from the days of the Chinese railroad workers and opium dens and ships that left to fur in Alaska on the way to the Far East. It was hard to get sailors to volunteer for the years it took for a China voyage, so crooked captains stole people. They'd get some poor chump drunk or drugged up on opium and smuggle him down through the tunnels and onto waiting boats — shanghai him, basically. When he came to, he'd be far out at sea, stuck for years sailing the Pacific. Evelyn said she'd even gone down into them, one night when she was high. She didn't seem to want to talk about it, but she told him one thing: there were people down there.

"With sharp teeth," she had whispered. "They had sharp teeth. I remember that."

The sharp teeth he wrote off to Evie's habit, but the tunnels . . . Nix understood why she was captivated. Being shanghaied didn't seem so bad to him, sharp teeth and all. It seemed the perfect solution to the mess he was in. He'd take one of those tunnels and go off into the sun and never come back. Out to some place you could never return from. A place where there weren't lights or dust. A safe place, where dreams and waking were the same.

A voice startled him.

"You're early."

He turned. A spare young man, square shouldered and long legged, had sat next to him on the park bench, his face obscured by a black hoodie and black wraparound mirrored sunglasses. Nix might have been surprised had he not been waiting for him.

"Yeah," he said. "Something happened."

The hooded man nodded, keeping his face turned so all Nix could see was the long nose and the tuft of his dark brown soul patch jutting out past a full lower lip.

"You got kicked out."

Nix bristled. "Fuck! How did you know that, man? That happened like less than an hour ago." He shook his head. "I don't know who you get your information from, but you can tell that mofo to get his head out of my ass."

The man did not turn, but his voice softened. "It's not important. What is important is that you decided to call me instead of Tim Bleeker. This is a very good step —"

Nix had heard the spiel before from his mysterious companion, whom he had met a few times. He was a dust dealer someone at Jacob's had recommended one night Bleek was up in Seattle. His product was cheaper than Bleek's, but he would meet Nix only here, in the open, in the park overlooking the city rather than in the seclusion of the forest Nix preferred. Though the mysterious stranger dealt in dust — nothing heavier, which

Nix appreciated — he didn't like to use him. Something about the guy scared him. The way he spoke to Nix as though he knew him, which, in a way, he did. He knew Nix was from Alaska and that he lived up at the squat with Finn and Evelyn. He knew that he washed dishes for Jacob, and he spoke to him like a brother might, as if he almost cared about him. Yet Nix didn't even know the man's name. The imbalance unnerved him. The stranger never showed his face and always wore the same hoodie, the same dark jeans, the same wraparound black glasses. All Nix knew about him was his cell number and that he had a soul patch and a tattoo on the inside of his right wrist. A tiny blue X, small enough to be hidden by the band of a watch. Nix had seen it once, when the man had passed him his dust, his sleeve riding up just enough to expose his pale skin. He never saw it again.

"A good step? Man, you don't even know me." Nix took his wallet out, passed the man the same bill he'd tried to give Bleek. He was irritated at him for knowing so much. "Here's your twenty. And keep the fuck out of my shit. I gotta go."

He started to get up but the man extended his right hand — the one the tiny X was on — and Nix felt impelled to sit down again.

"Just relax." The man took the roll out of his pocket and passed it to him without taking the twenty. "This is on me." He stopped. "Under one condition."

"No, man. I'm not helping you drum up new clients —"

The older boy shook his head. "Listen before you speak." He put his hands back in his sweatshirt pockets. "My condition is that you must not, under any circumstances, take any of it tonight."

"Condition?" Nix almost turned to look the man in the eyes, but the stranger averted his face, looking east toward the plains. "Are you kidding?"

"Request."

Nix had been planning to meet K.A. that night. D'Amici was taking him to a party at some rich girl's house — a friend of his sister's — in Northeast. It was the one thing he had looked forward to in this wreck of a day. He was going to get fucked up, and then he was going to get more fucked up, and then he was going to take dust, and then he was going to go to sleep. In that sleep he was going to figure out a way to get into those tunnels and out onto one of those boats in the ocean, to never come back.

"You can't tell me when to take this, man! That's none of your business! Jesus. What is your deal?"

"Those are my terms," the man repeated.

Nix covered his eyes with his hands. What was going on? How did this guy know him? Why was he even considering obeying his wishes? He felt confused again. Why couldn't things just be normal, like when he was small, when it was just Bettina and him and his vision hadn't started to change?

The man spoke softly but his voice was strong. He raised his right hand. "You must promise, Nicholas Saint-Michael."

Saint-Michael. The words echoed in Nix's head. *Saint-Michael.* How did he know his name? Nix was too confused to think. Something about that hand — that little X.

"All right. I promise." He got up to leave. "But I'm not calling you again, and I don't want to see you around. Ever. *Period*," he threw in, desperate to convince himself.

For the first time, the man on the bench looked at the younger boy. His eyes were obscured by his glasses, the rest of his face was in shadow — but Nix did notice two things. The stranger was smiling and, despite an odd curve to his incisors that gave him a hungry, wolfish look, that smile, for the first time, didn't fill Nix with dread.

ഗ ഗ ഗ

DARKNESS HAD SETTLED OVER THE WOODS at the edge of the ragged field past the D'Amici's white vinyl-sided house. Morgan sat on the front steps and waited for Ondine. She ran her hand along her smooth legs. The night was still. Owls lived in the woods beyond the house and Morgan could hear their solemn cries.

Ever since she was a girl, she had been afraid of those woods. K.A. and his friends had haunted them almost every day, building forts from scraps of board they'd steal from neighbors' back-yards, catching frogs, playing Indian. The few times Morgan accompanied them, she stayed close to her brother. He allowed it, but boys were boys, and once they had played a prank on her by disappearing. Though she had been alone in the forest, the green light clogging her vision like a flood, she had felt distinctly *not* alone. The forest was alive, swirling with a presence — many presences. She heard the owls and knew they were owls. She heard the creaking of trees in the wind. She could even hear the stifled giggles of her brother and his friends somewhere in the undergrowth. But what scared her — what made her never want to be in the woods alone again — were the whispers. Lisping swirls, a strange static she somehow knew only she could hear. The whispers seemed to be calling her. *Sweet,* she heard. *My pet,* in a horrid singsong. Her own name in the lightest of voices, lighter than the smallest child could utter, but in a tone that children would never use.

Morgana.

She began to cry: a hysterical, sobbing wail that never, some-how, ended in tears. She was eight or nine then, and though K.A. was a full year and a half younger, it was he who comforted her that day, led her out of the woods, and told her he was sorry for playing a dirty trick on her. From that day on, Morgan never played in the woods again. If their mother told her to get K.A. for dinner, she'd stand at the edge of the trees and call him in.

She never went beyond the first branches for fear of hearing the voices.

"Sweetheart, why don't you take this coat —"

Morgan was interrupted by her mother bringing one of her old blazers from her married days out onto the porch. Yvonne held a lit cigarette in her hand and her voice was husky. Morgan knew she'd already had a beer or two in bed, watching television.

"Because it smells like an ashtray."

Yvonne stood above her daughter, the coat limp in her hands.

"Jesus. Do you think you could be nice to me for a few minutes? I'm just trying to help."

"No, you're trying to stand outside with me until Ondine comes." She turned her head to her mother and a passing car illuminated a thin-lipped smile. "That's all right. My friends are your friends, Mother."

Morgan looked at the woman standing. Yvonne had changed into a pair of hip-hugger jeans and a fashionable, though tight, pink sweater. In the half dark they looked almost the same age — Yvonne eighteen years older than her daughter.

"Looks like you've even dressed for a party. Except your fupa is showing."

Draping the coat over the porch railing, Yvonne took a drag off her cigarette, and eyed the girl sitting on the steps.

"I'm going to Carla's, smartass. And don't think I don't know what you're talking about. *Fupa*." She tugged at the jeans that bulged below her belly. "Sometimes you're a real bitch, Morgan."

The girl ignored her. "Oh, you're not going to try to crash this party like you did the last one? Well, maybe I'll run into you later at the Laurelthirst. That's where your personal bartender works, isn't it? What is he — nineteen?"

"He's twenty-seven. And he has a name. Todd, remember?"

"Right. *Todd*." Morgan sniffed and turned to face the road. "It's disgusting." She looked her mother up and down. "You're hardly Demi Moore."

Yvonne stared. "You are so cruel. How did you get to be so cruel?"

Morgan ignored her, but it was hard. Somewhere inside she asked herself: *How did I get to be so cruel?* And she heard the voices in the forest. *Morgana.*

She dug into her purse for her mirror, a habit she had of looking at herself, as if to make sure she was still there, still the same person. A car had appeared down the road and was now pulling up the gravel driveway leading to the D'Amici house. Yvonne watched her daughter's expression melt into sweetness. She had seen her do it before when friends came to the house. The girls would be passionate friends for a few weeks, a month, maybe, then the girl would disappear. Yvonne would ask about it and Morgan would say they'd had a fight and she didn't like the bitch anymore. It never seemed to affect the girl's popularity, though. There was something so charming, so weightless about Morgan. Nothing stuck. Accusations slid off the dark-haired beauty and there was always yet another fawning girl to bring around. The latest, Neve, the pale, pretty daughter of Jacob Clowes, who owned Jacob's Pizza, had lasted the longest.

Shame *he* was married, Yvonne thought.

This wasn't Neve, though. It was Ondine, Morgan's other friend. Two at the same time — some kind of record. Morgan's interest in Ondine Mason seemed different, though. Less bored, more intrigued. Cropped ink-jet photos of Ondine lined her walls. Every time the girl called, Morgan took the call alone, in her room, careful to shut the door. It was as if she wanted to soak Ondine in, get as much out of her as she could.

Ondine was good for her, Yvonne thought. She was a good girl, a sweet girl, and Morgan's . . . difficult attitude . . . that was a phase. Her daughter's vulnerability touched Yvonne and she reached out and stroked her back as she rose to meet the oncoming car.

Morgan smiled and turned to her mother to hug her. The headlights of the car lit them up. Though Yvonne knew Morgan was being affectionate for the spotlight now, she still couldn't resist hugging her daughter back. She tried not to think about how cold Morgan's arms felt around her torso, how rigid and unfeeling.

"Bye, Mom," Morgan said and kissed her on the cheek, then grinned at Ondine and waved. She skipped down the steps to the car. Yvonne saw a slim brown arm and the top of a head peek out the driver's window.

"Hey, Mrs. D'Amici!"

Yvonne waved.

"Hi, Ondine. Be good tonight."

She nodded. "Don't worry, we will."

"Love you, Mom," Morgan called back, opening the car door. "K.A. and I will call you later."

Yvonne smiled. "Love you, too."

She did love Morgan, she thought, rubbing her arms to get the chill of the evening air out of them. She loved her daughter. It was crazy, Yvonne knew — but she was afraid of her, too.

∞   ∞   ∞

IN THE PARKING LOT OF O'BRIAN'S, Ondine looked in the rearview mirror, pulling a stray braid from her smooth brown forehead. She had put a little eyeliner on for the booze-buying excursion, but she didn't like makeup and anyway, nothing could make her soft, big-eyed face look older than the seventeen years it was. Clear cinnamon skin; those violet, almond-shaped eyes, fine eyebrows, and a mouth she thought was too pouty gave her the look of a perpetual child, though she was almost an adult. She looked at Morgan next to her, rummaging through her purse for the dark red lipstick she favored.

Equally delicate, Morgan arranged her face so as to telegraph its seriousness. Ondine was fascinated by the way that Morgan could shift, with the fluidity of wind across water, into a woman twice her age. Nothing about her face changed; its components only combined differently to make a different impression.

Right now she was becoming the kind of woman who bought alcohol for a party on a Saturday night.

"I am *so* twenty-one years old." Morgan smirked, raising an eyebrow. "What do you think?"

"I'm impressed," Ondine replied, opening the car door. Morgan followed and they walked across the glass-strewn pavement of O'Brian's — a run-down liquor store on a block surrounded by a garage and a few empty lots.

In the cashier's cage a middle-aged man in a maroon Windbreaker and soiled khakis sat on a stool reading the sports pages. He smiled and looked Morgan up and down, then waved at the girls as they walked in. Morgan headed straight for the liquor aisle.

"See." She smirked, jerking a thumb back at him. "This'll be a breeze."

Ondine stayed quiet. She had never tried to buy alcohol

before, never given a party. Trish and Ralph let her have sips of wine and beer when she wanted it, but Ondine didn't care that much for booze. It made her sleepy at parties and she always ended up the quiet girl on the couch, dozing, waiting to drive her friends home.

"I'll go get the wine," Morgan announced, heading off toward the back of the store.

"Yeah, okay," Ondine called after her. She didn't know much about wine so she was glad Morgan had taken the initiative, although the meagerness of O'Brian's selection suggested that she didn't have to know too much to make her choice. Screw top or carton? That about summed it up.

Something about Morgan's focused attention unnerved her though. She had turned back to Ondine and was staring at her. Ondine smiled.

"Um, Ondine?" Morgan asked, her voice hushed.

"Yeah?"

"Were you going to stand there all night *like a high schooler*" — Morgan's voice fell to a whisper — "or were you maybe going to pick up a few bottles of the hard stuff?"

"The hard stuff?" Ondine was a little shocked. Had the girl just ordered her around? "What? Oh, right. Of course."

She grabbed a cart and walked down a bottle-lined aisle, trying to concentrate. The party had been Morgan's idea, but it seemed a good-enough plan. Ondine always wanted to be older than she was, vested with more responsibility than she was given. Inside she felt older, always had. A sophisticated party with a few of the rising seniors seemed like just the thing to improve her mood.

But earnest as it seemed, Ondine knew that neither Morgan's friendship nor their proposed party would make up for the hole that had opened up inside her when her parents had left that morning. Why didn't she go to Chicago? Why was she so determined never to get close to anyone — even her family, even her father, who'd brought her into the world? She knew she couldn't trust people to share things she herself had a hard time accepting. She would never tell Morgan, for instance, the way she felt about her paintings or how lately she felt she'd been losing her fix on reality. But if not Morgan, her supposed friend, then whom?

Enough. Enough with your creative temperament, Ondine.

Browsing the aisles, staring at the rows of clear and dark liquor, she could almost hear her mother's voice, chiding her for indulging herself that one step too much. *Fuck it. I'm having a party.* She was determined to have fun and hummed a Flame song she liked, trying to get her spirits up.

Hurry — hurry — hurry! — ring of fire —
Ring of fire! Spin round, ring of fire —
Quick — quick! Wooden doll,
Hurry, lovely wooden doll, spin round —

She reached for bottles with her right hand, balancing them in the crook of her left arm. She made her choices by color as much as anything else. Vodka with its icy clarity. Warm brown whiskey. And what was it, Pernod — green, and *French*. She was examining a ridiculous bottle of liqueur claiming to taste like chocolate milk when a rustle of black and gray caught her eye. Startled, Ondine turned.

"Hello, Ondine."

The lithe older boy with wild dark-brown hair and green sparkling eyes — eyes that matched the bottle of Pernod nestled in her arm — laughed. "Haven't seen you around in a while." He was scratching a trimmed soul patch with his top teeth. He grinned and arched an eyebrow.

Didn't soul patches go out like ten years ago? That was about when James Motherwell was in high school. Since then he'd been a fixture around Portland's skate parks, bookstores, coffee shops, and parties. Never seeming to go anywhere.

"Hey, Moth." She smiled tightly and turned back to the liquor, which she took up with doubled interest. James Motherwell, or "Moth," as he called himself, had long tried to hit on Ondine and every other teenaged girl in Portland. Though she'd had a few conversations with the twenty-something boy, he seemed rather interested in checking out other girls' butts in between speaking to her breasts. An unfortunate tic, and she found him tiresome.

"You're looking enticing as ever," Moth continued, stepping closer. "What are you deciding between, my love?" He took the bottle of chocolate liqueur out of her hands. "I suggest something less sweet."

"Moth, don't you have some fifteen-year-olds to hit on?"

He laughed and raised his eyebrows.

"I'm *matooring*, Ondine. Everyone's got to grow up sometime." He stepped back and checked the black band around his wrist. Ondine could just make out the blue tip of a tattoo underneath the strap. She wondered what it was. Something "deep," like an om? Other than the watch, Moth was dressed simply: black jeans and a black long-sleeved T-shirt with a narrow collar, which flattered his slim face and high cheekbones. He wore a single heavy braided silver ring on his right middle finger. Even she had to admit there was something skeevily sexy about the boy.

Ew! What are you thinking, Ondine? She turned back to the shelves.

Moth continued unfazed. "So what time is our party starting?"

"What?" She whipped her head around.

He bent down and tied one of his shoelaces, still staring. "I said, what time is the party starting? I don't want to be late."

The girl narrowed her eyes and stepped closer. Moth didn't flinch. She was surprised. People normally flinched.

"There is no party."

"Sure there is, pet." He straightened up and smiled. "At your place. Your parents left today and you're having —"

Before Ondine had the chance to ask the older boy how the hell he knew about her parents leaving, Morgan rounded the corner. As soon as she saw their new companion she slowed, slinking catlike toward Ondine but looking at Moth, the bottles in her hands clinking.

Moth stared back. "Vision number two? Well, isn't this my lucky night!"

"Fly away, Moth," Ondine whispered.

"I'm Morgan," the black-haired girl intoned, tilting her head. "And you?"

He grinned. "James Motherwell."

"Like the painter?"

"Very good." He nodded. "A muse. But you can call me Moth." He extended a few fingertips, which Morgan grazed, her lips parting into a knowing smile.

"I was just asking our friend Ondine here what time your party starts this evening."

"The party starts at ten," Morgan replied, ignoring Ondine's shaking head. "We're just stocking up now." She held up four bottles of wine gripped in both hands.

"What lovely jugs."

Morgan threw back her head and laughed. "Why, thank you."

Ondine stared. "Oh. My. God. You're such an asshole." She turned to the boy then glared at her friend. "You're not invited, Moth. Moth tends to attract a difficult crowd. He can't come."

Ignoring her, Morgan eyed Moth up and down, a smile lingering.

"Oh. Too bad."

"Hm." He considered the loot. "There's no way you're going to be able to buy that yourself, though."

"*Au contraire,* my friend." Ondine pointed down the aisle at the cashier reading his newspaper behind the counter. "Morgan buys here all the time. That guy is *in love* with her."

Morgan shrugged, still smiling.

"Of course he is." Moth winked but shook his head. "Not tonight, though. Not without Moth's help." His face became serious. "And we might as well have fun tonight, before everything starts."

Before everything starts? What the hell was he talking about? Ondine ignored the mysterious comment. Moth was known for the kind of deep guy blather she hated. *Hey, are you going to Burning Man this year? Cool tats, man* — blah blah blah. Lines like these may have worked in Portland, but they were just ways of getting into crunchy girls' pants.

She waved her hand. "Dippin' into the dust a little too much these days, Motherwell? Let me rephrase. *You. Are. Not. Invited.*"

He only smiled. "Whatever."

"Come on, Morgan." Ondine started for the counter. "We don't need your help, Moth. We're just having a little gathering — a small, select group of people. From *high school*. But I suppose you can't be expected to remember back that far."

The boy laughed, enjoying the banter. "I'm just glad to be in your presence. Now, Morgan," he began, taking the wine bottles from the girl's splayed fingers and placing them in Ondine's cart. "Tell me about yourself. Who are you, lovely angelic creature of light? And would you like to run away with me?"

The girl stepped closer. She clearly liked the attention and was charmed by Moth. Ondine pushed faster. It felt strange to be ignored. It wasn't that she was jealous. No. Jealousy — an offshoot of desire, which for the most part seemed to have spared her (she had kissed a few boys at McKinley dances, but never really *dated*) — had always seemed ridiculous, something for bad reality TV. This was more like . . . like a hangnail. Irritating. *Stupid* irritating.

Still, there was a heat coming off these two, and she felt if she stood between them too long, she might also start to burn.

"Come on, Morgan," she said, walking faster.

The cashier made it known a few paces away that he had no intention of selling to the underage girls. Nevertheless, Morgan, prepared with a smile, began loading the bottles onto the counter. The man behind it shook his head.

"ID, young lady." He looked up from behind his reading glasses.

Morgan leaned over far enough to reveal a generous helping of milky breast under her black blouse. "I got my wallet stolen." She tucked a stray lock behind her ear and smiled. "Remember? Just last week I was in here and I told you I got my wallet stolen? As soon as I get it back I'll come in and show you —"

"No ID, no sale." The man tapped the "21" sign affixed to the counter. "And I suggest you put these items back on the shelves before I call the police and have you arrested for trying to procure alcohol underage." He pushed the bottles back toward her, one by one. "Hussy," he muttered, then coughed.

Too shocked to say anything, Ondine stood quiet. Morgan pretended she hadn't heard. Moth, however, who seemed to miss nothing, appeared delighted. He smiled and looked at Ondine as if to say, *What did I tell you?*

The cashier wiped his nose with the back of his hand, shook his paper out, and started reading it again.

"You, too." He nodded to Ondine.

"Excuse me?"

A thick, stubbled upper lip curled in Moth's direction. "And you can think again if you want this little turd here to buy for you."

Ondine and Morgan stood silent, hands at their sides. Ondine's mouth hung open as if she intended to say something but had forgotten what it was. A wash of pink seeped into Morgan's cheeks. Moth just laughed.

He stepped in front of the two girls, smiling calmly. Raising his right hand — the one with the silver ring, the wristwatch, and the tattoo — to his lips, he shushed the older man. The cashier stiffened for a second, his face knotted, then by increments he relaxed. Moth kept shushing and the man behind the counter softened. Ondine watched. Morgan watched. The softer and longer Moth shushed, his finger still to his mouth, the quieter and more passive the cashier became.

He lowered his fingers and placed his hand on the counter.

The cashier smiled as if he had never seen Moth before. "Well, sir," he said. "What can I do for you?"

"Oh, I think you can just ring us up."

Ondine felt dizzy and placed a hand on the counter to steady herself. She pulled it back when the cashier smiled at her, too.

"Yes, dear?"

"Nothing."

She didn't understand what was going on. One second the cashier was calling them hussies and turds, now this? She looked at Morgan. The girl was biting her lip, her eyes wide. Whatever was going on, it was clear she liked it.

"Never you mind, young Ondine." Moth didn't take his eyes from the cashier's. "Just put the bottles in the bag."

"No!" She turned and stared. "You tell me what's going on

or I'm out of here. And you —" She turned to face the cashier. "Why did *you* change your mind?"

"Shut up, Ondine!" Morgan whispered.

The cashier spoke, his phlegmy voice now kind. "A few chocolates for the girls, sir?"

"Excuse me, but what the hell did you do to this guy, Moth?"

"Make sure you still eat your dinner." The cashier spoke over her, reaching under the counter and placing a Hershey's Kiss in front of Ondine, another in front of Morgan. He nudged the candies toward them. "Go ahead, girls. They're all yours."

Whatever was going on, Ondine realized she would have to deal with it outside. Dazed, she took the candy and put it in her pocket. Morgan unwrapped hers at the counter and placed it on her tongue. Then she sucked on it, licking her lips.

"All mine?" she said, to the cashier or Moth, Ondine couldn't tell. "I *do* like the sound of that."

Moth's smile curled up on one side into a smirk, but he kept his eyes on the cashier's. "We can explore that statement in all its, uh, positions later. Right now" — his hand snaked into his back pocket and fished out a rubber-banded roll of money, which he handed to Morgan — "be a good little girl and pay the man."

Morgan looked so intoxicated you'd think she'd already drunk everything Ondine was shoving into plastic bags. She double bagged the bottles, concentrating on the practical details, because she didn't know what the fuck was going on, but she knew she wanted to get out of the store before it all exploded in their faces. Morgan peeled back twenties, one at a time. She looks like a stripper giving herself a tip, Ondine thought, then felt guilty. It wasn't like they were stealing — although it *was* the first time Ondine had ever paid for something by stuffing the money into a cashier's shirt pocket, which Morgan was doing now, leaning over the counter and throwing in a little kiss on the cheek.

"Since you gave us kisses," she cooed in his ear, "it seems only fair you should get one, too."

Her shirt rode up when she leaned forward, exposing the small of her back above her jeans, and Moth let the fingertips of his right hand play over the bare skin, never taking his eyes from the cashier's.

"It's kisses for everyone then," he announced. Then, in a firmer voice: "Now, let's get out of here."

Outside, Ondine stared at Moth, who was now helping himself to the trunk of Trish Mason's silver Jetta. She kind of wished she smoked, so she could light up a cigarette in anger.

"What just happened in there?"

"Magic?" Moth laughed.

"You asshole. Why don't you be straight with me? Can you ever tell the truth?"

He lifted his eyebrows. "I just did."

"You know, there's one thing I never understood about you, Moth. Other than chasing tail, what exactly do you *do*?"

"Help people, I guess. Isn't that what I'm doing with you?"

Morgan spoke up from the other side of the car. "Ondine? Honey? Your chocolate's going to melt in your pocket."

Ondine looked at her friend across the closed sunroof of her mother's car. She had wanted to open the sunroof on the drive over, but Morgan had said the breeze would mess up her hair. Now she almost seemed to be panting.

"Is that all you have to say? 'Your chocolate's going to melt'? Here then," she said, fishing out the candy and throwing it at Morgan. "Since you seem to like it so much."

Moth walked over to Morgan and whispered something in the girl's ear. Ondine noticed his fingers wrap around her waist. She felt a pang of something — not jealousy, surely not jealousy — despite herself. She had never been touched like that.

He turned to Ondine and smiled. "See you at ten, then."

She clenched her jaw and clicked her keys. The Jetta hiccuped in response.

"No. You. Won't." But he had already started loping away.

"Come on, Morgan." Ondine scowled, slamming the door. "Neve's waiting."

CHAPTER 5

IM BLEEKER KILLS OLD LADIES' CATS, my friend. Why the hell are you even talking to him?"

K.A. looked over at his friend, slumped in the passenger seat. Nix didn't say anything, just stared out the black Mustang's window at the soft yellow lights of Portland's low-lying neighborhoods. The early June air was soft and a little dewy from the rain earlier in the day.

"Hey, man. I'm serious. Why do you even mess with that stuff?"

"I can't sleep, man. I have these dreams." Nix looked at K.A., then back out the window. "And I wake up and can't get back to sleep again. The dust helps with the dreams."

"So you're saying you take dust because it makes your bad dreams go away?"

"Not go away," Nix said to the window. "Dulls. Mutes."

"Dulls," K.A. repeated. "Mutes. That's great. You're frying

your brain because it 'mutes' your dreams. That makes it all better, man. All better."

It occurred to K.A., not for the first time, how strange it was that he and Nix had become friends. K.A. was a delivery boy for Jacob, had worked for him since he was in ninth grade, running errands, stocking the pantry. He got bumped up to table service and then deliveries when he'd gotten his license the previous year. He liked hanging out late at Jacob's, shooting the shit with Neve and Nix. Neve, Jacob's truly smoking daughter, he'd seen around for years. They'd gone to school together until eighth grade, after which her parents transferred her to Penwick. Something about Neve needing special attention—true, as far as K.A. could tell. Neve was a total fox — smart, too — but high-strung. Which wasn't always a bad thing, in K.A.'s book. He still saw her at soccer games when their teams played each other. He had a distinct memory of her turning a cartwheel in a vintage cheerleading skirt; she'd worn it for the ironic value, but the look was perfectly executed, particularly the kneesocks and white cotton panties. Last summer at a party he'd watched her lose a makeshift, late-night limbo when the tips of her breasts nudged a Swiffer out of the sweaty hands of some Penwick seniors. But the thing that had really made him take notice was the day she'd slammed open the back door of her father's pizza parlor, where K.A. was hanging out with the new dishwasher while he smoked a cigarette. Every bit the boss's daughter, Neve had said, "Listen, D'Amici, if these three pies don't make their way over to Northwest Glisan *right now*, I'm gonna let you in on my father's special hippie recipe for making pepperoni without harming any pigs." Nix had snorted so violently his cigarette had flown out of his mouth, and Neve, not expecting an audience, had gone red. After she'd slunk back inside, K.A. had said to Nix, "You think I should tell her I just came in to get my paycheck?" The kid had replied, "I wouldn't risk it, man. Not while she's got access to that meat grinder."

Two relationships were born that day: a flirtation with Neve that had grown steadily, and a faster if weirder friendship with the slacker-vagrant-runaway dishwasher, or whatever the hell Nix was. The fact of the matter was, Nix Saint-Michael was the kind of guy K.A. was supposed to beat up, or at any rate, avoid. Instead he felt like the little brother K.A. never had — which was even weirder, since Nix was a year older than him. As the youngest employees of Jacob's, the threesome often sat around the same booth during the slow last hour — the pizza parlor stayed open till midnight on school nights, two AM during the weekends — sipping beer poured into soda cans in deference to Jacob, and sometimes, if it was slow enough and they'd managed to drink enough, K.A. would get Nix to tell stories about Alaska and his travels before he came down to Portland. He always stopped when the subject of his mother came up. All he would say was that she died young.

K.A. kept his hands on the wheel now, but looked over.

"So what happened today? With Jacob?"

Nix leaned back in his seat and sighed. "I don't want to talk about it, man."

"He likes you, you know. He told me once you reminded him of himself when he first got to Portland." K.A. saw the older boy smile despite himself and shake his head. He decided to press on. "No, man, I'm serious. He told me that."

Nix's expression darkened. He took a deep breath then kicked the dash.

"Dude! Drop it! I quit. That's all there is to it."

"All right, son. I was just trying to help." K.A. kept his eyes on the road. "Chill out."

They were quiet for a while, until Nix spoke.

"Look, bro. Things are just hard for me right now. I'm depressed. I can't take that job. These nightmares — I don't know what to do about them. And tonight Finn kicked me out of the squat —"

"What?"

"Finn kicked me out, man. I brought Bleek up there for a delivery, and Finn's into Evelyn now, and —" Nix traced the outline of the metal door handle. "Anyway, you know how Evie knows Bleek. Man, I totally fucked up. Today was a really bad day. Quit my job, got kicked out of the squat. I'm no good to anyone, including myself." He paused and looked ahead of him, his jaw tight. "I think it's time for me to head out."

K.A. took a deep breath, then spoke, still staring at the road.

"You can't run away from yourself."

He looked over at the boy in the passenger seat, waiting for Nix to say something. Nix's face was split by a wide grin, half mocking, half miserable.

"Dude. You are *way* too young to be saying shit like that."

The two boys laughed for a moment and then K.A. turned the music down — the Flame was playing — and shook his head.

"C'mon, man. We'll figure out something for you."

"I don't know."

"No. We will. Maybe my dad can get you a job at one of his stores, or — anyway. You're still studying, man. You've got the test in a few months."

K.A. had been helping Nix study for the GED and found him a good student. Curious, intelligent, probably smarter than he was, though maybe K.A.'s spelling was better. He didn't know what drew him to help the older boy. The dream of the rebel he never was? K.A. had the Mustang, the look — tousled blond hair, trucker's hat, dark jeans, chain wallet — but no matter what he did he would still be the straight-up soccer dude class council dork he always had been. The one with the steady job

82

and the cute girlfriend and the hyper-perfect older sister. The one who said things like, "you can't run away from yourself." He had gotten that one from one of Yvonne's self-help books.

"Dude!" Nix laughed. "Save it for Greenpeace. I'm a loser. You're a winner. Loser," he said, pointing to himself. "Winner," he added, jerking his thumb at K.A. "Got it?"

The squint in Nix's eyes told K.A. that part of him was telling the truth.

"Shut up, dude. For once you're going to listen to me. After tonight, no more dust."

Nix looked at his lap. "I'm not doing any tonight. Anyway, it's not your shit. You don't know what's going on in my head. Why I don't —" He turned again to the window.

K.A. ignored him. "And you're going to study for the GED."

"Study?" Nix smirked. "That thing is a joke."

"Whatever." K.A. tightened his grip on the wheel. "And we're going to find you somewhere to stay, and maybe my dad —"

Nix was shaking his head, but his eyes were bright.

"Why are you doing this, man?"

K.A. waited, the streetlamps throwing waves of light over his face.

"Honestly, I don't know." He turned to look at the young man he so little resembled, fumbling for reasons. Nix was cool; he was wild; he was the person K.A. was not. There was something else, though. Something about Nix that made you want to be near him. Some strange aura of protectiveness. Though K.A. told himself that it was he who was protecting Nix — team captain looking out for the benchwarmer, that kind of thing — at certain moments he wondered if it was Nix who was protecting him.

He cleared his throat and saw the boy's eyebrows rise.

"You're my friend. And I don't know why else."

"Well, I guess we'll see then."

"After Ondine's? Yeah, we'll see."

જી જી જી

MORGAN AND ONDINE HAD PICKED UP NEVE CLOWES from her house up in Southwest and driven her in. Neve's ultraprotective mother, Amanda, waved through the living room windows as the girls drove away; Jacob, of course, was down at the pizzeria. When they were out of sight, Neve took out a cigarette.

"God, she has *nothing* to do." Neve sighed, looking at Morgan in the front seat and raising her eyebrows. "I have to get back by one, okay? I told her I would."

Morgan just laughed, and as soon as they got to Ondine's, placed a beer in the younger girl's hand.

"You need to relax, young Neve," she instructed, bringing

84

the frosty bottle to her friend's glossed lips. Morgan winked and licked lime juice off her fingers, watching Neve sip slowly — but steadily, steadily — at the Corona she had given her.

"Thanks, Morgue." Neve giggled. "I *think*."

The girl was good-natured and cute in a turquoise fifties-style shift, which could've been vintage or could've cost five hundred bucks from one of those indie boutiques that someone like Neve always knew about. Amanda Clowes had a Saks card, and Morgan knew trips back to New York to see the Clowes clan in Brooklyn always meant at least a few grand dropped on some mother-daughter Barneys time. It irked Morgan to think that the nicest sweater she owned was one that Neve had bought her. And that hair. So blond tonight it seemed to glow. Neve swore she didn't dye it, but Morgan had her doubts. No one got to be that pretty just because.

"Hey, Ondine." Neve picked up. "How psyched are you that your parents are gone?"

Ondine smiled, but her eyes were downcast. "I guess I'm happy." She paused. "To tell you the truth, I kind of miss them."

"Yeah." The younger girl nodded, her brown eyes growing larger. "I always bitch about my folks, and then when they go away I'm like 'Where's Mom? Where's my dinner? *Waah* —' I end up ordering from Dad's restaurant just so I can taste his cooking."

Dad's restaurant. As if everyone didn't know Jacob's. He'd even been on the Food Network, for chrissakes. The thing Morgan didn't understand was how a three-dollar slice could make someone such a shitload of money.

She leaned against a corner of the butcher-block island in Ondine's kitchen and watched the other girls prepare. Her new friend, Ondine, sliced the limes, laughing with her old friend, Neve, who arranged chips in various bowls and unscrewed salsa tops. *How charming.* The girls' plans to make hors d'oeuvres had vanished once they came back from the liquor store, and they ended up ordering pizza instead — not from Jacob's, though. Dear Old Dad didn't need to have his delivery boys spying on innocent little Neve this evening. *Innocent.* Puke. Neve was already slurring her words and had shown both girls the new Agent Provocateur demi she got online. Somehow Morgan doubted that Neve was going to be so innocent when K.A. showed up.

What the fuck were they talking about? She watched the girls' mouths move but felt as if she were watching the scene through a mist. Things were too weird already. When they had gotten to the house and unpacked the alcohol, Morgan had been shocked to find a second keg in the trunk, though she would have sworn that the weird, cute guy with the roaming fingers and great lips — what was his name, Mouth? — had ordered only one. When she asked her about it, Ondine rolled her eyes and muttered something about Moth trying to send her to jail tonight. There were a dozen bottles of booze, several cases of beer, at least eight jugs of cheap wine. Who had remembered limes and lemons? And the rest of it? Morgan knew she'd been undone by the eerie presence of the handsome older boy, but for the life of her couldn't figure out how the rest of the loot had gotten to Ondine's. There was enough alcohol to blitz an army. Or a least the Salvation Army. Portland's kids were, in Morgan's opinion, underemployed.

Or rich, she thought, staring from behind an oversized red wineglass at the two girls chatting away in front of her. The glasses they held so casually cost ninety dollars a stem. She knew, because she was in charge of reordering at the Krak and got the catalogs. Riedel, from Austria. What did Ondine and Neve care? They'd never had jobs. They didn't know what five hours of wiping steamed milk off every conceivable flat surface, including the ceiling, felt like. Cleaning toilets stuffed with tampons, making a macchiato four times for an eleven-year-old punk and his yuppie Medusa of a mother because he "hadn't gotten it the way he likes it at home."

Spoiled brats. Morgan brushed it off. She could feel the slow warmth of the Bordeaux Ondine had opened from the Masons' wine cellar seep into her. She didn't drink much, and was nervous about the prospect of giving a party, but had to admit she was also excited. That Moth — at least *he* seemed interesting. Most of Portland's guys made her as cold as the celery Ondine and Neve were now chopping into little sticks and filling with salmon cream cheese in a halfhearted attempt to make the party appear classier than a kegger. Still, despite the strange turn of events, something seemed to be clicking, little puzzle pieces fitting together, though Morgan couldn't figure out what gave her that feeling. It was an early summer Saturday night like any other. She had to go to work on Monday at the Krak; Tuesday was the second class with sexy Raphael Inman.

And tonight at the liquor store: she knew from Ondine's behavior that James Motherwell was a prick, but then, she liked pricks. An image of Moth laughing, his green eyes crinkling, oozed into her head and she felt a flush down her center. That soul patch was so pseudo–Johnny Depp/I-live-in-France-and-have-many-tattoos that it made her want to hurl. Yet she could almost feel it tickle her lips as she —

Morgan shook the thought away.

"Tonight's going to be fun," she said. Ondine and Neve looked up from their tasks.

Neve *mm-hmm*ed. Ondine raised a thin eyebrow. "You sound like a girl who has something in mind."

Morgan swiped at her lips. She hadn't eaten dinner, and tried to pretend it was just wine on an empty stomach.

"Oh, I don't know. I just have this feeling." She held her wineglass with both hands, retreating farther into the corner. "Anyway, don't mind me, girls. I'm just, I don't know, *horny*."

Ondine laughed and continued slicing. Neve blushed.

"Neve gets embarrassed easily," Morgan teased, but her eyes were flat.

Neve took out a cigarette and started to light it. "Do you mind if I smoke, Ondine?"

"Not tonight, I guess." Ondine shrugged. "K.A.'s coming." She turned to Morgan. "Isn't that right, Morgue?"

Morgan grimaced. "Yeah, yeah. My little Kaka. I couldn't keep him away."

Neve smiled and Ondine tickled her. "*Oooh!* Neve's got a *crush.* . . ."

Morgan felt tired of the two girls. So — *young.* Even Ondine. But the irritation was balanced by another feeling. A kind of yearning so deep and complete she could almost feel herself salivating. *Ondine Mason.* Morgan wanted to be near her, almost devour her. She looked around the kitchen: the Viking stove, the glasses sparkling in neat rows in their cabinets. Everything clean and expensive. She contrasted it with her own kitchen: the old jelly jars that didn't match. The worn furniture set in the living room. Her mother's cheap plates, the ones they'd gotten from Grandma Lily that she used to think were pretty, with their blue flowers. K.A. didn't seem to mind. He cheerfully slept on poly-blend sheets and dug into Yvonne's three-bean dip as if it were caviar. Morgan couldn't stand it. She couldn't do much about the laminate walls and the adhesive plastic strips Yvonne installed on the windowpanes to make them look old-fashioned, but in her own corner she kept things neat; bought four-hundred thread-count cotton sheets and cleared her desk of the crafty crap her mother and grandmother and various aunts were always trying to give her.

Pretty, huh. Pretty trashy.

She realized she was digging her nails into the flesh of her forearms. When she released, half-moons of red stippled her skin.

"I'm going to go freshen up," she announced. Ondine and Neve, deep in conversation about some high school idiocy, merely nodded.

She looked at them laughing, standing close. Neve and Ondine weren't even friends. Neve was her friend. What kind of friend would poach her brother? Yvonne's cheap dinner plates flashed once more. One of the plates was chipped, and when Morgan was a little girl she would always make sure the chipped one ended up at her place, especially when they had company, so no one else would have to see it. At some point — Morgan couldn't even remember when — she'd started setting the plate at her mother's place.

When did she become that kind of girl?

The girls leaned closer and again Morgan felt ashamed. She needed to *do* something. Figure out a way to get Neve away from her brother and her new friend. Find that boy Moth and maybe have a little fun. But not just now. Now she needed to have a look around and get her head straight for later.

She walked up the metal stairway that connected the two levels of the loftlike house the Masons lived in. Trish Mason was an architect, Morgan knew, and the whole house showed it. Around one corner an alcove housed a few Roy DeCarava photographs; from the ceiling a wash of etched glass spires hung to suggest the Portland rain. It was a magnificent house and Morgan coveted it.

This should be mine, a voice inside her whispered, but she shook it off. There seemed to be two parts to her — the part on the outside: the perfectionist, the leader, the serious and funny girl never made a mistake; and another girl she didn't know as well. That girl moved the chipped plate to her mother's place, hoarded her friends only to dump them for imaginary transgressions, *wanted* things so badly it burned. That girl instructed her. *This should be yours,* the inside Morgan said at the Chanel makeup counter, admiring a thirty-dollar tube of lipstick the outside Morgan could not afford.

So she stole it, and because she was Morgan D'Amici, soon-to-be class president, straight-A student, she never got caught. Now what was that girl saying to her?

She wiped a hand across her face, her cheeks warm from the wine, located what she assumed was the nearest bathroom, and shut the door.

A light illuminated a recessed mirrored cabinet. A few vitamin bottles, Listerine, eyeliner, mascara, two bars of hand-made soap: nothing interesting. She closed the cabinet, studying her own face. She was pale, despite the wine, and her red lips looked sultry against her ivory skin. Morgan knew she looked lovely tonight but it gave her little pleasure. She thought about Neve. Neve was *cute*. So damned cute, with her pigeon toes and her shapely legs, and her always-perfect clothes, whether from Barneys or a thrift store. What did Neve have that she didn't? Morgan was prettier, smarter, more popular. She thought of her brother, his smiles reserved for her, and though she knew it was wrong, she felt a bitterness rise at the thought of those smiles going to Neve.

No. She shook her head, resting her hands on the marble of the bathroom counter. She felt dizzy and the smooth stone calmed her. Taking off her black silk blouse, she left just her camisole on. Maybe that would cool her down.

A little bowl of trinkets — earrings, necklaces, a few silver rings — sat next to the sink. Ondine's bathroom, Morgan reasoned. Plucking a plain jet strand out, she tried it on, looking sideways in the mirror. It suited her. She unhooked the necklace and dropped it into her purse.

"Morgan, Morgan!" Neve called from downstairs. "Someone's here!"

Shaking out her hair, she took one last look in the mirror.

Sometimes you're a real bitch.

Walking into Ondine's bedroom, she could see the moon rising in the big picture windows, the ubiquitous fir trees of Portland below. A single headlight flared and then dimmed. She approached the window to see who it was. Her eyes adjusted to the light and made out the lean figure of someone taking off his helmet. He stopped, put the helmet on his seat, and ran his fingers through his hair.

James Motherwell. Morgan's chest constricted.

He looked up. She was conscious of the fact that she wore only her camisole, but didn't move. Instead she stared. Moth grinned slowly and waved. She thought of Ondine and Neve inclining toward each other, laughing, their hands on each other's arms.

Let them whisper.

She slid her camisole off and stepped closer to the glass. Her nipples stiffened.

Looking up from the driveway, Moth smiled wider.

She waited till the bell rang to put her top back on, then headed down the stairs.

ဢ ဢ ဢ

FROM THE ONLINE, IM, CELL PHONE, CRACKBERRY, and good old-fashioned coffeehouse buzz, you'd have thought Ondine's was the party of the year. You wouldn't have known it from the outside, though. Things were quiet on N.E. Schuyler — a faint music coming from somewhere — but so hushed that when Nix and K.A. pulled up after getting a few slices — *not* from Jacob's, Nix noted — and talking more about Nix's plans for the summer, the boys couldn't tell whether the famed party they had heard about was happening. All they saw were a few flickering lights from Ondine's windows. Everything else was as silent as a Tuesday night in January.

"You sure it's tonight, bro?" Nix turned.

"Yeah, yeah. My sis told me for sure. A lot of kids know about it. It was all over MySpace." K.A. looked at the car clock, which read 10:27. "I don't know. Maybe Ondine decided to keep it mellow. She's the only girl I know who can give Morgan a run for her money being uptight."

The two boys walked across the lawn, hands in their pockets. When they got inside, the scene changed. It was dark at Ondine's, and though there were at least a hundred people lining the halls, sitting on the stairs, dancing in the sunken living room, the house seemed full of nothing but thrumming shadows. It was noisy — both could feel it — but it was a noise they could sense more than they could hear. Music played. People K.A. knew from school danced. Nix waved to a few folks from the squat. It seemed that all of young Portland was there. Finn and Evelyn; Rainy Alvarez, the twenty-something waitress from Jacob's; Li'l Paul, Morgan's manager from the Krak; tons of kids from McKinley; even a few from Penwick. Despite the awkward parting that afternoon, Finn waved and Evelyn smiled. Shadows and light undulated. People laughed, music hit Nix and K.A. low. Yet nothing seemed loud — and everyone seemed happy.

The perfect party, K.A. thought.

It was he who saw Ondine first. He knew her from soccer when they were younger. He'd always liked her and, from one overachiever to another, admired her. If someone had asked him, K.A. would have said that she was beautiful, but he'd never given it much thought. That changed tonight. For the first time Ondine's beauty impressed itself on him. There was something regal about her in the half-light, a playful smile glinting across her face, something undeniably sexy, too.

"Smokin'." He whistled under his breath and Nix looked in the same direction. "Her parents left her alone for the year," K.A. whispered, surveying the scene. "Seems to have had a good effect."

Like everyone else at school, he'd heard that Ondine's parents had gone away on sabbatical, leaving their seventeen-year-old daughter alone for her senior year, but it seemed to K.A. that Ondine was just now realizing the immense possibilities afforded by that absence. She seemed — well, she seemed grown-up. Self-confident and aware. Something K.A. yearned to be and didn't know anything about. She stood near the kitchen talking to a senior boy he knew, but she was also keeping tabs on her party — her house, her mother's art on the walls, the stereo people were plugging their iPods into. When she saw him she walked over.

"K.A.!" Ondine laughed and did a little twirl. "Pretty tight, huh?"

"Damn, Ondine." K.A. looked around at the dancing teenagers. "Who, like, *made* this?"

She smiled. "Well, your sister helped." She looked over her shoulder at Neve, who was standing in a doorway talking to another girl. "And of course Neve's here —"

K.A. tried to keep his face cool as he looked over, but he bit his lip. "Neve, huh?"

" '*Neve, huh?*' " Ondine laughed. "Yeah, Neve-huh helped. But really, it was Moth. He bought us the booze and spread the word — or so I gather." She shook her head and surveyed the scene. "You know Moth?"

He nodded. "James Motherwell? That guy's still around? I heard he got kicked out of U. of O. a few years ago. Some big dust thing." K.A. shrugged. "He made this happen, huh? I guess you never know about folks." He grinned, putting his arm around Ondine. "You're sure running with a fast crowd these days, little Ondine Right Wing."

She laughed and looked down. "I guess. Moth ran into Morgan and me at the liquor store, and what was supposed to be a chill thing for a few friends became the party of the year. I swear to god the kegs won't kick. And people keep coming. If I weren't

having so much fun, I'd be totally bugging. But no one is com-
plaining and everyone seems to be enjoying themselves. I have
Indra collecting keys at the door."

K.A. nodded, surveyed the pulsating crowd. "I'd say. Where's
Morgue?"

She waved a hand toward the dance floor.

"In Moth's clutches probably. I think he likes her."

She smiled then looked over his shoulder at Nix, who'd been
quiet the whole time. K.A. followed her gaze, lingering a moment where Neve stood chatting with two boys he didn't recognize. He fake-smacked his head.

"Jesus, I'm an asshole. Ondine," he said, "I want you to meet
someone. This is Nix." Nix offered a hand. "Nix, Ondine. Sorry
guys — just a little preoccupied." He tipped his head toward
Neve. "Now excuse me. I think someone's in need of a refill."

"Hey." Nix smiled. He had never seen a more beautiful girl.
Clear brown skin, big eyes, berry-stained lips. Impeccable 'do.
He noted the low-slung dark jeans and a tight black T-shirt that
showed just a bit of firm skin between hem and waistline. Silver
rings flashed on her long fingers. She was barefoot and had tied
her braids back with a red scarf that matched the polish on her
toes. Nix felt a sudden blush creep into his cheeks.

He looked at his shoes and wished that he owned better
ones.

Ondine stared back at the long-haired boy standing in front

of her and grinned. Too many boys had blushed like that in front of her tonight to count, and by now she was just chalking it up to something in the air, as if Moth had found a way to atomize dust.

"Hey." She leaned in, aware that she was flirting. "So, you work with K.A.?"

"Yeah," Nix said. "I mean, no. I mean, I quit tonight."

He felt peculiar. He never told strangers about his business — he even had a hard time trusting K.A. — but something about Ondine made him feel safe. *Her eyes,* he thought. They were purple-blue-brown and furry and they made him feel like he could rest.

"You quit? Why? I thought Jacob was cool."

"Yeah . . ." Nix trailed off. He thought about the light around Jacob and for the first time since he'd seen it a month ago, felt something else besides terror. Something like — power? Like maybe he could do something to change it? He didn't know what he was thinking altogether yet, or why it had hit him then, there, in the middle of a party where he didn't know anyone. It was just an instinct, somewhere low and unformed, but standing there next to Ondine, he felt calmer.

He waved it off. "You know, my accountant. He told me dishwashing's over; the real money's in garbage collecting. I'm gonna join the union Monday."

Ondine laughed. "Go Teamsters," she cheered. She could

tell the boy didn't want to talk about whatever was bothering him, but appreciated his attempt at a joke. For some reason she felt connected to him, though not in a sexual way — well, not quite. She found Nix attractive — with his widely spaced black eyes; his lean, toned frame — but there were a lot of guys in Portland who affected that look. He felt like something more. As if she had known him for a long time and was starting to know him again. She put a hand on his arm.

"Tonight is about relaxing."

He looked at the girl, felt her cool-warm hand on his skin.

Ondine stepped a little closer. "Do you like people watching?"

For a moment Nix imagined a circle of people standing around him and Ondine doing something he hadn't thought about doing since the sweetpea girl in Seattle. He thought about how good it would be to feel warm flesh up against his. The salt taste of sweat, the giggles as hair got in all the wrong places. Whenever he'd been with the sweetpea girl, Nix had always insisted on absolute darkness, because he wanted to be able to see even the faintest glimmer of light if it came. The thought of him and Ondine, and people watching, though — *mmm*. The two of them bathed in light, fused, glowing.

Nix felt a burst of desire — and power.

His cheeks caught fire. Ondine, seeing his blush, clapped one hand to her mouth and pointed at him with the other. For a moment he thought she was repulsed, but her laughter penetrated the deep throb of the music.

"I just meant —" Ondine began, but Nix cut her off.

"I know," he said, his cheeks still burning. "I mean, I know now."

Ondine smiled wider. "Well, come on then. Let's take a look around. Every freak in Portland must be here tonight."

She took her new friend by his thin arm — thin but muscled, she noted in the part of her brain that, like everyone else's tonight, seemed to be tuned to a sexual frequency. It seemed that everywhere they went, the shadows got a little darker, the air a little hotter.

Inside Ondine's hand, Nix flexed his bicep as hard as he could, and let her lead him into the fray.

CHAPTER 6

OMETHING CHANGED AT MIDNIGHT.

Morgan didn't know exactly when she realized she was the drunkest she'd ever been in her life, but she knew it was some time after James Motherwell placed his thigh between her legs on the dance floor. She was sweaty. He was hot.

He was sweaty. She was hot.

Sweaty.

Hot.

Something slipped inside of her.

"Mmm." She half moaned. That's about as far as she could get.

"You smell good," Moth said. His warm lips grazed Morgan's neck. She pushed against his mouth, willing him to bite.

The room seemed to swell and contract, swell and contract, as if it were breathing. Everything had gotten very loud. Something pressed against her thigh. Morgan was trying to remember where she was. Ondine waved at her as she walked by, and then she was gone and Morgan wasn't sure if she'd been there. Her eyes focused and she was staring at the side of Neve Clowes's face. Neve was gazing moonily at K.A. They were sitting on a couch that had been pushed off to the side of the dance floor. The girl had slipped off one of her shoes and was running her toes on the bare place between K.A.'s shoe and the bottom of his pants.

Slut. Morgan felt her stomach surge.

"I should check on my brother."

Moth moved closer. "Little brother's doing just fine, princess." He nuzzled her neck. "Some secrets no one should know, Morgan dear."

"What's that supposed —"

Moth's teeth were a little crooked and the tiniest bit pointed and they shone when he laughed. "Don't you worry your perfect head about it."

"K.A. knows everything about me —"

His thigh pressed against hers. "Not everything, sweet."

"Whathe*fuck* are you *talking* about?"

"Nothing, love. Nothing," Moth said louder. She whipped her head from side to side and he grabbed her shoulders. "My god, you want it, don't you? But it's too soon, Morgan. Too soon."

His hands felt hot on her skin and her head felt strange. What was he talking about? Too soon? She felt stuffed full of cotton. Cotton, or something heavier. Dirt. No, not dirt — dust. She'd heard the stories about Moth: that he dealt the stuff, talked about it as if it were the ticket to Nirvana. He'd been getting her drinks all night. Had he spiked them? Morgan doubted it. She'd had more than enough to drink to account for her disorientation. Somehow she felt Moth wouldn't make her do anything she didn't want to do.

His hot hands were kneading her shoulders and she realized she'd been quiet for too long. She looked up at him, smiling as brightly as she could, though her mouth felt rubbery. Moth smiled back.

"There she is," he said. "There's my wild child."

Morgan dropped her eyes. She liked him — liked his heat, wanted it to stay there, close to her, warming her, but her eyes kept returning to her brother and that little pizza-slinging bitch. She gawked, tripping on Moth's feet as she turned. The couple looked so — *disgusting,* Morgan managed to think before she swerved back to him.

"Shut up and kiss me," she said, though Moth hadn't been saying anything.

"Wait." He placed his head close to her ear and whispered. "I have something to tell you." He tugged at her earlobe with his teeth and she shivered. "Do you want to know about the Ring of Fire?"

Morgan felt her body soften to the handsome boy.

"Is that . . . the party? Around the solsshti — I mean solshstish — Sol —"

"Solstice," Moth instructed. "Your birthday." Moth's breath smelled like sugar and . . . more sugar.

"My —" Morgan was confused. Her birthday wasn't until September.

"Sshh." Moth's hiss was wet against her ear. "It's a secret. Secret solstice, secret day." He cupped her chin, turned her head until their eyes met. "You know how to keep secrets, don't you?"

She nodded. "Secret solstice," she whispered.

He smiled and leaned forward and Morgan closed her eyes. Her lips quivered; instead she felt him once more against her ear. He whispered something, finishing up by nipping her earlobe.

"That's just ours, then."

Morgan nodded. "Niney-ssshevn —"

"Shhh." Moth placed a finger on his lips. "Don't worry. You'll know when the time comes." He pulled back and eyed her. "Now. How am I going to take advantage of you?"

She smiled. Slippity slide. "You want to take advantage of me?"

"I do," he said and Morgan felt herself move closer.

The boy disengaged so quickly that she almost toppled over. He straightened up, readjusted a pant leg. "But not now."

"What?" Morgan felt the dirty red flush of shame across her face and chest. Hadn't he just said he wanted her?

"Where are you going?"

He was already walking away. "Wait here, princess. I've got to find someone."

What the fuck? She steadied herself. Morgan D'Amici was a virgin. Morgan D'Amici was an ice queen. Morgan D'Amici was a prize. Morgan D'Amici did not come on to anyone. She had been almost ready to give herself to a stranger — a drug dealer! — and now he was walking away from her into a party that seemed to have doubled in size in the last ten minutes.

She felt cold spots on each of her shoulders, where his hands had been a moment ago. "Well screw you, too!"

The strangest image filled her mind then. Wings — dark wings. Wings that would rustle and raise her clear above everyone. Make them look at her. Make them want her.

I'll rise. I'll rise.

She was drunk, she knew that. But the slight had sobered her. She wanted to go home. Fuck James Motherwell. Fuck him. She looked at K.A., cozy on the couch with Neve. Touching his knee. Throwing her head back and laughing. Her brother seemed far away and she wanted to go to him and rescue him from that backstabbing whore, but at the same time she didn't want him to see how drunk she was. She scanned the room for Ondine, spotting her near the kitchen talking with that loser from Jacob's. What was his name?

Ondine. This was all her fault. She teetered toward them.

"James Motherwell is a pig," she blurted when she got within shouting distance. Everything was blurry and had gotten very loud. She had to steady herself against the wall. She yelled and watched her former friend's face fall.

"Morgan! What up? What's wrong?"

"You shouldn't have let him come." She advanced uncertainly. "I'm leaving. I need a ride home."

Ondine looked at her friend. "Who? What are you talking about?"

"*Moth*. Your friend, James Motherfucker."

"I — you were supposed to stay over. There are all these people here. I've got to deal with this mess —" Ondine pointed around at the party, which was now out of control.

"The *mess* is that you invited that prick in the first place."

Ondine tried to put her hand on Morgan's shoulder but she shook it off.

"Invite him? Morgan, I couldn't do anything. You were at O'Brian's. You saw what happened."

She ignored her. "Thanks, Ondine. No I really mean it. *Thanks*. My brother and that little sausage-faced whore, and now you."

"What are you talking about?"

Blue flashing lights illuminated the packed living room.

"Oh shit!" Ondine cried. "The cops!"

Morgan didn't seem to notice. "Don't you worry. I'll get home on my own." She turned and nodded to Nix, who stared back at her, his dark eyes intent. "So you can get back to hitting on this loser. Though loser might be an exaggeration. More like a nothing. Isn't that what your ridiculous name means, Nix? Nothing? Zero?"

Nix stayed silent, his eyes fixed. Though the intensity of his stare scared her, Morgan waved him off and turned back to Ondine. "That's what you want, right? Someone you can push around? Or maybe that's Neve's role. I like how you pimped her out to my brother. Really classy. But hey" — she smiled and narrowed her eyes — "what's a little betrayal among friends?"

"No, Morgan . . . you've got it wrong —"

She had already turned to leave. Ondine tried to run after her, but Morgan was swallowed by the crowd. When she got back to the kitchen, Nix was still waiting for her. He frowned.

"What's he look like?"

"Who?" Ondine was exasperated. She looked around the room then covered her eyes. "Wait — wait. I have to think."

"That cat, Moth. What's he wearing?"

She put a hand to her brow. She was shaking. "He's tall. Black curly hair. All in black." She held up her right hand. "He's got a big silver ring. And one of those — you know, Fu Manchus or whatever."

Nix turned. The look in his eye was curious.

"I'll find him."

⁐ ⁐ ⁐

NIX WASN'T SURE HOW LONG he wandered around Ondine's house. It seemed like he'd just left her, and it seemed like he'd been walking for hours. At one point he stopped and asked himself what he was doing, who he was looking for. Then the name came to him: *Moth*. He closed his eyes, shook his head to clear it. It was a good thing he hadn't taken dust. Something about the night had him flying already — and, judging from the looks of things, everyone else.

Especially Neve and K.A, he thought, chagrined. Earlier he'd spotted the duo on the couch. They'd stopped teasing each other and were now looking as though they were attempting to stitch their mouths together. K.A. had pushed Neve's dress up, his hand resting on the smooth bare skin of her upper thigh. The curve of Neve's ass was visible, and the tiniest glimpse of underwear. At the sight of it Nix had felt a flash of something — lust? jealousy? — but not just for Neve. It had been the three of them up till then. Now Nix knew he would be excluded from the old grouping.

Moth. He snorted. And Morgan thought Nix was a stupid name.

He had a few questions for the older boy. Though he was pretty sure he wasn't going to like the answers, he was still determined to ask them.

Finding him in the swirling dervish of Ondine's first — and last, Nix was sure — party wasn't so easy. First there was the mass of dancing bodies in the living room to get through, now the damp crowd around one of the unkickable kegs. He was heading toward a black bobbing head near the front door when a bright light invaded his peripheral vision. He almost dropped his beer. The haloed figure of Jacob Clowes pressed through the crowd, on the hunt, the light around him burning brighter than Nix had ever seen it. For a moment he was confused. Who could Jacob be looking for if not him? The fire was so bright he couldn't think straight. . . .

Jacob was looking at someone, his heavy brow furrowed. Nix followed his gaze. At the end of it, in a dark corner, was Tim Bleeker. And on his lap — Nix blinked, not trusting his eyes — sat Neve Clowes.

Her spine curled like a young unstaked vine as she swayed on Tim Bleeker's knee. It was hard to tell if she was uncomfortable or just drunk. Probably a bit of both, he thought. Her arms clasped Bleek's neck, but it looked to Nix as though she were hanging on so she didn't fall to the floor, and the drug dealer had his face in her chest. Still, how the hell had she ended up on his lap in the first place? And where was K.A.? Nix caught a glimpse of Neve's confused stare and guessed that she'd already sampled Bleek's wares.

Another hand worked its way up Neve's narrow thigh. Asshole! Though that was not enough. Neve was barely sixteen, Bleek in his twenties. Nix didn't know what to do. Should he find K.A.? Do something himself? Jacob was now striding in his daughter's direction. The crowd seemed to split around him — almost everyone in Portland knew the man — and Nix saw Evelyn and Finn hurrying to keep up with him, Evelyn directing. She must have spotted Neve at the party and called Jacob. Evie, who used to babysit for the younger girl, had said more than once that Jacob Clowes was the closest thing she had to a father.

Nix looked again at the slight blonde. She seemed so young and helpless, so oblivious to the storm that was gathering around her. He thought of the sweetpea girl, of his mother, of all the women he'd failed to protect. His breath tightened. He dug around in his pocket, calming himself with the fact that the familiar roll was still there.

He started heading toward them, then felt a hand on his shoulder.

"Hold up, son." The voice was low but clear. "We need to talk."

Nix kept his eyes on the scene in front of him.

"Yeah? About what?"

"I think you know."

Nix gritted his teeth and turned to look at the speaker. He hadn't needed to see Moth's face to know it was the same man from the park — the same one he'd gotten his dust from earlier in the day. That the stranger seemed to be following him infuriated Nix, yet he did not walk away.

"I gotta take care of something."

He started again toward Neve and Bleek. He had to help, had to make up for —

Across the living room Jacob was untangling his daughter, shoving Bleek away. Neve slumped in her father's arms, and when he caught her, Bleek — the coward — melted into the crowd of onlookers. Jacob folded his daughter to his chest, staring over her pale head. His eyes seemed to drill through the air and find Nix, whose right hand — still in his pocket, still clutching the roll — squeezed so hard that the bag almost burst.

Again, Moth spoke. The voice was all too familiar.

"That's not your business, man. Not tonight."

Nix whirled. "What? What the fuck do you know about what is or isn't my business?"

"The time to help is coming, Nix. I promise. At the beginning you have to let the world be as it is."

Across the room, Jacob, fire-eaten, was carrying his trashed daughter out of the party. His eyes caught Nix's again, hostile now. He needed someone to blame — anyone but Neve — and Nix supposed he deserved it. Though he wanted to go to Jacob, protest his innocence and declare his guilt at the same time, Moth's last words stopped him.

"If you're fucking me, I'll . . . I'll *burn* you."

Nix didn't know what he meant, but Moth seemed to.

The older boy smiled, his soul patch sharp as a tusk beneath his lip.

"You'll light us all up one day, Nix Saint-Michael. I only hope I'm there to see it."

℘ ℘ ℘

"So it's you."

They were standing in a shadow near the back door, smoking a cigarette. Nix didn't smoke often but he felt he needed a cigarette now. The sight of Neve and Bleek and Jacob — especially Jacob, on fire, reproach in his eyes — had shaken him. He crouched on his haunches then straightened up, stubbing his half-smoked cigarette in a nearby bottle.

"I had a feeling it was you."

"Of course it's me." Moth nodded.

"James Motherwell, huh."

"No." Moth shook his head. "It's Moth. That's my real

name, just like Nix is yours." He paused. "But all of this is for later. Now. About the gathering in a few weeks."

"'The Ring of Fire,'" Nix said through a tight jaw, the quotation marks audible in his voice. It was as if someone had told him about it, but he couldn't remember hearing anyone saying the words.

"Exactly. You're coming."

Nix nodded.

"You need directions —"

"Highway ninety-seven . . ." He had a hard time believing the words were indeed coming from his mouth. He felt the cool beer in his hand, saw Moth standing in shadow in front of him. He stuttered and then righted himself. "I think — I think I know where it is already."

Moth smiled. "You're better than they said."

Nix was on the verge of asking "Who?" but he thought he knew that, too. Not a name, a face, but . . . he knew. It had something to do with the lights he saw.

"The Ring of Fire," he repeated. "But why Jacob? What about Jacob?"

"All in good time, Nix." Moth paused. "First things first: the time for explanations will come. I'm guessing I can trust you not to tell anyone."

Nix smiled, though he didn't feel happy. "No. I don't think I'll be telling anyone." Then again, speaking words that were barely occurring to him, he said, "Ondine's coming though, isn't she?"

"Yes, Ondine's coming. She has trouble finding places, though. It's a blind spot." Moth looked at him. "You'll have to help her."

He'd have to help her. Nix felt impatient — the turn of events, Neve's thin little arms, her helplessness, made him want to get back to Ondine, be close to her, protect her.

"Is that all? No one else?"

"You don't know? Interesting."

"Not Finn?" The question was a formality. Nix knew Finn wasn't coming.

Moth shook his head.

"Not K.A."

"No, brother. Not K.A. It would have been nice, but no, not him."

Nix's eyes narrowed. He thought of all of them there at the party: Ondine, Moth, K.A., Neve, Jacob. Even Bleek. The proximity was both completely random, born of life in a small city, and perilously meaningful. His mouth went dry and what came out was almost a whisper:

"Morgan?"

Moth smiled. "Yes. Yes, Morgan. Of course Morgan. Morgan needs to be tamed, true, taught, but yes, Morgan, too. But you. You are very precious. You are the most precious. Now, how are you with your . . . supply? You won't need any for the gathering, of course, and then afterward we'll start weaning you. Only when it's the right time, though. Only the right time." Moth's voice faded. "Oh god, she's going to be so happy with me. She's going to be so proud. . . ."

For a moment Nix thought Moth was talking about Morgan. Then he realized he was referring to someone else. Something about the remove of Moth's face — its glassiness, its vacancy — panicked him. Was he high? What had they just been talking about?

Ondine walked up. Nix calmed, erasing all expression. He knew he had to protect her — at least for now, until he knew more. At least until the Ring of Fire.

She was angry and shaking her head.

"Well, you did it, James Motherwell. The cops are here. The house is a total mess and there are about a hundred people here I don't know. Morgan's probably getting abducted somewhere between here and Southeast. She left without a car, you know. Pissed."

Moth's mouth was tight, but his eyes stayed unworried. "I thought she might."

"You know, you have a lot of nerve coming into my party, disrespecting my friends, then smiling and laughing at life's rich pageant. Who invited you, huh?"

"Morgan did, if I remember correctly." Moth rubbed his lips

together as if to erase a smile. "All right, all right, my lady. It's all good. I'll make sure she gets home all right. And don't worry about the mess." He looked around at the carpet of plastic beer cups, cigarette butts, red wine stains. "Moth will make sure this all gets cleaned up."

She turned to Nix. "Don't you love it when someone talks about himself in the third person? It's *so* cool." Then she shook her head, screwing up her face. She was about to let Moth have it, but something in Nix's eyes short-circuited her anger. "Right," she managed to spit out. "Whatever. The freaking cops are here. I'll probably get arrested. My parents will get called, and since they're somewhere in Colorado right now, I don't think they're going to be too pleased —"

"Your parents aren't going to hear anything."

Just then K.A. walked up. He had the too-earnest look of a drunken kid trying to appear sober. "Hey, did you she where Morgave — Neve — Morgan went? I saw her, I mean, I saw Jacob, and Morgan went . . ." The boy's voice trailed off in confusion. "Hey," he said then, "the cops are here."

Moth threw back his head and laughed. "Go home, hero boy. Your sister and your girlfriend will be fine."

"Who are you?" K.A. scowled.

"Moth."

"*Moth*," he mimicked. "Where's my sister, asshole?" K.A.

started toward the older boy, but quieted when Ondine put a hand on his arm. "I saw you macking on her earlier. Where is she?"

"Morgan went home," Nix interrupted. "On foot. I think you should go try to find her. Neve got taken home by her dad."

For a moment K.A. looked confused, then he straightened up and stepped again toward Moth. "Man, if anything happens to Morgan — to Neve — to either of them, you are hosed. By me. *Personally.*"

K.A.'s words would have been more effective if the last word hadn't come out *pershonally.* Before anyone could say anything else, a siren wailed and the doorbell rang. *Too much,* Ondine thought. There was too much happening. She was confused. Too many pieces — she needed time.

"Let me deal with this," Moth said.

Ondine was about to tell him to go screw, but remembered the scene at the liquor store, the cashier's sudden pliability. She stopped and quieted, her hands falling to her sides.

"Yeah, all right," she heard herself saying. "Yeah, why don't you tell them you're Dr. Mason. Dr. Ralph Mason, the geneticist. Dr. Mason, perhaps you'd care to offer a scientific explanation for the color of your daughter's eyes —"

Ondine's taunt trailed mid-word. She had no idea why she had just said the last few things — other than that she had been looking at Moth while she spoke, at his green eyes, and they made her want to lie down, as if in cool, soft grass, and weep.

His face was bland. He leaned in, whispering.

"You know why you're different from your parents, Ondine." She stiffened and he moved closer, his voice still lower. "Now listen carefully. Highway ninety-seven south out of Bend. The twenty-mile point. Paulina East Lake Road. The Little Crater campground. Park there. The Ring of Fire."

For a moment she could only stare. Her jaw hung open and she could feel K.A.'s and Nix's eyes on her. K.A.'s expression was confused, but Nix's was steady. She swallowed the lump in her throat and shook her head.

"You've ruined my house, screwed me, and definitely screwed Morgan, and you want to tell me about a party? A *rave*? So I can hang out with all the *cool kids*? Get the fuck out of here!"

Moth touched her. "I'm going. I'll take the cops. Don't worry —"

She fought back the urge to scream.

"Don't *worry*? Get out, Moth. Just get out —"

K.A. was between the two of them.

"It's all right," he began. "I'll make sure he goes." The boy turned to Moth. "I think you've done enough damage for one night."

Moth's eyes narrowed. "You don't know what you're messing with."

K.A. didn't blink. He seemed very sober all of a sudden. Very sober, or just drunk enough to pull this off.

"I said, let's go."

Moth put his hands up and smiled.

"I'm going, I'm going." He backed toward the door and his eyes found Ondine's one last time. "You *will* need me," he said, speaking over K.A.'s head — over the music and over the thrumming that filled the space between Ondine's ears. Though she knew he was almost whispering she felt as if Moth were talking right into her head.

"You will need me and I will come."

It was hard for her to speak but she felt she had to. Her voice emerged, jagged.

"*Need you?* No one needs you, Moth. You're extra. Good for nothing. The kind of thing you leave on the side of the road."

"Jesus. She's going to love you." Moth shook his head. Then he moved toward her one last time, too fast for her to withdraw. "You'll need the password. It's 'exidis.' E-X . . . I-D . . . I-S. You can remember that. And by the way" — he wasn't whispering anymore — "you did invite me, Ondine. Or at least Morgan did. I never fly to a light that's not lit."

With that James Motherwell bowed and slipped out the back door.

ை   ை   ை

THERE WAS A SHITSTORM TO CLEAN UP and Ondine wouldn't let her imagination freak her out any more than it already had. She made her way to the kitchen to check out the damage, which was significant: broken glasses everywhere, beer all over the floor, cigarettes stubbed out on the counters. Even one of the cupboard windows had been smashed. She threw cold water on her face, tied back her braids, and tried to shake off her mounting terror. One thing she knew: This party was *over*.

By the time she made it to the front door with Nix and K.A., most of the kids, spooked from the sirens and blue lights, had filed out the back. It didn't matter anyway. When Ondine opened the front door the cops just stood there smiling. The house smelled like beer and pot smoke and there were still drunk underaged teenagers milling past, but the police acted as if they were there to sell raffle tickets. They smiled, asking if everything was all right.

"Yes, sir," she said, and tried to look them in the eyes, but it didn't seem to matter. They were blank. She had seen the look before — from the guy at the liquor store.

"Well, all right then!" Both cops turned on their heels to leave.

Ondine looked after them, stunned. She felt like calling out — *Hello, I'm underaged! Hello! Alcohol is being consumed!* — but instead turned to Nix and K.A. behind her. "What the hell just happened?"

They shook their heads, just as confused.

"Did Moth talk to them?"

K.A. nodded. "I saw him out here for a second. But not that long. I don't know. Maybe he knows somebody on the force."

Moth didn't know any cops. It was something else. She just couldn't figure out what. Something about the way Moth controlled people, the way he rendered them powerless without lifting a finger — well, maybe a finger, remembering the way he raised his hand before the cashier in the store. The intensity, if not the gesture, was familiar. She recognized it in herself.

What the hell did he mean, *She's going to love you?* Who? How?

Ondine felt sick. She had done something wrong and hadn't had to fess up to it. James Motherwell or no, she should have gotten in trouble. Hell, she *wanted* to get in trouble. Her parents would have been called, they'd have been forced to come back, she'd have gotten grounded. Normal teenaged consequences. But instead Ondine's parents had left her alone for a whole year, she threw an out-of-control party on the first night of their absence, and except for some heavy cleanup and maybe a couple hundred bucks in repairs, she hadn't had to pay for what she'd done. It wasn't *right*. At the same time, she was relieved to have gotten off, and that relieved feeling made her feel guilty. This, too, was familiar.

After a few awkward good-byes and vows to find Morgan,

K.A. drove away, promising to come back the next morning to help clean. Then it was just Ondine and Nix, sitting on the second-floor landing, their legs hanging through the balcony bars, surveying the wreckage below. A dozen or so passed-out bodies lined the living room floor. It looked like a crazy Jackson Pollock painting, all squiggles of stains and dots of forties bottles and entwined bodies.

Ondine hung her head.

"What a mess."

For a while the boy was quiet, then he turned and faced Ondine, his raspy voice low.

"He told you about it, didn't he?"

"What?" Ondine pretended not to know what he was talking about.

"The Ring of Fire."

"The Ring of Fire? That awesome *rave* near the *solstice*? Where all the *cool kids* are gonna be? Jesus. Yeah. He told me about it." She scoffed, wanting to avoid the entire subject. All she wanted to do was be angry at Moth, think about how she was going to clean up the mess, and then go to sleep. But she couldn't. There was someone next to her who wasn't seeming to go away — nor did she want him to, which was sort of unbelievable since they were nearly strangers. But why Nix? Why all of a sudden was it just the two of them? Ondine let out an uncharacteristic sigh.

"Why? Are you going?"

He shrugged.

She grabbed the railing and shook it. "There's something weird going on. Something — I don't know what —"

She pointed to two boys in black baseball caps nestled side by side on her mother's favorite white leather couch.

"I don't even know those cats."

Nix laughed. "Hey —"

"No, I —"

Ondine looked at him. He was looking back at her, studying her, almost, though his eyes were kind and calm. She released her head and stared at the ceiling.

"What the hell am I doing? My parents just left today and already I'm in trouble."

"You're not, though."

She stared. "Right."

"Anyway, it's freedom. With freedom comes responsibility."

"Oh, please. Are you going to tell me to rock the vote now?"

Nix thought about his own conversation earlier that night with K.A. — *You can't run away from yourself* — and laughed. Karma was a bitch.

"Ondine. I'm your friend." He'd never said those words to anyone.

"My friend?" She felt her eyebrows rise. "You don't even know me."

He stared and she felt sorry she'd said the last words.

"I mean —"

"Call it friends at first sight."

"Oh, Jesus." Ondine put her hands over her face and sighed. "I'm sorry. It's just that I've always wanted to fuck up. I never fuck up and I've always wanted to." She pulled her hands away. "I guess I got a good start. God, I hope everyone makes it home okay. Indra really dropped the ball."

Nix nodded. "I think this might be your first and last party."

"Wanna help me clean?"

"I'm all yours. I don't have anywhere else to go."

She reached for the boy's hand and squeezed. "You're nice." Opening an eye, she still failed to address what was on both their minds—the Ring of Fire, the solstice. "James Motherwell's a prick, you know."

"Yeah." Nix cast his eyes down. He seemed to want to say something — both of them did — but without knowing what.

"I mean, I never fuck up. *Never.*"

He laughed. "I do all the time."

"Then we make a good pair."

"Yeah."

Thoughts whirled inside her head. Faces. Words. *Ring of Fire. Exidis. She'll love you.* Moth had said these things aloud,

124

she was pretty sure, or had they been there, inside her head? Waiting for her to hear them?

It was too much. She dropped back onto the white plush carpet, her legs still dangling from the side.

"What a mess." She sighed and closed her eyes.

Nix stared at Ondine's face. *My god,* he thought, *you are so beautiful.*

Which made him again think of Neve. K.A.'s Neve, his friend's, well, if not girlfriend, then steady crush. Lovely Neve. And the sweetpea girl, and what he'd felt in the dark, and how he'd run away from her before the light showed up, as it had around his mother, and Jacob, and all those people in between.

Ondine. Her eyes flickered behind her eyelids; she was asleep. Nix realized how tired he was. Tired of running, tired of being scared. Tired of being alone. He lay next to her, nestled his arm around her small shoulders. The girl's body was warm and cold at the same time, as if two forces were at war inside her. He knew that conflict, had known it all his life. It was peaceful, lying beside her, and he let himself close his eyes. He thought of the people in his life: Jacob and K.A. and Bleek — and Neve, the common link between them. He saw Neve's flushed cheeks when she swayed on Tim Bleeker's lap and he saw the edge of her lace underwear when she made out with K.A. on the couch and he saw her pale, pale hair disappearing into the light that emanated from her father when Jacob had taken her in his arms, as if the tiniest bit of the light had transferred to her.

No! He pushed the thought away.

Light stayed. That was the one thing he could count on. He looked down at Ondine again. Somehow he knew the light would never appear around her.

His hand groped in his pocket for the dust, but before he found it he relaxed. His right hand was in his pocket, inches from the roll, but his left arm was around Ondine. He was in her house. He knew he was safe there.

He managed to think before he dipped into the darkness that it was the first night in a year he wasn't afraid to dream.

II

Ring of Fire

ORGAN D'AMICI WOKE UP the morning after the best party of the year to the sound of someone banging pots in the kitchen. Or was that her head? Something smelled good. Bacon, she thought. And pancakes. She heard the familiar sound of her brother's lumbering shuffle and turned in her bed to face the window. Pain. Light. Pain. Sunlight grazed her face and she wiggled her toes against the silky smoothness of four-hundred thread-count sheets. Despite her headache, she registered that K.A. was making breakfast, just like the old days, and it made her happy. She nestled deeper under the all-white covers. She was warm and safe and —

Her eyes opened and her stomach seized.

Last night. What happened last night?

Her last memory was of dancing with James Motherwell. She asked him to kiss her and he walked away. She yelled at Ondine. Then she left the party. The road was black. Streetlights. A car passing.

That was it. Everything after that, she realized, was a wash of nothingness. She must have blacked out, or —

No. Moth wouldn't have done that.

Or would he have? Would she have let him? She put her hand between her thighs. Panties still on. Nothing out of order. The thought of James Motherwell taking advantage of her while she was drunk made her angry, but the thought of him keeping a trophy made her *crazy*.

How could she have drunk so much? Morgan never drank. She didn't like how out of control alcohol made her feel, and she certainly never blacked out. So how did she get home?

She looked out the window at the yellow roses her mother had planted beside her window years ago, just after her father had left. To brighten your day, Yvonne had said. Normally the flowers cheered her up, but today Morgan could only notice the leaves that had been eaten; the dead petals; the way the scraggly, thorny canes never managed to disguise the fact that she lived in a house one step above a trailer. Tracing a finger along a stray lock of hair on her pillow, she felt clogged, fuzzy, scared. A stick was lodged there. She looked at it then felt the back of her head, finding a speck of dried leaf. She pulled herself out of bed. Her legs and her feet were mud splattered; tiny red scratches flecked her arm. My god, she thought. Had they done it in the dirt, like animals?

She'd pretend as if she hadn't seen anything. It's a Sunday

like any other, Morgan told herself. I'm home. Kaka's making breakfast. *Everything is fine.* She went through her normal routine. Walked over to her vanity, yanked on a pair of paisley-print pajama bottoms, dragged a brush through her tangled hair, ignoring the bits of leaves and sticks that fell from it, then put on her favorite Japanese blue-and-white *yukata,* tying it neatly at the waist.

Everything is fine. If it isn't, I will make it so.

She rubbed her eyes, pinched her cheeks to get the color back into them, and walked barefoot into the kitchen, smiling. K.A., Sunday-morning casual in a black T-shirt and jeans, looked up from the stove.

"Well, if it isn't the midnight rambler —"

Morgan panicked until she realized he was joking about the way she'd left the party. She cast her blue eyes down, playing sheepish. K.A. opened his arms and she leaned into his chest, small and quiet. There was the old comfort there, but other faces intruded: Moth's, and Neve's. The tramp.

Her brother must have felt her tense up, because he squeezed her, then stepped back.

"So what happened to you? Last I heard you were with that Moth dude, then you were gone. I looked around Portland all night. I kept calling but Mom was at Todd's. No one answered and your cell was off. . . ."

Morgan stayed quiet. She tried to match her breathing with

K.A.'s. Tried to concentrate on where she was now: in her kitchen, in the morning, where everything was bright and fine.

Her brother cupped her chin with a flour-dusted hand, tilting her face upward. "Hey, Sis. I was worried about you."

She managed a tight laugh. "Well, I'm here now."

He held her gaze for a moment longer, then looked down. She followed his eyes. Her feet weren't dirty, they were filthy, blackened by a crust of mud.

"Oh, man."

She pulled away, wishing she'd showered first.

"That was when I was a kid, K.A." She opened the fridge and peered into it, not knowing what else to do. "I just took a while getting home, that's all."

"Barefoot?"

He was looking at the silver sling-backs sitting next to the door: Manolos, her one pair. Her eyes followed his. She tried to keep her voice light. "Anything for the shoes! Now where's the OJ? I'm starving!"

K.A. gestured to the dining room, though his face was still worried. "Table's set." He stopped. "Were you there when Jacob showed up?"

She shuffled to the table, pulling the cotton robe closer around her. "Clowes? Isn't he a little old to be crashing high school parties?"

"I guess someone told him Neve was there."

132

Pouring herself some juice, Morgan kept her face impassive, but inwardly she was rejoicing. So Neve hadn't gotten into K.A.'s pants after all! Thank god for small favors.

"What happened?"

"I don't know really. I mean, one minute Neve was with me. And then she got up to hit the can —"

"Charming," she interjected, but K.A. didn't smile.

"And she just didn't come back. The next thing I know she's sitting on goddamned Tim Bleeker's lap, and before I could break his face, Jacob showed up and took her home. It was, I don't know, *weird*."

Morgan couldn't help herself.

"That doesn't surprise me."

"That Jacob was there?"

"That Neve is, you know, into drugs. Dust."

K.A.'s face clouded, and she knew she'd pushed too far.

"How can you say that? Neve is your friend!"

Morgan tried to wave it away. "It's just . . . whatever. I've heard some things. Look, you're the one who saw her on a dealer's lap, not me."

"I'm sure there's a perfectly good explanation —"

She shook her head. "It's too early for this moment-of-truth crap, Kaka. I need coffee."

Morgan set about making coffee in the French press she wouldn't let anyone else in the house use or wash (she had a line about ruining the oils in the bean, but the truth was, she was afraid it would get chipped or broken, like her grandmother's plates). She liked making coffee. She'd have to, working at the Krak. The place was packed seven to eleven and Morgan was assistant manager. She liked the method of it, the precision of the process. Right now, she liked the fact that it got her away from K.A., gave her something to do with her hands, which were trembling.

When she came back to the table, he spoke of light things — his time at the party, who was there. He must have known something was up. Or maybe she'd pissed him off with her insinuations about Neve. What did she care? Neve was an unloyal double-dipper. A slutty little Penwick ho. How easily the lie about dust had rolled from her lips. Anyway, the bitch had it coming. You don't make moves on your best friend's brother. Not without asking first. And if Neve had asked, the answer would have been a resounding *hell no*.

While K.A. prattled on, she ate mouthful after mouthful of his signature blueberry sourdough pancakes soaked in maple syrup, much more than she'd usually eat. Food wasn't so interesting to Morgan. She blamed it on working in a restaurant, though she'd been that way her whole life. Really, she wanted to seem busy so K.A. wouldn't talk about anything heavy. Still, somewhere behind the bittersweet pop of blueberries in her mouth and her brother's plans for his upcoming soccer trip to

California, the events of the night before kept looping through her mind: buying booze at O'Brian's, getting ready at Ondine's, standing in Ondine's bedroom window showing Moth her —

There again: that slicing in her torso. Pulling her yukata tighter, she took another sip of coffee and tried to concentrate on what K.A. was saying. She couldn't. The beginning of the party, the low music. Seeing Moth; dancing with him in the pulsing shadows; the hot, soft kisses, then—nothing. What had she done? How far had she gone? Come on, Morgan, *remember.* It wasn't the blacking out that scared her. She was home; she was safe. It wasn't even Moth that pissed her off, or — *ugh* — Ondine, whom she knew she'd have to apologize to.

It was her dirty feet.

Her dirty feet and the sticks in her hair and the slashes of mud on her ankles and calves, the tiny red pricks, as if she had been running through —

She placed a hand around her brow and looked down. The dark wood of the table opened up and Morgan let herself sink into it.

"Morgue? Morgue?"

She looked up. She had sunk halfway into her chair. The long black hair she had brushed minutes earlier trailed through the syrup on her plate. K.A. cleared a strand from her face.

"Where'd you go?"

Where had she gone? When would she go there again?

"I didn't —"

K.A. furrowed his brow. "You were sleepwalking last night, weren't you?"

She shook her head and opened her mouth. Nothing came out.

He put down the fork he was holding and cupped his sister's hand in his own. "How long has it been? God" — he winced — "six years?"

Morgan took her hand away and dragged a piece of pancake through a pool of syrup.

"Five," she replied. "And I didn't sleepwalk last night. I was drunk. I blacked out." She stared at her brother. "Look. I'm home, aren't I? I went to a *bar*, K.A. I left the party and went to a bar. I got plastered, okay? *My name is Morgan and I'm an alcoholic.* Okay? Then I walked home." She set her fork down and pushed her plate away. "Barefoot."

K.A. frowned. "Look. Something happened last night and you're not telling me what . . ."

Morgan tucked a stray lock of hair behind an ear, her ever-present nervous habit, though she knew how ridiculous she must have seemed. Had she even gotten all the sticks out? She pulled her feet under the chair. She remembered mornings like this years ago, when their father was with them, when she was sleepwalking almost every night, so often that her mother and father kept watch over her in turns. She'd hear them fighting in the morning about how much sleep they'd gotten. Phil Jr. had always wanted to take her to see a psychiatrist — "It's not normal," he'd said — but Yvonne never let him. "She's just got a lot of energy," she'd argued. "She'll grow out of it."

Grow out of it she did. Not because she got older. She grew out of it because one night she woke up on one of her walks. She was twelve. It was dark — the deepest, blackest dark she'd ever seen — and she was in the middle of the forest. The place Morgan was more terrified of than anything.

She was standing over something. She couldn't tell what it was, so she picked it up. It was warm, soft, wet — *gross* — but she made herself carry it to a place where the trees were sparse and the moonlight filtered through. She saw that it was a little animal. A rabbit, she figured, though she couldn't be sure. Its skin had been stripped from its body. All that was left was a bloody carcass: lidless eyes; lipless mouth, snarling. When she dropped it she saw that there was blood on her hands, and she told herself that it had gotten there when she picked the animal up. Later that night, though, in the shower, she had to use a file to dig the scarlet flesh out from under her nails.

From then on Morgan stayed awake at night. She'd drink coffee, study. Her grades had always been good, but after seventh grade they were perfect. For a full year she went to sleep when the birds started chirping; she'd sleep just a few hours before school started, until she was convinced she'd broken the habit of sleepwalking. They let her come to school late because of her "sleep disorder," though Yvonne would never admit her daughter had an actual problem.

She could hear her mother's voice now, explaining to the school counselor: "She's just got a lot of energy."

Now Morgan was looking down at her dirty feet. Red scratches embroidered both ankles; one big welt embossed her right calf. Although she had just eaten, her stomach felt empty.

She got up from the table. "Listen, I've got work to do today. I'm on at the Krak this afternoon and I'd better do the dishes —"

"Morgue." K.A. stood. "Don't worry about the dishes. Listen, maybe we should tell Mom. I don't think we should just let this go. I don't want this to start again —"

"I *told* you. I'm *not* sleepwalking. I was drunk, I walked home, I stopped at a bar along the way. And you definitely do *not* need to tell Mom." She paused, shaking her head. "Anyway, according to Coach Gonzalez, you shouldn't have been within a mile of that party last night. You have soccer camp in two weeks. Drinking will get you kicked off the team, Kaka. So I wouldn't be telling too many people — especially Yackity-yack Yvonne — about how big sister got trashed at a party little brother was not supposed to be at." She picked up her plate and lifted her chin. "Don't you think?"

K.A. sat down and set his jaw, crossing his arms over his chest. He was used to Morgan bullying him. "Yeah, I guess."

"That's what I thought." She started clearing the plates like her mother usually did, stacking them in her arms. Their weight felt good. "Now let's move on. I think I've got some apologizing to do to Ondine. She's probably worried —"

"Uh, *yeah*. You were a real bitch last night."

Morgan flicked her hair over a shoulder. "I'll deal with that."

"And Neve? You were really mean to her, too."

"Of course." Neve's china-doll face popped up in front of her and she felt like slamming it down again. *The little maggot.* "I'll apologize to Neve. Neve's my friend."

She picked up the last of the dishes and headed into the kitchen, feeling better, clearer, more in control.

"Listen," she called out, "don't worry about me. And don't worry about the dishes, I'll take care of them." She poked her head past the doorway. K.A. was sitting at the table, his arms still crossed, eyes down. "Thanks for the p-cakes, Kaka."

He didn't look up. "Yeah, whatever."

Morgan frowned and returned to the kitchen. She'd deal with him — and Ondine and Neve — later. Right now she needed to get her head straight. She needed to figure out how long she'd been gone last night. What had happened after she walked out. Why she had left. How long she had been in the woods.

She poured the lemony soap out — *clean, clean* — and started wiping the dishes, silverware first, then glasses. Then plates. She liked the feeling of the warm water running over her hands, but she was still angry. She wanted to do something, make something change. Why now? Why the sleepwalking again? Morgan let her eyes roam around the room, looking for an answer. They lit on a band of knives, hanging on a magnetized strip above the sink, like a column of fat medieval soldiers in a line. A vision of that old movie *Carrie* flitted through her mind. What if they came at her? Realistically Morgan knew they wouldn't, and anyway, she'd prefer them to be aiming at Moth, the disgusting creep. Shaming her like that. She pictured his face, terrified, as a phalanx of knives sailed toward his head. It made her feel better. If she could just . . . if she could just have a little more control —

She found herself whispering while she moved the plates back and forth under the stream of water. *"Move move move —"*

Nothing did, of course. Not the slightest. She tried speaking it quickly, like a machine. She tried slowing it down. She tried saying please. Finally she just screamed.

"Move, you motherfuckers! *Move!*"

"What?" K.A. called from the living room, the sounds of Spanish *fútbol* in the background. "Morgue, you okay?"

"I'm fine. Just trying to scrub a pan."

How long had it been since she'd cried? All she could manage were the same dry heaves. She felt ashamed and powerless — a powerlessness made worse by the memory of the night before.

Abruptly she turned from the sink. *Fuck him. Fuck Moth. And fuck Ondine.* Past the dining room table she walked, swiping her keys up, then putting on her jacket.

"I'm going to the store," she called back. "I need to get some soap."

What she needed to do was find Moth. She'd feel better once she'd seen him.

She slammed the door behind her, and whether from the force of the door or something more sinister, the knives, the entire phalanx of them, clattered into the sink.

's 's 's

"That jerk!"

It was the first thing Ondine managed to think the morning after her party. Even before she fully woke up, James Motherwell's jade eyes crowded her thoughts, along with his voice, reedy, overconfident: *I never fly to a light that's not lit.* What was his problem? He talked like a comic book character. *Moth.* He disgusted her. Greasy hair. Flavor Saver. She sat up and got her bearings. Somewhere downstairs music was playing — the

Flame. Again. *Orange wings — white wings — blue wings — green. Filaments of fire — unspoken and unseen.*

God, she was so sick of that band.

Though Ondine knew all the words to every song on their first collection, *Fly,* something about the voice of their kittenish, spacey lead singer made her feel cold.

Her eyes drifted to the other side of the bed. It was rumpled, the pillow slept on. Who had put her there? Who had slept next to her? She knew she had fallen asleep on the landing last night. She was even in the same clothes — black T-shirt, jeans — she'd worn the night before, but someone had taken her lace-up black sandals off and, she realized as she ran her hands over her shoulder-length braids, untied her red scarf. She put her hand to her ears. Who had taken off her earrings?

Another name popped into her head.

She sniffed at her tank top, expecting the reek of cigarette smoke with a nice undercurrent of dried sweat, but instead smelled Trish's fabric softener, as if the shirt had just come out of the dryer. *Huh,* Ondine thought. *Well, at least I don't stink.*

Again she heard the music from below. Though the singing irritated her — it seemed so aggressive, taunting her, boring into her head like some insidious worm — she couldn't help but hum along. *I will make you happy. You will rue the day. You and I became one. A stranger and a twin.*

Shaking off the last bit of drowsiness, she headed downstairs.

"Nix!" she called out from the landing. The silence that greeted her made her feel less confident. "Nix?"

She scanned the living room below. He wasn't there, nor were the kids who had passed out the night before. In fact, nothing was in the living room — no backwash cups, no cigarette butts, no empties. No Jackson Pollock painting of red-wine stains, no ashtrays. Everything had been cleaned up and was exactly the way it had been when Trish, Ralph, and Max left the day before.

It was as if the party had never happened.

Ondine was trying to figure out how she'd slept through the vacuum cleaner, when the phone rang. Considering most of her friends called her cell, Ondine knew it was Trish or Ralph. She thought about the cops and felt her stomach flip-flop as she ran down the stairs.

"Hello?"

"Ondine, honey!" Ralph Mason's voice was warm and crackly over the unsteady line. Ondine could tell he was in the car, driving. She looked at the clock on the kitchen wall. It read eleven. They must have reached the Midwest, she reckoned.

"Dad! Where are you?"

"We just got out of Nebraska. Jesus, that's a big state. We

143

didn't have cell service forever, and then we hit Omaha. You wouldn't think Midwesterners drive like bats out of hell, but they do. But things have calmed down, and I wanted to call and make sure your first night went okay, before we disappear into another dead zone." He paused. "Miss us, baby?" Ralph chuckled and Ondine could hear the wind over his voice. She imagined clean Midwestern air streaming in through the open windows.

She laughed. "Yeah, Dad. I do. I miss you a lot. Is everything . . . okay?"

"Okay?" He pulled away from the phone. "Trish, hon, is everything okay?" She heard a distant "Sure is," and then it was Ralph's voice again. "Well, yeah, honey, everything is fine except for the fact that we haven't seen anything much higher than a Jesus Saves billboard in a day and a half and we miss our only daughter and Ivy crapped in the car twice. Other than that, everything is fine. But you? You okay, hon?"

"Oh yeah." Ondine found a confident note and turned it up. "All good."

"*All good*," her father repeated. "What'd you do last night?"

She looked around at what she hadn't noticed before. A clean kitchen. No. Spotless. Hospital clean. Her voice raised its pitch. "Hung out with Morgan D'Amici?"

"Uh-huh."

"That's all."

"Good. Sounds good." Ralph's voice had gotten patchy. "Listen, sweetheart. We're headed into the cornfields now, so we're probably going to get cut off. We just wanted to tell you we love you and we're thinking of you and we'll call when we get to the hotel tonight. Okay, hon?"

"Okay, Dad —"

"Everything all right?"

"Yeah, yeah."

"Well, good. I knew we could trust our little girl. Not so little though, now, huh?" Ralph laughed. "Anyway, sweetie. We'll call tonight, from Chicago. Kay?"

"Okay, Dad."

With that her father hung up. The conversation suited her father to a T, she thought, placing the phone back on its cradle. Unselfish in everything, but always efficient — even when it came to love. She realized that not only had her parents not heard anything about the party last night — cops and all — but looking around, it was clear everything had been cleaned up in the kitchen, too. Glasses sparkled on the shelves, floors and counters shone. In fact, everything was cleaner than it had been before, which was a hell of a statement in compulsively tidy Trish Mason's house. Ondine opened the refrigerator. A single orange juice container sat on the shelf. One of the last things she had done before the cops showed up was make a pair of screwdrivers for a giggling couple she hadn't recognized, and hadn't wanted

145

pawing through everything. The fridge had been a mess, splashed with beer, soda, red and yellow juices; crammed with a dozen empty cartons. Now there was just that single carton of unopened orange juice, sitting next to a virgin half-pint of half-and-half on the gleaming white shelf. The OJ was explainable, but the half-and-half was Trish's. *My daily indulgence,* she'd always say, patting a stomach that was still as trim as her daughter's, and Ondine had watched her mother pour the stuff into her coffee the morning before. Though she could imagine that she'd missed an unopened carton of orange juice when she'd pawed through the fridge last night, she had a harder time imagining a Portland high schooler bringing half-and-half to a keg party.

Ondine closed the fridge. Her eyes moved to the shelves over the counters. The glass pane that had been broken was now in one piece. She placed a hand on the butcher block to steady herself. What the hell was going on?

"Nix!" she called once more over the music. "Are you still here? Nix!"

She was trying to remember the night before. What had she and Nix done? They'd ended up in bed together, even if she woke up in her clothes. She knew she liked the mysterious dark-haired boy, but hoped she hadn't gone there.

"Out here!"

A voice floated in from the backyard, and Ondine wandered through the sunny room, as if it were Nix alone that gave her

146

direction. He was sitting on the steps of the slate terrace, staring at Ondine's maple. He had one of Ralph's Eddie Bauer jackets on and his long hair was pulled away from his face with Ondine's signature red scarf. She followed his eyes. If she hadn't known better, she'd have sworn the lawn had been mowed.

He spoke. "The leaves are so red —"

Ondine stood over the boy. Both were quiet, and far more serious than the sunny day called for.

Her words came in a rush. "How did you clean the house up so fast? And that cupboard in the kitchen. That cupboard got broken last night. Smashed. I saw it with my own eyes. Casey Martin broke it. I saw it, Nix. How did you fix it? You have to tell me what's going on."

He turned to look at her, his eyes squinting in the midmorning sun.

"I just want to know." She continued, faster now, almost hysterical. "There's something weird going on. Ever since yesterday, since the party. Since I met you. Since . . ." Ondine stopped herself, because she knew she could keep going back and back with those *since*s. Since she could remember. Since she had been born.

She took a breath. "I'm confused. I just want —" Her hands felt like pieces of meat, her legs, weak. "I just want to understand."

She had a hard time focusing on his face, the tree, her own

house. Something was in her vision — something making it wavy and incandescent. She felt silly asking him what was going on, as though she were in some ridiculous horror movie: *Hey, let's go down to the basement to check out that scary noise. No, we don't need to put any clothes on. We'll be fine in our underwear.*

An undulating Nix looked back into the yard. He shook his head.

"Ondine, I didn't do any of this."

"What?"

"I didn't clean up. I didn't —" He turned back to her. "I woke up in your bed; music was playing. I came downstairs and everything was clean. Everyone was gone. I walked out here and a few minutes later you came out. That's all I know."

"But I was in bed. We fell asleep on the landing. There were bottles everywhere; the house was a mess. I remember all of it."

"Yeah, me too." He shook his head. "I didn't put you there. So either we sleptwalked together, or someone — and I think we both have a pretty good idea who — came in and moved us and did" — Nix waved his hand at the house and yard — "all this."

She couldn't help herself. She put her small face in her hands and started to shake.

"What's happening? What's happening? Why are you here?" She was wailing now, rocking back and forth, shaking into her hands. "I don't even know you. And that creep. How did he get into my house? I — I don't know what's going on. I'm confused. I don't — I don't understand . . ."

She felt it. On her hands. The silken wetness. The taste, salty and heavy and sweet.

"I'm just —" She shot her hand out, pushing Nix away. She was crying. But why now? Why not when her parents left?

He moved closer, and though Ondine was still sobbing in shaking heaves, he held her. This time she didn't move.

"I don't know what's going on either, but whatever it is, we've both known about it for a long time. I knew it the second I saw you. How I was supposed to . . . How we were supposed to . . ." Nix faltered.

"What? Supposed to what?"

"I have no idea what's going on, any more than you, but I do know something. It has something to do with Moth, and that . . . that party around the solstice that everyone's been talking about." Nix looked away, almost ashamed. "The Ring of Fire. I know. I know it sounds ridiculous, but we might as well sit tight here until —"

Ondine stared, her red-rimmed eyes seeming to fill her whole face.

"Till?" she whispered.

"We're not going to get any answers until then. So look. I'll split. You go back to your life. Try to forget about this for a while and in three weeks —"

"No!" Her choked voice fell in the empty backyard. "No! I want everything to just go back to the way it was before my parents left. I don't understand what's happening . . ."

Nix pulled her closer, trying to calm her. "Things will be clearer after the Ring of Fire."

"How do you know?"

He didn't answer.

She ran a hand over her hair and across her eyes. "You're going to stay here," she said.

"Here?"

"Till then. You're staying with me."

Ondine pulled Nix to her and leaned on his shoulder. She felt the solidity of his flesh, and beneath that, something warm. She was crying — for the first time in her life — and she needed a hug.

"We'll know then."

Nix nodded, though he didn't know anymore what was right. He just remembered Moth's words, how he had to get Ondine there, how she got lost easily.

"I'm not going anywhere," he said, and drew her closer.

They stayed that way for a long time.

CHAPTER 8

HE NEXT TWO WEEKS PASSED QUIETLY. Though Ondine's
had been, as Morgan divined, the party of the year, summer had started, days were getting longer, and Portland's kids
were heading to the mountains, to California, to summer jobs at
resorts along the coast, or on fishing boats in Alaska. Morgan
called Ondine and apologized — she had been *so drunk,* she
said — and Ondine forgave her. They didn't make a plan to meet
again, though, and while they stayed friendly in Raphael's class,
Morgan always begged off hanging out afterward. She had to
work, she said, or help her mom at home. Ondine let it pass. She
needed to clear her head, too. As Nix said, there was no use asking the same questions over and over when there was no possibility of answering them. She worked on her painting and helped
Nix study for his GED. She also bracketed off his habit of using
dust, just as she didn't acknowledge the glass of wine she'd drink
while cooking dinner, or the glass she had while eating dinner, or

the glass she'd have after, talking to Nix in the backyard with the lights off, the leaves of the maple shaking in the night breeze.

In the darkness they whispered their stories to each other, unsure of whether they were awake or slumbering, or somewhere in between. Nix told her about Sitka and fishing with his grandfather. Ondine told him about the first time her mother took her to Italy, to Venice. They slept side by side; sometimes facing each other, sometimes apart. Ondine might rest a hand on his back; he might cuddle close enough to smell her hair. There were times when Ondine would look at Nix's lithe body stretched out beside hers, covered only by his boxers, and she would want to reach out and pull him onto her, but something always held her back. She could sense Nix felt the same way but he never made a move. They were chaste but loving. Neither brother and sister, nor Romeo and Juliet, but lovers all the same. It was as if they had found their other half, the wing that allowed each to fly.

Fly they did, at night. Next to Nix, Ondine's dreams became electrifying, dizzying experiences. She plowed through colors, fields, flowers, forests. Creatures and beasts of great complexity and beauty formed and then disappeared. Whole worlds were created. Not ones Ondine had seen in real life, but ones that inhabited her mirages. Cities filled with people she'd never seen. Animals that spoke and trees that cried and people who sat as still as stones. Nothing made sense — quite. Yet it did, or seemed to be heading toward making sense. As if Ondine were learning something, like how she felt when she first learned to draw. Her ideas, her thoughts and strange imaginings interpreted, given meaning and shape.

She felt all-seeing, lucid, perfect — close as she had ever come to whole — and when she awoke she somehow knew it was Nix who had been guiding her. They were *his* visions, too, that Ondine was channeling, transforming.

Awake, they never said a word.

To Nix, those three weeks before the solstice with Ondine were the most peaceful time he had spent since leaving Sitka.

The girl calmed him, made him feel safe, protected, and most of all, she made him feel like he had a purpose. The nightmares did not come when he was with her. Nor did the lights. He used up almost all the dust he had bought from Moth and didn't buy any more. He was even able to put Jacob out of his mind, though he could not erase the vision of Neve, frail little Neve, swaying on Tim Bleeker's lap. He chalked it up to his fears about Jacob, felt that if he could just figure that one out — use whatever was going to happen at the Ring of Fire and with Moth to help Jacob — he'd help Neve, too.

He was full of Ondine. Her moods, the way she fingered her braids, her smell. He slept close to her, breathing her in. As if, in dreaming, he could become her. He never told her about Bleek and Jacob and Bettina and the lights, but when Ondine and he awoke in the morning, Nix knew they had communicated, shared something over the course of the night: something profound, something neither of them understood.

It felt a little like falling in love.

The Masons called every day. They had gotten to Chicago, settled into a big house in Evanston with a porch and a swing. Ralph liked his colleagues at Xelix there; Max had already started classes at the conservatory. Ondine had a bedroom if she changed her mind.

She didn't tell her parents anything about Nix, but instead, how her art class was, how her summer job search was going. Ondine almost felt as if Nix didn't exist as Nix. Rather, the mysterious boy was part of her, and she of him. They had Neve and K.A. over a few times for movies. Though Morgan was always invited, she never came. They passed the first part of June in a frothy dream state. Ondine painted. She listened to Nix. He cooked. They ate and slept and the next day it started all over again.

Somewhere in the back of her mind Ondine knew that she'd have to get back to her real life, the one that included working and Raphael's class, finding that summer job she kept promising she was looking for in nightly phone calls to Chicago, her parents, her other friends, but for now she let it be. Something was happening. A chain was being forged between her and Nix, a link in preparation for —

Here was where she stopped.

Other than the gathering near the solstice, she had no idea what was in store. What would happen next was a line Ondine, for the first time in her life, chose not to step over. She and Nix didn't speak of the Ring of Fire, though they both knew it held the key to the strange events of the last few weeks. To James Motherwell's presence in their lives and to their meeting each other. But they had already said everything those first nights in their dreams.

ᔕ ᔕ ᔕ

DUDE, *I* HEARD IT'S OUT AT CANNON BEACH.

No man, it's down in the tunnels.

They're gonna hand out dust there, dude. It's a government thing. They want to bust all the kids.

I heard all the chicks are gonna be naked.

The one thing everyone could agree upon about the Ring of Fire was that the Flame was going to play and it was supposed to be huge. People from all around the Northwest were supposed to be going — Washington, Vancouver, Cali, even. Yet no one seemed to know where it was. The connected kids pretended they knew, but even they were clueless. Dealers were paying dollars for any solid information but the leads all turned out to be wrong. It was anyone's guess where the Ring of Fire might be.

Anyone but Morgan. She didn't need to guess. What she did need to do was remember.

Just like on the PSATs: A perfect score the first time. Then in ninth, she "forgot" — consciously, unconsciously, she wasn't sure. Just a few questions, a hypotenuse here, a fill-in there, but enough to keep her from getting tagged by Penwick or any of the other geekeries she had no interest in attending. She wasn't up for any special schools stinking of nerd B.O. and the drool of overinvolved parents. No, McKinley was fine. Morgan liked being a big fish in a big pond. Any other role would have bored her, and the slower pace at Portland's biggest high school left her time for her job as assistant manager at Krakatoa, which she pretended was a drag, but wasn't. Morgan liked any position where she got to tell people what to do. She was good at it, and the owners trusted her to run shifts after school, adding a few mornings during summer break.

Though the seventeen-year-old was still too young to serve the wine and beer the Krak proffered along with the best macchiato in Portland, the place attracted a crowd Li'l Paul, her boss, liked to attribute to his "chill vibe," but Morgan knew was due to her own policy of attracting — and limiting admittance to — Portland's coolest. "Think of it as popularity by death stare," she once confided to K.A. "It's ridiculously easy. You just make the weeds feel as unwelcome as possible."

"The weeds?"

"The geeks. The losers. The people that ruin the garden."

Morgan needed only to raise an eyebrow to silence him. Anyway, the ends justified the means, or whatever. K.A. loved the Krak, and spent most school days hanging there when he wasn't at practice or studying, as did any Portland kid who wasn't stared out of the place by the impossibly hot girl behind the counter.

Morgan was proud of the scene, and though she enforced carding, she didn't mind if there was a little dust passed around on weekends, just to enliven the mood. She'd even volunteered to work an after-hours thing on Saturdays, a party-before-the-party kind of thing. The place closed at eleven, but Saturday at midnight always found the Krak full, someone DJing, Morgan keeping one eye on the door, one eye on the bar. They'd even gotten written up in *Vice* for "best place for a sprinkling."

The night Tim Bleeker walked in looking for information on the Ring of Fire was no different. She spotted him slinking through the front door, turning his head both ways to scope out the room before he strode over to the bar, where Morgan was covering for Li'l Paul, who was out for one of the smoke breaks that always took enough time to get some "business" done — there was always a preponderance of handsome young dishwashers at the Krak.

Bleek smiled when he saw her. They'd met once before, and she knew the guy from a party he'd thrown down in Eugene. Morgan had been fifteen and it was the first time she'd gotten trashed. She'd even tried dust, which made her sick, and she'd vowed never to do it again. The party — and Bleek — skeeved her out.

She nodded but kept wiping the water glass she had in her hand.

"Morgan D'Amici — looking good as usual."

Morgan said nothing and Tim Bleeker sat down at the bar.

"What can I get for you?" She wiped the countertop, where Bleek's strawberry blond matted forearms were now resting. He had *a lot* of hair — except on his head. That and the puffiness around his eyes and gaunt look made him look old, almost rancid. And there was something weird about his teeth.

"Doppio, babe. I know it's late but I've got some parties to improve."

She let it pass, but inwardly she shuddered.

"Skim milk." He smiled an oily smile and patted his nonexistent belly. "Weight Watchers. I think it's really the safest of all of them. Atkins makes your breath stink."

"Huh," she responded, noting Bleek's did already. She turned to the machine behind her, tapping her feet in time with the music that drifted in from the other room.

"So, Morgan" — fake casual — "where ya been hiding? I used to see you around all the time."

The girl shrugged, going through the well-practiced motions

of making yet another espresso. Dump grounds, fill, tamp, lock in place, flip switch. Get little pitcher, fridge for milk —

"Working a lot."

Bleek frowned. "All work and no play —"

"Makes Morgan very happy." She turned. "Look, Bleek, what do you want? I haven't spoken to you since you came in here with doped-out Evelyn Schmidt hanging off you." She worked the pitcher up and down to foam it. In one deft movement she scooped some of the foam off the top and into a waiting cup of espresso. She pushed it toward the boy and firmly smiled. She was a professional, after all.

"Three bucks."

Bleek pushed it back to her. "A sprinkle of chocolate on there, sweets. Just a *dusting,*" he said, picking the tiny spoon up and balancing it between his thumb and forefinger.

She stared. She got the reference. Morgan had bought the stuff from him that night at the party in Eugene and always sensed that he'd use any chance he had to leak the information to her ultra-square student council faculty leader, who was always around the Krak checking in on the McKinley kids. Morgan was going to be class president senior year and didn't want anything screwing her up.

"Well, I want some information . . . love. An address. Wondering if you've heard anything about a certain . . . gathering."

Gathering. What was it with the lame code words? Yet the mention of the Ring of Fire made her stomach tighten. The morning after Ondine's party she'd asked around at the Krak for Moth, even thought of calling Ondine or Neve to ask if they'd seen the boy, but then decided against it. Neve she didn't much want to talk to, and Ondine she didn't want knowing her business. She heard Moth had gone back to Eugene, where he was from. So she had decided to wait. He'd turn up sooner or later. Every day she tried to remember what he'd said, but all she could come up with were a few images: confused stumblings in the dark, blue lights flashing. Then nothing. She gave up thinking about it and let herself disappear into her work at the Krak or spent her time daydreaming about sexy Raphael Inman. The party was ancient history, she told herself. The party? What party?

Which made her response to Bleek that much weirder. Even as the words spilled from her mouth, Morgan wondered whether she was saying them.

"Highway   ninety-seven . . . twenty-mile   point . . . Little Crater. Park there."

"I knew you'd be the right person to ask," Bleek countered.

"Sometimes it's not good to be too . . . clean," she said, lowering her voice but unable to look into the older boy's eyes. She watched her right hand wipe circles on the counter in front of her. It wasn't quite that she was in a trance, but something peculiar was happening. She hadn't told a single person what she had learned from Moth about the Ring of Fire, barely remembered it, in fact, and wasn't planning to go. The Flame? *Right*. Morgan's favorite local band was the Berms — an experimental suburban slacker outfit from Beaverton, of all places. Raphael Inman said he even jammed with them a few times on his electric cello.

"Fantastic." Bleek smiled, and pushed his empty demitasse toward her. "I'm so glad I came."

Morgan took the cup and saucer in both hands, conscious of it trembling. She turned to the sink behind her.

"See you there, darling."

She hung her head. He might as well have had her neck in his jaws.

"Feels good to be a little dirty, doesn't it, Morgana?" Bleek whispered. The song playing over the speakers ended. "Yeah, it does."

The next thing she heard was the light tinkle of the Krak's back door ringing as he left.

ᔛ ᔛ ᔛ

It was K.A. who brought it up.

It was a cool night in mid-June and Ondine had invited the crew over for K.A.'s last night before a weeklong soccer camp in California. He was leaving for Stanford in the morning. Scouts were going to be there; he could come back with the scholarship

161

that would determine where he'd spend the four years after high school.

They were watching movies. Neve and K.A. snuggled on the couch while Nix and Ondine lazed on the floor, picking at the last slices of pizza from Jacob's and sipping root beer in sympathy with K.A., who couldn't drink before camp. Nix kept one eye on Neve. She seemed normal, giggly, all her attention focused on K.A., but Evelyn had sworn she had seen "Clowes's daughter" hanging out a few times with Tim Bleeker by the river. Nix kept the knowledge to himself so far, though it worried him. Once was a coincidence. Twice, a mistake. More than that, a habit. And Nix knew all about habits.

Morgan had been invited, of course, but she said — through K.A.; she didn't return Ondine's phone call — that she'd picked up a few extra shifts and couldn't come. Neve, guileless, or perhaps just less inhibited than everyone else, had asked if Morgan was mad at her. She hadn't seen or heard from her since Ondine's. At the mention of the party everyone got quiet, until K.A. said, "Aw, you know Morgue. She's moody. Sometimes she just likes her downtime."

"Dude!" he said now, stretching back onto the couch and smiling at Nix. "You have to admit, Jacob makes a mean pie."

"Yeah," Nix replied, uncomfortable at the mention of his old boss, but grinning anyway. Ondine winced. Two weeks together alone on N.E. Schuyler had made Ondine feel joined with the boy, and it was almost painful to have other people around, even ones as close as K.A. and Neve. Sensitive to her friend's moods, she tried to change the subject.

"So, K.A., next World Cup. Think you've got a shot?"

K.A., unfazed, unclasped the arm he'd draped around Neve and reached down to tousle Nix's long hair.

"He misses you, you know."

"Who?" Nix said, though he knew who K.A. was talking about.

"Jacob, man! I was just telling Neve today how Jacob was asking after you."

Neve nodded and trailed a long rhinestone-studded fingernail — she was doing ghettofabulous that week — around the lip of her root beer glass.

"Yeah." Her pierced tongue clicked. "K.A.'s been wanting you to come back, Nix." She tickled the boy's shoulder with a stripey-socked foot. "He misses you."

From the floor Ondine watched with a protective half frown. "Nix is taking it easy. It's been a rough spring."

"Yeah, well," K.A. resumed, "it would help to have him around so that he could run interference for me with Tim Bleeker —"

Nix looked up at the mention of the dealer's name.

"What?"

"Yeah, man. He's been around almost every day since On-dine's party, macking on Neve. And let me tell you, Jacob is *not* happy about it. He knows Bleek is bad news. But you know how Clowes is with Neve. If she wanted to walk on Mars, he'd figure out a way to get her there. But man, Bleek is *lame*. I'm like, dude, that is my girlfriend, and that is my girlfriend's dad, and you are a lame-ass drug dealer, and he's all like, it's cool, dude, it's cool. And he's always asking me if I know where you are. He wants to get the four-one-one on the rave — for some reason he's convinced you know where it is and so he's always bugging me. 'Nix coming by?' 'Heard from Nix, man?' One time Jacob overheard him asking, and after he left, Jacob was like, 'Is Nix all right? Why is he hanging out with Tim Bleeker?'"

Throughout his speech Neve had been still, her eyes aimed at the TV, but glazed. Nix thought it was weird that K.A. would think Bleek was hitting on Neve, and that was the end of it. Love truly did conquer all. Tim Bleeker was a drug dealer, though, just like K.A. had said. His first priority was his next sale, and not even premium tail was enough to put that out of his mind. When Nix caught Neve glancing his way, she fixed her eyes on the TV again.

K.A. sighed, readjusting his lid. "I have enough drama at home with Morgan and Mom fighting constantly."

Nix looked back. "Tim Bleeker's an asshole, Neve."

His voice came out harsher than he'd intended, and K.A. glanced at him, then at his girlfriend.

She sat up and pushed K.A. away.

"Jesus Christ, boys. I've got one daddy. I don't need two more, okay? Jacob is up in my shit enough. He got to have his fun and now he wants his daughter to be the good girl? Yeah, well *fuck* him."

Silence swelled after her outburst.

Finally K.A. spoke: "Neve?"

A panicked look came over her face, as if she were as surprised by her words — by their vehemence — as everyone else was.

"Oh, don't pay attention to me. It's just that Dad's been riding my ass ever since the party. I mean, you have a little too much to drink *one time* and suddenly it's homeland security. I mean, I caught him checking my odometer. My *odometer*. When I called him on it, he said he wanted to know if I was doing more driving than I should." She snickered. "I told him Bleek has his own car; I didn't need to drive mine if I wanted to sneak around."

"Neve," K.A. began. "You're not . . ." His voice indicated he didn't know which was worse: the idea of Neve fooling around with Bleek, or the idea of her doing dust.

"Oh, relax," Neve scoffed. "It's just a little taste to mellow me out." She looked at Nix but spoke to K.A. "What, your best bud can do it but it's too good for your girlfriend?"

Nix tried to piece through what he was hearing. He knew when he saw Neve at the party with Bleek that things were bad, but not so bad she would flaunt it in K.A.'s face.

"I'm off it, Neve."

She threw back her head and laughed. "Yeah, right, Mr. I-Wore-Sunglasses-to-Wash-Dishes-for-a-Year. Tim told me all about your *intake,* man. I don't see you going cold turkey."

Ondine smiled at everyone and no one. "Is it true, Nix?"

Something seemed to have come unstuck in Neve. In a wild voice she let fly, "Man, don't try to put this all on me, Miss Goody Two-shoes. You were the one who threw a party attended by not one but two of Portland's biggest dust dealers. If you serve it up, don't be surprised if your guests *partake.*"

K.A. was looking at his girlfriend as though she'd zipped off her skin.

"You — you know about Moth?" Ondine asked, her arched brows high.

"Yes, I 'know about Moth,'" Neve mimicked. "And don't tell me you don't." She stared at her three friends. "Tim told me about him. Figures he knows about the party, wanted to see if I could get it out of him."

"Who in the hell is Moth?" K.A. said.

"'The Ring of Fire,'" Neve scoffed, ignoring his question. "Somebody needs to hire a new ad agency. And the *Flame*? What is this, last year? Everybody knows the Flame sucks now."

Ondine stood up. "I'm getting some water. Does anyone want anything? A beer? Some dust? Maybe a couple shots of heroin?" She walked out of the room.

Her departure seemed to silence Neve, who sat picking at a loose thread on her perfectly tattered jeans.

K.A. got up, looking at his girlfriend. "We'd better get going. The bus leaves at seven tomorrow. You ready?"

Neve stood up, half sullen, half coy. She took his hand in a mock-flirtatious way. "Don't be mad at me," she said in a baby voice. "I'm a good girl, really I am. I'm just playing is all."

K.A.'s mouth opened and then closed. He turned to Nix. "So you'll talk to Jacob?"

Nix scanned the room for Ondine, who stood in the kitchen doorway with a worried frown on her face. Then he looked at Neve. He didn't want to talk to Jacob, didn't want to see the light again, but he knew now that Neve was in serious trouble, and that Jacob was her only hope. He wished it was something K.A. could take care of the way he took care of everything, but even if K.A. weren't going away to soccer camp, Nix knew that Jacob would never believe these things from K.A.'s mouth. Nix was the transient, the slacker, the "user." He would take the blame and might have to leave Portland, but at least Jacob could get his daughter away from Bleek. Moth, of course, was another question.

"Yeah, man. I'll talk to him."

When K.A. walked to the door with Neve in tow, it was hard to tell if he was holding her hand, or if she just wouldn't let go.

ண ண ண

NIX DIDN'T TALK TO JACOB. When he went into the restaurant the next day, Leon — Portland's self-proclaimed best pie maker — told him that the Cloweses had taken off that morning to the coast for a vacation. Leon was an ageless waxy-haired hippie who had known Jacob "since Altamont, man," and Jacob had confided to him that the main purpose of the "vacation" was to get Neve as far away from Tim Bleeker as possible, especially with "the square" out of town for a week. Nix assumed Leon meant K.A.

"Hey man, mellow out. Why do you need to see him so bad, anyway? You knock up the pepperoni princess or something?"

If Nix ever had doubts about when to quit dust, one look at Leon reminded him. The man coughed, passed a burning joint to him, raising his eyebrows. Nix waved it off, shaking his head.

"Suit yourself, man." Leon let a stream of smoke trickle from his dry lips. "But it's better than that shit you do."

Later that day, Ondine got a surreptitious phone call from Neve. She almost hadn't answered because she didn't recognize the number on caller ID. "I'm on a fucking *pay* phone," Neve said, half pissed, half amused. "We're at some gas station halfway between hillbilly central and B&B hell — ugh. I *hate* bed and breakfasts. All that fucking *lace*. And my loser dad confiscated my cell. He said we need some 'family bonding' time, but I know it's just cuz he doesn't want me calling Bleek."

Ondine exhaled. "Nix said he heard the cops are on Bleek's trail."

"Yeah," Neve cooed. Ondine didn't like her tone. It was almost wistful.

"Neve," she ordered in her sternest seventeen-year-old voice. "Tim Bleeker is pathetic. Must to avoid, girl. *Must. To. Avoid.*"

Neve laughed, a breezy tinkle. "Aw, he's like a lost puppy, moping around the Krak asking anyone he sees where the Ring of Fire is gonna be. He just needs someone to take him out to play."

"What he wants is to sell dust to a thousand blissed-out Flame fans."

There was silence on the line, and then Neve whispered something.

"What'd you say?"

"And me," Neve repeated softly. "He wants me." Then, annoyed — and louder: "Jesus, Dad, back off! It's just Ondine! *Ondine*. Gotta run, baby," Neve said into the phone. "Love ya!"

With Neve and K.A. gone, and Morgan in avoidance, Nix and Ondine were on their own. Phil D'Amici had gotten Nix a job at the Burnside D'Amici store, working in the stockroom, so he spent his days leading up to the solstice there, coming home late, when Ondine was already in bed. Nix had always been a loner, but Ondine wondered what had happened to the girl who just a few weeks ago had to turn her phone off, it rang so often. She had always been the popular girl, the one who walked into a roomful of strangers and walked out with a new posse of friends. Now when the phone rang — if it did at all — she answered it only if it was Ralph or Trish, and the idea of calling someone to grab a cup of coffee or go shopping or catch a movie didn't even occur to her. The girl who did those kinds of things was someone else named Ondine, not her. This Ondine stayed close to home, cleaning, cooking — though she had never made anything more complicated than ramen noodles before — spending long hours maintaining Trish's flower beds. Gardening was Trish's passion, but not something Ondine had ever shown any real interest in. There were magazines and manuals everywhere, but she ignored them, just as she eschewed tools. She wandered into the garden and sank to her knees and worked the earth with her fingers, pinching off a leaf here, a twig there; she whispered to a cupped leaf, "Grow." Under Ondine's watch the Masons' yard exploded. It was almost eerie how every plant seemed to bloom at the same time. How the flowers didn't fade, or rust, or even close when the sun went down. Ondine knew, because she had looked. She had gone to the window late one night when Nix still wasn't back from the store, and seen an army of roses and peonies and irises all staring up at her window. When a breeze stirred them, it was as if they were bowing. Ondine felt like Evita of the flora. She would have laughed, if she hadn't been so creeped out.

She thought about telling Nix, but didn't. At least not out loud. What could she and Nix say to each other that they hadn't already said in their dreams?

Ondine didn't know what to do with all the fractured thoughts, the hints of imaginings, the subtle intuition, and the plain anxiety she felt alone that last week, so besides gardening and cooking, she painted. She finished her first piece for Raphael Inman's class; her crit would be on June 19. She hung her canvas in her bedroom against the sliding doors of her closet, covering the oak floors with D'Amici paper bags to catch the paint. She worked from sense — from feeling — wasn't that what Raphael had told them that first day? His hazel eyes had burned under a frizz of gray hair. *Find out what is in your heart first. Then shape it with what is in here.* He had touched a finger to his chest. *The head only knows what the heart feels.*

Ondine had looked at Morgan. She missed her friend, yet didn't know how to ask what had happened at the party to drive a rift between them. She watched Morgan's eyes narrow when Raphael said those last words. Had he noticed, too? Morgan was by far Raphael Inman's best pupil. A genius, almost, in her rendering. Ondine envied her talent — her lines, her gesture sketches that seemed to walk off the page. Though Raphael had been speaking to Morgan then, he had also been speaking to Ondine. What had he been saying to her?

Alone in her room, she painted. This painting was blue. All the blues she understood. The blue of sadness. The split blue of the sky meeting the sea. Her mother's favorite blouse. The blue of emptiness. The Virgin's dress she had seen in a Giotto painting. The blue of the ocean of Alaska, of Nix's home. A blue waiting to be filled.

Something emerged. The painting was still wet when Ondine pulled it off the wall and headed to Raphael's class.

෨ ෨ ෨

BITCH.

Staring past the heads of her classmates at Ondine's impossibly beautiful painting on the opposite wall, Morgan couldn't stop the word from springing into her head, straight from the pit of her stomach. *Bitch bitch bitch.* She looked at Ondine's painting, watched Ondine nodding at Raphael, Raphael beaming — beaming! — back at Ondine. A proud smile that usually only Morgan received during one of Raphael's harsh crits.

Stop, she told herself. *Stop it.* She couldn't.

He hadn't even spoken. When Ondine tacked up her painting, still wet, Raphael Inman was so moved he couldn't speak.

He had cupped his hand to his mouth as if his guts were caught there, and he hadn't even spoken. The whole class just stood there, following Raphael's lead like a bunch of stupid cows while Ondine stared at her shoes.

And blushed. The bitch blushed.

Morgan herself would never have shown something so messy, so unfinished, so raw.

With a trembling hand, she tucked her hair behind her ear and wiped away the veil of sweat that had gathered at her temples. It was hot in the room, odd since it was almost nine at night. She was about to throw up. At least she had been late and couldn't assume her normal seat at the front of the classroom. At least there was that. But it wasn't fair. Morgan wanted Raphael Inman to favor her. Not the skinny bitch at the front of the class. Spoiled brat. Was there anything Ondine *didn't* get?

"Well, Ondine." At last Raphael spoke. "Would you like to tell us about this?" Morgan swallowed hard to quell the sick bulge in her stomach, noting Raphael's barely concealed smile, his proud-father look. That look should have been hers. That smile should have been hers.

Ondine looked at her feet, then at the painting. "I —" She faltered, uncomfortable with the attention.

Revolting.

"I was just thinking about what you said last time, about the heart and the mind. And our assignment was to use one color, understand one color. And I had been feeling, I don't know . . . alone — and I understood that for me, blue was the color of that loneliness. Not a sad loneliness, but a loneliness that wanted company."

Morgan couldn't listen to any more of Ondine's blather. The fey looks, the earnest nodding. Raphael's devoted attention. She knew her teacher adored her work, she didn't need to feel jealous, but she couldn't help it. Everything had been so awful at home. K.A. busy 24–7 with Neve, then jetting off to soccer camp, her pathetic mother irritating her about school and college apps and whether she had called her dad. Her "dad." The bastard took her to Jake's Crawfish once a month with Bree, the "athletic dancer," during which time he spoke entirely to the woman's tits. They wanted to have a baby, he told Morgan in a rare moment of looking her way. *A little sister for you, Morgue, honey!* Just what Morgue honey wanted: a slobbering brat siphoning off what little Phil Jr. claimed to be saving for her and K.A.'s college education. *Fuck them.*

But what really bugged her was that she couldn't get Bleek's visit to the Krak and her own odd behavior out of her mind. She thought of the night of the party, the missing hours, creepy Tim Bleeker, and — once more — Moth. What did it matter if she knew where some lame, Red Bull–sponsored rave was if all it did was help a saggy drug dealer find it? She'd already made up her mind: no way she was going. The last thing she wanted to do on

174

the longest day of summer was spend it driving to the middle of nowhere. *Bend,* ugh. Condos and housewives in Uggs and bear shit. No, thank you.

So she had stayed up late painting, working on her college applications, getting ready for her senior APs. Work started early at the Krak and she was exhausted. Everything was ass and Raphael's class had been the summer's only solace. Now Ondine was ruining everything — again.

Morgan slipped out the open door of Raphael's studio. Not a head turned, though the sweet pair of black Sigerson Morrisons (two months' tips at the Krak) she had worn to class clacked down the linoleum hall. She didn't care. Legs were the animal part of a woman. Hadn't Raphael said that about Ingres's *Odalisque*? She wore miniskirts every day after that.

But even the most scandalous hemline couldn't do anything about the stifling air that was choking her tonight. It was damn hot. Morgan felt another wave of nausea. She needed to get outside. She needed fresh air.

The car's clock read 9:02 PM. Twenty-eight minutes left for Raphael to slobber all over Ondine. Morgan felt the rush of a dry sob but swallowed it, instead starting the used Lexus she had bought by scrimping and saving every penny of every job she'd had since her paper route at eleven, and screeched out of the parking lot. She was too distraught to even play the radio.

The road was clear. Instinct guided her home. Streetlights,

darkened stores. She would not cry. Scratch that: She *could* not cry. What was wrong with her? All her life Morgan D'Amici had awaited her senior year. She would be class president. She was considered the most beautiful, intelligent girl in school and yet here she was at the doorstep of the rest of her life and all she felt was confused, and lost, and sad.

And angry. Why was she so angry?

She pulled into the long gravel driveway of the house on Steele Street. No one was home. K.A. was at Stanford; Yvonne was at Todd's. *And Morgan is in a trailer, where she belongs.* She turned off the ignition. The lights faded. She let herself go.

She sobbed, grasping the steering wheel with her delicate hands. She hated crying. Not so much because of the weakness, though she resented that, too, but because nothing came out. No tears, no snot. Just cracking heaves. It wasn't the way she used to cry. Before the nights spent sleepwalking, she had tears. Wet, luxurious tears. Then one day they went away.

It was dark, no one could see her. She sat and shook and wailed; she didn't know for how long. Snatches of memory flashed. Scenes of death, of things she felt like she had seen, but how could she have? She was a nice girl. A good girl. Raphael told them to paint what was in their hearts, but how could she? How could she paint the tableaux of destruction that sprung, unbidden, in her mind? A wolf eating her young. Worms twisting in the earth under moonlight. The cruelty — the senseless, feelingless cruelty of nature? How could she paint the baby bird taking flight only to drown in a puddle an inch deep under the nest, to be gnawed on by vermin until there were only bits of feathers and bones left?

She stared into the blackness, at the even blacker forest beyond. How could she express what she knew was hidden there? How could she paint the dark things animals do?

CHAPTER 9

THE MORNING OF JUNE 20, NIX WOKE UP BEFORE DAWN. It was Wednesday. Ondine had gotten in late from class the night before and he didn't want to wake her. It had been a hot night and so he'd slept downstairs on one of the couches that faced the backyard, and when the sun rose to reveal a coming storm — a bloody smear rising into a mounting anvil of gray — he knew it was the day. Moth had told him he'd know, and he did, though he wasn't sure how. Something about the unusual weather. No kid who wasn't invited was going to venture out to a rumored party in the mountains today. Not on a Wednesday. Not with a storm coming. He took a shower, packed water and blankets and a change of clothes, his pocketknife and a tent. He included a sleeping bag, flashlights, bug spray. Wrapping Ondine's leftovers in sheets of tinfoil, he felt like a husband almost. Confident, excited. Prepared for anything.

In the kitchen he washed apples and carrots and celery for snacks, running his hands under the cool water, thinking about the events of the coming day. He let Ondine sleep. Getting her there was his job.

It wasn't so much that he expected something in particular as he knew that whatever was at the Ring of Fire — whatever James Motherwell was leading them to — might be able to answer questions he'd harbored about himself all his life. Nix wasn't sure what this meant to Ondine, but he felt a double edge of anticipation and anxiety. He'd been wandering in darkness. The loss of his mother, a father he never knew. Visions that terrorized him. Now he sensed he was heading toward something that would complete him — or at least chart his course toward completion.

He wasn't surprised when Neve Clowes's small face appeared before him, hovering above the sink. She wore a sparkling collar around her neck and she was crying. Then Ondine. Her eyes were closed, her face blank. *Nix,* she summoned. *Nix, cover me.*

He opened his eyes. He was standing at the Masons' marble sink, an apple in his hands, the water running. The sun peeked over the trees at the border of the backyard.

"Nix?"

He turned to find Ondine behind him. She wore jeans, a hoodie mini, and a black RVCA jacket. Her hair was tied back in her red scarf and she wore a baseball hat. She held a backpack in her hands.

"I got a text from Moth." She took a deep breath and stared. "I'm ready whenever you are."

∽ ∽ ∽

MORGAN AWOKE TO A MUFFLED THUMP on the windshield. A toad had plopped there from somewhere and was now trying to get off by scrambling across the dew-slicked glass. Each time it tried to hop it slipped. *Just my fucking luck.* Outside the sky was scarlet tinged with gray and the air seeping through a small crack in the driver's-side window smelled swampy and burnt. A storm was coming. She felt achy and prickly and tired. The sandals she wore for Raphael sat muddy, straps broken, on the seat next to her. She didn't have to look in the mirror to know that there would be sticks in her hair, that her feet would be dirty.

She turned the ignition and watched the headlights seep into the semidarkness. How was she going to get rid of the toad? On her fucking Lexus, which she had cleaned *by hand* just the day before? It tried to climb the windshield — when the lights came on it sensed something had changed — only to slip again on the sweaty glass. *Stupid piece of shit. Dumb beast.* She didn't want to touch it. She turned on her wipers, thinking maybe that would dislodge it. All it did was confuse the thing, causing it to scramble faster. Find a stick, Morgan thought, push it off. Instead, she turned up the wipers and the blades started to whip faster across the glass. She wanted to punish it for being so dumb. For spreading its filthy toad-juice all over her car. It hopped for a while, avoiding the metronome of the blade, but soon it tired. A leg caught, then tore. She flicked again. It started to quiver. Pressed against the glass, its tiny heart pulsed. *Good.* Again, faster. It slipped under the blade. Green and brown guts trickled. Finally its flat, ugly head. Then it was dead.

She sat for a second. Couldn't she have gotten a stick?

No. It needed to die.

She pressed the little button at the end of the wiper and a solid stream of fluid — Lexuses were good like that — skimmed over the bloodied glass. She waited and pressed again; the wipers wooshed, and everything washed away. Only when it was quiet did she hear the soft buzzing.

ഗ ഗ ഗ

"RIGHT. NO LEFT. NO. THE TWENTY-MILE MARK. Linus Road? I can't remember what he said. Something about a campground —?"

Nix glanced over at Ondine while she stared at the map, turning it around in her hands to get her bearings. She had let him drive, saying that she needed to be in charge of directions, though she hadn't looked up once since Bend. They'd passed the town twenty miles ago and Nix was looking for Paulina Road, as

181

Moth had promised. A few hundred yards more and there it was. He took a left. Oaks and feathery pines arced into the road, soon giving way to craggy rocks, thin combs of trees, and crusty black soil.

"I've been here before," she said, looking around. "We're near Sisters. The mountains. I came here in elementary school once to see what a volcano looked like. A flank was bulging or something —" She looked at Nix and they both smiled. "The area is due for an eruption any day now. Give or take a thousand years."

"You don't say." He squeezed her knee, and Ondine smiled again and looked back at the map, tracing the contours of the volcano near the campground, its crater now filled with two perfectly round lakes.

"That must be Paulina Lake," she said, remembering the twin sapphire lakes surrounded by black rock. "It's beautiful there."

The drive off the main road was longer than they expected and soon the radio was just static. Ondine checked her cell phone; a few bars still showed. When they got to the promised parking lot, they were already twenty or so miles in. Nix turned off the ignition and Ondine looked up from the map in her hands.

"Great!" She smiled. "We made it!"

Nix nodded. It appeared they were at the right place, though the thickening clouds behind them made him marvel again that a party would be held on such a crappy day. The presence of a few VW buses, dusty Toyotas, SUVs, and the like — the geeky-funky-crunchy mix of any Northwestern campground parking lot—confirmed that Moth had advised him correctly. Nothing was unusual about the scene except that the lot wasn't full. A few people unpacked coolers and backpacks from trunks. No one looked much over twenty-five. Kids appeared in the lot as if they had walked down the dirt road, though Nix hadn't noticed them on the way in.

A dark patch in the scrubby forest showed an entrance to a trail.

"I guess it's in there." Ondine pointed and Nix nodded again.

"Let's go then."

He didn't feel much like talking. In the distance, black hills swelled and Nix smelled sulfur. A strange place for a party, he thought again, and as if in answer, Ondine said, "There's a state park here." She looked up at the gloomy sky.

"What a day for a party."

The two ducked under the low branches. A few kids were ahead of them in rain gear and hats. She hadn't seen any cars she recognized, but the air of the place felt familiar.

"Doesn't seem much different from the Oregon Country freaking Fair." Ondine scowled. "The silver statue people are going to come out any second."

Nix turned. "Including the rain. Hey —" He stopped. "What's wrong?"

"I don't know. I just thought this would be . . . different."

He thought the same thing, but his anticipation stopped him from agreeing aloud. He wondered if he'd know anyone, someone from the squat or Jacob's, but there weren't enough people around, and the ones who had passed them in the parking lot kept their heads down against the rain.

"Moth said it was today. You saw it on the text." He squinted up into the sky and then into the trees. "Where do you want to go?"

Ondine peered at the faces of a couple passing them on the path, but they had their hoods pulled up.

"Your guess is as good as mine. I'm not sure where we're supposed to . . . um . . . get comfortable?" She looked around at the rocky grass. "Anyway, *this* was the party everyone was trying to find out about? Am I missing something?"

Nix shrugged. Ondine could tell he was just as confused.

"Maybe it will pick up later."

She raised an eyebrow. "Whatever. I don't think you could get a Phish bootleg here it's so lame. I guess we'll just wait till Moth shows up."

Another couple passed them on the dirt path, heading toward what Ondine imagined was yet another clearing like the one they were languishing in. Farther on, a group was setting up a blanket under a tree and unpacking a cooler, which was weird, since it had started to mist, and the clouds above them were making low, faraway rumbles.

"What?" Nix tugged at her wrist. She waited, then turned.

"Maybe . . . maybe we should go. It's going to storm."

His eyes shifted to the clouds. Shaking his head, he picked up the cooler and rucksack he had set down. "No. We're here. Let's go find ourselves a place to chill and I'll look for Moth."

They found a place under a spindly pine a few hundred yards down a twisting rocky path and started unpacking their stuff. Ondine was tired. The ride had been long. Not as long as she remembered from the field trip in second grade, which she identified now as the one time she had gotten scared and had to go back and stay in the bus with the teacher's assistant. Despite its beauty, she hadn't liked the queer, lonely landscape then and she didn't now. Still, no harm in seeing, she told herself while Nix set up the tent, though the lack of people and the terrible weather unnerved her. What, exactly, had she expected? She watched Nix and felt the familiar warmth and understanding, the closeness they'd shared in the last few weeks. "Relax," she whispered aloud. It appeared Nix was thinking the same, for as soon as the tent was up, they scrambled in. It was still morning. Whatever was supposed to happen didn't have to happen now, Ondine reminded herself. She burrowed into her sleeping bag. Nix, beside her, rolled over and did the same, mumbling, "I'll look for Moth in a little while."

They sank into a dreamless nap from which they awoke hungry, Ondine thankful that Nix had remembered to bring food. She despised falafel. That is, if they could have found any at this strange failure of a party. She looked at her watch. It was past noon. A few hours had gone by, and the area was as quiet as it had been when they got there that morning.

Ondine was starting to think it was just a crappy Rainbow Gathering fizzled when Nix looked up from his PB&J and said, "Let's go look for him." She nodded, happy that he'd suggested it. They left their camp as it was, taking the rest of the gear and heading down a path toward a deeper wood, where light strains of music floated through the increasing rain.

There *was* more activity in the forest, but it was still quiet. Small groups of people sat under tarpaulins or around modest campfires, not paying Nix and Ondine particular attention except for the one time Ondine had looked back and seen a short and somewhat stocky Asian girl peering after them. The girl had ducked into a tent from which Ondine thought she could hear the hum of a tattoo needle. After that, she didn't see the girl anymore.

For a half hour they wandered. Incense trailed out of glowing makeshift tents stippled with the shifting silhouettes of their inhabitants, and a few tables seemed to be set up to sell something. People crowded around, but when Ondine tried to push her way through to see what was offered, she could never get close enough. She wanted to ask Nix to stop, but he was busy scanning the huddled groups for Moth and she felt shy to ask. A few boys passed her, juggling Hacky Sacks or twirling Frisbees, and there was even some music from what sounded like the ubiquitous Peruvian flute ensemble — though eerier in the darkening wood — yet most faces were averted, so she had a hard time seeing her fellow partygoers. No one laughed, no one danced. Mostly everyone seemed to be waiting, like she and Nix were. For the Flame, she supposed, though a concert was going to be hard in a downpour.

When they passed the same patched army tent the third time, it was clear that they were walking in a circle.

"Nix." She stopped and tugged at her father's Gore-Tex she had lent him. It was a gesture that made her feel young, like tripping after Ralph in the hardware store, and that feeling, combined with the realization that they had no idea why they had come or what they were supposed to be doing — besides not knowing a soul — made Ondine feel powerless. It wasn't that she didn't want to stay. It was that whatever she'd thought she would find at the Ring of Fire — answers to questions she hadn't yet formulated about mirages, the party, Nix, Moth, whatever — seemed hopeless: a girl's fantasy.

"Nix! Hold up!"

"What?" He looked irritated and barely slowed, so she had to scamper to catch up with him.

"What are we *doing* here?"

"Does it look like I know? I'm trying to find Moth. Like I'm supposed to. I don't know any more than you. But unless you walk a little faster or help me find him, we're never going to know. Is that what you want, Ondine? To just *stay like this*?"

The look on her face must have exhibited a fraction of the hurt she felt, for he quieted then, though his mouth stayed gripped and his hands remained jammed into his pockets, not looped in hers as they usually were when they stood close.

"Look. I think we just need to find Moth."

"Okay, it's just —"

"It's just what?" He was a few paces from her, but his voice was more tender.

She swallowed a sigh. "It's just . . . this doesn't feel right."

"What does? What does feel right? Or should I put it this way: have you ever 'felt right,' Ondine? Because I sure haven't." Nix's voice hushed. "I thought that's what we were doing here. I thought that's why we were trying to find Moth."

A distant crack and, a few seconds later, faint light in the sky, and she knew they were in for a full storm.

"I mean this isn't safe," she said over the crunch of their feet against lava dust.

"I'm not sure it's meant to be."

"What the hell is that supposed to mean?" She stared at him.

"Nothing," he mumbled, and kept walking.

Behind Nix, she checked her watch. Time had passed, and the storm that had threatened them all morning was now a reality. Branches tossed, wind howled, thunder rumbled. Ondine was no Girl Scout, but she knew that a tent in a clearing under a tree wasn't the place to be during a storm. Nor was the path back to the car. They had hiked a ways into the forest already. Nix had the tarp, the flashlight, and a blanket in the rucksack he carried.

"Let's set something up here. You have the tarp. We can wait out the storm and see if Moth shows up."

"We'll have to find some twine —"

"It will be a good chance to speak to someone."

For the first time that day she linked her hand with his, and he took it, and squeezed it, and didn't let it go.

∽   ∽   ∽

MORGAN SAW THE GIRL WITH FANGS outside her car window — a Japanese girl with long, shiny blond dreads — as soon as she woke up. She had fallen asleep soon after she'd arrived at the campground, late from getting lost somewhere around Bend and spending two hours retracing her route along winding mountain roads, still icy at the edges from the late spring snows. At a truck stop she'd almost turned around, and if it weren't for the leering fat-ass down the counter she might have, but a glimpse of his swollen face reminded her that she had zero to lose by going to the mysterious party-gathering-concert-whatever-it-was, and talking to Moth. The heated words with the strange boy at Ondine's still puzzled her, as did the resurgence of her night walks since meeting him. It wouldn't be so bad if the Ring of Fire were some kind of a rich-boy, culty thing crawling with Moth's higher-end clients. Maybe she'd meet someone from Penwick. A weirdo who liked parting with his cash for a few spankings or whatever. Rich boys were always into freaky shit.

But this was too idiotic: A short chick with fake vampire fangs staring into her window? To sell T-shirts or bumper stickers or bottled water or programs or fucking glow sticks? Or maybe, if it was just Morgan's luck, to beg for cash. *Got a dollar, lady? I need to buy a hash brownie.* When had her Lexus turned into the vermin motel? And what ever happened to manners?

She rolled down the window and the girl edged back. She was pretty enough, solid and curvy, with black eyes and a ripped T-shirt that slipped over a tanned left shoulder. Outside it was a gray, rainy afternoon, and Morgan thought she heard thunder somewhere in the distance. She moved to open the door, but her seat belt restrained her.

The girl with the dreads smiled, not quite nicely.

"Excuse me, do I know you?" Morgan said through the crack.

190

The girl said nothing, but her hands fell to her sides, and Morgan noticed she had a tattoo on her wrist, a little blue X. She felt like she'd seen something like it before, but wasn't sure where. The girl didn't move and kept staring. Morgan thought she detected a high-pitched whine coming from her throat.

"What the fuck? I said, *Do I know you?*"

Great, Morgan thought. She's rolling and wants to make friends.

Though the girl's face didn't look friendly. Her nostrils flared and her eyelids fluttered every time she inhaled. Was the chick *smelling* her?

Morgan wished she didn't feel so disoriented. She'd been up since five because of the toad incident, and though there wasn't anything going on in the half-empty lot, she should have checked out the scene earlier. The remnants of a slippery, bothersome dream knocked around in her head. Something about a cave, or a tunnel. She was walking in darkness toward a dull yellow light, but the memory of what was there kept floating away from her. She was reaching toward a wall, which gave way to an adjacent room. Each time Morgan grasped, she fell farther into thick black nothingness. She reached once more —

She unbuckled her seat belt and glanced at her cell. Moth's one-word text of TODAY was still there on her screen, so she deleted it and clicked back to the clock. It was three. Whatever was supposed to be happening at the Ring of Fire had probably already started. It irritated her that she was late. What irritated her more, though, was the freak standing outside her car.

"Go away," Morgan said to the rain-slicked girl. "I don't feel like company."

She didn't move, though her eyelids still fluttered and the weird humming heightened. Thunder clapped and a brief burst of lightning illuminated the afternoon sky.

"What are you, a fucking *'tard*? I said *go away!*"

What was the bitch doing? That sound she was making. If she didn't stop, Morgan was going to have to —

She opened her car door. She *tried* to be careful but it bumped the girl anyway. Not that she was sorry, though she mumbled an apology while she flipped through her keys for the alarm. She was cut short by a sudden flurry of movement. Morgan turned and there the girl was, in front of her, on her haunches, grabbing for her ankles like a demented dog.

"Fuck!" She moved back, trying to disengage. "You are not what I need right now, bitch!"

She wouldn't have kicked the weirdo had the girl not held one of Morgan's ankles in her grasp. It seemed that she was trying to drag her toward a line of scraggly trees at the base of what looked like — was that a volcano? Where the fuck *were* they?

"Stop it!" Morgan yelled, still kicking.

She started to walk in the other direction, but the girl —

Morgan couldn't believe her eyes, but it was happening — the girl was grabbing for her other ankle in an obvious attempt to keep her rooted. In one swift motion Morgan grabbed a handful of dreads and pulled. Then she swiped, hard. She had never hit another person before — well, besides K.A. and her mom — and when she felt her palm meet her opponent's cheek, then the ragged, serrated bump of fingernails, her own, scraping into flesh, she was surprised how good it felt.

She only had to whisper.

"I said, don't touch me."

The freak was breathing hard now, whimpering. Morgan pushed her to the ground, scrambled with her backpack, and headed for the dimming trees. There was music in there. She could hear it. She turned back and saw the girl watching her leave, still holding her cheek. Morgan looked down at her nails, which she could swear were an inch longer than they had been in the morning, and coated with a red-violet shimmery substance she figured was blood mixed with the freakazoid's makeup. *Man! What is going on today with the slime?* She wiped her hands on a passing weed. Heading down the rocky trail, she concentrated on the sound of her heart pumping. Loud and quick and even. She didn't much feel like thinking.

∽ ∽ ∽

"Excuse me."

After twenty minutes of walking, Ondine stopped in front of the first person who met her eyes: a handsome, dark-haired boy who sat with his arms around his knees, surrounded by a few other hollow-eyed kids on a blanket under a tarp. The boy did not return her smile but nodded to show that he was listening, and Ondine, motioning to Nix, who had found a nearby tree and was now unpacking the blue tarp, continued.

"My friend and I, we'd like to set up our camp. Do you have some twine?"

A few words passed between the boy and the group behind him in what sounded like Spanish. He dug into a nearby bag and handed her a roll of brown twine. He smiled this time, and nodded, but still didn't speak. Even weirder, he kept his eyes on the ground as he passed her the rope, as if he didn't want to see her.

"*Habla inglés?*" She tried again, pissed that her scientist father had encouraged her to take Latin. "Do you know when the band starts? Mi amigo and I —" She gestured to Nix again. "We want to see the band. *La música.*" Ondine did a little desperate dance and snapped her fingers. "*La música?* La Flama?"

Nothing. The boy continued to look at the ground.

"*Gracias,*" she said, frustrated, and trudged back to Nix.

"They could only speak Spanish." She shrugged. "Weird. I didn't know the Flame was popular with Mexicans."

"They might not be Mexican," Nix corrected her peevishly, taking the twine that Ondine passed him but continuing to look at the small group, who were now in conversation with each other, their backs turned.

"Oh sorry. Maybe they were from *Béleeth*. Or *Guatémala*. Jesus. What is your problem?"

"Nothing."

Ondine sighed and shook her head. She didn't feel like fighting. "Anyway, they were kind of shy," she added, trying to bridge the gap that had opened between them, but Nix stayed silent, concentrating on their temporary arrangements. She watched him go through the motions of hanging the tarp. Lightning struck again, closer this time, and she ducked under. When Nix had finished, he too crawled under the low ceiling, his face a pallid blue, his eyes squinting in the dimming light. Despite his proximity, she felt desperately alone.

"I'm going to return the twine," he said. "Wait here. I'll be right back."

"Whatever." She watched him walk down the path. She lay on her back and looked above her. Rain pooled in the center of the blue square, forming a circle. She aimed one of the flashlights toward it and it illuminated a watery nimbus, shaking with every splash. She flicked her flashlight on and off, thinking.

She *was* disappointed. Though she was sure there were a few more kids somewhere among the rocks and trees, the much-whispered-about Ring of Fire, by her reckoning, was a party of no more than a hundred kids. No alcohol, no dancing, and a storm. What was everyone waiting for? For it was clear, from the hush that had fallen in the forest — only somewhat enlivened by rolls of thunder and the cracks of approaching lightning — that everyone was waiting for something. The Flame? There was no way the band was going to play. Not with an electrical storm close by. So this soggy affair on a Wednesday in June: this was the rave that everyone was talking about? The momentous occasion she and Nix had dreamed about side by side for the past three weeks?

Whatever. The whole thing was a bust. That she had expected something different, something shocking, was pathetic. What she got was yet another confirmation of her father's advice to never trust what you can't observe. *Things are as they seem, Ondine.* Yes, things were as they seemed: wet and gray and dull. Nothing to do now but wait for it to be over. She would have asked Nix what he was feeling, what he thought, but he was returning the twine, and, she noted, taking his sweet time. She sat up, cupping the flashlight in her palm.

One by one, lights were being extinguished in the scattered tents. Despite the storm, Ondine thought she saw fireflies twinkling in the moist air. Her jeans were soaked so she took them off and rolled them neatly into her backpack, leaving just her hoodie mini on. She leaned back against a tree and closed her eyes. Just for a second, she thought, but when Nix's face appeared in the dim blue of their lean-to, she realized she must have dozed off, for his flashlight was on and behind him the sky had darkened to a smoky black. The rain had stopped but the thunder had not, and every so often the sky was lit up by viscous yellow.

"The Flame," he said. "They're playing."

She scrambled up, her heart beating.

"They told you?" Remembering the way the boy with the twine had remained so silent.

"No, no. I just heard it. I checked it out. There's a clearing by the crater. That's where they are. Everyone's going over there. Come on."

She was watching Nix so intently she didn't realize she, too, heard the music playing. A faraway seasick sound, like a carnival heard from down a country road.

"Come on, Ondine. It's time."

It was . . . time? Nix barely allowed her to think before he turned and started walking down the sloping crunchy path, following the skipping flashlights ahead of them. Maybe there *were* more than a hundred people. Ondine could see at least that many lights in front of her, moving down a hill and then up another, heading toward where she imagined the lake was, at the top of the crater. There were quiet murmurs of song and then the ever-louder beat of a single, deep bass drum. The Flame. She and Nix came to an opening, and below them a sort of crater, rudely lit by a few bonfires, opened up. The lake, she figured, must have been just above them.

"I guess we're in the right place."

She looked down at the plateau. A stage was surrounded by a hundred or so people, undulating like water rocked by the passage of a boat, and another hundred hung around the edge or near the fires. The figures on the stage itself were hidden by lights and smoke — liquid nitrogen? — and Ondine couldn't tell how many they were, what they were doing, but she could hear their music now.

Hurry — hurry — hurry! — ring of fire —
Ring of fire! Spin round, ring of fire —

So it was a concert after all. Though a lingering fear tugged at her, a voice whispering, *Don't go down there,* they had come all this way, and what was she going to do now? Go back to the car? A crack of lightning behind her nudged her farther.

"Come on. We'll be safer down there," Nix said, pointing to the rock formations that poked out of the sides of the bowl-shaped crater, like gargantuan fingers protecting it from the wind and — she hoped — from the lightning.

This time he smiled. A smile that Ondine remembered.

"You ready?"

All she could manage was a halfhearted shrug.

He turned back to the scene in front of them, his eyes glowing in the light from the bonfires. That's when she knew she was scared. Everything had gotten just a little too weird. She looked at Nix, holding the flashlight, smiling as if a party in an electrical storm in a volcano in the middle of the wilderness were the most normal thing in the world. She had known the boy for three weeks. Knew *no one else* at the concert, if that's what it was. She pulled her cell out of her pocket and was relieved to see it still showed a few bars. She tucked it away before Nix turned back toward her.

"All right." He tried again. "Tell you what. You wait here. I'll go find Moth. I'm sure he's here now. See that fire?" He pointed to one near the middle of the gathering. "I'll meet you there. Or if you want, go down there and I'll find you. Stay near the front left of the stage."

Ondine could tell Nix was feeling antsy, and though she didn't want to be left alone, she didn't feel like running after James Motherwell, either.

"Okay," she said. "Front left of the stage." She called after him as he started to lope down the hill, a raggedy figure in black against a ruddy, firelit night. He didn't answer. Maybe he was going to do dust, she thought, but buried the suspicion.

"Front left," she called out again, louder.

"Front left!" Nix shouted back.

It was how they said good-bye.

CHAPTER 10

MOTH SURVEYED THE CROWD. Things were coming together nicely, he thought, though he stayed hidden under an outcropping of rock, away from the light rain and roving eyes. They would be looking for him and they would be confused, as they all were, as he had been the first time. They would have to wait. Preparations still had to be made: the finial had to be raised, liquid nitrogen placed, and it was crucial to maintain the illusion of normalcy now, before everything started.

They couldn't have asked for a better storm. The lightning was strong from the recent warm front, yet without the torrential rain that sometimes accompanied such gatherings.

Two hundred or so had come from around the Pacific. Even a few from South America. A VW bus was one thing, an airplane, quite another. It was a bigger gathering than Portland had ever seen, and one ring would be initiated. His. Or to put it more precisely (Viv was always telling him he needed to be more precise): Ondine, Nix, and Morgan.

The three had behaved just as he had wanted them to. Moth had watched Nix search, only to separate from Ondine and weave through the crowd, as he was now doing, alone. Looking for him. Good. The first time would be easier to witness solo.

Morgan — he'd heard — had fallen asleep in her car and Rei, from San Francisco, had been sent out to pull her in. Done, Rei reported, shortly before Moth found his rocky perch. He imagined he'd spot Morgan soon, wandering through the crowd, a little dazed, a little charmed, solitary, just like Ondine.

Just to make sure the daze was permanent, Moth had dispatched Jinn, also from S.F., with some dust. Nix, he knew, would already have had some. Usually they took it willingly; the Ring of Fire was the perfect opportunity to sample the stuff. They'd be less suspicious then. With what they were about to find out, this was crucial.

The only one that was missing was Bleek. Moth knew the dealer had been asking around Portland about the location of the gathering, and there was a good chance of his making his way here, however dangerous. The proximity of so many uninitiated would be enough to outweigh the risk, but so far there had been no sighting.

If he could eliminate Bleek here, Moth thought, his problems would be solved. He hadn't been feeling well lately — at twenty-two, the small window of years past eighteen was closing on him, and he could feel the end coming, like air being squeezed out of a tire. He had lost weight and shrunk from the small amounts of food he allowed himself. The constant, grinding energy had made a mess of his teeth. He didn't like the devilish cast they gave him, but what little he sold in dust wasn't exactly enough for cosmetic dentistry. He almost envied Bleek his tidy business, but reminded himself that Bleek was evil and selfish and dark, and it was his duty to eliminate him — a task he had not yet managed to complete.

He sweat involuntarily in his small hiding place at the mere thought of passing before his time. His fate then — nothing less than infinite cosmic pain — was enough to keep him to his given tasks.

Moth looked at the stage where the Flame played. They would be leaving soon, too. He had known a few of the members from his own inititation a few years ago. They worked in Seattle mostly, and he thought their trick of becoming a band ingenious. Rings sometimes played tricks before their time and this one — an anonymous, unsigned band that had risen to the top of the download charts — had kept them in the world just long enough to cause problems. One member had died. A pet they had gotten to dance was starting to become inured to the effects of dust and had to be chained. Some pathetic abandoned human thing.

Where had they kept her, this big, Brunhilde-esque blonde?

The Northwest was Viv's territory and though she was good at hiding things, Newberry National Volcanic Monument wasn't exactly an airport Hilton.

Around the smoky, fiery scene below him, night had fallen. A flash lit up the stage and he counted. *One-one-thousand, two-one-thousand, three-one-thousand.* Thunder boomed. The eye was less than a mile away. Nix, Ondine, and Morgan would be given their dust and the finial would be covered and ready. The great ring was forming. The exidis was near.

Moth stretched out his legs and readied himself. His sign flashed by him as he moved his hands toward the earth, and he thought again of Bleek and what it would finally feel like to go. One look at the scene below — the blinding lightning, the billowing fires — was enough to scare him. Because of the mess with Bleek, he'd had to wait longer than most. Would he still be able to see himself from there? What would it feel like to be unbound? Would he miss . . . himself? These were questions that only Viv could answer, and though he'd asked her a million times what it was like, her answer was always the same: Like everything and nothing, like forever and never, all at once.

Lightning cracked again. He dislodged himself from his narrow ledge and headed toward the stage.

ဢ ဢ ဢ

ONDINE WAS BORED, and Nix hadn't returned with Moth, so she decided to make her way alone to where the Flame was playing, to meet them at the place Nix had designated. Closer to the stage, past the fires, she was able to make out the band. A typical four piece: one girl and three guys — drummer, guitarist, bassist, singer — and a fifth figure, a woman, who held no instrument, stood away from any microphone, and swayed. She was a big, striking blonde, larger than the skinnier, smaller, black-clad people on the stage. Ondine felt like she had seen pictures of the woman on some blog, but only parts of her face. Now here she was in the flesh: not quite Valkyrie material, but Ondine hadn't expected the infamous Flame dancer to be so tall. She moved quartertime to the music, her hips tracing wide figure eights, her hands carving the air like a child scooping handfuls of bubbles off her bath. The boys and girl behind her shook their hair and gyrated, but the woman just swayed and smiled. Her eyes were wide and happy and welcoming and empty, seeing everyone and no one at the same time.

It was only when Ondine got up to the stage that she saw the thick rhinestone collar around the woman's neck. Her smile was fixed, but while she moved — spacily, stonily — one of her hands pulled at her collar, as if she were curious about it.

Quick — quick! Wooden doll,
Hurry, lovely wooden doll, spin round

Was she really that tall? Ondine took in the crowd, which

she could see clearly now for the first time. Girls and boys, long hair, short hair, curly hair, no hair. All young, all different colors. Blue eyes, green eyes, brown eyes, black. Brown skin and pink skin and tanned and freckled and pimpled. They were smiling and laughing, dancing with each other with a kind of buoyant, blissful energy Ondine had rarely experienced. Or, at least, not since she was a child. Not since running around the yard chasing Celeste at Irvington Montessori. For that's what she was reminded of: childhood. The innocent, boisterous freedom of being a kid.

So this *was* what everyone was waiting for. The Flame *rocked*. Ondine was surrounded by strangers and Nix was nowhere in sight, yet for the first time that day, she felt at home. Had he . . . ? No. She banished the thought, losing herself in the tangle of glowing wet bodies, in the endless waves of sound that washed over her, tossing her and spinning her and twisting her. She was having a good time. She couldn't deny it. Maybe she was sick of Nix. Maybe they were too close.

A flash drew Ondine's eyes back to the stage, and behind the music a low rumble sounded. The storm must be close, she reckoned, yet no one around seemed worried. The rain had ceased and there in the bowl of the crater she felt protected. Familiar pinpricks of color swirled around the band. She thought they were fireflies at first, but realized they were butterflies, their iridescent wings throwing off glancing sparks of red, green, blue, orange, and yellow, shifting under the spotlights.

Butterflies? That must have cost a pretty penny.

Ondine laughed, delighted, and caught the eye of a cute brown-haired boy who'd wrapped his shirt around his waist and was eyeing her, edging closer to her, sensing her openness.

Orange wings — white wings — blue wings — green.
Filaments of fire — unspoken and unseen.

Her arms were in the air. She was dancing. She couldn't tell who moved closer to whom, but she and the boy pressed together, bumping, and one of her hands dropped down to the small of his back and one of his hands dropped to the small of hers and then lower, holding her butt lightly, easily. After all the chaste nights she'd spent with Nix, like a geriatric couple on an Alaskan cruise, Ondine felt lust like pepper in her mouth. She nudged one of her legs between his, inched up his thigh. She had to pull her mini up to ride higher and she did it, her bare skin feeling the coarseness of the boy's denim-covered leg.

His hands clasped hers and she looked down. A small tattoo of an X traced the inside of his wrist.

"What's your name?" She leaned toward him and smiled. Never in her life had Ondine Mason asked a boy his name.

He smiled back. His teeth were white and very straight. "Jinn," he said.

"I'm Ondine."

"Right." He grinned again.

She said it louder. "My *name* is Ondine."

The boy nodded and pressed closer. He removed something from his right pocket, a small packet of paper, and emptied its contents into his other hand, dancing all the while.

"Do you want some?"

Ondine had never actually seen dust. All the times with Nix, he'd gone into the bathroom. She knew it didn't require anything — one just ate it, like sugar — but to see it there, in his hand, gave her a singular feeling. Not scared. Not comfortable. It glittered and had a vague goldish cast. It looked, she thought, like powdered Crystal Light.

"You just lick it," Jinn said, holding out his hand. "It's not strong."

Never in her life had Ondine done drugs. But dust was harmless. Nix was finished with it. What might a taste do? She was having fun. She wanted to have more.

"It's sweet. You'll like it."

She licked his outstretched palm. It tasted like salt at first, then sugar, then something chemical, like Advil. She swallowed and waited.

"Don't worry." Jinn bowed his head to look into her eyes. "It's really not strong at all."

Her newfound friend's smile grew as wide as the girl's on-stage, and Ondine could feel it mirrored on her face. She was confused and ecstatic at the same time. It was incredible, this thing — the Ring of Fire. Who had thought of it? Why had she been invited? All the waiting — yes, it had been worth it. She hoped no one would ever discover this secret thing — her thing now — but not just hers, all of theirs. The connection she had been yearning for, it was here. She was scared, but her fear felt liberating rather than imprisoning. Jinn's grip tightened; he whirled her around. Faces flashed. A small group of people had separated from the rest of the crowd to dance closer to a nearby fire. Above them a kind of pillar had been raised. Twenty or thirty feet high, white, with silken streamers billowing from its stem. Ondine felt momentarily nervous but couldn't remember why. A dozen or so kids held hands around it, then started moving, as if around a maypole. They held the streamers in their hands. Some of them Ondine recognized, though she didn't understand how till she discerned that the music had stopped. On the stage only the dancer remained, still swaying, looking out into the crowd, but sadder now.

Before Jinn's mouth covered Ondine's and her eyelids fluttered closed, she saw the word on their lips, the same word that was coming from her.

Exidis.

With her eyes closed and the taste of Jinn on her mouth, she saw the thing she had not been able to see with her eyes open. The girl on the stage. Swaying as if floating. But not *as if.* She *was* floating. Two feet above the stage, wading through the air as if through water. And the people on the ground, the richly hued, impossibly beautiful ones, spinning in a great circle, chanting the word Moth had given her.

She was in Jinn's arms, on his thigh, in his kiss.

A figure appeared from the twilight: a cloud, a whirl, a moonbeam, hanging for a moment in the air. Ondine watched Jinn's face crack, then fall in wonder. He had separated from her now, and was staring up at the woman's oval face, crowned by a ring of black-and-silver hair. Her purple-gray eyes glittered, her lips parted, revealing the serrated edge of small white teeth. Her voice shimmered. Dappled silver coruscation.

"Welcome to the Ring of Fire."

Everyone around Ondine silenced. She felt light-headed, confused. Dust, she thought cloudily. This must be the dust.

"You will hear this from me only once. The rest of your teachings will come from your guide, the one who told you about this gathering, the great gathering of our kind. You will be scared. You will doubt us. But you know who you are and you must listen carefully, starting now."

Ondine felt her knees begin to quiver and buckle. She could not make out any distinct faces in the crowd. That boy — with the little X — where had he gone? She felt something sharp on her knees. She tried hard to keep her head up but could not. And still, the woman's voice, like a beautiful snake.

"You've known it since you were young. You inhabit a world that is not ours, yet — but not theirs either. You are different. You

209

have felt it since you were children. People give you wide berth; they want you. They want to be you."

Ondine felt as if the woman's voice were being piped into her ear. Then sound very far away. Then close again.

"You've been given the responsibility of furthering our tribe." Now the woman with the strange braided hair was looking coldly at the dancer on the stage, who was sitting, head in her hands. Had her voice darkened? Ondine tried to hear what she was saying, but her voice kept moving in and out again, as if on a tide.

"You are changeling fay . . . Not human. . . . The fire that runs in your veins, in your bodies . . ."

She smiled, bowed her shining head.

"We must give you a chance to enter. It is decreed: Those who are fay must be allowed a choice to pass through the Ring of Fire."

Ondine felt her hands hit rough rock.

"We changelings travel through the mortal world and endure its tests." A shadow passed over the woman's flickering eyes. "We remember love; we taste the sweetness of mortality, and pass on the cup. Very soon, when your time comes, you will have to choose: mortal or fay. A tortured humanity or the power of the illuminated." Her voice hushed. "The incandescent."

The shroud on the giant pole at the center of the gathering fell away and the sky turned fluorescent. Thunder shook Ondine's bones. She rose with great effort. Was the crowd parting in front of her? And the woman, was she floating? Like the Flame dancer had been before? The chanting twisted its way into her brain, till what she heard and what she thought were indistinguishable. *Exidis. Exidis. Exidis.* The butterflies had grown and turned into whizzing balls of multicolored fire. She felt one pass, its stinging. She would have run if she weren't so very tired. . . .

When the bolt struck, its path had been so clear in Ondine's imagination that she was not surprised to see the twelve people holding the cloth-wrapped spokes fall to the ground, their eyes rolling into their heads. Only one stood apart, a girl with long red hair pulled back in a low ponytail. When the lightning cleared, the redheaded girl rushed over to a blond boy Ondine had noticed earlier in the forest. He was still holding one of the white-wrapped chains. A little blood leaked from his mouth — it looked to her like chocolate syrup. The crowd stilled. The air smelled like burnt meat and rain.

CHAPTER 11

WHEN YOU FIND SOMETHING OUT about yourself that you've always known, how are you supposed to feel? Not shocked, because the knowledge isn't wholly a surprise. Nor at ease. Consciousness rarely breeds ease. Maybe you feel tentatively located, as if you had just moved into a new house. Not a home yet; the place doesn't exude that kind of wear, comfort, and memory. But it's yours now and you must live in it.

Nix Saint-Michael had rarely felt at home in his life. Maybe with his mother and grandfather in Sitka, but that was long ago, and other than a few memories — like half-forgotten movies now — home eluded Nix. He had come to feel that he didn't need a home, and he didn't believe any bullshit about how home is where the heart is, or if he were at home in himself, he'd be fine. Nix knew nothing was ever really fine, even before he started seeing the lights.

The woman who had come out of nowhere right before the lightning struck had said the word *fay*. *Changeling fay. The fire that runs in your veins, in your bodies.* . . . Then a lot of other insanity that Nix couldn't hear because he was backing away by then, running, in fact, from the whole ugly fiasco. Someone had died in front of him. A kid. His age. An innocent. When Nix saw him there at the edge of the gigantic maypole or lightning rod or whatever it was they had raised, holding a spoke that was clearly metal wrapped in cloth, he had tried to run toward him but the bolt had come too fast.

We taste the sweetness of mortality, and pass on the cup . . .

He hadn't stayed long enough to hear any more. He had run. Though the rest of the kids around the pillar, incredibly, had survived a direct lightning strike — they were moving, shaking, trying to wake up; Nix could see that much — that one kid, the blond boy whom he had seen in the forest earlier, the fire around him already blazing, that kid had died. Nix had known he would. That's why he'd been so quiet earlier.

He had brought her here, his friend, Ondine. It was his fault they were there. It was his fault a person had died.

You've known it since you were young.

"No." Nix said it aloud. "No. No. No."

He walked toward the trees. The last thing he heard was the woman in the long black coat telling someone to call an ambulance. By then he was yards away.

The storm had passed over the mountain and he could see it in the distant dark like a flashlight underwater. The moon had risen. It was a little less than half full, and its light shone clear in the mountain air. *No.* Nix said it again. This was Moth's fault. The one who lured them there. The one he'd been looking for and could not find. Yet he could not explain the profound sadness that rose from his stomach, wrapped its tentacles around his chest, and squeezed.

He had heard more than he had wanted to. Seen more, too. He had walked into this nightmare on his way down the dark well of madness and here he was. What was the real Nix doing in the real world? Was he having a conversation with himself on a street corner somewhere? Was he down in the Shanghai Tunnels, loaded? Was he even in Portland? Was he even himself?

He had to get his head clear before he could help Ondine. And Morgan, he remembered suddenly. She was supposed to be there that day. What had happened to her?

Nix's legs felt weak so he stopped, putting a hand on a nearby tree to steady himself. Like the first day on the water with his grandfather during the salmon run. But that was a good memory and this was bad. Worse than bad. Nix felt the tree's trunk, rough. A needle grazed his cheek. He looked around him, seeing a dark path, illuminated only by the moon and the faraway storm. He could hear the low buzz of people talking through the trees, but no one word was distinct. His mouth felt dry, his forehead moist.

He crouched on one knee, feeling the wet sponginess of dirt

mixed with pine needles and leaves and sticks. *Now I'm a real Injun*. He put his face down and inhaled. It smelled like his childhood: sweet and thick and mineral. What was this if not real?

The beating in his chest slowed.

The woman in the long black coat had grayish eyes. Her hair was black, pulled back, ringed by a single line of silver. She was small and older. She had been pretty once and carried a cane in her right hand. He'd have to identify her eventually. She'd be charged with murder.

Someone scuffled on the path behind him; a hushed male voice floated around the trees, more like an odor than a sound. Nix turned. Whoever it was hadn't rounded the bend. He strained. The voice was familiar to him, its rasp, its conspiratorial tone.

Without thinking he slipped behind a tree, pressing his back to it, feeling its rough striations. He felt for the last of the dust in his jacket pocket and reminded himself that he hadn't taken any that morning. Or had he? Was this withdrawal? Was this a hallucination? If it was, he was still in it. It wasn't going away. Nor, Nix recalled, did any of them, no matter how much dust he took. All that crap about forgetting: Nix didn't forget anything. Daddy Saint-Michael and him on a boat on the glassy sea, his mother sitting in Koloskov's singing, *I can't stand the rain*, her idea of a joke. The smell of buses and public bathrooms and death. The hallucination that was his life.

215

He could make out the soft shuffle of two pairs of legs and he pressed closer to the trunk; the passersby approached. The single voice had gotten clearer. Nix could make out the barest hint of a higher voice, too: light, girlish. He was afraid to peer out beyond the trunk to see who it was, but words slowly took shape.

"Here, pet. Eat it. You'll feel better."

Nix cringed. He knew what was being offered. The man's voice was thin and reedy, placating yet aggressive. The girl with him moaned.

They paused beyond the tree. Nix placed himself so that he could get a partial view.

He could see only the backs of their heads, but in the moonlight he knew immediately who he was looking at. That receding corn-husk hair. The squat neck. The red jacket. He would have known that fucking jacket anywhere. And the girl next to him, whose slight shoulders Tim Bleeker bearishly grasped, whose little sock, Nix noticed, had dropped sadly on her thin ankle. Not embracing, but pulling her closer, weighing her down so that she had to lean on him to stay up; that pathetic little thing was Neve.

Nix didn't need to think much before he stepped out of the woods toward them.

⁊ ⁊ ⁊

MORGAN D'AMICI BIT THE KNUCKLES of her pointer fingers to keep from smiling. Hard. Or at least, she thought, hard enough for it to hurt. She liked a bit of physical unpleasantness every once in a while. Some might call it pain. But pain was so messy. Anything taken to an extreme was unpleasant. A little bit of pressure — combined with that ice cube feeling of sharpness — it kept one's will strong. It kept one from slipping — Morgan cleared an imaginary strand of hair from her brow — into messiness. Cloudy thinking. The miserable in-between.

She took a breath and tipped her chin up, looking straight at the empty stage. Already people had started to dismantle it. So that was what had accounted for the jury-rigged nature of the Ring of Fire. The gathering had to be broken down quickly, in case something went wrong. Which, tonight, it most certainly had.

Morgan had been at the outskirts of the mysterious circle when it had started to shift. She had watched the pillar rise: the stakes hammered into the ground, the cloth-wrapped spokes lying like ribbons on an Easter bonnet. She had spoken to no one and no one had spoken to her. Her experience with the freak in the parking lot had prepared her. When that boy from San Francisco came around with dust, Morgan had taken it willingly, despite her bad experience in Eugene. Something very out of the ordinary was occurring and she wanted to take full advantage of it.

When the Flame left the stage and took up their posts at the pillar with the others, Morgan almost swallowed her tongue. She was that excited.

Exidis, they had chanted. The word she had been trying to remember all those weeks after Ondine's party. The one Moth had whispered in her ear.

Just before the lightning struck, balls of electricity, many-colored orbs, like giant sparkling Christmas balls, burst from the stem of the pillar and tumbled to earth, rolling willy-nilly through the pulsing crowd. Not among them. *Through them.* Through their bodies: in one side, out the other.

That only one died seemed a miracle. When the bolt came, it was as if the sky had parted and delivered a pure blast of un-imaginable cosmic heat straight to the center of the earth. The entire structure of the ring — for that's what it was, Morgan de-duced from looking at its unshrouded shape, a rather primitive superconductor ring — flashed blue, then red, then dirty orange, its human attachments frizzed off like so many burnt husks.

The others were struggling to awaken. The woman in the black coat had emerged from the crowd, giving brisk orders for someone to call 911, and had then spoken directly to her. Or so it had seemed. For the crowd had parted around three lone bod-ies as soon as the chanting started, and Morgan had understood, in an instant, the answer to so many questions: Why she'd been attracted to Ondine Mason. Why Nix Saint-Michael had shown up at their party that night. Why all of them were in the mountains together. But now Ondine was passed out, having danced pathetically right in front of her, and Nix — whom she'd spotted earlier at the edge of the crowd casting his eyes around as if he were looking for someone — was nowhere to be seen. Not that Morgan much cared.

"Listen closely," the woman had said. "Starting now."

So she did. Morgan always had been good at following orders.

"You are called a changeling." Her voice was metallic and raspy, like a bell rubbing against a cheese grater, and she spoke quickly, without ceasing, so Morgan had to concentrate to remember the terminology.

"Your human body is used to hold what you truly are, which is not of this world, nor of humanly conceivable proportions. You belong to another dimension: Novala. The never-ending, the one. The everything and nothing. Your time in the human world, everything you've known thus far, is but an intermediate state in your ultimate evolution. What you have just witnessed is the exidis of a group of your kind, leaving their bodies and entering their true home. We call it Novala. New Land. Be advised. These are all simplified ways of understanding what is beyond any human's ken."

That's when Morgan saw James Motherwell, whispering something to the woman before he progressed to Ondine.

"The ring is a superconducting vortex. At its center is cold fission. Lightning is used to power the conduit, liquid nitrogen to keep it cold. The exidis takes immense energy and preparation and that is why we are here. The ring is your cocoon. You will be reborn into Novala as a being of such unimaginable power and greatness there are no words to describe its awesome totality."

Here her voice softened.

"Soon you will know it. You will see it. You will come so close. . . .

"Human life is ending. You have already witnessed its initial corrosions. Is Novala a safe place? Should we doubt it? You have a chance to join the existence of a higher plane. The fay. The one. The ever changing and immutable. We have been with you through all time. The bodies you inhabit are our conduits. You, the changelings, are chosen for your fitness and intelligence and energy."

Her voice became colder, though her eyes remained quiet. "You have only a year to learn and organize. There will be those who will try to disrupt your progress. Family, friends. They will ask why you seem different. Why you seem, perhaps, oddly happy. Or sad. You must tell no one. You must live as you have lived. You are safe in your ring. After your body reaches its mature state, which is soon, the pressure of the inhabitation will start to wear on it, and it will rapidly deteriorate. If your corpus dies before the exidis, your fate will be of the harshest proportions."

She paused. Morgan held her breath.

"Study well the exidis and the laws of the fay. The boy's fate you saw tonight" — for the first time the woman cast her opaque eyes down — "could have been averted. Each of you has a monitor. A ringer. You probably already know him." She stopped and Morgan saw her eyes dart around, as if looking for someone. "A person who can read the health and fitness of your human corpus and advise you of its life force. Remember that your ringers are there to help you. Use them well."

Ringers? But before Morgan had a chance to wonder, she took up again.

"The police and the ambulance will soon be here. Before then we will disperse." She flicked her eyes to Moth, now back at her side. "You will want to know if you have 'powers.'" The cold look resumed. "And you will find out. Your guide will help you. Remember that you must not allow your body to be harmed. There are chaotic, insidious forces out to hurt you. Changelings who have chosen the path away from their one fate. One is familiar to you already.

"You will know us by this mark." And here she held up her wrist, upon which Morgan could make out a small tattoo of an

X, the same one she had seen on Moth, the same on the rabid girl in the parking lot. "It is tattooed upon us after our initiation, and the radiation from the exidis completes its design. There are those in the world who have it. Humans. It means they were once inhabited. You will know the completed design when you see it. You mustn't speak to them or show them your own sign. They have no memory of the experience. They have no memory they had once gone through the ring of fire.

"I am Viv. I am a scion. We are the bridges between changelings and fay. We stay in the world longer, and the threat of elimination is greater for us. Do not think that you will see us often. We come out rarely for fear of the evil ones."

"Cutters," she whispered, and for the first time Morgan felt the full weight of the woman's obdurate gaze.

"The humans over there." She looked in the direction of the young men and women trying to rouse themselves. "They will soon awaken. You will not speak to them. You will allow them to be led back to their homes by their guides. They will wake up and believe that this was all a strange, singular experience. A party. Which, until ten minutes ago, it was. This is the effect of the dust that was given to you at the beginning of the night, and that will again be given to you at your exidis. You will take nothing in between.

"Finally." Here the woman who called herself Viv looked behind her, at the stage. "The pet there. She is human." The blonde was still standing, big and vacant, and Viv looked away. "The changelings used to have a practice of keeping uninhabited humans in bondage, under the influence of dust, for their . . ." She paused and searched for the word. "Enjoyment. This is absolutely forbidden. That girl should not have been here tonight."

With this she turned to leave. Moth was at her elbow, leaning in, whispering. Around Morgan, order was resuming. She knew the woman must have been giving them time to take in what they had just learned, and of course she would need to check on what was happening with the dead boy in the ring.

The dead boy in the ring.

The people on the ground around the pillar were starting to rise, and Morgan knew instinctively that she should not be nearby when they woke up. The red-haired girl — their guide, she reasoned, or a ringer — was attending to each, gesturing with hands pointing at the sky, then hugging them. Others huddled around. The members of the Flame — for that's why they had looked familiar, Morgan realized — searched in the half dark for their things. Another young man, a roadie type, had jumped onto the stage and was collecting backpacks. The blonde with the dreads from the parking lot was still there, staring at Morgan but keeping her distance. She didn't see Nix. And Ondine, head in her hands, had made it to a fetal position. Nearly everyone else was gone. Morgan knew she should be, too.

She needed a moment to think.

A pretty face in the mirror. That's what everyone thinks I am.

She crouched on the still-wet earth, then drew her legs to her chest and wrapped her thin arms around them.

"Tooth fairy," she whispered, and laughed.

She had been right all along. She *was* different from other people. All those . . . *mortals*, with their Odor Eaters and their rotting teeth. She would be — the word seemed smaller than the feeling it inspired — a scion, like Viv. No, *instead* of Viv.

Though she knew she was getting ahead of herself, an early memory sprang before her. It had been tucked away somewhere, from a long-ago venture into the forest. She must have been younger than twelve, for the trees rose up high around her. A bird — her adult eye named it a falcon — circled above, looking for prey. Morgan could feel its hunger, its cold heart, the thin stream of air through its dagger beak. Each feather ruffled and the fine hairs on Morgan's girlish arm distended in sympathy. She sensed and smelled and swooped. Another bird, helpless under an uncaring sky, had crossed its path. In a vicious instant the falcon had dived, caught the other in its talons, pierced its breast, and killed it.

K.A., she thought suddenly. Morgan pictured him, and a cold burning in her sinuses started. What was he, then? Were they related? Were they blood? She recalled the words Viv had used, still strange on her tongue: *Changeling. Ringer. Corpus.* There

224

were so many questions. Who would answer them for her? Moth? The night of the party seemed far away. She shoved him and her brother out of her mind. Her mother, too, though it was painful. Yvonne and her out-of-date coats and slutty sundresses and cheap shoes.

Then she lit on it, as a child might on a toy she did not want to share. A half-formed word Viv had spoken at the end, in a tone so low it seemed it had oozed from the volcano around them. The ones who were evil, chaotic. The ones who were out to get them.

"*Cutter,*" Morgan pronounced half audibly, and pushed herself up from the rocky ground.

∽ ∽ ∽

AT THE EDGE OF THE STAGE, Moth felt in his pockets for the keys to the car he'd driven. He was already thinking of what was next: the first moment he'd be able to talk to his ring. What would he say to them? He looked at the dissipating crowd, a scene he was so familiar with after his years in training. He was anxious to do things right, to avoid the mistakes his own guide had made, and that anxiety made him more jittery than usual. He scratched his chin where his beard should have been, jingling the keys in his pocket.

"Stop fidgeting!"

Viv scrutinized the younger man. Nothing on her face moved. She stared, her hand on the stick she always carried, but never leaned on, rather grasped, as a fighter would.

"Where is your head?"

Moth looked at his boots, then up again, trying to meet her eyes. The scion made him nervous, but he tried to quiet himself by running his thumb over the edge of the keys.

"Attend to what I say."

Viv, intense and steely, was nevertheless not haughty. Her authority came from somewhere more rooted, some deep, certain place that allowed her to fixedly stare at the young man she was now addressing, calmly, precisely.

"You have been doing very well, Moth. You have made . . ." She rolled the stick in her right hand as she looked for the words. "Marked improvement. The responsibility has been good for you. You're lucky. You might have been left behind. You know who I'm referring to."

Though Viv was paying attention to the activities around her — the humans were gathering now; Moth could hear them asking about their friend, whose body had since been taken to the road — she kept her eyes locked onto his.

"Look at me." He did. "Did they check his sign?"

Moth nodded. "Yes. Still the X. The exidis was not complete."

A shadow passed over the woman's face, but she recovered herself and resumed.

"What happened to that corpus is not your responsibility. As we speak, the new ringer is about to depart the gathering, having missed most of the first lesson. That cutter he is drawn to is more powerful than either of us acknowledges. No one has been able to track him, even though we know he is here, with the girl. There is an active ringer here, Moth. Need I remind you? And though yours does not yet understand his power, Bleek does. Had I known Nix would be so" — Viv stilled her twisting cane — "*flighty*, I might have been able to intervene in such a way that at least he would have been able to hear the first lesson. Now he is leaving, and the burden will be on you to transmit the information that he missed."

She narrowed her eyes. "Not to mention to make sure he gets home alive."

Moth bit his bottom lip. His arms were crossed in front of him in bottled frustration. He seemed to want to say something, yet he remained silent.

"What is it?"

He shook his head, a brief but strong tremor.

"I will not tell you that you are forgiven," Viv continued. "You have not earned it yet. Since the failure of your ring, you have been a model changeling: your actions just and true, your intent pure. But how is it that you managed to elude eliminating Bleek? How is it that he is here now, pet in tow, to disrupt a peaceful gathering of our tribe, a welcoming of the new change-lings? How is it that this area, your territory since birth, has stayed mysterious enough to you that you did not know a cutter was gathering power in your presence?" She blinked, the inten-sity of her stare deepened, and Moth coughed.

"I don't — I don't feel well. I'm feeling sick. I'm tired. The schedule —"

"The schedule nothing. You are allowing your human traits to dominate you. You must be stronger. Your will must be more aligned, you must be clear and leave off what belongs to your corpus. You are not human, Moth. You are fay. Nothing humans have is what you want." Viv abruptly pulled a slender stiletto from the folds of her billowing black coat. She held it in her palm for a moment, as if balancing it, then smoothly, with one deft movement, flipped the blade in her hand and drew it across Moth's cheek. He looked down; a purple-red slash carved into the bone below his left eye. It welled a moment, threatening to spill.

"Do you feel that? No. You don't. That is because it belongs to your corpus. You are incorruptible. Incandescent. Fay. You are not 'sick.' You cannot be sick. Unless you are not what I think you are." She raised a dark and slender eyebrow.

Moth looked up, his eyes steadier now.

"I am exactly what you think I am." He shook his body, took a breath. "I'm sorry."

Viv tsked. "Are fay sorry, Moth?"

He hated it when she played her games with him — hated it most of all when she won. "No. I am not sorry. I must speak more precisely. I have been worried about the ring. They are not an easy group. Getting them here today took more cunning than I am used to. And Ondine —"

She nodded once, silencing him. "Yes, Ondine is different." She smiled, then blinked exactly three times. "Ondine has the potential to be a scion. You know that." With that Viv looked at the guides ushering away their humans, and behind them, the lingering changelings responsible for dismantling the finial before the authorities arrived. To the police the Ring of Fire would appear like a teenaged party gone awry.

"Moth," she said, almost as if talking to herself. "You are perhaps the most indefatigable changeling I have overseen. But you are not human. This is the hardest thing for a ling to understand. That what you were born with, you in fact are not. I know." Viv looked pained then, her eyes darker. "This is the great sadness of our kind, that we cannot hold on to what we've been given. That sending you off is so —" She looked up to the sky then. It had begun to lighten from the moon, and the bowl of the heavens was turning a dusky purple, speckled with the milky seeds of stars.

"I remember the feeling. I remember . . ." She paused, as if searching for the word. "Pain."

For an instant Moth's eyes joined the scion's. He winced, touched his cheek, and returned his hands to his pockets.

"At any rate, the cutter has already begun. Now we must be on the defensive."

Moth nodded. "I'll find Nix. I won't let him leave without the first lesson."

Viv returned his nod, but didn't move.

"And I will eliminate Bleek."

She nodded again, and with her eyes slightly downcast, spoke once more.

"This is not easy for me. I have known Bleek since he was first changed, as I have you. Your guide failed you both. That you made the correct choice speaks to your true fay nature. You will be rewarded in Novala."

Moth knew he was free to go, and yet he waited a moment more, inwardly doubtful he'd be able to do either of the things he'd promised. The scion's sentries stood by, waiting for a sign, but Viv only stared. She stood looking at the sky, at the tops of the trees, seemingly oblivious to the hushed activity around her, the stick she always held twisting in the dust this way and that.

CHAPTER 12

NDINE COULD NOT MOVE. Everything had shifted around her. The people that had surrounded her earlier, in motion — hugging, clapping backs, chanting — were gone. Jinn — she shuddered to think of the boy's mouth on hers — was gone. Nix was gone. Only Ondine remained: curled in a fetal position, having passed out, she realized, sometime after she saw the blood coming from the blond boy's mouth. Not early enough, she rued, to have missed the psychotic blather of the head of this sickening cult. Gone was the riot of bodies, dancing, jumping, spinning, replaced by a sparsely populated and dark miasma of treachery.

Nothing made sense. None of it: not the trees, not the mountains, not the moon. Moth there, talking to that woman. She wondered how much dust Jinn had given her. Had she actually thought she was flying?

And Nix. He had fallen into her life when she was weak. To think she had opened herself to him. Let him into her bed. Where was he now? She felt disgusted, wanted to get the memory of his touch off of her. The touch of all of them. *Fay*. Whatever these drugged-out lunatics called themselves.

She looked around. The gathering was almost empty. She'd have to find her way back to the car alone.

Except Moth, of course. Moth was still there. *Moth never goes anywhere*. He nodded and knit his brow, listening, hands in his pockets, to the freak in the long black coat. The woman was around fifty — sickeningly old to be chasing after teenagers, whatever she wanted them for — with a creepy hairstyle. All black, with a strong widow's peak that gave way to a tight, smooth crown, lined, like rims on a car tire, with silver. One huge braid coiled near her nape six, seven times. Like those bumper stickers: MY OTHER CAR IS A BROOM. It would be useful for the police later.

Ondine had to turn away. She was in the middle of a nest of madness, without a way home. She was shaking and weak, but most of all, she needed to regain control over her own mind. An image of her father dropped into her head. *Look for the strings, Ondine. There are always strings. What was the girl on the stage wearing? Was there a girdle? A shoulder strap?* She flipped through her memory of the time before the lightning struck, when she had been so out of it. Yes, there had been a thick belt around the Flame dancer's middle. *That's right*, she heard her father say. *Things are as they seem.*

Ondine Mason had been raised by a scientist and an architect. One showed her the foundations of things: the beams and pulleys and flying buttresses that erected and supported wonder; the other taught her about truth.

She shivered and pulled her red scarf closer around her ears. *Fuck it*. She didn't need to analyze these people. What she needed to do was find Nix, get the keys, and get the hell out of there. She wished she had her jeans on. Her eyes darted to Moth again. He was touching his face, which wore an expression of controlled surprise, though she was too far away to tell why. She wondered what was going on between him and that lady. Probably sleeping with her, Ondine thought grimly. Was there a cult in existence that didn't have an "initiation"?

Things are as they seem.

The thought, repeated now as she pulled herself off of the ground, gave her confidence, and a mission. She could see how kids got sucked in here. They were all — she could only come up with a string of adjectives — glassy, removed, otherworldly, drugged, beautiful. Yes, they had seemed beautiful. That was the dust. Beauty was seductive; Ondine knew that. So she repeated the mantra to herself — *Things are as they seem* — as she walked toward Moth and the woman. She needed to find Nix, get her keys. She needed to drive home and figure out what to do next. She needed to call the police and bust Moth's ass for everything he'd been doing over the last month. She was underage and he had procured alcohol for them. He had taken her to a place where there were drugs. Someone had died. Ondine didn't care who else she brought down. All she wanted was for all of the weirdness to end, and for things to go back to the way they were the day the Masons pulled out of their driveway.

ᔓ ᔓ ᔓ

Tim Bleeker was now stooping over, administering a few more shakes of dust to a nearly asleep Neve. If Nix were crazy, he'd do what came naturally. What came naturally was to get Neve — little wayward Neve, his best friend's girlfriend, his old boss's daughter — home.

He was glad he hadn't thought much, because as soon as he stepped out of the bank of trees, Bleek turned and came at him, a knife drawn, as if he were expected. Neve, freed from his grasp, weaved, stumbled, and fell to the darkened ground.

"Well, fancy meeting you here," Bleek sneered. He flicked his knife back and forth in his hand.

"You." Nix didn't know what else to say. Everything had gotten so strange; actions sped up, fast-forwarded. He barely had time to register the thin curving blade before he jumped out of the way. He felt light, and noticed nothing about what was around him except for that shining blade in Bleek's hand, the lattice of silvery green and black behind him, and the dark

234

moonlit sky. Nix moved his fingers and they trailed through the air as if through oil, as if he could feel every molecule of oxygen. How very odd, he managed to think before Bleek lunged again. The knife parted the air to Nix's side.

Everything — the air, the knife, himself, even Bleek — was made of the same substance. Equally solid and weightless, equally light and dark.

"So now you know." Bleek punctuated his words with a scowl and a bullying parry. He cut near Nix's face, close enough for him to feel the heat of his opponent's hand near his cheek. Bleek snickered, still lunging, but slicing around Nix, almost as if he were trying to miss him.

"Now you know the story. The tale. Yes, Dorothy, there are good witches. And bad ones. And ones who are fucked up." Bleek's upper lip was pulled back in a tight grin, revealing a row of glistening sharp teeth, like a rickety fence. "And it's just like the real world. Some of us are liked, some aren't. Some of us get the girls —"

Nix let his eyes flick to Neve, struggling to push herself up, her small hands, heavily ringed, grasping the ground. He looked back at Bleek.

"And some don't. Ha!" The older boy lunged, and Nix, taken off guard, leaned back. He felt supple, and he found his head near the ground, his feet still planted. Had he just done a back bend?

"That's some Matrix shit you got going there, boy." Bleek laughed and just as quickly, pulled in the long slender knife and lodged it inside his jacket. Nix, steadier now, waited for Bleek's next move. He could hear his own breathing, and Neve's next to him, and Bleek's. Bleek's was the tiniest bit labored.

"Let me fill you in on a little secret, Nixy. Maybe you weren't listening when the boss bitch of the silly fay did her welcome-wagon speech, but you don't need to waste your energy jumping away from me." He tapped the knife hidden in his jacket. "I don't want to kill you, dumb-ass. In fact, I'd like to be friends. Or did you miss that part?" He advanced, stepping so quickly that Nix found himself jumping back again. He could smell Bleek's breath. Liver and onions. He sidestepped to where Neve sat on the ground, and he crouched, trying to look at her.

"I don't know why I'm reminding you of this. Maybe because I see a little of myself in you." Bleek laughed. "Something around the chin. A certain weakness." Then he stopped and his face got serious. "Get up."

Bleek was addressing Neve, but his words had none of the sycophantic cloying Nix had heard earlier on the path. Neve stirred, but not quickly enough. Bleek kicked her, a brown Timberland nudging the space where her shirt met her low-rider jeans. She toppled again.

"Look how pathetic she is." Bleek snorted and smiled.

"Dumb, dumb animal. Stupid bag o' bones." He looked up at Nix. "Look. I know you've come for her, and since I'm not going to do anything to stop you, you might as well take her. She's a dumb bitch anyway." He paused, grinning. "But she's mine. *Badapba*." He nudged her harder. Another half-moon of dirt darkened her white baby tee. "Aren't you, pet?"

Neve said nothing. Nix, crouching, kept still. Obviously he had missed something.

He tried to breathe without outwardly moving, then spoke softly. "Come on, Neve. Let's go home." He grasped her under her moist armpits and raised her up, ignoring Bleek's sixth-grade snickering.

"Nix has a crush!"

He balanced Neve, trying to look into her eyes to see what condition her mind was in. They were half closed. Her head bobbed like a junkie crashing in a bus stop, but her legs were clearly trying to stand. He put an arm under her shoulder and stared at Bleek, who stood square in the middle of the pathway.

"Move," Nix said. Anything louder than a whisper and his voice would have felt unused, husky.

Bleek, smiling again, shrugged.

"Why should I?"

Nix considered the question. Then Bleek did something strange. He blew. Like blowing out a candle. A gust of hot, oily air rushed at Nix and he could smell its rottenness. Neve's hair blew back.

A strange challenge, but Nix's mind was taken up with an object coming from the sky. What was it? Coal black, a scribble, beating, attended by a dark, cold wind. Then, faster than he could even think its name, a bird — a crow — looped from nowhere, aiming for Bleek's head. Its claws were black and sharp as barbed wire. Its wings, six feet across. It scratched at Bleek's shoulders, his cowed face, and he shriveled in front of Nix, yelling "No!" until he was just a tiny ball, head buried in his knees.

Nix heard himself speak. "I said move."

He held Neve while Bleek, shielding his face, crawled to the shelter of a low bush. The crow retreated. Nix stared at the space where it had been for a moment, wondering what Bleek knew about him that he did not. How long had Bleek been feeding him dust to keep him quiet? He felt in Ralph Mason's jacket pocket for what was left of the supply he'd gotten from Moth that afternoon weeks ago, and tossed it into the forest. He picked up Neve — he had never held her before, or at least not like this — and noticed how light she was. Were all girls this light? Or was it just her?

"Come on," he said gently. "Let's get you home."

∽   ∽   ∽

ONDINE STRODE TOWARD VIV AND MOTH, looking neither right nor left. Her stomach spasmed. She desperately wanted to be home.

Things are as they seem, Ondine. She put one foot in front of the other.

James Motherwell smiled as she approached. His smugness disgusted her, but the anger made her stronger. She set her jaw and stopped a few paces away, not looking at the woman in the black coat. She did not want to be too close.

"Where's Nix." Command, not question. Ondine could feel her teeth baring, her skin stretched tight across her neck.

Moth tilted his head and grinned sheepishly. He stepped toward her then checked himself, as if he knew she would stop him. The lid of his right eye trembled. It seemed so obvious; she wondered why she had never seen it before: his fear. How he always put his hands in his pockets when he was nervous. How they bent outward at the wrists, like a boy's. She noticed his shallow breathing and the fact that beneath his narrow black jeans his knees were locked. She looked again. His smile was big and white and charming and dimpled. It telegraphed kindness and sympathy — and worst of all, understanding. It revolted her.

"Hey, Ondine," Moth beckoned quietly. "We're not going to hurt you."

"Where is Nix?" Desperation tinged her voice. She steeled

herself, trying to fight it, and failed. "Look, just tell me. Please. I just want to go home."

It hadn't occurred to her until then that she could be in any real danger. What had happened to the blond boy, despite her outrage, she had construed as a strange cult ritual gone wrong. The woman at its helm, more dangerous in her misguidedness than in her person. And Moth had never struck her as particularly violent, just narcissistic and crass. But now she felt her heart surge and a diffuse, sweaty heat prick the palms of her hands. Ondine was alone. The few strangers around were just that — strangers. She felt unprotected and small.

"I want to go home." Her voice emerged a clenched squeak. "Now."

Moth shook his head and reached out to her, but she flexed her hand and he backed off.

"Listen, Ondine. I don't know where Nix is right now." He looked at the older woman as if to know he was doing the right thing. "I know this is all —"

Her words crashed out.

"No, Moth, you don't know. You and I are strangers. And after I find Nix and get the hell out of this Hansel and Gretel dust-coated candy house you've brought me to, I don't ever want to see you again. Unless it's in court, when I have your ass arrested for harassment and endangerment. This is bullshit. You and everyone here. I'm a minor. And you . . ." She took a step toward him, emboldened by her words. "And you are going to make some murderous maximum-security ape who makes Jeffrey Dahmer look like the Dalai Lama very happy when I get you locked up."

She took a breath and was about to turn and head into the forest to look for Nix, when she felt a hand — not Moth's, no, lighter than Moth's, lighter than any hand she'd ever felt — on her shoulder.

The woman's voice was calm, raspy, almost shiny, if a voice could be that. Despite herself, Ondine turned to face her. *Viv. Her name is Viv.* She looked at her. There was a slight distortion about the woman's face the girl could not pinpoint.

"Nix is taking the pet who came with Tim Bleeker back to her human home."

The woman stopped, and Ondine ran through the implications of what she had just told her, true or not. *Tim Bleeker. Tim Bleeker is involved with this.* And the person with him, probably a girl. Probably — the associations were becoming far too incestuous here — Neve.

Ondine said nothing. She could feel herself being studied. She thought of the mice in her father's lab, wondering if it would be more food today, or the needle that administers the killing serum. The woman's choice of words: *Pet. Human home.* Heat rose to her face and she nearly covered her cheeks with her hands, then stopped herself.

241

"Moth is your guide, Ondine," Viv continued. "His task is to help you. He has passed through the stage you are experiencing now and has acknowledged the truth about himself. Let him lead you to the light."

It was the way she held her lips. The violet-gray pool of eyes. Ondine shook her head, signaling no, but she could not speak.

Her vision narrowed to a pinprick, at the end of which was Moth's face, leering in false compassion. She felt the undulation of what had been solid ground beneath her — *Oh my God, I am actually going to fall down again* — when a nervous, bony arm encircled her shoulders.

"Nix!"

The word erupted from Ondine's mouth, and as she whirled to embrace him, she registered her relief at his return. But instead of Nix's narrow face and nervous eyes, she saw a mane of lustrous black hair that seemed to have a life of its own, apart from the pale, eerily calm face it wreathed.

"Morgan." Her mouth opened and closed. "What are you doing here?"

The girl looked into her old friend's eyes, ignoring the two people behind her. "I'll take you home."

"But — why are you here? How did you get here?"

"*Later.*" Morgan whispered.

"I —"

Why was she hesitating? A moment ago, all she had wanted

was to leave. But Morgan: she was the last person Ondine expected to see.

"I saw Nix leave," Morgan said smoothly over her silence, then looked over her shoulder, coldly, at Moth. "He left with Neve."

"That's what —" Ondine broke off. *That's what Viv said,* she thought, but didn't say it aloud.

Morgan's eyes returned. "Ondine? Honey? Let's just go, okay?"

She wanted to say yes. But more than that, she wanted Morgan to tell her why she was here at the gathering. Who had told her, though she already knew. All Morgan said was, "Neve looked pretty trashed, and Nix, well, he seemed to really want to get her into his car."

"My car," Ondine whispered.

"What, sweetie?"

"Let's just go." She started walking in the direction of the forest she and Nix had come through earlier, stopping to tie a shoelace that had come undone in the chaos. She heard Morgan tell Moth and Viv that she expected a complete reckoning when they got back to Portland.

"What's your last name?" Ondine heard Morgan say, presumably to Viv. The woman laughed. "I think you know you won't find me in the phone book."

Then she felt Morgan's tense little arm guiding her back up

the hill, through the forest. Ondine let herself be led. It had gotten dark; the only light came from the moon.

"Waxing crescent," she heard herself say.

"What?" They had passed out of the clearing where she and Nix had first settled when they arrived. The tent was gone. Nix must have packed it up. *How thoughtful.*

"Waxing crescent," Ondine repeated. She made a vague motion toward the sky. "The moon."

"Oh," Morgan replied. "Right." Then she did something strange. Something Ondine had never seen Morgan do in the half year she'd known her. She stopped and turned toward Ondine and took her hands in her cold smaller ones, squeezing, and said, "I think we shouldn't talk about this for a while. I think we should wait till we get home to do anything."

Ondine swallowed. She waited for an explanation but none came. Given a choice, she would've preferred that this night had never happened. But laws were laws and someone had died. She had been a witness. To have Morgan request a silence — Ondine didn't want to use the word "suspicious," but Morgan's hands were squeezing hers harder now, and she felt that if she didn't agree, the girl whose hair was so dark it seemed to grow out of the sky would squeeze her hands until the bones crumbled.

"Okay," Ondine whispered, forcing herself not to yank her hands from the girl's grip.

"Okay!" Morgan repeated brightly, squeezing one more time.

With that the two girls exited the first line of trees and headed toward Morgan's black Lexus, which beeped comfortingly when she clicked her key ring, as if the car had been waiting for them. Otherwise the lot was empty. The headlights cut a narrow swath through the darkness, and Ondine kept her eyes focused on the bright part and ignored the blackness that pressed in all around. When Morgan said, "You wanna listen to the radio?" Ondine jumped a little in her seat and bit back a scream.

"Okay," she said, and kept her eyes on the hard light in front of her.

III

CHANGELINGS

EVE CLOWES SLEPT THE WHOLE WAY back to Portland, her forehead forming a filmy spot of warmth and grease against the Masons' Jetta window. Nix zipped up the jacket — Dr. Mason's — he'd given her and covered her cold hands with socks, making sure her boots were laced and her cuffs were rolled down. His gestures were tender, and with each he thought of Ondine, whom he knew he had abandoned. She'd have to understand. He'd explain everything later. Now he needed to help Neve — and Jacob.

Nix didn't actually think the words "He needed to help the humans," but they were there anyway.

He tried to give Neve water, but it just dribbled out of the side of her mouth, coiling around her bare neck like a translucent snake, and she coughed and sputtered, not really waking up. Nix wiped the water from her mouth, making sure her nose and her throat were clear. He'd learned to do these things from Finn at the squat. It was how people choked, Finn told him. How they most often died when they were OD'ing. Doing these things felt good, or at least real.

The moon at the lip of the window, the low music he was playing (a Bill Evans CD was still in the car, from Mrs. Mason): these things made him feel grounded, actual, intact. Nix even found himself tapping one of Evans's silky melodies on the steering wheel, keeping time with the clicking orange road markers and an occasional pine outlined against the black-blue sky.

It was a familiar feeling, this getting used to things. He had done it many times before. Even as a child, when he first started having his visions. It was the perpetual truth of his existence, the one thing he could count on. Eventually he would take in stride whatever strangeness the world threw his way.

The Evans CD came to an end. Nix was still tapping. He thought about Ondine. She knew him. At least one person understood a little of what he had experienced. Ondine, he trusted. Now to find himself locked in this situation with her, and — he almost tripped on her name — Morgan D'Amici of all people. The girl's intensity threw him. How unlikely that the three of them would be bound together here, in Portland, in this place, next to these hills.

The mountains. What is in them? He recalled again what his grandfather had communicated silently to him those days on the water. They rose up black and still in the moonlight, massive and ancient, surrounding Portland. He thought back to something he remembered the woman in the black coat saying: *We inhabit the Ring of Fire,* and Nix knew instinctively that she meant these mountains. But who was "we"? And what, exactly, did "inhabit" mean? He shouldn't have left so early, but he had to, for Neve's sake.

He had heard one name just as he left, *Novala.* Was it a place? An actual place, with a geography, yet unmapped? Or was it a place like in that children's book about the lion and the closet, where only the border was important? At the gathering, the trees at the edge of the parking lot had marked a line. Once he'd stepped past it, everything had felt more solid; sounds had rung clearer; Neve's body had been heavier. Was that Novala, too?

Even if it were a hallucination, Nix felt the loosening of all of this thinking work its calming effects on his brain, and for a while he was happy to just sit there, music-less, Neve's head bobbing to the beat of the ruts in the road. He started to replay the little he'd seen. There was the girl on the stage . . . then the lightning struck . . . the boy . . . then the woman in the black coat . . . and Bleek . . . and the bird.

He felt gravel and rocks under the Jetta just prior to hearing them. Neve moaned, and his hands responded to the wheel even before his mind did. Nix braked, hard. He must have fallen asleep. They were on the shoulder, a few feet from the trunk of an oak. He glanced at Neve. She was drooling, the seat belt across her chest splitting one small, perfect breast from the other. She was safe.

His hands trembled on the wheel, and his second thought, after Neve, was, *So we can feel fear. If not for ourselves, then at least for humans.* He took a breath. They hadn't run into anything. The relief made him drowsy and he realized how long he'd been on the road that day, then out in the rain. Weeks of staying up with Ondine had caught up with him. He was tired and confused. It was late. Neve was still sleeping, her breathing more regular now. He needed to get her home, but a quick check of the dashboard clock told him that there were another two hours to drive, and as the moon was just setting, it would only get darker.

He'd deal with Jacob in the morning. Now he needed sleep. Nix looked behind him on the road. No cars approached and he was off the shoulder enough to be safe. He'd just rest till dawn, then get back to Portland, where for once, everything might turn out fine.

∽ ∽ ∽

MORGAN AND ONDINE WERE QUIET MOST OF THE WAY HOME. Ondine stared out the window; Morgan played the radio: an oldies station, something Ralph Mason would have chosen. Almost as if she knew it would relax the girl beside her. In fact, Ondine realized, as she ran through the little things that Morgan did during the drive, they all seemed chosen, calculated, to please her: the relaxing oldies station with its repetitive commercials for weight-loss supplements; Morgan asking her more than once if the temperature was all right, even turning on the seat warmers. Ondine fell asleep, and when she awoke they were in the parking lot of a gas station. Morgan had left the car — gone to the bathroom, probably — and sitting in the holder was a Styrofoam cup of hot chocolate. Ondine drank it, realizing the last thing she had eaten was Nix's PB&J in the tent the previous morning. That is, if you didn't count the dust she'd licked off a stranger's palm. The memory of her eagerness, her idiotic abandon, shamed her.

Morgan came back a few moments later, coffee in hand, the car beeping softly. She had locked Ondine in. "How are you?" she asked, devoid of her normal irony. "You fell asleep for a while. That's good."

Ondine nodded into her hot chocolate. She couldn't look the girl in the eyes. She felt embarrassed even sitting there with her.

"All right. Just tired. I want to get home."

Morgan hadn't said anything. She regarded Ondine in the semidark and smiled. Then she rested her hand on Ondine's knee, a startling gesture coming from a girl who rarely touched anyone. They started off and, despite herself, the gentle rocking of the car and the familiar crackling of the AM oldies station lulled Ondine back to sleep. She awoke in her driveway on N.E.

Schuyler. Morgan was already out of the car, stretching. The sun was rising and everything was a little pink.

Red sky at night, sailor's delight. Red sky at dawn, sailors be warned.

It had come to Ondine unconsciously, the aphorism. She didn't even know where she had picked it up. She shook it out of her head and watched Morgan stretching, lifting her bony arms into the air. Skin showed where the girl's shirt separated from her jeans and Ondine had shivered, as if she, too, were standing in the cold morning air.

"You're up." Morgan smiled, opened the door, and ducked her head in to look at Ondine, who felt embarrassed to have been watching her. She fumbled for her bag in the backseat and stood up too quickly, hitting her head on the roof of the car as she emerged.

"Ow." She touched her crown and laughed nervously. Morgan, draping her forearms across the top of the Lexus, rested her chin in her hands.

"Long night." She squinted and cocked her head. "You okay?"

"Yeah, yeah." Ondine rejiggered the knapsack on her shoulder. "Just . . . out of it."

Morgan nodded, her eyes serious. "Me, too."

Ondine had not known what to say then. Everything felt reorganized; the slight edge she had always had with the other

254

girl, she realized, was gone. Even the way Morgan was shrugging now, rubbing her shoulders to warm herself — a familiar gesture from afternoons spent walking around the track at school, talking — had taken on a new confidence. She felt silly and small. She didn't know what to do with her hands, so she tucked them into her still-damp jeans and looked at the ground.

"Well, I'm gonna go in. So . . ." She turned on her heel. "I'll call you. We have to —"

Her words came out stiffer than she intended, and Morgan acknowledged this, yet so subtly Ondine wasn't sure if she was imagining the minute shift that had taken place between them.

"We'll talk." Morgan looked away, out into the street and then back again. She smiled. "K.A.'s coming back tomorrow."

"Oh, good. Good. That'll be good." Ondine panicked. What had happened to her vocabulary? And K.A.? What did K.A. have to do with any of this?

She remembered Neve Clowes. Neve had been at the Ring of Fire, too, with Tim Bleeker. A known drug dealer. Probably already a felon. It all seemed too complicated. Too messy and screwed up. Ondine had been there, too, had willingly taken dust. Had even believed that she was there to learn something, to find something out about herself, like the rest of them. Was she an accomplice? Could she be arrested? She felt weak and scared and hoped it didn't show. She didn't trust Morgan D'Amici, she realized. Never had.

The last words came out in a rush. "Anyway. I'll call you later."

"Yeah, yeah — okay." Morgan waved brightly and Ondine felt released. She turned and walked toward the gate leading to the back door. She wasn't sure why she hadn't gone in the front door, as she usually did. It was almost as if she were a guest now.

Just as she started to turn and raise her hand to wave, she saw Morgan in the car, staring at her through the windshield. The girl smiled. No. Had already been smiling. Sitting in her Lexus, beaming. *She believes this.* Fear seized Ondine's body, gnawed at the delicate unity of her mind. She forced herself to wave. Morgan waved in return, glanced behind her, and pulled out. Neither girl looked back.

CHAPTER 14

DAWN CAME EARLY ON THE DAY fate had marked Jacob Clowes to die.

The sun climbed above the Columbia River valley and spread its rays across the Willamette, infusing everything in Portland with a pinkish orange glow. Jacob Clowes liked this time. He was at work early during the summer. Everything was twice as busy and people liked eating pizza for breakfast — post-club, pre-crash snack — so early morning, six, seven AM, was the only time he had to himself.

The Cloweses lived up at the base of Forest Park, amid a tangle of ivy and blackberry. Their house was a ramshackle white affair built during the late twenties, and eighty-odd years later it still possessed a wide-open view of downtown. The view was probably the finest thing about the place: despite the fact that Jacob seemed perpetually to be fixing it up, the Cloweses' house was the least fancy on their road, now mostly populated by whatever it was dot-commers called themselves these days, as well as a few people whom his daughter referred to as "*cool* parents." He thought he was one.

Jacob had bought early, when you still had to dodge sleeping bums along Burnside. The only people who came to his new pizza shop then were the hippies and gay boys that lived in Northwest; the proto-punkers (Theatre of Sheep, Poison Idea and the Rats); and a shy, friendly guitar instructor with curly hair named Ritchie, who said his girlfriend's Mormon grandmother had written that druggie book *Go Ask Alice.*

Jacob had loved the roughness of Portland then. Not as rough as the New York he'd left behind, which he appreciated, but rough enough to be . . . what? Unformed. Maybe a little haunted, if you could say that in 1976. Portland in the year of the bicentennial still had the air of a nineteenth-century city, a place where a man had to live by his wits. A bet had given the city its name: One of its early American residents had been from Boston, the other from Portland, Maine. They tossed a coin; Maine won. And it *was* another country then, teeming with loggers and wayward Forty-niners; Indians; sailors; and Chinese railroad workers; salt dogs and rascals; men with names like "Bunco" Kelly, who, it was said, passed a wooden statue of an Indian through the Shanghai Tunnels to a waiting captain desperate for one last man.

A century and a half later, hobos still came to town in

boxcars, but the "hippies" showed up in Mini Coopers and BMWs spackled with SCREW BUSH bumper stickers and, as far as he knew, liked dust more than pot. "Hipsters" — whatever those were — and yuppies were Jacob's mainstay now.

Portland had softened a tough Brooklyn kid, and though it was the Brooklyn in Jacob that had said, "What kind of redneck do you take me for?" when his best friend had invited him to a *barn dance* of all things a year after he'd moved, it was the Portland boy who trimmed his beard and put on his lucky underwear and went anyway.

Of course this was a barn dance Portland style. Most of the dancers *were* wearing overalls, but without shirts underneath — or bras, for that matter. Jacob would freely admit to not knowing much about the modern world, but he was sure nuder was always better, so when the wild-haired woman with the ear-to-ear smile told him the price of admission was his shirt, who was he to say no? Three years of slinging pies had not yet had the expansive effect on his stomach that it would later, especially after Neve was born. Jacob still looked damned good with his shirt off in 1979, or at least he thought so.

More important, so did Amanda.

She was the strongest woman he'd ever met. She'd had three miscarriages in as many years, which made the first years of Jacob's marriage both the happiest and saddest time of his life. It turned out she had a heart-shaped uterus, and despite the heart-ache it caused them, there was some part of Jacob that loved the fact his wife's womb was made that way — kind of like how Amanda said she liked Jacob's pizza gut (well, maybe she'd said "didn't mind"). Reaching over a sleeping Neve to rub his soften-ing stomach in bed — after three false starts they'd been too spooked to buy a crib, and so Neve ended up in bed with them for the first year of her life — Amanda said Jacob was a big man, inside and outside. The less romantic way of looking at it was that Jacob didn't have the willpower to stick to a diet, whereas Amanda had the strength to go under the knife, and, with more courage than he could fathom, have the corrective surgery that eventually brought them Neve. Jacob didn't even like to go to the doctor for his physical, for god's sake. He'd managed to miss his appointment for the last three years. Amanda would pin the card to the bulletin board over the phone, and Jacob would somehow "accidentally" cover it with an invoice for firewood or a sauce-spattered business card from some guy who said he could fix that leak in the kitchen for cheap. If Amanda reminded him, Ja-cob would mutter something about still being a young man, and he'd find some yard work to do. He didn't need a physical *every single year*. He wasn't even fifty yet. If it was true what they said about parents — that you're only as old as your youngest kid — then hell, he was still a teenager.

Neve was why Jacob was up now. Not the beautiful morning.

Not puttering around the kitchen making coffee. Not reading the paper, or staring out the window wondering if next week was the week he'd start running again, or filling the hummingbird feeder like he used to, or weeding the garden, or splitting firewood (there was just something about swinging an axe). No. This morning Jacob was cutting the grass.

Whacking it, actually. Ferociously attacking it with an unmotorized hand mower he'd picked up at a barn sale fifteen years ago — having met his wife in one, barns remained forever dear to Jacob Clowes's heart, often to the detriment of his wallet. The mower was an antique, slightly ridiculous contraption. He'd bought the mower during what Amanda called his "green" phase. He'd put in the woodstove and started splitting firewood around the same time, made a big show of turning off the boiler, which he promptly had to turn back on when he realized it also heated the hot water. Later he installed solar panels on the roof of the house, but he was pretty sure they warmed nothing besides a family of raccoons, and he'd even planted a vegetable garden, which now bore only the tomatoes and cukes that reseeded themselves each spring. But neither nostalgia nor Jacob's eco-consciousness had led him to pull out the mower this morning; rather, the simple fact that his neighbors would kill him if he fired up the Lawn-Boy at six AM. Besides, he needed to work off some of his frustration.

He was sweating now, pushing the heavy machine up and

down the hill of the Cloweses' decidedly un-lawnlike yard, which was narrow but long and steeply pitched. The year Neve was four there had been snow, and Jacob had made his daughter a sled out of the curved plastic lid of one of the trash cans. She had slid the length of the yard, whooping and screaming the whole way. Maybe it was the memory of that better time that had Jacob pushing the mower up and down the hill rather than across its slope, which would have been easier, or maybe he wanted to tire himself out, take out his aggression on the lawn so he wouldn't take it out on Neve when she *finally* decided to drag her ass home. He had spanked his daughter only once, when she was three and tried to light her own hair on fire. He had smacked her hand and sent the match sputtering through the air (you could still see the burn mark on the carpet in her room, if you knew where to look), and a startled Neve had burst into tears then run to her father's arms for comfort. Jacob would give anything to be able to swat this new threat away from his daughter, but he knew that wasn't going to happen. So, lacking a better substitute, he attacked the lawn.

It was early and no one could see him, so he had taken his shirt off and let his stomach hang over the waistband of the cargo shorts Amanda had picked up for him at Old Navy, which Jacob, to preserve his manly identity, pretended actually came from the Army-Navy supply store. He dropped the mower and fished his cell out of the side pocket of the shorts: 6:43, and his daughter *still* wasn't home. He had never learned to program the thing — he couldn't tell one silly colored icon from another — and so, with damp, blunt fingers, he punched in the ten digits of his daughter's number and pressed the phone to his sweaty ear. His pulse pounded in his temples and he knew he was going to have another one of his headaches today. He'd been having a lot of them lately.

Correction: Neve had been *giving* him a lot of headaches lately.

Hey, you've reached Neve . . .

His daughter's innocent voice leaked into his ear without so much as a ring. She had turned her phone off. Jacob had to stop himself from throwing his onto the flagstone terrace at the edge of the yard. After all these years of testing his boundaries, she had found his line and marched across it without looking back.

Jamming the phone back in his pocket, he picked up the mower and attacked the lawn again. Neve was a good girl, he told himself as he panted up the hill. Loving but shy, like a new puppy who wants to jump in your lap but needs coaxing. A little spacey. Her SATs weren't exactly Berkeley material, and though part of Jacob wondered if it was all that pot he'd smoked, neither he nor Amanda had the aptitude, let alone the attitude, for college. But when Neve started going out with Phil D'Amici's son, K.A., Jacob had had a brief moment of calm. In six months of "hanging out" — that's what Neve had called it — with his daughter, the boy had never pulled into the driveway later than 10:59. Of course, they spent another hour and a half fogging up the windows, but he was sure K.A. valued his balls too much to take them out of his pants in his girlfriend's father's driveway. Her grades even improved. When she showed him her A in history at the end of the year, Jacob had made a big show of holding it up to the light to see if the letter was doctored, but it survived inspection. The punch in the gut Neve gave him afterward was surprisingly painful, however, and even as he wondered aloud when his daughter had turned into such a brain, he wondered silently when he himself had turned into such a wuss.

The yard was long. And steep. And uneven. Jacob had to push the mower over the same strip of grass three times to cut it all. He could feel sweat pooling in the seat of his boxers, and tried not to imagine what he looked like from the back. What do you call the Jewish pizza maker's version of plumber's crack?

He was a "cool parent," wasn't he? A dad you didn't have to be ashamed of? He didn't even care if his daughter smoked pot — he knew she'd grow out of it eventually. And he wasn't stupid enough to tell her not to have sex either. Like a good modern father, he'd sat right beside Amanda at the kitchen table while she and Neve had the talk about making your own choices and saying yes only when you want to and using various methods of contraception. Only after Neve had fled to one of her girlfriends' houses did he go out on the back porch and drink his way through the last third of a bottle of scotch to erase the words "negotiated sexual contract" from his ears. Amanda had pulled the phrase from a book called *So Your Teenager Wants to Have Sex*. God bless the woman — but come *on*.

He'd managed to drink the words out of his head, but try as he might to beat the nagging sense of failure and doubt away this morning, he couldn't eradicate it. Maybe his mother had been right about raising her out here. His Brooklyn friends were stockbrokers and lawyers now, despite their wild youths. And real estate. Jesus, what that modest brownstone he had grown up in in Cobble Hill would fetch now. His friends back East sent their kids to private schools, or magnets like Bronx Science or Stuyvesant, where Jacob himself had gone. Amanda had enrolled Neve in some extremely expensive "self-directed" program at Penwick, and even though their daughter left the house every morning, he had the sense she wasn't always "directing" herself to school. It was all so "unstructured," and as the years passed and his daughter grew further and further from him, Jacob found it hard to remember what it was exactly that he'd loved Portland for, back when he'd been not too much older than Neve was now. Then they'd decided Neve was going to be the picture of the Rousseau child — Amanda's phrase, of course. In Jacob's mind it was even simpler: his daughter was going to have the exact opposite of his experience in New York, with a father who expected too much of him, and a mother who expected nothing at all. His daughter was going to be supported, encouraged, *loved*. There was no way she wouldn't be the perfect child. And maybe that's what would have happened, until Neve, as all children do, grew up.

And discovered dust.

He leaned into the mower to make it up the last incline leading to the forest that bounded their property. He almost wished he *could* spank her. But once your daughter has lain out in a string bikini in the backyard, that option is definitely off the table.

Neve. String bikinis. Contraceptives. Dust. Amanda once reminded him that she'd been wearing less — at least on top — the first time he saw her. And that she'd been on the Pill, and that the joint she'd handed him at the barn dance had come into her hands from a complete stranger and for all she knew had been laced. Twenty-four years later she'd traded the braless overalls for linen shirts, gone off the Pill after Jacob had consented to a vasectomy. And most important, she reminded him, they had both outgrown drugs. So would Neve.

When it's two against one, a man gets used to conceding to the women in his life. But as Jacob leaned his aching back into the mower — damn this thing could take it out of you — he decided he had to do something. This wasn't pot. Pot grows in your backyard. This was a chemical made in a lab by some greedy, amoral little shit who got his formula off the goddamned

Internet. Or at least Jacob thought it was. The truth was, he didn't know what dust was. The few times he'd asked some spaced-out customers at the pizzeria about it, he got answers along the lines of "Dust is totally mellow, man," or "Dust is, like, *magic*," or, his favorite, "Yo, dude! Dust!" Whatever the hell it was, he didn't want his daughter on it. He didn't want her hanging around with that asshole who peddled it either. *Bleek.* What a name. The thought of that boy pawing his daughter was the final straw. He wheeled the mower around to head back down the slope and decided he had no choice. Neve would be grounded.

He stopped to wipe the sweat from his face. Though it was barely morning and Portland was still cool and dewy from the storm the previous night, Jacob was steaming. Even his head. *Especially* his head. He felt steam pulsing from his temples, and he knew from recent experience that neither Advil nor Tylenol nor aspirin would cure it. A drink might, or two or three, but the last time Jacob had gotten drunk in the morning was the day he woke up to discover Ronald Reagan had been reelected. He would have to tough this one out.

He was at the high point of his yard now, looking over the city. A slight haze was developing over downtown, but everywhere else the sun shone indiscriminately, brightly, mocking the darkness that had sunk into him last night when he realized that Neve wouldn't be coming home, yet again. Amanda, better able to separate from her daughter — and more capable of expressing anger — drank four glasses of wine in quick succession and went to sleep. Jacob, so mad he refused to drink, felt his wife was passing the buck, leaving it to him to stay up waiting for their daughter — as though *that* would make her come home sooner. He put on a Zappa album and turned it up just a little too loud, then watched a bad movie on television, then whipped up a calamari salad for himself around five AM. *Nothing like the smell of squid in the morning.* While he stared out the window munching it, he decided the lawn needed to be mowed. It was too early though. His neighbors would kill him. (Actually, they'd probably write a letter to the community board.) Then he remembered the push mower. Cursing Neve — as though she had somehow *forced* him to mow the lawn at this hour — he fished Amanda's iPod from her purse and went outside in his cargo shorts and rooted around the garage until he found the mower, buried under three bicycles with four wheels among them, all of them flat.

Joni Mitchell got him through most of the job. Amanda had never lost her taste for her, through all those years, even though those talky songs sounded like a page — several pages — ripped from her diary. He almost jumped out of his skin when some strange caterwaul came on after "Don Juan's Reckless Daughter." The iPod said the singer's name was "Björk," which sounded to Jacob more like a brand of bike tire, and, wincing at the screeching, he sifted through Amanda's albums till *Blue* came up. He had to wipe the sweat from his eyes three times before he admitted that it wasn't sweat that was blurring his vision, making it hard for him to read the words on the tiny screen. He closed his eyes and tried to tell himself it was just anger or fatigue making his fingers tremble like an old man's, but he wasn't fooling himself. His head was throbbing and he hadn't even turned on the music.

Jacob Clowes did not pray. He did not believe in god. But he was praying now. *Dear god, please bring my daughter back to me. I will come home from the restaurant early. I will tell Neve I love her every day. I will lose thirty pounds. I will call my mother more often. I will donate twenty pizzas a week to God's Love We Deliver. There are things I will do, god. I will change. I will. Just let me have this —*

Jacob stopped. He asked himself what "this" was. What he wanted most. Just let me see this through, he prayed. Until Neve is safe.

He opened his eyes. His vision had cleared but his hands were still shaking. A strange tingling pulsed in his arms and legs. It didn't hurt as much as it felt as though someone were touching his skin with a mild electrical current, and when he bent over to pick up the mower, yellow-ringed black spots danced in front of his eyes. He started back down the hill. He knew he couldn't power his way through this, but that's how he'd dealt with every-thing in his life. What the hell was *wrong* with him? He was forty-nine. He was a young man. He chastised himself for even thinking about his own problems at a time like this, when all his thoughts should be focused on Neve.

Jacob was halfway down the hill when he saw her wobbling through the back gate on the arm of a slight, black-haired boy. He had to squint to focus.

Nix.

The lawn mower's handle fell from his fingers and he stepped over it. All thoughts of beer guts and plumber's crack and the pounding in his temples vanished. Neve's head hung like a bro-ken puppet's, but Nix had looked up and seen him before drop-ping his eyes back to the ground. *Trying to sneak her around back.* Was the little shit just going to dump her in the yard, wait for someone to wake up and find her? The ungrateful punk. To think that Jacob had once cared for the boy. Given him a job. Had tried to *help* him.

Jogging downhill, he pulled out his earphones and fumbled with them, not knowing where to put them. He looped the white cord around his neck. Neve was hanging off Nix while he tried to close the gate. In this, as in all things, the kid's priorities were assbackwards. He was trying to cover his tracks when he should have been concentrating on speed. Get in, get out. That's what the punk should have been doing. Get the hell out before your victim's father rips your head off and stuffs it down the neck hole from which it had grown. Jacob was so angry he wanted to beat Nix like he'd beaten the kids in elementary school who'd called him a dirty Jew. Thank god he wasn't using the Lawn-Boy — he'd have fed the kid to the blades one limb at a time.

First things first. He grabbed his daughter and pulled her to his side. Neve managed to register that it was her father whose hands had grabbed her, then her head fell again.

"Hey, Daddy," she whispered, and giggled, a distracted, tinkling sound, like glass breaking in another room. He tilted his daughter's chin up. Her eyes had that same glassy glow she'd had for months. But at least they were open, and focused. If his daughter had OD'd, Nix really would be dead.

He looked at the boy. The punk refused to meet his eyes.

Jacob cleared his throat.

"Right now you should be thanking my wife."

Nix didn't say anything. He still didn't lift his head. It was almost as if he were scared to look up. First smart thought the boy had yet.

"A couple of years ago I wanted to buy a rifle, take up hunting. But Amanda wouldn't allow a gun in the house. You should thank her for that, because if I did own a rifle it would be up your ass right now, blowing your brains out the top of your fucking misbegotten skull."

With a visible effort, Nix roused himself to speech. "Look, Clowes —"

"Don't you call me that! People who work for me — people I didn't fire — call me that. But not you."

Defiance flashed in Nix's eyes, which almost — but not quite — rose to meet Jacob's.

"You didn't fire me. I quit."

You had to hand it to the skinny punk: he *almost* had a backbone.

"Mr. Clowes," he was saying now, still looking at the grass, "your daughter and I were at a . . . party. Out past Bend. Far out. In the mountains. Neve got fu — I mean, Neve got messed up. I found her with a guy." He faltered. Jacob continued to stare, and Nix continued to avoid his eyes. "He's not a good guy, Mr. Clowes."

Without warning a siren seemed to go off in Jacob's ears, a high-pitched sound that burned from one side of his skull to the other. Nix's voice was drowned out and his face blurred like a wet painting. Jacob sank into a squat, almost fell. He managed to catch himself just in time, his hands slipping from Neve and smacking down hard on his knees.

What the . . .

The spasm lasted only a moment. When it passed he heard a

sound coming from the boy. Like the kid was moaning. Breathing deeply, Jacob managed to stand again, though he had to grab Neve to make it up all the way. The two of them leaned into each other like a pair of uprooted trees.

"He — he — he's not a good guy, Mr. Clowes." Nix was stuttering. "You need to keep your daughter away from him."

The siren was receding. Jacob knew who Nix was talking about: goddamned Tim Bleeker. He was the one responsible for the way Neve was now. Nix's destructive tendencies had always been directed at himself, which is why Jacob had cut him so much slack at the shop. But Bleek wasn't here right now and Jacob needed an object for his anger. He needed to feel as though he were saving Neve, even if it was with his dying breath.

"I don't see Tim Bleeker here," Jacob said when he could finally talk. His voice sounded thin, as though it were coming out on a long string pulled from his mouth. "I see you. What the hell were you doing with Neve anyway? K.A. is in California."

Nix's eyes flitted up, down, sideways — everywhere but at Jacob's face. "It's not what you think, Mr. Clowes —"

Anger was the only thing holding Jacob up now. "Listen to me, Nix," he said, again hearing the stretched-out sound of his voice, which came in little uneven spurts. "I've cut you breaks in the past. But you cross a line when you mess with a man's daughter. Neve is my only child. If one skin cell is out of place on her body, then you'd better pray. Pray the cops throw you in jail before I get my hands on you. Because I will make you hurt in parts you didn't even know you had. I —"

A stab of pain cut off his voice and his vision dissolved again. He wiped the sweat from his brow, but his eyes refused to focus. "You —" Nix's body wavered in front of him like a candle flame, and Jacob closed his eyes. "You . . . little . . . *bastard*."

When he opened his eyes again, he saw that Nix had taken several steps back, as if starting to run away. And he was looking at him. Straight at him. Finally. The fear in his eyes scared even Jacob, because it didn't seem to be *him* the boy was afraid of. Rather, it was almost as if Nix were afraid *for* him. The boy was trembling, and Jacob would have felt pity, if he hadn't wanted to neuter him.

Jesus Christ, he was thinking. Jesus, Jesus, Jesus Christ. What the hell is *wrong* with me?

Jacob clung to his daughter. He wanted to get Neve inside now, then lie down. If he could just catch his breath, calm himself, stop the pounding in his head, the ringing in his ears, the fire on his skin.

"Mr. Clowes." Nix was talking slowly, over-enunciating. "I did not hurt your daughter, Mr. Clowes. I just brought her home. She's in trouble, sir." Nix swallowed and Jacob could see his Adam's apple bounce. "Do you know Tim Bleeker? Bleek? Bleek's got Neve all strung out on dust."

Jacob felt his stomach drop. It was disgusting to hear it from someone else. He tightened his grip on Neve, who giggled again. She even pointed at something, though her eyes were closed.

"Flying!" she exclaimed. "She's flying!"

His daughter's laughter coiled around Jacob's heart. A good father would have been strong enough to save his little girl.

"Look." Nix was still talking. "Bleek's bad. He's, like, *dark*. You do not want Neve hanging out with him."

Jacob could hardly hear Nix, nor could he understand him. He seemed to be saying things, yet he wasn't saying anything. *He's, like, dark.* What the hell was that supposed to mean?

A sound came to Jacob's ears. Over the ringing and the panting of his own breath and Nix's cryptic words and the occasional giggle from Neve: Joni Mitchell, jangling softly, tinnily out of the earphones looped around his neck. She sounded far away, like his daughter and his youth and everything good in the world. The only thing close to him was this little punk, who was now staring at him as though he were some particularly grisly piece of roadkill.

Jacob's words came in short, wheezing gusts.

"Listen to me." He had to concentrate to pronounce each word. "If I ever see you around my daughter again, I will kill you. You won't walk. You won't eat. You will wish you couldn't breathe. I will make your life . . . *over.*"

Somewhere in the middle of his words, Nix had begun to back up. He backed through the gate, terror on his face, his head shaking. The kid's mouth was moving but no sound was coming out — it took Jacob a long time to be sure of that. He had to focus so he could read the boy's lips.

No. No. No.

He wanted to follow him, but he couldn't lift his legs. He realized he wasn't holding Neve anymore. She was lying behind him on one of the lawn chairs. Curled up like she used to when he and Amanda would be at a party and she was tired and ready to go home. How had she gotten there? When had she left his arms? He stared at her for a long moment, wondering if she was all right. Was she cold? Did she need a blanket?

He turned back to Nix, who was standing on the other side of the gate, still shaking his head.

"It's all right, Mr. Clowes. I'll take care of it. You'll be okay. I'll do it."

What the fuck was the kid talking about? *He* would be all right?

Jacob tried to shake his head, but it only vibrated. He had a sense of himself, stooped, half curled. The throbbing in his head had become one steady shaft of pain. He couldn't see out of his left eye. He tried to lift his left arm to rub the sweat out of it. He couldn't.

"Get out of here, little shit. Don't ever let me see you around my daughter again."

His voice sounded strange to his ears. *Getowaheerlilsshh. Donevlemmeseeyewrownmydaweragay.*

Nix was backing down the sidewalk now.

"I'll fix it, Mr. Clowes. I'll make it all right."

Jacob managed to stumble to the gate, his left foot dragging through the grass.

"I'll tell K.A.," he called to Nix. *Aylltellkayay.*

"Hold on," Nix was saying. "Hold on. I'll do it. I'll make it all right. I will."

"*Kayay* —," Jacob began, but couldn't say anything else. His dragging foot caught and he twisted, fell against the gate, his weight knocking it closed. The slamming blocked out Nix's face, his voice. Jacob leaned against the gate, but his legs weren't strong enough to hold him. He was . . . sinking. That was it. That was what it felt like. Drowning in air.

He saw Neve on the lawn chair. She had turned on her side, facing him. Her eyes were closed and she was smiling. He was glad his daughter was the last thing he was going to see.

He waited for the pain, but felt nothing now. Instead he saw a figure in the distance, wading through fire. Just a shadow at first, walking toward him against a tidal wave of searing orange. It drew closer.

"You'll be okay," the figure said. His voice was calm. Sure.

Nix.

What the hell kind of name was that anyway?

∽ ∽ ∽

NIX RAN DOWN THE CUL-DE-SAC, away from the Cloweses' house. He didn't know what was making him run, but he knew he had to first get away from Jacob before he could help him. He had to have a moment alone to understand where his power lay. What he could do and what he couldn't. He had to go into the woods.

An uninterrupted line of stockade fences barred his entrance to the forest, shadowed by pines that raked the sky like towers. Now the house, eerie, pale, luminescent as a ghost in the early morning light. Now a dog barking somewhere. An opening — a crooked alley between two yards, narrow, smelling of uncollected garbage. Blackberry bushes grabbed his pants, scratched his ankles. A thorn stung his face and something ran down his cheek. Blood? But it was only sweat. Nix wiped it away, still running, wondering when was the last time he'd been cut. When was the last time he'd bled? Had he ever?

He dove into the forest, quick, light, circling back toward the Cloweses'. He didn't know where his body ended and the woods began. All he knew was that he had to see Jacob to help him. He didn't have much time.

He stopped. The light was hot enough to feel it through the fences and trees, a few hundred yards away. It had gotten so bright around Jacob those last few minutes that Nix couldn't see the man through the flame. At the end his voice had been an unintelligible slur. But the brighter the flame got, the more it had called out to Nix. *Take me. Shape me.* The ring of fire was not Jacob's death. It was simply death, and Nix sensed he could lure it from Jacob, maybe to himself, if he could just see the man from afar, where the light wasn't so blinding.

Nix was not afraid of taking it. Even if it meant that he would die.

An image of the woman in the long black coat rose before him. Was that just yesterday? *You've known it since you were young. You inhabit a world that is not ours, yet — but not theirs either. You have felt it since you were children.*

It was all Nix had heard her say before he left to help Neve. But the ring of fire . . . what was it? His gift, the halos — that was real. He knew it was real. He'd lived with it his whole life. And that moment in the forest with Bleek. The man had known something Nix did not, but what? Had the woman told them what it was? Had he, in looking after Neve, lost his chance to save Jacob? No. No, he could do it. He would find a way. He had to trust his vision, which had led him to Portland in the first place. Which had united him with Ondine. Brought him to her house that night, introduced him to Moth, even Morgan. It was all part of something bigger. Wasn't it?

Was he cold? He didn't know. It was misty that morning, dark beneath the clotted limbs of the pines. He looked for the edge of the forest. Nettles thrust toward him, finding his face, the naked places on his arms. A bird called and it was as if it came from inside of him. How long had he been running? A few minutes only. The world entered his eyes frame by frame; his vision clicked like a camera. The micrometers of empty space between the slivers of pine needles against a rising sun were as focused as the entire canopy of leaves and branches above him. He looked down at his own feet running; they jerked staccato. Time itself had slowed. Yet it was not the familiar shoe that he saw; it was the fecund undergrowth below. The tiny pale shoots of grass, the wedges of shale and bark, the millions of pebbles.

Nix reached the edge of the forest and stopped next to a tree, concealing himself. There was Neve, lying on her back, her left arm still flung across her face. Then Jacob. His old boss was almost invisible inside the cocoon of light that engulfed him. He sat against the closed gate, unmoving. The light had taken on the physical presence of flames. They burned and shimmered, and Nix knew the shimmering was Jacob's life melting away.

He could hear his own breathing. It was labored. Not from

fatigue but from sobs. He was crying — for himself and for all those people he hadn't saved. Frank Shadwell, his mother, the people on his way down from Alaska. The girl from the squat, the boy at the gathering. Nix understood why he'd been using dust all that time. This was what he had been trying to control. This yawning sadness, the most profound helplessness of seeing someone about to die.

He wanted to pray, but to whom? Who were his gods now?

He forced himself to peer through the flames. He could see Jacob's eyes. They were open but unfocused. Nix stepped closer. He was standing up, wiping the back of his hand with his chin, blinking in the light. Were they meant to meet? To touch each other? Was that how the light moved? Nix didn't have time to think further, for the man was striding toward him now, his steps evening out as he approached. The light bent and wobbled around him like liquid wax, reaching out toward Nix. He stepped closer to grasp it.

Jacob's mouth moved.

Nix's arms spread, welcoming the flame.

Jacob spoke. "I thought I told you to stay away from here —"

The last thing Nix saw was Jacob's fist flashing through the light. And then, finally, darkness.

CHAPTER 15

T HE SUN HAD GONE DOWN. It was the first thing Nix thought when he opened his eyes: the sun had gone down and turned the summer grass around him a dark bluey green. He must have fallen asleep. His whole body ached and his eyelids sagged as if someone were pressing down on them. Where was he? He tried to move his head but the slightest tensing of his muscles caused pain, like razors notching slits in his spine. Had he passed out? Jacob — it was coming back to him now. He had gone to Jacob's. But he was so tired. Nix shut his eyes and when he opened them again the sun had come back. How long had he been on the ground? With all his strength he pulled his fingers to his eyes and rubbed them. He propped himself on his elbows and again focused on the shadows on the grass, trying to deduce what time it was. His head throbbed, his back ached, his legs felt unattached to his body.

"You okay?"

Somewhere behind him Jacob's voice broke the seal of his

temporary amnesia. He had brought Neve home. He had tried to pull the fire from her father. Then the man had knocked him out. The last thing he remembered was Jacob coming toward him with his fists clenched.

Nix touched his face. Blood, still warm, congealed under his nose. He touched again. His right eye was tender, swollen.

So he could feel pain. *Your body is a vessel. It is used to hold what you truly are, which is not of this world. . . .*

He turned, even though it hurt. Jesus it hurt.

"You gonna answer me or what?"

Jacob Clowes stood in the same position, Nix realized, as he had after he punched Nix in the face only a moment before. The iPod cord was still wrapped around his neck; his left hand idly rubbed the knuckles of his right. His eyes were just as slightly sad, slightly droopy as they'd always been. And everywhere around him:

Nothing. No light.

The ring of fire was gone. Nix had made it disappear.

He felt his face warm and, despite himself, a smile crept onto his lips.

"You think it's funny, kid? Maybe I should hit you again?" Jacob's voice was unconvincing. He sounded more guilty than angry. He was rubbing his head now, and Nix knew he must be wondering what had happened to him, where the pain had gone.

"No, Mr. Clowes. I'm just — I'm dizzy. Slaphappy." He

paused, glancing at the older man, who shook his head and pretended irritation. "I'm fine. I deserved it."

This time it was Jacob who smiled. "I'm sorry, kid. I overreacted. Neve told me what happened."

"Neve?" Nix looked over at the lawn chair, which was empty.

"She went to get some ice. You've got a helluva shiner on the way." Jacob reached out to touch Nix and, for the first time, the boy did not pull away. "Though it seems like it's going down already." Jacob half grimaced as he stroked the tender spot. "Huh. Weird. I can't believe I hit you. It's just that I was . . . feeling strange. I dunno. Anyway, I'm fine now. And we're fine, too, you and me. Neve told me it was that Bleek kid. She told me you just brought her home. I'm sorry, Nix. I was feeling so . . . screwed up. But I'm fine now." He repeated, "Fine."

"You're fine?" Nix echoed. It seemed true, yet he couldn't believe it. Had it been that easy? Was that all he'd ever needed to do? To just . . . meet the light? Touch it, take it inside himself? His mother, could he have saved her? What he had just been through was exhausting, sure, painful — every muscle in Nix's body ached — but this . . . this was *cake*. Too easy.

Nix looked up. He tried to make his voice light but wasn't sure if he succeeded. "Neve was pretty out of it. What — what did she remember?"

"You can ask her. She just went inside. Listen — I don't

284

really know what happened there. I was just so . . . out of it. I'll tell you." Jacob chuckled softly. "I thought I was having a heart attack or something. I thought I was about to . . . you know. Croak. But I feel fine now. No. Better. I feel better."

"I'm sure Nix is glad to hear that your punching him made you feel like a young man again."

Both turned at the sound of Neve's voice.

"We didn't have any packs so I put some cubes in a plastic bag."

No, Nix thought.

"I even made one for you." She smiled and tossed one to her father. "As soon as the adrenaline fades, your knuckles are gonna start throbbing."

No. Oh, god — no.

"I feel fine," Jacob said, staring at Nix. "You sure you're okay?"

Neve had reached them now, stepping close to Nix to press the bag of ice against the side of his face.

"What do you think, Daddy? You weigh about three hundred pounds and you socked him right in the face. Of course he's not *okay*."

Her voice was clear, her eyes focused. You would never know she'd been high a moment ago. Everything about her seemed fine.

No no no —

"I want to apologize for both of us," Neve was saying. "It's my fault, really." She was taking Nix's lifeless hand in one of her own — warm, soft, alive — and pressing it to the pack on the side of his head. She was stepping back. "I got really messed up. It was — well, you know who it was." She was squinting now. "Do you want to sit down? You look a little spacey."

Nix felt his jaw open. Heard a word leave his mouth.

"No."

The bag of ice fell to the ground.

"I'd appreciate it if you didn't tell K.A. —" she was saying.

"No," he repeated, and began backing away from father and daughter, toward the forest from which he'd sprung.

"Nix?" Jacob said.

"What the hell, Nix," Neve said. "Are you okay? You're freaking me out."

He squinted against the sight of her. Her pretty hair, a moment ago mashed to her skin with sweat, light and dry now, waving when her head shook, glinting. Her tilted dark brown eyes. Nix had always thought brown-eyed blonds were the prettiest. The shaking, buzzing, unholy light around her that grew with every second passing. Her obliviousness to it. Her perfect, stupid innocence.

Pet.

Neve Clowes was going to die. Soon.

"Nix," Jacob repeated as he backed away faster. "Listen, I'm sorry. Come back. You need some ice."

He did not stop. He stumbled over something, fell, and scrambled up, then turned and ran into the trees, their voices echoing behind him.

"Nix? What's going on?"

He heard Neve's call but didn't stop. He was running through the trees again but didn't know where. Just away. Away from Neve, now burning in the light that had been around her father. He had not made it go away, only moved it. He had saved Jacob, but condemned Neve.

Light and shadow whipped around him. Pine needles and empty space. A universe of light and shadow, mutually dependent, balanced. How had he thought he could just make part of it go away?

CHAPTER 16

THE DOORBELL OF 1515 N.E. SCHUYLER RANG, just as it had countless times before. A pleasant two-tone peal that normally made Ondine happy. She liked visitors, even talked to the Witnesses once in a while. But not now. Now she felt like being alone.

Never had Ondine felt so little like seeing another human being. She wanted to sit in her dining room doing exactly what she was doing now — erasing her mind, erasing what she had seen, so that she could at some point go to sleep. The snatches of rest she had caught in Morgan's car were just that: torn and ragged bits of something like sleep, but terrifying and confusing, not at all soothing. She was dead tired and needed to think about what she had to do after she'd rested.

The bell rang again. Ondine let her hands drop from her eyes to the table in front of her. It was Nix at the door, she knew. He'd come to apologize. She'd have to speak to him, go through the motions of kindness that had once seemed to her as effortless as breathing. She didn't want to be kind. She wanted everything to return to the way it was a few weeks ago, before her parents had left. That's what she wanted. To be a girl again, safe at home. To be Ondine.

She reached the door and pulled it open.

"You've got five minutes."

The words shot from her mouth, but she swallowed them almost as quickly. Moth stood in the sun squinting, his bug-eyed black sunglasses perched atop his head. He was playing the penitent, but Ondine knew it was an act.

"That's a bit long for me."

She was almost too shocked to speak. "I have nothing to say to you," she replied tersely. "Especially not a comeback to one of your sick attempts at a joke. Get out of here before I call the police." Before she could shut the door and pull the cell phone from her jacket pocket, Moth took a step forward and placed his hand against it. Ondine could feel the strength in his hand, the resolve. He'd push if she did. Harder.

Her legs weakened. In the mountains there were people around, but here, on N.E. Schuyler, it was a quiet Thursday morning and everyone was inside. An image of her brother Max — thirteen and nearly six feet tall — flashed before her. How could she have wanted him to go?

The smile faded from Moth's face, and though his hand was still on the door, his voice turned soft, almost pleading. "Ondine, please. I know this is painful."

"No —" She was shaking her head, still trying to shut the door. She heard herself begging, her voice jagged. "Please . . . just leave me alone."

His hand dropped. "I can't."

Though she should have slammed the door in the boy's face, she didn't. Instead she paused, hand still clutching the cell phone she'd retrieved from her pocket.

"What?"

"This is real. We're — real. Please. I can prove it to you."

Ondine stared. His fragility gave her strength.

"I don't know who you are, James Motherwell, or what you've gotten yourself into, but I don't want any part of it." She was calmer now, her voice more measured. She'd tell him what he wanted to hear. "I'll pretend like none of this took place. But if you try to call me, if you come here again —" She breathed and remembered the conversation she'd had with Moth the night of her party. "Please, just stay away, Moth. Otherwise, I'll go to the cops and have you arrested."

The boy's eyebrows furrowed, not from fear but exasperation. He blinked, hard. She swallowed.

"It's not going to do anything, Ondine."

She watched him move away from the door. He was preparing

to leave. What she said about the police must have convinced him. She wanted to believe the scene was over, but something about Moth's voice as he spoke made her look at him one last time. The sun was behind him and his green eyes were trained on hers.

"This is not a joke. You're in danger. To know what you know now, and not to do anything . . . you have to be prepared. You have to understand what you are. You were passed out for a lot of what Viv said and we don't get many chances. Now Bleek knows it's you and he'll come and get you, Ondine. He'll come to kill you. Your ring and I are the only people who can help you." Here Moth paused and stepped closer. Ondine was afraid to move. "You're not alone," Moth whispered, and she found herself, incredibly, listening to him, though she knew she shouldn't.

"I'm calling the police right now. . . ." She flipped her cell open but waited to press the buttons.

"I only want you to hear this. We *know* you. Viv has known you since you were born. She saw that this would happen, that you would have to go through this — this confusion. You belong with us, Ondine. Viv —"

Ondine could barely speak. "You're crazy, Moth. You're crazy."

For once he stayed quiet. He looked out to his right, down N.E. Schuyler, and shook his head. He was muttering.

"She told me how hard it would be. I don't know why I didn't listen —"

"You have to go now. Please. Go. Go tell someone. Get help. You're sick. You've been brainwashed."

He swiveled his head back to her and said one more thing as she was closing the door. She managed to do it — close the door — but not before she heard Moth's last words, the words that now had her breathing hard, crying, losing the strength in her legs, letting herself slowly sink to the ground with her back against the door, where she sat rocking herself, not knowing what to do next.

"Call your father, Ondine. He'll tell you where it started. Ask him if he remembers Viv. Your father knows."

∽   ∽   ∽

IT STARTED WITH A HISSING from the steaming thicket around her. *Morgana.* The forest breathed and Morgan with it.

The bank of green and black shimmered and expanded. As far as Morgan knew, she was alone. She had dropped Ondine off, dumped her things at home (or was it the other way around?), then just as quickly headed into the trees — awake — for the first time since she was twelve years old. Here was where it had started, and here was the only place she knew to run to.

Something seemed to be straining to come out. *Morgana,* she heard again, and wheeled, but when she turned, the same disorienting vegetal chaos greeted her: twisting vines; overlapping leaves; and behind it, an inky, mysterious blackness so dense that even the shafts of morning light that fell from the sky like shards of milky glass could not pierce it. Night ruled here, and Morgan began to wonder whether she was asleep, whether this was just one long dream — the toad, the girl with the fangs, the Ring of Fire — when from behind a screen of nettle came Bleek, smaller than she remembered. Instead of his red fleece and Gap khakis he wore a black-leather fighting costume with straps and buckles and what looked to Morgan like metal-tipped scales. He was clean-shaven and his receding corn-husk bowl cut had been shorn so close to his head that his bald skull seemed to glow when he crossed under a slice of light toward her.

Morgan stopped and waited. Even from several yards away, the man's tensile strength and tarry eyes unnerved her. She held her breath and tried not to move, though she could not help but shiver in the misty coolness, cursing herself that she had dropped her jacket along with her backpack at home. Bleek appraised her: tennis shoes to thin white sweater to black, still-damp hair. Morgan felt the hair on her arms stand up. She knew what her nipples must have been doing under her sweater and she hugged her arms closer. She was frightened, but sensed he would not hurt her.

His feet scraped the muddy ground.

"Morgan le Fay." He smirked and slithered nearer. "Humans

can be so —" He smiled crookedly, his eyes downcast in some imitation of flirtatiousness. "So *instinctual*. So beastly instinctual."

Bleek looked her up and down again. She felt her stomach turn.

"*Morgana*," he whispered.

She waited, unsure what to do next. What had Viv told them? *There are cutters out to hurt you. Changelings who have chosen the dark path. One is familiar to you already.* Of course the woman had meant Bleek. And Neve — Bleek must be using Neve somehow, she reasoned, untangling the associations that had formed among her small group over the last weeks leading up to the Ring of Fire. But why? For simple enjoyment, as Viv had said? The hassle hardly seemed worth it. If Neve *was* at the Ring of Fire, as Morgan had overheard Viv telling Ondine, she must have been brought by Bleek. But for what purpose? And what did it all have to do with dust?

She stared at the older boy — *cutter*, she reminded herself. Evil, chaotic, insidious. But what was he, really? And why was he dangerous to the others, but not to her?

Or was he?

One thing Morgan was sure of was that she wasn't going to do anything until she had more information. Whatever Bleek was, and whatever she herself was, were more similar than Viv imagined. *Bleek* — Morgan winced inwardly at the improbable name. And they say you can't judge a book by its cover. He was a dark disturbance, a shadow after her own heart, which was beating shallowly now, fluttering.

Morgan knew that what would ultimately happen depended on moments like these. Each decision stacked up like a line of dominoes. If one fell, everything would be lost. She was not stupid. Bleek's . . . what was it? Flirtation? It was hardly as sweet as that . . . had little effect on her, though she knew she'd use it.

Coyly, so coyly, she spoke.

"Fancy meeting you here."

Should she smile now? Bleek was so close she could see the open pores on his hairless skin, the ripples of wrinkles around his black eyes. She breathed, inched her chest forward, tilted her head, and lowered her eyelashes.

Bleek blinked.

"Disgusting little slut. Stupid bitch."

He struck her. Not with his hands, Bleek was not meant to use his hands. He struck her with a bolt of something, an electric current that transfixed Morgan and sealed her to her place. She felt her hair fly about her. She felt her feet fasten to the ground. She tried to raise her hands but they would not move.

"Deceptive minx." Bleek opened his mouth and his jagged white teeth shone. Despite his harsh words, he was smiling.

"Don't think I don't know what you're doing. Do you know what your problem is, Morgana?"

She looked down. The ground seemed to move in waves beneath her.

"You think you're special. You think there hasn't been anyone like you. An ambitious girl with a beautiful face and a blessed body." He sneered. "The thing is, your tits won't get you anywhere in Novala. There are thousands of you burned at the door."

He spit the last words and Morgan felt the air shake around her.

"Fuck you, you pathetic drug dealer, dumb redneck —"

"Quiet!" He jolted her again. This time she felt her tongue lock to the top of her mouth. She tried to move it but only gagged. "Do not underestimate me, Morgana. Let this be your first lesson. You like lessons, don't you?"

He circled, yellow-rimmed eyes upon her.

"We have not chosen the dark path for nothing, love." She felt the coffee she'd had on the drive with Ondine inch up her gorge. "There's very little that a cutter won't learn, or do, for his own gain. Or hers." He smiled condescendingly. "Our instincts are sharper, for we've had to hone them on creatures just as lightning quick as we are."

He stopped, walked up to her, and flicked a taut nipple.

It was a shocking gesture, both intimate and violent. Again Morgan felt a current root her to her place, though not as painfully as before. Though she had to restrain herself from smacking him across the face, she stayed quiet, as she knew Bleek wanted her.

"You're here because you already know what you are. Well, good. It usually takes longer." A shadow of something passed over Bleek's face but he shook it off and crossed his arms over his chest. He started sucking on something between his teeth. "Of course, not me. I knew. I knew like you did."

Morgan tried to remain still, though every nerve wanted to bolt. She had not expected this reaction. She had expected to feel more powerful. Herself, but better. Bleek smelled swampy, and Morgan, despite herself, wondered whether she would have to become ugly like he was if she were to be a cutter.

"It's obvious what you want, Morgana." He sidled close again. "Power, isn't it? Come on, sweet. You can speak now. Bleek is listening."

So this was what he wanted: submission.

"Yes." The word sounded like a yell but she knew it had emerged a whisper.

Bleek whispered back. "And I will teach you."

She held her breath.

"You will learn much more, and much faster, than the other

lings in your ring will from that disaster, Moth. Viv's little charity case." He whipped around. "I could — and I will — tell you a few things about him."

Morgan almost responded but checked herself, and Bleek, infatuated with his own words, moved on.

"But you." He moved closer, brought his mouth to her bare neck. She felt his soupy breath against her. "You are quite another creature altogether. I've been watching you since you were an itty-bitty thing, Morgana."

Watching her? Was this how it started then? Had Bleek been there all those nights in the woods?

"And you've turned out very nicely indeed."

She was disgusted by the insinuation. She had been only a child. What had they done to her? Despite her revulsion, she forced her face to be blank, pursing her lips. "Thank you."

Bleek laughed. "It wasn't meant as flattery. We'll have to work on that. You know" — he turned to her — "cutters aren't *sex-shual*. Dear, vain Morgana. Your pretty face is as compelling to me as that puddle over there." He pointed and the water shivered. "Well," he smiled. "I should amend that. We can procreate. If that bitch-bot Viv wasn't running the show, we would. Check that: *Will*. Will run the show. Power is what turns us on, dear. Power and trouble. Here. On earth. Now. Not in never-never land. But perhaps you've already gotten an inkling of this?"

He traced a long nail down the thin fabric of her sweater and she shivered again.

"I know what makes you tick, Morgan. I hear the same bomb as you. Now." He paused, clearly ready to give her some instruction. She was about to ask him about Viv, what made her a scion, but thought better of it. The confines of the relationship had been settled, the terms agreed upon. Bleek had been seduced — by himself. He would teach her, and in return, she would do his bidding. She had only to be patient.

Apparently he read as much on her face. He started humming a crooked little tune — where had she heard it before? — and began.

"Tomorrow your idiot of a brother returns from *soccer camp*." Bleek shook his head. "Unbelievable that you had to share a home with him. And that one! That trailer. I would have caused an accident some time ago. A pinch of arsenic in those *p-cakes* Kaka is so good at making? A goose-down pillow over the mouth just before bedtime? Eh?"

Despite her dark intentions, Morgan clenched back a scream. How dare he? She loved her brother, as much as she could love anyone. How did he know about the pancakes? The pillow she'd spent two hundred dollars on as a birthday gift for K.A.'s sixteenth? He had been spying on her. Drawing her into the forest night after night. Morgan knew she hated the cutter then.

Hated him more than she hated anything. And she knew that this was what he fed upon, this anger. Power wasn't Bleek's elixir. Hatred was.

She stared. He was testing her commitment to him, and though inwardly she rebelled, she stayed quiet and listened to his spew.

"You're harder than I thought." He tossed his head. "In any case. You know the little slut called Neve? Your brother's seriously misguided choice of a girlfriend?" He smiled evilly. She nodded and spoke.

"Neve. She's a trashy whore."

"I've got my eye on her. I've been trying for years to find a suitable human. Cutters, as you can imagine, aren't first on the list for pets."

Morgan must have seemed confused, though she was trying to conceal any emotion from her face. Bleek's tone had become sarcastic, almost infantile. He pursed his lips, sniffed, and continued.

"Viv must have given you the spiel, sweetheart. She did the rest of us. *So long ago . . .*" A faraway look came into his eyes but it did not last. "The humans, love. The pets? Some of them were used for reproduction. For more changelings." He looked at her. She shook her head to indicate that she did not fully understand. "For the initial change. For the ringing."

"That's where we're from?" Morgan whispered.

"Some of us." He frowned and looked away. "Not you. You were born into a *real* family, and the change had to be done later, in secret. In the forest." He gestured grandly to the green canopy above her. Morgan had almost forgotten where she was. "Don't even try to remember. You won't yet. You were out of it and the ringer wasn't a very good one. But you remember afterward, don't you? The little games you used to play? With the animals? Remember that, Morgy?"

Bleek folded his hands over his chest and regarded her.

"That's why you kept coming here. To be with your kind. A baby ling trying to learn how. It was almost . . . sweet. If you hadn't been so cruelly *abandoned*. Viv was busy playing patty-cake with her favorite, Ondine, and didn't have time for you. And your human family . . ." He inched closer. "They certainly sucked ass, didn't they? But that's all right. All of that is gone now." He reached out a yellowish finger and trailed a sharp nail down the mound of Morgan's wet cheek. "Uncle Bleek's here now."

"Don't touch me." She choked. Was she — crying?

"Don't speak until spoken to. And wipe those tears off your face." She tried to swallow a low whimper. The show of weakness obviously irritated the cutter, for he stepped back, wiping the hand that had touched her on his leather jacket and tucking it into his side. "Not me, of course. I was born to a stinking pet in one of the scia's hideous little corpa factories. But you. You

301

were raised by loving Yvonne, the Rose Queen, and doting Phil Jr., the prince of paper products. That's where he stocked, didn't he? Aisle ten? Burnside D'Amici's? Quite a *provider*, that Phil."

"Fuck you."

Bleek ignored her. "At least you had plates to eat off of. Clean sheets to wrap around your pretty corpus. And what a lovely one, too, eh? A perfect ten. Too bad none of it is yours."

He scowled and wagged another long-nailed finger in front of her face.

"You didn't think that you actually *looked* like this, did you?" He was close to her and she could smell him again. She breathed shallowly. "You aren't human, Morgana. Get this through your shallow fay reflecting pool of a brain. This —" He grabbed a bit of flesh at her hip and tugged. "This is just temporary. Your costume. Your cocoon, pretty butterfly . . ." Morgan pulled away and Bleek laughed bitterly. "I know I disgust you. You really need to work on your acting skills. Unfortunately, dear, if you're going to be a cutter, you better get used to looking and smelling like one. Invest in some deodorant. Teen Spirit, perhaps? In the human world, we take human form. And humans rot. Especially if something's in them." He blew at her and Morgan could smell his putrefaction. She remembered the girl with the dreads from the parking lot at the Ring of Fire, sniffing her. Was she already turning?

"Soon everything will be ours. Novala, too."

Bleek unfurled his hand — his wrist marked by that same little blue X, Morgan noted, the same that she had seen on Moth, the same on the girl in the parking lot, the same on Viv — and a spinning sphere of blue and yellow sparks almost a foot across emerged from his palm and whizzed past her, shearing her left shoulder as it spun by. She watched it bounce through a tree trunk and into the dark woods till she couldn't see it anymore. When she looked at her sweater, it was brown from where the ball of lightning had skimmed her, and the air smelled like burned wool.

"We are of the greater sphere, love. And that's where we'll return." He waved a hand around majestically and Morgan followed but could only see darkness, and the barest outline of an even blacker darkness. "We inhabit the larger universe — the one that humans can feel only the lightest pricks of. When they are afraid of the night. When the hair on their arms stands up. When they walk in the forest and understand that they are not alone. We are fay. We come from the holes — in the earth, in the trees, the graves, hurricanes and tornadoes and storms. The black holes that swallow stars.

"Cutters, too." His voice lowered. "The invisible world makes room for good and evil and everything in between."

For a moment he almost seemed sympathetic. Morgan eased.

"Cutters . . . what are they?"

But speaking before she was spoken to was not welcome, so

instead of answering, Bleek coughed and shook his head, sighing.

"Did I say that it was question-and-answer time? No. I didn't. Listen to me. Wipe that pathetic little frown off your mouth and listen to me. That crying of yours — *puh-lease*. Must have taken some energy to do that. We don't cry, Morgana, in case you hadn't noticed. Since that first time in the forest, have you cried? No. The inhabitation dries us all up." He snorted and laughed. "But why am I letting you waste my time?"

And then, as if to show her that she'd be sorry if she allowed the kind of softness she'd always, in a sense, longed for in her life, as if to show her that yes, he did survive on hate and cruelty — he scratched her with a long nail, just on her cheek. Morgan felt wetness, and after putting her hand there, she drew it down and looked at it. There was a black, thick substance coated with phosphorescence that she recognized as whatever had seeped from that girl she had scratched at the Ring of Fire. Just as quickly, it disappeared. Had she never seen her own blood before? No, never. She had never been hurt. Her period hadn't yet come — something she had just chalked up to being thin — *amenorrhea*, it was called, though she still told her mother to buy her tampons so that Yvonne, the nosy bitch, wouldn't ask.

"Corpa do bleed, my dear. It isn't easy, but they do bleed." Bleek moved closer again. "Nasty, stinky things, aren't they? Our human bodies? Especially when they get old. I mean, look at me." He pulled a particularly saggy bit of flesh from his jowls and wiggled it. "I used to be quite handsome. I used to get all the girls."

He continued, pacing in the small clearing. "Cutters don't want to leave. We like it here. We have power on earth. In Novala we'd be just one of many. At the ring we decide, *nah*, why take what power we have *there* when we can use it right here on earth?"

"What kind of power?"

"You like the sound of that? Never mind. Soon enough you'll find out. In any case, it's verboten to stay, Morgana. Changelings are required to join the exidis, even though she pretends like it's a 'choice.' Problem is, Viv wasn't lying when she said that the inhabitation — it wears on us. To put it lightly." Bleek opened his mouth and bared his horrifying muzzle. "My poor teeth, for example. Our human corpus — it can't handle it. We break down starting at eighteen. I'm twenty-two. And how old do I look?"

Morgan started, but Bleek waved a slender, long-nailed hand.

"Don't answer that. I've even considered a face-lift. They're much less invasive these days. . . ." He sighed and shook his head. "But what I smuggle in dust can't pay for it. And though I'm a good dealer, a man's gotta eat. So I've lit on another . . ." He paused and looked at Morgan directly, as if to suss out her trustworthiness. "*Avenue.* Much tidier. Much more *fun.* But I'll tell you about that all later. No need to spoil you so soon. Of course, this little tutoring session we've set up, it's not free. You realize that don't you?"

She said the words deliberately, fighting her dizziness. "What do you want me to do?"

He paused again, retreated and turned away, then began reciting his instructions.

"That darling little tinfoil-for-brains Neve Clowes is close to becoming my pet. I have been feeding her dust now for long enough; she is my slave, or close to being so." He turned, looked at Morgan. "It's not easy getting a human to become one's pet. Don't let Varicose Viv fool you. They have to want it. And your farm animal of a brother is my main concern here, since she must be alone, and while he is around, they seem to be attached in a most inconvenient way. I suggest, then, that you occupy him or otherwise distract him over the next few days while I snare this particular prey."

He snorted and shook his head, almost mournfully.

"She is really second-rate, this one. The first girl . . . Evelyn. Much better — would have given me a strong corpus to inhabit, but she was terribly" — he paused, searching for the right word — "stubborn, and there was that insect, Finn, and I lost her. And that other one. *Ugh*. I had to eliminate *her* right away." He drew a line across his throat and widened his eyes. "Who knew she'd be such a bleeder?" He shook his head. "But I am really not well and must do something about it. Neve is almost *too* easy, unfortunately. Not much fun at all." Bleek eyed the shivering Morgan. "But I am talking too much. You turn your brother's head for me." He smiled evilly. "But you know how to do that already, don't you, darling?"

She felt heat creep up her neck.

"Of course you do. It's so — exciting that the two of you aren't *really* related, isn't it? I mean, tell the truth, Morgana. You've always thought he was a little cute, huh? The perfect guy." Bleek's voice raised in imitation of a teenaged girl's. "Smart, handsome, nice, *funny*. Shucks, too bad he's my *brother*."

Morgan stared.

"Closer's better, huh? But that's your business. Mine is much more simple: deliver Neve to me and I will give you your first, well, second, lesson — this wasn't exactly a chat at the Krak, was it? — which will give you a distinct advantage over that self-righteous little twat in your ring, Ondine. Viv's favorite, need I remind you. Whom Moth, by the way, seems to like a great deal as well. Too bad. The two of you seemed to hit it off at that little party. God, that was a disaster. Moth really can't do anything right."

The memory of Moth shaming her made Morgan's face burn and she stepped closer.

"How do I do it?"

"You'll need to figure that out. Be *creative*. Jesus." He rolled his eyes. "But just do it. The sooner the better. And I don't need to tell you that you aren't to speak of me with anyone, especially that other one, Nix. But you wouldn't do that, would you? Because you know where that cold jewel of a heart in you lies, and for that, there is only one way."

She didn't need to say a word. Bleek stopped. His eyes were very black, and his skin pale.

"The one that I am on. The dark one."

He smiled and turned to leave, but Morgan stepped after him. "Please just tell me. Why are we called cutters? What does that mean?"

"We? *Me*. Morgana, *I* am a cutter. You are nothing yet."

She shook her head, amended herself. "I mean, you. Why are you a cutter? What do you do?"

He grinned and tipped his head back, rocking on his heels. "Of course she didn't tell you. That's good. That means she's afraid." He paused. "We're cutters because we cut the current that effects the exidis. We short it. We stop the ring. No one gets in until we're eliminated. *Thereby damning us to existence as an everlasting particle of pain, passed from one being to another, for eternity,* blah blah blah. She told you that part, right? Gentle Viv *loves* that part. 'Forced to relive the entire history of the universe,'" he recited, "'as an original particle of pain. Searing, hopeless, unimaginable pain.' Yawn. Easy for her to say. There are more of them than there are cutters. Usually it's easy as pie to defeat us. And Viv has extremely nice ways of selectively directing the circuits at the Ring of Fire."

Morgan's eyes narrowed.

"The way that blond boy died? Almost every year someone dies like that. Viv pretends it's an *accident,* something about how the guides didn't prepare them, *et cetera,* but it's happening more and more as they're bringing changelings in. She wants to eliminate anyone she thinks might endanger the exidis. Anyone who slightly reeks of cutter."

"But do you believe it?" Morgan spoke quickly, remembering the girl who sniffed her in the parking lot. "The exidis? Do you really believe that we're" — Morgan struggled with the word — "fay?"

"Oh yes. It's real. It's happening. The exidis is growing. Human life is" — Bleek put his tongue between his lips and blew — "*pffft.* Don't you doubt that." He sneered. "But you think Viv cares about you? You're a common morpha as far as I can tell — expendable. You might have a few trifling powers, birthday party tricks, basically, but you can't come back. Like me. Ringers like Nix — they take a little more care about them. Prepare them better. But you and me? We're nothing. Believe me. Viv doesn't care about you and neither does her lackey, Moth. That's why I joined the cutters. It's dangerous — we're often eliminated, but I've proven extremely hard to catch. See, I was born into this sick in-between world and I know every nook and cranny of it. Why, I even sort of like it. *Me dam, she was a whor-ish pet,*" Bleek sang, slipping into a cockney accent. "A lazy, squalid piece of ass for the scia. Very soon that will change." He eyed her. "There are many of us left, Morgana. Many who could be made to remember what they once were . . ."

Morgan tried to let the tide of information soak into her, but she couldn't stop her questions. She wanted to get started. She felt there was no time to lose.

"When do I get my first lesson?"

"Impatient, aren't you?"

She nodded.

"Good. One thing cutters don't have a lot of is time. Meet me in the tunnels tomorrow morning. You'll get your first lesson there. Of course, you'll have to do that little thing I asked of you before then —"

"That's not a problem." The words had barely left her mouth before he turned. She realized she did not know what he was talking about.

"The tunnels?" Morgan called out. "Bleek?" Morgan listened for his footsteps, but the cutter had already sunk into the inky woods around him and disappeared.

CHAPTER 17

T FIRST IT FELT LIKE A VACUUM had sucked his insides out; Nix was clean as a seashell on the beach. Then the memories came, fast, like notes of a song. Splashes of his life: silver fish in a small white boat, his mother laughing, the smell of cedar and blood. Traveling from Alaska down the coast. Run, walk, hitch, hop a train, take a bus, a car, a plane if you could scrimp and had ID. The sweetpea girl, apple picking at sunrise. His SpongeBob sleeping bag, Finn, K.A. The first time he'd seen Neve. Her sleepy brown eyes. The soft tangle of her whitish-blond hair. He'd fallen in love with her — Nix knew that now, though he'd never do anything, out of respect for K.A. Then, just as surely, he'd damned her. Was it always going to be like this? As soon as he loved someone, as soon as he got close, they'd be marked to die?

He who giveth, also taketh away.

He needed to get to Ondine's. Ondine would be able to help

him. He'd tell her all about it, about Jacob and Neve and how he'd made the light jump. If she'd just remember what they'd shared. Was it only a few days ago? Nix thought of Ondine's smooth body next to his in her shaded and cool bedroom, the light slanting in, and felt ashamed. Though nothing had happened — at least not *that* — their bodies had wanted something else, and those weeks were such a dream. . . .

Ondine had stayed. She had heard what Viv had told them. She'd know what to do.

He careened away from the Cloweses' so fast he forgot that he'd driven Ondine's car there and had to take the Burnside bus along with the rest of the crazies. No way was he going back to face Neve until he knew what to do. An Indian man was sitting in one of the front seats: slumped, handsome in a way, with long hair, which meant that not so long ago maybe he'd lived on the rez. His face was red, his nose pocked. A drunk. *My father,* Nix thought, faster than he could hold on to it. Then the undeniable: a thin glowing light, white and electric, surrounded the man, not gaining, not lessening, just hovering there. How had he missed it when he got on the bus?

He had ignored it. That's what dust had allowed him to do. That's why he had taken it. Then he did it out of habit. But now his eye was keen. He wasn't going to blind himself anymore.

When Ondine's door opened, he was surprised to see her eyes red, her nose, too. She didn't look well. She shook her head and looked at him coldly — "God, Nix" — but held the door steady, and without a word he stepped inside.

For a moment, nothing passed between them; Nix kept his head down. He wasn't sure what he had been expecting. He had left Ondine at the gathering without so much as a good-bye.

"Where are the keys?" She wiped her nose and stared at him, but her eyes were unyielding.

He passed them to her, head still down. He noticed she was careful not to touch his hand. "I . . . I left the car at Neve's." He raised his eyes to hers.

"At Neve's? Great. That's just great." Ondine shook her head. "And all that time I trusted you. How much dust are you doing, Nix? Huh? Does Moth give it to you by the truckload now?"

When he spoke, his voice was soft. "Ondine, I need your help."

She stood a moment, then sighed. He felt the weight of all that time together slip out from under him.

"I can't help you." The girl looked away. "I'm sorry; I can't be involved in whatever happened out there. It's not good for me. And it's not good for you either." Her voice became more tender then, but it was clear none of their former closeness remained. "I know you take dust. Whatever you're hooked up with, those people . . . they're dangerous. You need to get help. Professional help."

She spoke slowly, as if the last bit of energy in her body had already been sucked from her. Nix realized — too late — that he had not even thought about how she got home. Morgan D'Amici must have driven her. But what was going through her head now?

He didn't need to guess. Ondine stepped over to the door, picked up Nix's backpack that was sitting there, and handed it to him. "I care about you. No. I *cared* about you. But you left me and I can't be involved in this anymore."

"Ondine —"

His eyes pleaded with her and he wondered whether she could feel their pull. They had looked into each other's eyes when they were both naked, vulnerable.

"I know this is weird. I know. I'm sorry. I'm sorry I left you. But there's something going on that neither of us understands." He took a breath and held it. He had to ask. "I think this is real, Ondine. I have to know what Viv said at the Ring of Fire."

"Viv? You mean the cult leader that has hundreds of kids messed up on dust? That Viv?" Ondine shook her head. "Nix, that was a messed-up place, and that was a messed-up thing Moth did to us, bringing us there. None of that is real. You realize that, don't you?"

Nix was begging now, his voice a thin whisper. "No. You don't understand. This is real. This is real. It's already started for me and I need to know what I missed. I have a problem. I need you — you're the only one who can help me. You heard

314

what she said. I . . . I see things, Ondine. Light. I see this light around people. And then they die. When I see it." Nix knew he sounded confused, but her eyes — they were so hard, so unlike before. "Please, Ondine. I need to know what I am."

She stiffened and started to inch backward, shaking her head.

"You need help. And I can't give it to you."

He was scaring her, he realized. This girl whose bed he had shared, who had opened herself so sweetly to him. He was a monster now. She was shaking her head, slowly at first, but as he continued, begging with her, coming closer, deeper into the house, she started trembling.

"Leave, Nix." She put a hand to her mouth. "I don't want you or anyone else here anymore. Not you, not Moth, not Morgan, no one. Please. I want you to leave."

She was sobbing soundlessly, but he couldn't stop moving toward her. He had to get her to understand.

"Please . . . Ondine. There's something wrong. Something with Neve. I have to explain it to you —"

He was close to her now, and he felt her fear. She was shaking. She thought he was going to hurt her.

"I'm going to call the police."

"I'm not going to hurt you. Ondine —"

She pulled the phone from her pocket and he could see her fingers hovering above the numbers. Her hands shook, but he knew she was going to do it. She pressed three digits and then held the phone to her ear.

"Please," Nix begged. "She'll die if you don't help me."

"Leave, Nix. The police are coming . . ."

Her eyes flicked away.

"Yes, my name is Ondine Mason, 1515 N.E. Schuyler. There is an intruder in my house and I am in danger. I need a police car here right away —"

Her last words were a whisper, and Nix, though his eyes pleaded, said nothing more. Ondine held the door open and he put his backpack on and ran away.

∽ ∽ ∽

"Welcome to Cingular Wireless. . . . Para español, marque uno. For English . . ."

Ondine shut her cell and slammed the door, not wanting to see his face anymore, not wanting to watch him as he ran, lonely and friendless, down the street. She had been about to call the police. She was going to dial the numbers. Why, at the last moment, hadn't she? Nix was not her responsibility, she repeated to herself as she slid her back down the door, sinking into a ball on the floor. She was hysterical now — tearless, convulsive sobbing — and yet part of her, the part that was always there, stood outside and looked at her own pathetic, crumbling self.

Light. I see this light around people. And then they die.

The cool tile floor calmed her, and soon she was breathing regularly, the small hiccups of hysteria receding. She knew what she had to do.

Her cell phone was still in hand, her fingers gripped around it. She scrolled through the names till she found the one she wanted, and dialed. Ralph Mason picked up on the second ring.

"Honey!"

Something about his voice — its warmth, its sanity — undid her, and she found herself moaning again, except this time softly, keening into the phone, before she could get a word out. She didn't want to speak anymore. She just wanted to cry. Yet try as she might, the tears wouldn't come.

"Ondine, honey, what's wrong? What's wrong, baby? Are you all right? What's going on?"

At first she could only whimper in response, but when Ralph asked, "Is this an emergency? Should I call nine-one-one?" she managed to eke out a *no*. She didn't need an ambulance. She obviously didn't want the police.

"Daddy, I want to come to Chicago."

"Sure, honey, sure. We'll buy you a ticket right now. But what's wrong? What happened? Ondine, you need to tell me what's going on so that I don't worry." His voice cracked. "You've got your dad pretty worried here, sweetheart."

"Dad." She rubbed her eyes to think straight. "Dad, something's wrong with me. Something's wrong." She started moaning again and Ralph tried to soothe her.

"What do you mean something's wrong? Did something happen with one of your friends? With a boy? Ellen said someone has been over. Are you all right? Please tell me, honey —"

"No, no. That's not it. It's me." Her voice was choked. She wasn't going to tell him about the night in the mountains, or about Nix — she knew that. At least not now. She couldn't. Ralph, with his scientific mind, wouldn't understand.

She calmed herself and tried to explain. "It's me. There's something wrong with me. I know it. I just don't know what it is. I don't . . .

"Dad —" She didn't register the fact that she was saying the words until she heard her own voice say them. "Dad, do you know someone named Viv?"

Ralph spoke, his voice more serious than she'd ever heard it.

"Did she try to contact you, Ondine? Did Viv contact you?"

"No — no, I mean yes. I mean, I don't know."

"Hold on." She heard the sound of a door closing. He must have been at the lab, she reasoned, and looked at her watch. Ten AM. Of course. It was the middle of the day in Chicago. Dr. Mason came back to the phone.

"Ondine, love. Joy of my life. Your mother's at home right now and we made a promise to each other that we'd talk about this first, before — well, anyway. Listen to me carefully. There is nothing wrong with you. You are perfect. You are as perfect as a child could be, and your mother and I — not to mention Max, and Nana, and Aunt Vita, and everyone else — love you so much, sweetheart. So much. We want to protect you, and I think your mother and I made a mistake in protecting you too long —"

"I don't understand." Ondine's voice betrayed her panic. "Protect me?" For an instant she had the thought that her father was in on the Ring of Fire; that she had walked into a circus fun house where everything she trusted, everything she felt safe and secure about, had been twisted. Even her father. Even the one she depended on the most.

"No, no, sweetie. Don't get upset." Ralph took a breath. "I promised your mother we would do this together and I am breaking that promise, and I hope I'm not doing the wrong thing. But you already sense . . . I don't want you to worry any longer. Please, Ondine. Know that I love you more than anything in the world. I care about you more than I care about myself, and I would do anything for you, honey. Anything."

She didn't know what to say. She couldn't picture what her father was about to tell her. Did she have an awful disease? Was she about to die? Was she really born a boy? *Ask your parents; they'll tell you who you are.*

"Honey. I do know someone named Viv. Jesus, I can't believe I'm telling you this on the phone. I can't. Ondine, just get on the plane. I'll —"

"No. No. Tell me now. Who is she?"

"Please promise you'll get on that plane."

"I promise, Daddy."

Ralph Mason took a breath and continued.

"When Xelix was first starting, there was a nurse there who worked for me. Her name was Vivian Greene."

"What?" Ondine gasped. It was not what she expected, this announcement. Not at all.

"Honey, I told you. I don't want to do this over the phone —"

Her voice was flat. For some reason, all she could think about was her mother's toes.

"Just tell me."

"She was my nurse. She assisted us with the transfers."

"Did you have an affair with her?"

"No, no, honey. No. Nothing like that. Your mother. She was . . . we had been trying to get pregnant for many years and it wasn't happening. The technology was less advanced than it is today, and we couldn't . . . we couldn't extract your mother's eggs. Viv knew about this and — she offered to be a donor. She offered —"

"But I have the same toes as Mom! We have the same toes! You said we had the same toes!" Everything had gotten mixed up, and when Ondine closed her eyes she felt dizzy, the colors behind her eyelids a mix of orange and blue, black, green, the colors of her ceiling upstairs. Her dreams. The whizzing balls of light. It was all too much.

"I'm black! I'm black! Viv's white!"

Her father's voice dropped. "You saw her?"

She stopped. "No. No. I mean, she told me she was —"

"Your skin comes from me, Ondine. Listen. This is too painful for over the phone, sweetheart. We need to be together for —"

"No." Ondine's voice was suddenly cold. "No, you need to tell me now. Then I will get on the plane and we will talk about it more. What happened? What happened then? What happened at my birth?"

Ralph was quiet for several moments; finally he spoke. "Not your birth, honey. Your conception." He paused, then continued. "Everything was fine. Your mother was under sedation, the egg had been harvested. Then the power went out. It was very unexpected. We had backup generators. There had been a storm — anyway, that's not important. I rushed to check on what was happening, and when I came back I found the other attending nurse missing and Viv in her place. She had been wanting to — I don't know — do something to your mother. Maybe she was deranged. Some women get like that when they know that the egg is going to be implanted. She ran out before I could stop her. Nothing was amiss, and your mother was already out. I had to continue with the operation. Viv . . ."

"What?"

"We looked for her, and we went to the police and everything, but I never saw her again."

"She's my *mother*?" Ondine pictured the woman in the long black coat — her insane hair, her bruise-colored eyes. She covered her face with her hands.

"No, no. Sweetheart. Your mother is your mother. Trish is your mother. My wife. Your mother. Darling, please. Please forgive us. It was all so new — the technology. And we wanted a child so badly. We didn't know what to do. We never knew how to tell you."

Ondine heard herself speak. "I don't believe you."

"Oh, sweetheart. I know. I know this is hard. But it's true." He stopped and sighed. "Get the folder, sweetheart. It's in the folder. The one I gave you with all of your insurance information. There's an envelope in there marked 'for hospital use only.' Open it. It tells the whole story."

By now Ondine had wandered into the kitchen, where the folder that her father had left three weeks ago was sitting in a

322

drawer by the door. She cradled the phone on her shoulder and opened it. There was the envelope her father had promised, with the Xelix logo of a double helix on its side, like the sign for infinity, neatly headed with the words FOR HOSPITAL USE ONLY. He must have known she'd never look in there.

"I've got it," she whispered.

"Go ahead and open it."

She broke the seal. The single sheet of paper inside was the original of her own birth certificate, which she suddenly realized she had never seen. Trish Mason, mother, Ralph Mason, father. Date of birth, eye color, weight, and length. But under "Special Circumstances" were written the words: Egg transfer from donor Vivian Greene, nurse, SS # 262-98-8766, 1202 N.W. Glisan #4, Portland, OR 97209. And under her blood type, the words: RARE. CANNOT RECEIVE O.

"But my blood type — what's my blood type?"

Ralph cleared his throat. "You have a very unusual blood type, Ondine. I'd never seen it before; it's in the Lan group. I'm sure there's someone out there in the world who has it — well, Viv, maybe — but I still haven't been able to locate it."

"But why didn't you tell me? Why didn't you tell me until now? How could you? Daddy, why?"

"Sweetheart, I'm so sorry. It just — it got too late. Mom got pregnant with Max. It was all — normal. Like it had never happened. And of course we wanted you to be ours, really and truly. You *were* ours and so we just — we lied. We lied to you. We wanted to protect you. I'm sorry, honey. I thought maybe if we waited — long enough — we'd never have to tell you. But when you called . . . I just couldn't take hearing you cry like that. I wanted you to know that there was an explanation. . . ."

Ralph was crying now and it made Ondine quiet.

"Dad, no. Dad, don't cry."

"This means nothing about how much we love you. But it probably explains why you feel different. This is what you feel." He sighed and his voice cracked. He sounded far away. "God. They express themselves in the end, don't they?"

"What? What do you mean?"

"The genes, honey. Of course you would feel it. I think I was just in denial. We, your mother and I, we were in denial." He cleared his throat and spoke again, this time deeper, with more control. "Ondine, I'm buying you a ticket right now. Don't worry about packing; just bring yourself. We'll get you some clothes here. Just drive to the airport. I want you on a plane and I want you here. We need to deal with this as a family. Together. Do you have the number Viv called you from on your cell phone?"

"No. No . . . no, there's nothing."

"That's all right. We'll figure out what to do. She's not bad. She's just . . . she was just —"

"It's okay. You don't have to explain." Ondine was almost

324

too shocked to do anything but follow orders. She'd pack her backpack. She'd have to get a taxi.

"I'm so sorry. I'm so sorry I didn't do this better."

She had heard her father apologize before, but this felt different. She was . . . *a test-tube baby?* She tried the word out in her head. It didn't sound right somehow — too eighties. But that was what her father was telling her, and that's what she had to believe. What Moth said, what he had warned, Viv must have told him about. A ploy used by people like them to try to convince people like her. No. She amended herself. People who were weaker than her.

A little clarity came in — some hint of blue sky out of the storm of the last week, month, too long. She was heading toward her parents, and something, some hint of what all this was, would be explained. At least there was an answer. She had felt something, and here was a perfectly logical answer as to why. Things were as they seemed.

"It's okay. I'm leaving now. Just call me and tell me what airline and when. I'll be at the airport." Her voice softened. "I miss you, Dad."

"We miss you, sweetheart. And don't worry, we'll figure this all out."

With that they said good-bye. She didn't have much to put in her knapsack — her sketchbook, wallet, cell charger, toothbrush. A jacket. She called a taxi, cursing Nix. Everything else she left as it was. She turned off the lights, set the alarm, locked the front door behind her, and walked steadily toward the curb. Each leaf seemed to stand out to her, each puddle on the asphalt; each mailbox stood in sharp relief. She was seeing clearly for the first time in a while. She was ready to find out the truth.

IV

THE INVISIBLE WORLD

FTER FOUR YEARS OF STRUGGLING with the lemma of the fay, Moth had only begun to delve into the delicate art of "seeing," as Viv called it — and quite elegantly, he thought, for a tribe obsessed with taxonomy, with lists, and with the largely meaningless (at least to him) web of particles and gases, plasma bodies, and electromagnetic phenomenon Viv studied for communication from the invisible world.

As one of the thirty living scia in the world today, Viv's main task was to read, capture, and utilize the energy that leaked between the dimensions (and branes, in string theory) in the form of geophysical phenomena: tornadoes and hurricanes, lightning, aurora, earthquakes, as well as any number of smaller occurrences that might indicate interstitial dimensional activity, such as ball lightning, even fire — a relatively low-temperature plasmic occurence. It was an ability she learned from the scia before her, the ones who trained her, an ability she would then pass on to the scion she would train: most likely Ondine. Viv told him she had known the girl since her birth, and in the years leading up to Ondine's initiation, she had returned to Portland, from where she had been living in the mountains of New Mexico, specifically to prepare the girl — as well as to protect the ringer who had migrated down from his original territory of Alaska. That Viv had been Moth's leader as well was an accident of timing. A lucky one, Moth reminded himself. At other gatherings — in L.A. a few years ago, once even in New York, where he met lings from the Atlantic whorl — Viv was spoken of as a scion with great cosmological insight and wisdom. Revered, almost, though changelings were strict in their use of words with religious connotations. *We are magnetic, physical entities,* Viv always reminded the young man. *Not angels, not gods. Our time in this dimension is enough only to gather consciousness.*

Viv had gotten a PhD in physics from Berkeley to help her. In New Mexico she read and studied the signs, coming out for gatherings only when she had to. Moth was far less adept and his seeing had little to do with his "superhuman" powers — the phrase still made him smile — which he'd learned enough about in the last few years since he himself went to a clearing, in a forest, one summer solstice, and had his mind blown, just like Nix, Ondine, and Morgan had.

No. His ability to read the signs was more mundane. More human.

His ringtone was set to Michael Jackson's "Thriller" for unknown callers, and there was only one person who called him who was unknown. From a pay phone, just like in the old days.

"Nix."

Despite himself, Moth couldn't disguise the gruffness in his voice. An initiate's leaving his first gathering was, of course, a possibility every guide had to prepare for. But Nix's departure had been so early and sudden, and so clearly tied in with Bleek. Till now, the cutter had kept to himself, and though Moth lived in fear of his own elimination, he knew Bleek feared the same thing. Any meeting would have resulted in danger for both of them. Now Bleek was taking more chances, sensing that a ringer existed close by. Why else would a noted scion like Viv have come out of isolation, endangering herself? Moth chided himself that he had not prepared for the possibility that Bleek would actually show up at the Ring of Fire, dragging a pet along, no less. But then, that was Bleek. That was how the cutter had always been.

There was no sound for a moment, then Nix's scratchy voice broke the silence.

"You bastard."

It shocked Moth, how angry they were. Had he been so angry?

"Calm down, Nix. We've got a long road ahead of us and I suggest you get used to the fact that we're on it together."

It was something like what Moth's own guide had said at the beginning, though less obtusely. Viv had nailed it: His and Bleek's guide had failed them, though it had been a failure of attention rather than intention. Theirs had been more interested in using his newfound knowledge for his "practice" — Moth shuddered at the word the older changeling so favored to describe his human calling — than for preparing the very real, very scared, and, except for a gathering every so often, very isolated changelings for their exidis. Bleek had seen the advantage in the situation; Moth had just foundered. But failure was failure and their guide's had created potentially deadly consequences. Moth had to only look in the mirror to know that.

He was going to be different: a better teacher, less egotistical, more compassionate. Still, talking to Nix and Ondine, Moth felt like a sixth-grade punk trying out his first cigarette. He wondered what it would be like when Morgan finally contacted him.

"Where are you? Where's Ondine?"

"Ondine won't speak to me. That's your fault."

Something had changed in the changeling's voice. Though Nix had always been defiant, this new tone shaded into something darker.

"Are you listening?"

"Of course. What's happened?"

"You must know. You have to. You're our *guide,* aren't you?"

Moth took a breath. The rebelliousness in Nix's voice set his teeth on edge. Had he been so bold?

"Slow down, soldier. I don't know anything. I am your guide, but I'm not a mind reader. I know only a little more than you do. Something you would have known had you stuck around and listened to what Viv had to say —"

Moth knew it was wrong to bring it up — Nix was looking after the pet Bleek had brought, a local girl Moth recognized by sight but did not know well named Neve Clowes — but he couldn't help it. Nix's aggressiveness, his accusatory undertone, pissed him off and made it hard for him to play the role he was supposed to. He could hear Viv now: *No. Not this way. You've done it wrong. Once again. Pay attention. Focus, Moth, focus.*

"It's Neve. She's in trouble. I don't know what to do. I see — I see a light around her."

"You see a ring?" Moth's voice emerged tighter than he'd intended it. "You can see it now? On that girl?"

"I guess I can," Nix replied, offering nothing more.

"She was right," Moth said under his breath.

"What? Who was right?"

"Nothing. Listen, Nix," Moth interrupted. "There are some things I need to tell you about. Involving . . . the light you see. And Tim Bleeker. The stuff you missed when you left. Meet me at the park at sundown. Morgan will be there, and I'll get in touch with Ondine. The same place you used to meet me, up by the clearing —"

It was Nix who interrupted this time.

"Ondine won't be there. She wants nothing to do with you,

man. You have to know that. She kicked me out this afternoon. She called the cops."

Though he didn't want to acknowledge it, Moth knew it was true. He took a breath. Ondine he'd have to convince later. He had to meet the others. Bleek was planning something with the girl, Neve. Viv had surmised as much, and his ring had to be aligned so they could negotiate a response. Besides, the chain of events that would hopefully end in his own long-awaited exidis had already begun. The spark had been lit.

"Sundown," he repeated at last.

Nix responded in kind. "Sundown."

Moth closed the slim silver phone, heard its satisfying little click. What humans accomplished with nothing — no scia, no dust, no mancing — somehow, it was much more impressive. This was the hardest thing for Moth to accept when he first was initiated. There were no tricks to being a changeling. You either were or you weren't. He never liked the rigidity of it. Still didn't.

It made his heart hurt, thinking he'd leave this world, the one where tricks got played and fantasies were nurtured. In Novala, everything had an explanation. *No one gets away with anything. Ever. All things are transparent in Novala.*

And here, in preparation: only rules to follow, lemma to memorize. Scia to obey.

Heart. That he still felt his testified to the pull of his adopted tribe.

Moth knew his time was almost over. Whatever was happening with his ring, it would lead him back to the exidis, where he would finally be released. It had been promised to him for so long — its delay so harsh on his body — that he almost could not wait for Nix, Morgan, and Ondine to learn their lessons so he could join them. His door to the invisible world had been harder to find. Now it was just there in front of him.

It scared him, though, the thought of entering Novala for good. No fixed body. No death. No pain. Only total and everlasting consciousness, permeable through each brane in the bulk, able to slip in and out of lower dimensions at will. Fay. Even thinking about it made him dizzy. He had won Viv's trust, finally. Overcome his ring's early mistakes. Proven to her that he was worthy. She promised him that soon he'd have his glimpse. Now there was just this last task, and it was revealing itself so quickly that he was stunned. Somehow he'd expected to — what? Get an e-mail about it? *No, Moth.* Viv had placed him here, in Portland, to ready him for these three. A ringer and a potential scion were rarely paired, and never before in this part of the human world. Even Morgan, though a common morpha like him, was no slouch. It signaled a new opportunity in the long battle against the insidiousness of the cutters. That Moth was given the task of initiating the three meant something.

This was just as it should be: fast and furious. At the end he'd know what he was meant to know. He'd be ready — really and truly ready — for the exidis. His door would show itself, just as Viv had told him. The person who had just called him — *Nix, who comes from nothingness.* Nix was one of the keys.

✍ ✍ ✍

MORGAN KNELT BY THE BATHTUB, watching it fill, occasionally dipping her hand into the bottle–bluish green water to check its temperature. Her brother would be home soon, and she wanted to be clean.

K.A. She let his image float around her in the mist while she undid her yukata, hung it on the hook at the back of the door, and climbed into the bath. *You know how to distract him, don't you Morgana?* There was the sudden scalding, the bright pain so hot it was almost cold, and then a warm flush up her back. She sank farther. The water cupped her breasts and settled there.

Just an hour before, she had called Neve Clowes. She told her that she was calling for K.A. "He wants you to meet him at the Krak in forty-five minutes," she had told the girl, and Neve, happily, breathlessly — it was guilt Morgan heard in the younger girl's "Oh great! Sure!" and relief — agreed. K.A. wouldn't be using his phone — Coach Gonzalez outlawed cell phone calls on the team bus — and though Neve said she'd been grounded "for some lame party in the mountains she didn't even remember," Morgan knew Clowes wouldn't have anything against Neve meeting up with "the square," as she knew the old man called her brother.

"Thanks, Morgue," Neve had said. Then whispered: "I miss you." Morgan mumbled something like, "Me, too" and hung up.

She called Bleek. Told him if he wanted the pet he'd better take his chance.

"What do I owe you?"

"Just what you promised," Morgan answered.

"Tomorrow? Are you sure you're ready?" Bleek's voice had slipped into his skeevy, mocking approximation of flirting. "Do you even know where you're going?"

"I'll find out."

"Good. Good. Very fine." He laughed and his mouth moved closer to the phone. "I like the attitude. All right. Here's something that will help you, since assface will likely teach you nothing of importance anytime soon. You're a morpha. Like I am, like Moth is. Like many of the changelings are. What inhabits you can also inhabit other corpa you tame and utilize. It's your" — and Bleek paused here, turning his voice saccharine — "*gift.* Problem is, it's really, really not easy to get control of. And it's a bummer when it gets out of hand. I think your little experiments on the bunnies might remind you of that. But Moth has come along fairly well in his studies and so I suggest you listen to what he has to say in that department. And use it to our advantage."

"Okay . . ." Morgan's voice trailed off. *Our* advantage?

"Not what you were expecting, muffin?" Bleek's laughter stung her ears. "This isn't the fucking Force, Morgana. You don't get to learn all of this in a montage. You want knowledge, you work for it. You keep your eyes open and you learn."

"That's supposed to be a tip? I deliver your precious bitch to you and I get fucking meditation advice?"

"Watch your mouth. I suggest you practice listening for a while. You really have no idea what you're saying. And I've got to run. I've got an appointment to keep. Oh, and if you can, bring Nix. No. Strike that. Bring Nix. Or else."

That was all there was.

Morgan slipped back into the water, trying to let it relax her. Gift? Morgan D'Amici *defined* gifted. The problem was not *a* gift, but *which* one? *Concentrate, Morgan.* She closed her eyes. *Morpha.* The screen of her mind was a white field, thick with mist. Shapes emerged, but Morgan could not make them out. She felt her body sag into the warm water. The shapes seemed to be nothing more than denser spaces where the white coagulated, making oblong figures — nothing so recognizable, densities spun of snowy foam.

Bit by bit she felt a cold drying. The hairs on her arms stood

338

up. Her shoulderblades chafed against something hard. From somewhere not near and not far a blackness ripped. A crack, tiny at first, barely noticeable, a fissure of loneliness and foreboding. A sucking. She was not alone. Then a single black shaking tendril emerged — quivering, dark energy.

It had happened in the forest, when she was young. That's where it had all started. There were others there, older than she, in a ring. She had tried to run away but only backed against something cold. . . .

Sacrificing Neve: It was the first truly evil deed she had done.

A sudden draft sucked the air from her chest and her eyes sprung open. Water was in her mouth, in her eyes. She sputtered and coughed. Black split the edge of the door.

"Sorry!"

Morgan only had time to register the confused and bashful expression on her brother's face before he shut the door again and said from the other side: "Um. Sorry about that. I didn't know you were in the habit of taking baths in the middle of the day, Miss Hilton."

Morgan was silent. She was sitting up now, staring at the water.

K.A. coughed nervously. "Mom called. She's on her way home. She asked if we wanted to go to the Spaghetti Factory for a late lunch. I told her I'd ask you if you were working." He scraped a finger on the door, just like he would do when they were kids and he wanted to be let in. "You know. Like a family. I was gonna call Neve and see if she wanted to come, too."

Morgan lifted her head. She was aware of something instinctual happening inside of her, something tied to the vision she'd just had. *Morpha,* she repeated silently. The nights in the forest. A rattling cocoon.

"Morgue? You okay in there?"

She stood up dripping, plucked her yukata off the hook, and wrapped it around her. Its thin cotton clung to her still-wet body. She ran her fingers through her hair and looked at herself in the cloudy bathroom mirror. Black eyebrows, black shining hair, blue eyes. She was still there, and she was clean.

She opened the door and stood in the light, her yukata plunged low across her breasts.

"Hi, Kaka." She smiled a sisterly smile and touched her brother on the forearm. Mist curled up around them.

"Hey." K.A. blushed and reached over to give his sister a kiss on the cheek.

How soft she must feel, how good she must smell.

"Welcome back, bro." She reached into the bathroom and got a towel and started casually drying her hair. Seconds passed deliciously. How easy, how *right,* it all felt. Not harsh at all, nothing like disgusting Bleek with his onion breath. She'd be a different kind of cutter — a quivering slender leg emerging from a white cocoon. Foxy.

Morgan smiled and turned to walk into her room. K.A. followed.

"Lunch would be great with Mom. I haven't seen her in a few days." She looked at her brother. "So busy. *Ugh*. But nothing compared to you. How was camp? God, welcome back, Kaka! I missed you."

A shadow passed over his eyes, slight, but discernible.

"I'm good. Coach gave me hell, though, something about being toughest on the strongest or some bullshit. I love it, but man, I'm looking forward to doing something else after college. I don't think I'm going to try to go pro after all. Four years of college and that's it for me." K.A. cleared his throat and turned over a silver snake paperweight on his sister's desk. "Did Neve call when I was gone? We talked when I first got down there, but for the last few days I've been trying her cell phone and it's been off."

Morgan looked into the mirror at her brother, who stood behind her as usual, eyes downcast.

"Anyway, I was just going to go by Jacob's and pick her up, surprise her so that we could all go to lunch." He checked his watch.

She cleared her throat. It was mostly for effect, but it worked. K.A. looked up again and spoke.

"Sound good?"

"Listen." Morgan paused, biting her lip as if to signal, *I know how hard this must be. I don't want to tell you this, but I have to.* "I didn't want to get into this with you till you were back for a while, but —"

"What?" K.A. searched his sister's face. She willed herself to flush.

"I'm sorry I'm the one to tell you this, but . . . Neve's been really out of it. She's been hanging around with Tim Bleeker since you've been away, and last I heard —" Morgan turned to face the doorway, pausing tactically. "She was with Nix. At the party everyone in Portland was talking about. Someone saw them together."

K.A. narrowed his eyes. "The Ring of Fire? How do you know? Did you go? Who saw them?"

"Look, I just heard. It was going around at Krakatoa. You know I don't spread rumors." She stopped. "Nor do I believe them . . . usually. But I haven't heard from Neve since you left. She just split. Disappeared. No one really knew where she went, but I kept hearing stuff about her and Bleek, and then Nix. Look, everyone knows Nix uses dust. Gets it from Bleek, in fact."

K.A. put his hands to his eyes. Morgan knew her brother was about to cry, and though she knew it didn't really matter whether he did or not, she didn't have the stomach at the moment to soothe him.

"K.A., she's fucked up. You don't need that in your life."

342

"I'd better call her."

"Why? So you can listen to her druggie apologies? You know what they're like. Out for themselves. *Selfish*." Morgan stepped closer. "You remember. I know you remember. When Dad was drinking? How bad it was? How he didn't care about anyone else but his pathetic, red-faced self? Look. If Neve is out of it, if she's not calling you back, it means she's hitting bottom of some sort, and you know what? That's exactly where she should be. She needs to be there before she gets her life together and recognizes what she has — what she should be thankful for."

She emphasized the thankful part.

"But I can't just not call her. I —"

"Why the hell not? She hasn't called you. And Nix? Come on, Kaka. He's *supposedly* one of your best friends. What the hell do you think they were doing together? Crossword puzzles? They don't hang out. You know they don't. And wasn't Nix all up in Ondine as of last week?"

A blink confirmed her question and she continued, faster now. "Something's up, you know it, and the last thing you need is to get involved. You have a future, K.A. You're meant for better things. We both are. You can't get hung up on someone who just triggers the same shit Dad brings up in you. It's just not fair. You deserve more."

She watched him, coached him the way she had since they were kids. Morgan, the one who was strong, who could take it, who could wake her father up from where he'd passed out in the middle of the living room and coax him into bed with another PBR. Who comforted K.A. when Yvonne took off for the night. Who was her little brother's mother and sister and best friend.

She cupped a hand around his nape and let her fingers run through the darker curls there, pulling his head close to her to hug him. Gentle and firm. Sisterly.

"It's going to be okay," she whispered. "Just let her be for a while. You've done what you can. She has to make her own decisions about what she wants." Morgan squeezed her brother once more and tilted her forehead toward his till they touched. "I'm not going to let you get hurt, little bro. I'm not. I just won't."

An old-fashioned ring — "Provence," it was called, and Morgan set her phone to it because she thought it sounded classy — sounded in her bedroom and the girl released him, her hand lingering on his cheek.

"That's me. Now call Mom and tell her that we'll meet her at the Spaghetti Factory. Just us three, the family, huh? Garlic bread. *Mm.*" She smiled at K.A. and he tried his best to smile back. Then she sidled past the vanity, toward her bedroom. "I'll be ready to go in five minutes." Morgan stopped and regarded her brother thoughtfully. "We'll get through this. We always do."

K.A. wasn't smiling when he turned on his heel to go looking for his own cell to call their mother, but Morgan knew she'd done the trick. She'd gotten him to cry, at least. That was something. That would stop him from calling Neve again, or looking for her, at least till tomorrow when she could see what was really going on. By then the tart would be Bleek's problem.

In her bedroom she was pleased to see the clothes laid out on her bed, ready for wearing. Morgan had forgotten she'd put them there before her bath. She searched around for her cell phone, but when she found it the ringing had ceased. Before she could scroll down the list to see who had called, an SMS arrived.

"Private," it read. She opened it.

THE PARK AT SUNDOWN. BY THE LOOKOUT. M

She didn't need to know who wrote it, though the single M confirmed it. K.A.'s voice floated in as he spoke to his mother, giving a rundown of the bus trip back home, setting up their meeting together for lunch. *So innocent.* Morgan shook her head and half smiled. How easy this had been. Even with Bleek.

Moth was a different story. She was glad the sun set later in the summer. She would need the time.

∾   ∾   ∾

NIGHT WAS FALLING, out past the plane's wings, in the distance toward Chicago. Darkness swallowed the horizon. Ink, oil. Permanent marker. Her mother's hair. The color of the woods in winter, hearses, expensive suits, top hats, and widow's weeds. Long coats and lava rock and that woman's hair. Black. The name she — Ondine — was called. The color of her mother and her father. *Mother and father,* suddenly and irrevocably made uncertain.

Ondine leaned her head against the window. She had begun to make a drawing in her journal of the darkening sky. "Night that comes too fast," she had scribbled below the sketch. Nothing special, a technique of crosshatching she'd learned from Raphael that intensified darkness while allowing for the light necessary to give a drawing depth. For there was light in pitch-black, Raphael reminded his students. "The light is in you. If you're there seeing it, you will detect it, even as slight as it is."

Ondine needed that advice now; she was moving too fast. But what could she do? She had asked the question, *What's wrong with me?* and her father had answered it: *Nothing.*

From her father and mother she'd learned to trust not just what was visible, but what could be demonstrated, proven. For her fourth birthday party, Ralph had helped her blow up balloon after balloon till father's and daughter's cheeks were both sore and their tongues tasted like rubber. A typical-enough occurrence, but Ralph Mason had used the occasion to demonstrate the fact that air, though invisible, still had mass. If it were "empty" or "nothing," as men once believed, then the tautly stretched red and blue and yellow balloons would remain slack no matter how much they blew into them.

Physics and birthday cake: just another party at the Masons. That same air held aloft the wings of the plane that sped her to her parents. Except that what her parents had told her about her very birth, the circumstances that defined her, wasn't real. They had lied to her, the one they loved the most.

For the second time in her life, Ondine felt a tear roll down her cheek and she wiped it away self-consciously, glancing over to see if the woman reading a magazine next to her had seen. She hadn't; she was actually asleep, the magazine open in her lap, her head tilting toward the aisle, a line of drool beginning to bubble out of her open mouth. The woman's obliviousness somehow depressed Ondine even further. Why the tears now, after so long? She thought about that one day with Nix, after the party; she had cried then, too. Was it that she wanted someone to notice her? At the same time, she wanted to pull a tissue from her purse and wipe the woman's drool away. She wanted to mother her. She wanted her mother.

Now there was no stopping the tears. All Ondine could do was cover her face with her hands and try to keep her shoulders from shaking.

"Are you all right?"

The voice was soft and female and seemed to come from

somewhere far above Ondine, but when she opened her eyes she saw that it was a flight attendant leaning over her, speaking in her practiced flight attendant voice.

"Can I get you anything?"

The woman was pretty, slight and spry with tilted brown eyes and soft, coiling brown hair gathered in a bun. Ondine found herself surprised that she was black. She figured the woman was about her mother's age. Usually she didn't go for ethnic solidarity stuff, but today the fact of the woman's brown skin — and her big liquid eyes, understanding and compassionate — calmed her.

She straightened up and nodded. "Yeah, yeah. I'm all right." She pointed to her nose. "Allergies."

A knowing nod signaled that both of them knew her wet eyes and red nose had nothing to do with allergies, 30,000 feet above the earth. But the flight attendant played along anyway.

"Recycled air," she whispered, mindful of the sleeping drooler. "Terrible for the sinuses. Can I bring you something? A juice or a soda?" She smiled. "Might help clear something up."

"That's okay." Ondine straightened again, pulling her shirt down and adjusting the collar of her jacket. She was aware that she hadn't changed clothes since the trip with Nix. Her mother would *tsk*.

Her mother. And who, exactly, was that?

The flight attendant paused, frowning, and Ondine thought she was going to try to help again. But all she did was reach into the jacket pocket of her fitted uniform and pull out a cocktail napkin, and, with an amazingly deft touch, wick the moisture off the chin of the woman sitting next to her. The nonchalant tenderness of the gesture nearly sent Ondine into a fresh spasm of sobs — if only her problems could be fixed so easily — and it was all she could do to smile at the flight attendant before the woman pocketed her napkin and continued down the aisle.

Ondine turned to the window. It was dark, so all she saw was her blurry reflection. She closed her eyes lest the image set off a fresh bout of existential confusion. It wouldn't be bad to get a little sleep. She felt her limbs unwind, loosening her seat belt so she could slide deeper into her seat. Not a minute later she felt a rustling. Her neighbor must be getting up to go to the bathroom, she figured — but when she opened her eyes she saw that the drooler was still asleep. Ondine's tray table had been lowered, and on it sat a glass of club soda — her favorite drink on a long flight — complete with a lime and a swizzle stick, a white cocktail napkin beneath. On the napkin were written the words:

Tomorrow morning. Grant Park, the rose garden. We can talk there.

Her lips felt dry, her throat and mouth parched. She had wanted that club soda.

She pulled the napkin from under the drink and crumpled it up and put it in her jacket pocket. She looked to her neighbor, who was in the same position she had been last time Ondine checked, her mouth slightly open, her head listing to the left, almost to her collarbone. Everyone else was asleep.

A bell chimed. The FASTEN SEAT BELT sign had been lit. A woman's voice came over the PA.

"Ladies and gentleman, Captain Thomas has turned on the fasten seat belt sign in preparation for landing at Chicago O'Hare. Please return to your seats if you're moving about the cabin and —"

Tray tables, seat backs. Ondine was just about to take a sip from her club soda when a flight attendant appeared to collect her cup. This one had frizzy blond hair and coral lipstick and a smoker's ring of wrinkles around her lips. Ondine rose to look for the earlier stewardess, bumping her tray table and causing her seatmate to wake suddenly with a small "Oh dear!"

The woman started, her hands flying. The glass of club soda spilled all over Ondine's lap.

"Hon, tray table up." The blond stewardess reached across her for her empty cup.

Ondine, sopping, forced herself to speak.

"I'm sorry. Can you call the stewardess —"

"Flight attendant?" the woman corrected, her eyebrows raised.

"I mean flight attendant. Can you call the flight attendant who was just here? Who gave me my club soda?"

"I'm sorry, hon, but we're about to land. Can I help you in

350

some way?" As she spoke she deposited Ondine's cup in a trash bag and locked the tray table up in one continuous, well-practiced motion. She even managed to push Ondine's seat-back button, so that she was propelled suddenly forward. "Sorry," the woman said through a tight smile. "FAA regulations. Here are some napkins."

"It's okay; it's okay." Ondine readjusted, trying to keep the woman's attention. "She's black, the stew — the flight attendant. She gave me my club soda and I wanted to ask her something."

The blond woman's face was blank. She shook her head and pursed her seamed lips. Ondine felt her seatmate trying to pat away some of the water that had spilled on her knees, mumbling, "Oh dear, I'm sorry. I'm so sorry."

"No flight attendant on this aircraft who's black, darling." And, smiling blandly, she turned down the aisle.

Ondine pulled the napkin from her jacket pocket with wet fingers and looked at it. The words were still there: *Tomorrow morning. Grant Park.*

She looked out the window at the sky, completely dark now. Her heart beat faster. In the reflection she could see her neighbor pulling a packet of tissue out of her purse.

"I am really such a klutz. God —"

"It's okay. It's okay." Ondine turned and showed her the napkin. "Can you read this to me?"

The woman looked up once, as if to try to understand why

she wanted her to do the task. She put the soaked tissues in the seat-back pocket in front of her and began to pronounce the words:

"Tomorrow —" She paused, cleared her throat, and started again. "Tomorrow morning. Grant Park, the rose garden. We can talk there." Her accent was slightly nasal: *tawk* for talk. Ondine figured she was from the East Coast. "Okay?"

"Thanks. I'm just . . . I'm just having trouble with my vision."

The neighbor nodded knowingly. She had curly brown hair and deep-set, pinkish eyes. "Happens all the time on flights. Believe me. I used to sell industrial chemicals — traveled all over creation. Good *gawd* my eyes were dry. Drops?" She rifled through her purse and pulled out a bottle of Visine.

"No. No, thanks." Ondine waved it away.

"Listen, I'm really sorry about the drink."

"It's all right. Don't worry about it." The water was the last thing on her mind. She concentrated on what was happening around her. The woman talking. The lights of the grid of Chicago rising up to meet the plane, the dimming cabin, movements of one of the flight attendants somewhere ahead. A baby's cough.

"Well, it was just really klutzy of me. And I deprived you of necessary hydration! These long flights, they're killers. When I was in corporate, I told my husband, Mike, I said, 'Mike, remind me to buy Visine before I go on a trip.' Of course, he's the forgetful one. . . . I typically am the, you know, anal one. Virgo. But Sagittarius moon, which makes us get along well, Mike and me. Anyway . . ."

And the saleswoman of Ondine's former life continued this way until they landed. Mike; astrology; Des Plaines, Illinois; Visine versus propolis eyedrops; the Midwest; O'Hare; and reverse commute. Chicago hot dogs versus East Coast franks. *The rose garden in Grant Park. Oh, that is beautiful.* Ondine didn't have to speak once. Normally she would have been irritated to the point of nausea. But tonight — with the lights of Chicago approaching quickly under them, like hieroglyphics explaining some future self Ondine would not, could not, understand — she was grateful for the distraction.

CHAPTER 19

THE MIDLEVEL BRICK BUILDINGS of Portland's seamier district bordering Burnside tapered to a sprawling D'Amici's, a car dealership, cell shop, pizza parlor, and finally, the pretty, shaded streets heading up toward Forest Park. The apartment buildings ended, yielding bigger, handsome houses, and Nix stayed to the outside of the sidewalk, avoiding eye contact with the few desperate housewives and their mini SUV strollers out on a cold, windy day. He would keep his eyes on the ground, but not for long. He was coming into something and he knew it.

Without much effort he gained the top of the first hill and started to move through the forest pathways that afforded a shortcut to the lookout. He remembered these trails. He thought of Finn, and missed him, and Evelyn, and his old, dust-mellowed life. It was late afternoon; the sunset that was supposed to define the meeting time was more of a hopeful projection than a reality; the sun was no more than a vague splotch of lighter gray sinking somewhere toward the hills behind him. There had been a brief break in the rain during the morning, but it was coming again, from the north, and Nix knew that whatever meeting there was would be a short one. He imagined Morgan D'Amici wouldn't tolerate the whipping rain for more than a minute or two. Her carefully blown-out hair wouldn't stand for it.

He pulled his jacket around him, conscious of the fact that he'd now worn these clothes for several days straight and didn't smell a thing. *Crazy fairies' shit don't stink.* The unlikely thought made him laugh. He'd had a sense of humor once.

The bench was there, right where it used to be. On it, Moth, with his back to Nix, looking a bit more hunched than usual. Next to him sat a figure in a toxic orange Final Home parka, the hood pulled up, smaller than Moth. Morgan. On time, of course. Little Miss Can't-Be-Wrong. They looked like any other disaffected, partially employed, overly educated young Portland hipster couple, watching bad weather for kicks. Nix half expected Moth's arm to casually drape around her. They'd kiss. Then some entanglement involving facial piercings.

He walked up sideways, careful to let them see him first.

"Nix." It was Morgan who spoke, almost kindly, a greeting he did not expect. Then Moth offered a hand. Nix was surprised to see the little X tattoo still there, as if all the signs of the world had changed since their last meeting. Which, in a way, they had.

Moth, seeing his gaze, exposed his wrist.

"That's the mark. You probably recognize it already. All

lings have one. You'll be getting one at the next gathering. You too, Morgan." Moth moved his eyes to the girl.

Nix took Moth's hand and shook it, and nodded to Morgan. She nodded back, her face warmed from the reflection of the orange parka, against which her eyes, he noticed, looked particularly large and blue.

"So," Moth said.

He's never done this before, Nix thought, and as if in answer, Moth cleared his throat and began.

"I've never done this before. So —" He moved his eyes side to side. "You'll have to forgive me if I fuck up now and again. The first fuck-up is that Ondine isn't here. And that you, Nix," Moth said, nodding at him, "missed the initial lesson. Neither of these things is unmanageable." He smiled affably and Nix realized this was his great gift. Moth's smile was big and white and winning. And until proven otherwise, not very trustworthy.

"You'll realize that fay like to speak in precise terms, so *unmanageable* is one. *Fatal* would be a misstatement, since very little is, in fact, fatal to us. To our bodies, yes." He switched his glance to Morgan and grimaced. "But that's for later. Right now I want to make it clear to both of you that besides Ondine, you are it for this ring. There are no other new changelings right now in Portland. And since you already sort of know each other — that makes my job easier. It's the one good thing about smaller places. In New York, god, I've met guides that have ten, fifteen lings they have to deal with. Not that this is so awful, but man, it's a lot of work. Anyway . . ."

Moth's tangents and shaking knee irritated Nix. *What about Neve Clowes?* he wanted to scream. *And Tim Bleeker!* Standing listening to Moth ramble, Nix wondered whether he had missed Viv's instructions for a reason. Was he meant to figure this out by himself, using his own senses? Otherwise, he would risk faltering under the shaky guidance of the one who was now moving erratically, circling, circling, into a long story about his experience with the bust in Eugene, a story complete with keg stands and vomit.

"He was fucked *up*, man." Moth laughed. "*So* fucked up — I think he was pissing on someone's stereo when he finally passed out —"

Nix interrupted him. "Moth, *dude*. We've already heard this story in several versions. You're kind of — legendary, you know? Can we get to the point?"

Moth's face got serious and Nix sensed something there he hadn't noticed before. Hardness? Protection? Morgan, too, watched the older boy from the corner of her too-blue eyes.

He stood up. "Sit down, son."

"Naw, I'm fine."

"No. You're not. Sit down."

Nix felt his legs weaken and then burn, as if exposed to some chemical. He reached down to touch them, but Moth shoved him toward the bench and Nix, unclear as to what was happening to him, unwillingly took his seat.

"Good. Now. Some people take a little time to get into things. Don't be a punk, all right? I'm your guide, and that's how it's going to be for the time being. Like it or not. If you're as good as Viv says you are, you will learn from a changeling as clumsy and simple as me. Then you'll go on to heights I can only dream of. Got it?"

Nix nodded and the burning in his legs ceased.

"You arrogant fucks. The reason why I was telling you that long-ass story was that Bleek was my partner. Okay? I know Bleek. I've known him for a long time. Bleek was in my ring. He and I were close — as close as the two of you will get."

Morgan and Nix looked at each other, and Morgan dropped her eyes.

"Our guide was terrible. Not really interested in preparing us for the exidis. Which is, as you already know . . . well, it's more than a little scary. Anyway, we didn't understand. We had this idea — this first idea. Why not see what this dust stuff the scia were giving to us at the Ring of Fire would do to the general population? We already knew it had once been used for the pets — this wasn't exactly broadcast, but our guide —" Moth shook his head. "Our guide, he trusted us. Too much. So that's what we did. Bleek got a supply and we started leaking it. Just a little at first, mostly for girls at parties, or to make something happen."

He looked at the two. "It's the worst thing about this; I'll tell you right now. The boredom. While you're waiting for the exidis. All you want to do, once you find out, is see what it will get you. Nothing in the human world seems off-limits anymore." Moth's eyes were glazed. "Can you imagine how boring that is?"

Nix and Morgan stared, mystified, and Moth shook it off and continued. "Anyway. You will. So it was kind of a joke, see? A *lark*. Except it wasn't. Bleek had it all figured out. He'd found out way more about what the stuff could do to humans than I had. The man had a plan, you know? Me, I was just having fun."

Morgan spoke. "And what happened?" Nix was surprised her voice was so measured.

"You know."

"I *know*? What are you talking about?"

"You were at that party, Morgan. I remember. And Bleek remembers, too. We've known about you for a long time. You were too young to be at that kind of party, by the way." Moth smiled, and some touch of big brother came out. "But then, you always were a little precocious."

Morgan looked away and Nix wished he had access to the girl's thoughts. He couldn't read her in the way he did Moth, or even Ondine, despite those clear, light eyes.

"Anyway, for your edification, Nix, since you were in Alaska — we got arrested, no one posted bail, but Bleek got off somehow. I spent three months locked up. *Jail,* man. I couldn't do anything about it. There are things we can do, with magnetization and electricity — what I just did to you — and some stuff using the bodies of other living creatures . . . morphing, basically —" Nix saw Morgan look up then and thought of the burning in his legs a few moments before. *Morphing?* Was that what the crow was, in the clearing with Bleek and Neve, at the Ring of Fire? But Moth was speaking quickly and Nix realized he had better pay attention if he was going to do anything about Neve.

". . . But I didn't know any of that then. I was just getting started. And Viv did exactly *nada* to change my situation. Maybe she was trying to teach me a lesson, or test me." Moth observed the two, looking into their eyes to make his point. "The scia are very careful about getting found out. They have to live in their bodies much longer than the rest of us and must conserve their energies. They are also very particular about who undertakes the exidis. If your will is not aligned, you don't go. If you have a cutter in your ring, you don't go." He paused. "Until the cutter is eliminated. But we'll get to that."

Moth sighed and wrapped his arms around himself. "Anyway, you can imagine it had quite an effect on my ring. The time for our exidis came and went. Our guide — he fell apart — and Bleek was designated a cutter. Now I figure it was all a setup on Bleek's part — the whole thing. He chose his path. And since then" — he cleared his throat and looked up at the mountains — "he's been using it for the hunt."

Nix looked over at Morgan. Her eyes were as blank as his probably were.

"The hunt," Moth repeated, then shook his head. "It's not something the scia like to advertise. The hunt is what we call —" He looked embarrassed. "It's what we call mating." He cleared his throat and restarted. "For reproductive purposes. Totally unsanctioned."

Morgan and Nix must have continued to look confused because Moth stopped and stared. "Bleek's been trying to capture a pet. So that she can have his offspring . . . or something like that. I'm trying to figure it out. It has to do with the change, the initial habitation."

"Oh," they said, almost in unison. There was a knowing tone to Morgan's "oh," but Nix's was uncomprehending. He had no idea what Moth was talking about.

"He'll need a ringer for that."

"A ringer?" Something about the word sounded familiar.

Moth held up his hand. "He doesn't want to leave the human world, obviously. He doesn't want to give up his mortal body. The practice is *forbidden*," he emphasized. "There's no reason for it. In the old days, when the technology was worse and the exidis relied on natural events, random lightning, that kind of thing, the scia kept humans in bondage, used them to reproduce and then effected the inhabitation. That's what a pet was: just genetic material for a new changeling." His eyes darted to Morgan's, and Nix thought he could detect the faintest blush. "We're not strong enough to reproduce on our own . . . together." His eyes fell. "Nor do we have time. The period between finding out and the exidis is short — a year or two at most. Anyway, now, with dust and with the Ring of Fire it's different. A few pets are still kept, I know, and some are used by cutters to do their bidding —" He frowned. "But the practice makes me sick.

"They're kept in horrible conditions." He spoke earnestly. "Underground, in caves. In places . . . outside of the normal world. It doesn't happen so much anymore — there are plenty of corpa around and inhabitation techniques have improved — but Bleek grew up like that, in the limina — the edge places between this world and the next." Moth shook his head and looked at the ground. "Usually they just spend their lives in a kind of dark haze, but Bleek was special, intelligent and good at identifying potential changelings."

He moved from Morgan to Nix. "That's one of our tasks while we're here, along with preparing for the exidis. We must . . . to increase our kind. We must give consciousness its chance. Humanity, it's not strong enough. Look how we've messed everything up."

Moth took a breath. "In any case, they let him out into

the human world. He became part of my ring. Usually cutters cause trouble for a while and then die, which you do fairly quickly if you don't go through the exidis. . . . Nix. You heard that part, right?"

Nix shook his head and Moth blanched.

"You can't let your body die, Nix." Moth spoke very slowly. "It's absolutely forbidden. The worst thing that could happen to a changeling. What becomes of us — it's more horrible than any human can imagine."

"*A particle of pain*," Morgan whispered sarcastically, "*passed from one living being to the next, for eternity.*"

Moth stared at her. "It isn't funny. It isn't even something we should talk about." He turned back to Nix. "You will never, ever die. You will just keep hurting. Over and over and over again. And you will always be conscious of it. That is the burden of the fay. We need a living creature to inhabit while we're in this transitional state. Only in Novala can we take our true form."

Both were silent. Nix tried to look at Morgan but she was turned away.

"So the cutters. Their bodies die or they're eliminated, by changelings who are trained to do that kind of thing. They're usually easy to spot. They have the sign" — he showed his wrist again — "but they're old. Much older than they should be. And they smell." Morgan stifled a laugh and Moth again shot her a look. "If they've been given a pass by the scia —" The guide faltered a little here and Nix wondered what he was omitting. "They have a cross through their X. Wicklings. Weak, not evil. Bound for death. Fast. But Bleek is different. He's a cutter through and through. He's smart and powerful and wants to stick around. He knows the limina, and he'll do anything to survive. Clearly he's planning something. I just don't know what it is. So Bleek tried with your friend Evelyn first." Moth nodded to Nix curtly. "But she didn't work out, so now he's on to Neve Clowes. The pet needs to be out of it, pliable. Addicted, basically. To dust. He'll take her somewhere —"

Moth turned and faced Nix. "The ring you're seeing is some indication of her demise. Bleek won't keep her alive long after he's used her for what he needs."

Nix felt his mouth go dry. The businesslike tone Moth slipped into when he mentioned Evelyn and Neve struck him. As did the easy way he spoke about the rings Nix saw; as if it were the most normal thing in the world to see light around people when they were about to die.

"The ring?"

"You're a ringer. You monitor the mortality of the body at the beginning and at the end. During the change and during the exidis. Every ring needs you; without you it would be too dangerous. We've been waiting for you, Nix. Your ring has been waiting for you. You're a seer. You've got the power of life and death. Your gift is . . . it's a necessity."

"And yours is important, too, Morgan." Moth hurried to include the girl. "Have you had a sense of it?"

She shook her head — too quickly, Nix noted — but Moth didn't seem to notice.

"You will. Soon. I'll help you." His eyes turned back to Nix. "The whole thing about being a cutter is that you're addicted to this life. The human world. Even though it's doomed." A shadow passed in front of Moth's eyes. "But I guess that's why Bleek wants you. That's why he's been giving you dust. That's why he lured you to him at the Ring of Fire. That's why he didn't kill you. If Ondine had been with you he would have eliminated her, surely. Both of you." Moth nodded at Morgan and she took the news without blinking. "He needs a ringer for whatever he's planning to do."

Moth delivered the news as if he'd been reading the weather report. Nix let his mind unravel the tangled thread of what he was hearing. Pets he understood. Dust — yes. It was needed to effect a measure of control over the human body as it was inhabited and during the exidis to Novala. And the ringers — those made the most sense, since he'd been living with his visions his entire life. He even understood the importance of keeping his body alive. But the body he lived in, had spent almost eighteen years in . . . If Nix and Morgan and Ondine were inhabiting human bodies, if the bodies had been "inhabited" sometime during their childhood, then there was something — no, *someone,* a human being, an actual person, stuck in his body — or he was stuck in someone's body, or —

Here is where he stopped. Where? Where did the real humans go?

"But, the human, me . . . where do I go? Where am I?"

Morgan spoke over him. "How long has this been happening?"

Though Nix couldn't see her face — the orange hood obscured it — he felt she must be as confused as he felt. Moth chose to answer her.

"Since . . ." He looked up at the sky and shrugged. "Since I don't know. Since whenever. Since forever. We've been here since humans developed consciousness. Since they learned to tell stories about things they didn't understand. That's what the legends said. Fairies, fay, pixies. All the same thing. Just not how they pictured it. No wings. No Tinker Bell. 'Fay' means spirit — energy — intelligence unbound from matter. A power, but fractured, manifold. But we need the human body, the human brain, to take shape, to organize ourselves for the higher spheres. Otherwise we would simply be diffuse energy, no more powerful, singular, or lasting than a puff of wind, a crackle of static. That mountain over there." He pointed to Mt. Hood in the distance. "But changelings — us." He locked his eyes to Nix's, then Morgan's. "We are a median step to the next dimension. Our brains act as gatherers and conduits for the current that electrifies everything. That defines life itself. That's why we're called changelings. We change energy. We create focused spirit. We are the only hope universal consciousness has. Humans used to kill us, okay? Roast us, beat us. They knew we were different. Not like what we should be. They'd throw us in fires, boil us, keep us tied up. We died by the thousands, millions, who knows. Look." Moth stared. "Nix. Morgan. You have a year or two, max, to learn what you need to. Then you get pulled in. The shortness of the changeling phase is so that the experience isn't too hard on your body. This is a long-evolved process. The fay don't want to hurt the humans. They *need* them. They need them to gather consciousness together. There isn't enough heavy matter in Novala —"

He paused and waved his hand. "This is all in the lemma — the knowledge. You'll learn it soon. But in answer to your question, Nix: Your body — the human you're inhabiting — won't remember any of this. That's what the dust was for. Ondine — her parents will come back and she'll resume her life. Morgan will go to Princeton or whatever. You'll go back to Alaska if you want to. We've made this all so it isn't hard on your body. That's why it's so important that we deal with this thing with Bleek immediately. After he uses you, he'll eliminate you. Kill your corpus. Do you understand?" Nix nodded and Moth mumbled, "Fortunately, I don't think he knows about Ondine yet —"

Morgan spoke. "He knows about Ondine."

"What?" Moth faced the girl. "How do you know that?"

Her eyes were flat, but Nix saw the slightest tensing in her neck muscles. Right then he ceased to trust her.

"He told me."

Moth tightened. "You saw Bleek."

The girl blinked her assent. "He tried to corner me. In the forest. I fought him off." She stared at Moth, and Nix could feel the barely concealed contempt in her eyes. Did every ring start off this badly? "No thanks to you. This little mountaintop picnic. It's a little late, isn't it, Moth? Considering what you think Bleek has planned?"

Moth's silence made Nix feel that there were worse things than Tim Bleeker in this new world.

"Fortunately, I happen to know he's wrapped up in another matter." She gazed at the older boy calmly. "Yes, he's after Neve. My brother's girlfriend. The girl Nix so valiantly tried to save at the Ring of Fire. So I imagine he's not going to have *too* much time to chase after Ondine." She sighed and faced Nix for the first time since they'd started talking. "So let me get this straight. You see some kind of ring or something around Neve Clowes, which means that she's going to . . ." She let the sentence hang there. Moth looked at the ground, speechless. Nix knew he'd have to fill in the pertinent information.

His voice was flat. "Die. Once I see the ring, people die."

"Oh." Morgan bit her lip but didn't move her eyes.

How strange it was to finally talk about it. After so many years of keeping the biggest secret of his life, here Nix was, revealing it on a Portland hillside to two kids barely less screwed up than himself.

"So what are you going to do?" Morgan asked, her voice merely curious.

"What am I going to *do*? Well, I guess that's why I came here this evening, to ask this asshole" — Nix flicked a finger at Moth, standing with his hands in his jacket pockets, still looking at the ground — "what the hell I'm supposed to be doing here. *How I'm supposed to help.* But if you haven't noticed in our little conversation, gothic ambience aside, our quote unquote *guide* doesn't have a clue about what to do next and how the hell we're supposed to settle into this new *identity* of being *changelings*. Fairies, Morgan. In case the word 'fay' threw you. Flying fucking fairies —"

"I said we didn't fly —" Moth started. Nix ignored him.

"Now" — he shook his finger again at Moth, who was squinting at the younger boy, leaning back but his feet still planted in quiet defiance — "there is a girl who all of us know, your supposed *best friend*, Morgan, who is in serious trouble. Not to mention Ondine. If you can't help, Moth, then we need to talk to that lady — Viv or whatever her name is."

Moth shook his head. "Scia can't see what's going on. They are not omnipotent. They're changelings, like we are. Just more trained. Only the fay can hear all, see all —"

Nix started. "Then how the hell do you know —" But Morgan cut him off.

"Anyway, Neve can't be my friend," she said flatly, "because she's a human. And," she added, sneering at Nix, "you're an asshole."

Behind the defiant, unambiguous stare, he could feel Morgan's real confusion, even a trace of fear. Out loud she was claiming this new identity because her other life — her human life — had little to offer. He could relate. Besides, he knew even less than she did. But still. Matterless creatures from another dimension who you couldn't speak to, couldn't communicate with, just had to believe in . . . ?

He peered at Moth. "I don't believe you. I don't believe anything you're saying."

Moth didn't look surprised. "No. You wouldn't."

He grabbed Morgan by the shoulders just then, drawing her to him till she stood under his jutting chin. At the same time, he drew a knife out of his jacket pocket, which he immediately brought to the girl's throat, just inside her parka. The tip of the blade, Nix could see, edged into her pale skin, drawing a wisp of bright blood. Instantly she started to burn, a thick yellow ring around her that was different from the ones he'd seen on other people. She looked to the side once, then straight ahead at Nix. Her eyes bore the raw fear of an animal that knows it's about to be put down.

"How could you —"

"You're sick," Nix whispered. Moth only stared.

"So what explains it, Nix? Huh? A second ago Morgan wasn't going to die. But right now, she will, even if I have to doom both of us. And you know it. You can see it. I know you can. I swear I'll do it. You're that important, Nix. You're a ringer. You guarantee our making it through. Otherwise we're stuck. Larva with brains, bound for the grave. That's all we are."

"Nix, please —"

Morgan was choking against the blade and slowly the fire around her lessened. Nix knew he was being convinced.

"We have the ability to plug into the godhead. That is fay. Each of us knows it. Morgan knows it — has known it since she was a child. You know it, Nix. You've been inhabited, endowed. You out of everyone. This is your burden and your responsibility. This world is not all there is —"

"No!" Nix cried. "I can't —"

He turned on his heel to run when a beam of light hit his eyes, temporarily blinding him. He raised a hand to shield his face and heard a familiar, raspy voice blow toward him in the rising wind and rain.

"Nix? Is that you?"

He dropped his hand. He heard Morgan behind him, calling. Then she abruptly stopped.

"Jacob?"

"Nix . . . Nix!" An agitation moved toward him and there was Jacob Clowes's raincoat-covered midriff, lit by the reflection of the flashlight, now skipping around, checking the faces of the people behind Nix.

"Morgan D'Amici?"

"Mr. Clowes —"

"Have you spoken to your brother? Is he home from camp?"

For a moment Nix was confused. Why was Jacob Clowes in the park? Why did he have a flashlight? Before he could think further, Morgan answered. Her voice was calm and polite, as if meeting in the park at dusk in the rain were the most normal thing in the world. As if Moth hadn't just been holding a knife to her throat.

"Yes, Mr. Clowes . . ." Only a slight tremor betrayed her. "He's home. He's there now. I was just . . . we were just meeting here. We were going to the movies. We're all going to the movies."

Jacob obviously didn't care about movies or anything else. His voice was high-pitched. "Do you know if he's spoken to Neve?"

"Not that I know of. Wait — yeah, I remember him saying he called her cell but it was off."

"Oh my god." Jacob's voice broke. "Oh my god. Nix." Jacob turned. "Have you seen her? Has she called you?"

"I haven't seen her since . . . since this morning. With you. I — I thought everything was —"

"Neve is missing. She's gone somewhere. We had an appointment. She said she was going to the Krak, to meet K.A. I called and she's not there and I can't — I can't reach her. Her cell — oh, god." Nix felt a desperate hand on his sleeve. "Please, you've got to help me. She left around noon. She said she'd be back in two hours. After we saw you. She . . . I don't know. I took a nap and when I woke up she was gone. I called her cell but she never picked up, and she hasn't come home. Nix." Jacob was pulling on him now, shaking his arm. "You have to help me."

He felt Morgan beside him, moving toward the older man.

"Mr. Clowes, I work at Krakatoa. I can ask the manager."

"The police, they can't do anything yet. I came up here thinking I'd find someone who knew her. This guy — Tim Bleeker. Do you know him?"

"I've seen him around," Morgan answered.

"I thought some of her friends might know where to find him. Like K.A. K.A. knows where she goes —"

"Yes, yes. Of course he does." Nix noticed Morgan's pale white hand squeezing and smoothing Clowes's arm. He himself couldn't have reached out that way to the old man.

"Do you have any idea where she might have gone?"

When Jacob spoke his voice cracked. "No. I don't. I just — I didn't want to know about it — what was happening to her. I didn't want to see it. Now —"

Morgan's face bowed and Nix could see the girl willing him to believe. "It's not too late, Mr. Clowes. It's just been a few hours. We'll find Neve. Go home. Nix and I will call K.A. and get started tracking her down. We'll call you when we have a plan. In the meantime," — she looked at Nix as if getting his confirmation, and then turned back — "you go home. Talk to your wife, call the police, and we'll call you in an hour or so, when we have more information."

Jacob was nodding, staring. Nix found himself wanting to believe Morgan, too. She was so — he searched for the word. Convincing. She was so convincing, he realized. No matter which role she played.

There was a confused shaking of hands, and Morgan and Jacob Clowes hugged, as if they had known each other for years, and within a matter of seconds the old man was walking off toward the road, the only evidence of him in the mounting dark a flashlight skipping over the grass and darkening foliage ahead of him. Nix could only whisper.

"Morgan. What's going on?"

"We're going to find her. We're going to find her, wherever she is. Bleek is taking her somewhere. Moth already told us that.

So we're going to follow her." She paused, her silvery voice finally quiet. "Moth will know where to go."

Nix could hardly see her anymore in the gathering darkness, but he could feel her eyes on him, staring.

"Moth," Nix called out, half whispering. "Moth."

No one answered.

"He's disappeared." Morgan's voice was flat. "He's testing us. That's why he grabbed me. Now this." Her voice had gained in intensity and Nix felt afraid. Then it lowered to an eerie whisper.

"You're the only one who knows how to find Bleek. You're the only one who knows where he's gone. You're the ringer."

Nix was quiet for a moment, his head tight, as if he were underwater. Test? Why would Moth be testing them? Wasn't he supposed to be helping them? Wasn't he their guide?

"The tunnels," Morgan said. "Maybe he took her to the tunnels."

"The Shanghai Tunnels?" He stopped. "I need to talk to Evie." Though he could not see his companion's face any longer in the dark, he knew she was listening. "Nothing can happen tonight. It's too late and too dark. I need to find Evie and talk to her and find out exactly where Bleek might be taking Neve." He paused again. Morgan was silent. "Evie will know."

"Do you want me to come?"

The eagerness in Morgan's voice grated at him, but Nix reminded himself that they were in this together. They were a ring; that's what Moth had called them.

"No. You go to the Krak and then home and see what you can find out from K.A. Evie wouldn't want to talk about it in front of someone she doesn't know, and for both of us to go would be" — he hadn't thought of it this way, but it was true — "it would be suspicious."

Her short, low laugh cut through the dark. "Suspicious. Oh yeah. That."

Nix didn't know how to respond. He wasn't yet sure if he believed anything Moth had said. He squinted, trying to locate Morgan's shape.

"I'll talk to my brother." Her voice was still a little hoarse, but the sarcasm was gone. "Call me tomorrow. Early. Wherever you're going, I'm going."

Somehow Nix doubted this, but he nodded in assent, forgetting she couldn't see him.

"Tomorrow, then," he said quietly, but Morgan was already gone.

CHAPTER 20

MOTH STILL KNEW THE WAY. It had been four years since he had last buzzed the second floor apartment tucked into a back lane in Southeast with the red front door and no name on the buzzer, but he knew the way even now, in the dark. He parked his motorcycle — a beaten-up Kawasaki he'd bought from an old biker in Olympia — on the side of the concrete, sixties-modern apartment building and for a moment stood outside the red door wondering whether he really should ring. It was forbidden to contact the rare ones who'd received the pass to stay — and die — in the human world. Wicklings weren't cutters, but they were still weak, since their death would result in more pain in the world.

Besides, it was late. Moth had ridden around the city awhile, trying to figure out what to do after he'd left Morgan and Nix in the park. He wasn't proud of what he'd done to Morgan, but he had had no choice. As soon as he heard it was Jacob Clowes approaching, he had crept away and sprinted down the hill. He couldn't risk leaking to Bleek where his meeting place was. Nor was it a good idea for Jacob to know that Morgan and Nix were associated with someone who'd spent time in jail. Whatever happened in the coming year, it was most important that everything in the changelings' lives appear to be progressing normally. He'd already screwed up with Ondine and wasn't going to take any chances with Morgan and Nix.

He had known, but also not known, that this was where he'd end up. The saguaro cactus that stood like a guard by the door was still there, he noticed, as was the sign, written in a neat, slanted hand, that reminded visitors to REMOVE YOUR SHOES, PLEASE — though it had faded in the intervening years since he'd last seen Raphael Inman.

Moth knew his old guide had left Portland after the fiasco with Bleek and the bust down in Eugene. Once Moth had started retraining in earnest, he learned from Viv that Raphael had chosen to remain in the human world, even if it meant being branded a wickling. He returned to New York to work on his art, then came back to teach at Reed a year ago. He lived a human life. Lonely and hermetic, terrified, Moth was sure, about his impending fate, guilty for robbing his corpa of consciousness and a life, but human — aging all the while.

He rang the doorbell and waited, unable to control a slight shaking in his right leg, a nervousness and restlessness that had accompanied him since he was a kid. He could hear Viv now:

Stop, Moth! Get control of yourself. Master it before it masters you. Or variations on the theme: *One must not fidget. It wastes fay energy.* Or his personal favorite: *It's called bruxism. It has a name. If you grind your teeth, get a night guard.*

A man's voice, crackling out of a plastic intercom, surprised him.

"Yes?"

"Raphael?"

"This is Raphael. Who's there?"

"Raphael, it's James . . . Motherwell."

There was a pause and the buzzer sounded. Moth tried to gauge whether it sounded angry — could a buzzer sound angry? — but he couldn't. Raphael had always been inscrutable to him. Why would it be any different now?

He opened the door and bounded the short flight of stairs up to the second floor. Raphael was on the landing, the door to his apartment open. Not smiling, but not angry either. His face — still generous, big-eyed, smooth-skinned — wore the intensely calm expression of someone trying very hard to be at peace. The only change was that he had aged. Moth had expected it. He knew it was what happened to those who stayed. They got old, fast. He himself had already started to experience it. Raphael's black hair was now softly silver; his bright, excitable demeanor more solemn, more thoughtful. Clear, plastic-rimmed glasses magnified hazel eyes and crinkled lids. Though the man, Moth surmised, couldn't have been older than forty, he looked middle-aged. He stood in the hall, wearing a long-sleeved gray T-shirt, his hands in faded jeans pockets, his head cocked. Finally he spoke. Moth thought he could detect the faintest whiff of cinnamon Altoids.

"You know you're not supposed to be here."

He nodded. "I'm still working on the lemma. I didn't exactly receive traditional training." Raphael smiled and Moth remembered that he had once liked his old guide. "Do you still see Viv?"

"She drops in occasionally." He squinted. "I am a wickling after all. She has to monitor my whereabouts. But you know that." He looked behind him and then again at Moth. "Would you like to come in?"

It was odd, this formality, with the man whom he had once felt — wished — was family. That's what it had been like between them, their small ring: he, Raphael, and Bleek. Two brothers and a father. Except Bleek — poor, mistreated Bleek, talented Bleek, clever Bleek — was the favored son.

"I know I'm not supposed to be here," Moth announced at the door. "But this is important. I have to ask you a question."

Raphael nodded. "You can do it here. We're alone."

For some reason Moth longed to touch the man standing in front of him. Not in a sensual way. He just wanted some of that calm.

"I need to know where Bleek is. I know you're not in it anymore; I know you're not even supposed to be speaking to me. But you know him. I mean, you knew him. And he's endangering my ring. I'm a guide now. I want to go through the exidis. You know there's only one way —"

Raphael eyed the younger man. His face had lost its softness and was now just hollow and sad. He lifted a hand out of his jeans pocket and scratched a day-old-stubbled cheek.

"You're prepared to eliminate him?"

"I am. It has to be now. Bleek is hunting. My ring — there's a ringer in Portland and he knows the girl. He sees her death and he's intent on saving her. I know Bleek is using it as a way to lure him into the limina. He's going to use him somehow. There's no other explanation. I have to stop him. Or else . . . or else I can't —" Moth looked at his black boots and suddenly thought how small they looked, how silly and contrived compared to the manly easiness of the person facing him. "You know what I can't do. Raphael, I don't want to stay. I'm not a cutter. I want to go to Novala. I want to go through the exidis."

Raphael shook his head, his face saggier now, and shifted his eyes to a glass-block window in the stairwell. "You don't know anything, Moth. You won't know what you'll decide until you're there making the decision. Don't overstep yourself." He looked back at the boy. "That's always been your problem."

"I know I didn't listen before, but I'm different now. I —"

"I don't need an explanation." He sighed. "I'm not involved anymore."

"But —" Moth felt liquid fear spread down his legs. He was shaking. "Please. This is my only chance." He looked at his old guide. "I was *your* responsibility."

The wickling's face dropped then and he stared vacantly in front of him. Then he covered his eyes with his hands and for a moment just stood there.

"Raphael, I know you felt protective of Bleek, but he's a cutter now. He's evil. He wants to harm us. All of us."

Moth knew it might be overstepping his bounds to insinuate danger, but he felt trapped and didn't know what else to do. Raphael rubbed his eyes and shook his head.

"Of course. Yes. I've been waiting for this. It's the last thing I have to do. Now I'll be released." He scratched at his arm and continued to stare in front of him. "Okay," he continued, and opened the door wider. Moth saw a low couch, plants near the windows, a coffee table, and pictures. Pictures everywhere. On the walls, stacked against doorjambs, in rolls on the floor.

"Come in. We have to talk. I have to tell you some things."

Raphael met Moth's eyes.

"About where Bleek is?" He looked around hungrily. So this was what it was like . . . after.

"That, too." The man started toward what Moth imagined

was a kitchen. Then he stopped and turned, the distance between them seeming to lend him strength. "And a lot of other things you know nothing about. I'm going to make some coffee. Want some?"

Moth shook his head.

"Well, I do. We're going to be here for a while. There's a lot to explain."

ဢ ဢ ဢ

NIX WAS LOST. It wasn't the darkness; he'd walked almost every trail in Forest Park a hundred times when he lived in the squat. It was something else. A kind of confusion brought on by everything that had happened to him since he'd last been there. It was as if his vision itself had changed. On dust he'd been single-minded, focused on getting from here to there. Only the departure and the arrival were important. The road, with its lights and constant heartbreaks, with the loneliness he wore along with that same coat, those same boots, Nix wanted to pass by as quickly as possible. So he found shortcuts and memorized his goat path, blinders secure, head down.

Now the darkness opened up around him, revealing a world he had slowly shut down since he was a child. He remembered: this was what it had been like to see, before he had trained himself not to.

The sky cleared and a half-full moon appeared, hung like a pendant above the hills. He walked. Minutes, hours later — he didn't have a clear sense which — he caught the reflection of something on a branch, a white piece of something, toilet paper. He was near a camp. He stopped and listened and thought he heard the tinkle of a girl's laugh. He moved toward it and saw the glow of a fire reflecting on leaves. He whistled the warning tune Finn had taught him, then he was walking through the last scrim of trees, and Finn, in red long johns and flip-flops, was heading toward him, thin arms outstretched.

"Nix, man, where've you been? We've been worried sick about you, dude." Finn clapped his old friend on the back and then hugged him tight. Had Finn always hugged him? He still wasn't accustomed to being touched.

He let Finn disengage first, then nodded and smiled to Evelyn, who was crouching near the edge of the squat, her hands full of suds, washing dishes out of a plastic washtub. She waved and smiled and Nix nodded back.

"I've been around." He put his arm on Finn's shoulder and smiled. "Getting my shit together. Miss you though, man. How're you?"

Finn shrugged and grinned. "Not bad. Evie got a job at Borders and we've pretty much just been saving money. Mac and cheese like every night. We want to get a place. And I'm thinking of going back to school. Engineering or computers or something. But hey — sit down." Finn pointed to a camp chair near the fire. "Want some tea or hot chocolate or something? Swiss Miss, dude. Little marshmallows —"

"No, no." Nix laughed. "That's all right." He shook his head, still nervous but feeling calmer. The fire crackled and warmed him, and he realized how tired he was, and tried to remember when the last time was that he had slept. Yesterday? The day before? Did he — they — even need sleep?

Finn settled in beside him on a log, mug in hand. "It's like I can't go to bed without a cup of the Miss. Totally weird. Addicted." He winked at Nix. "Not anymore though, I gather. For you."

Nix shook his head. "No."

For a moment Finn's eyes sharpened and Nix realized he was testing the truth of his statement. Then his gaze softened and he smiled and took a sip of his cocoa.

"Hey, Evie!"

Evelyn Schmidt, a somewhat shy, dark-haired girl with plump arms and sloping shoulders and a supple, curvy waist protruding slightly over tight jeans, looked up from her washing.

"Come over and join us, babe."

"All right." She hiked up her jeans, dried her hands on her

thighs, and picked her way over to the boys, joining Finn on the log, a little behind him. "Good to see you, Nix." She nodded at the boy and he smiled back.

"You too, Evie."

Nix breathed deeply and exhaled. He might as well start now.

"Listen." He looked both of his old friends in the eyes before he started. "I know I've been less than dependable in the last while, but I'm cleaned up and, well, there's something going on and I need your help."

Neither Finn nor Evelyn spoke, but they were quiet, and he took it as a sign that they were willing to listen.

"Neve Clowes is missing."

He was looking at Evie when he said it and the expression on her face — eyes wide and sad, but more than that, afraid — confirmed to Nix that he had come to the right place.

"I came straight here because I knew that you'd be able to help." He leaned in closer to the couple. "Evie, I knew you'd be able to help me find her."

Evelyn moved her eyes to Finn. After a moment, he nodded.

She looked back at Nix. "It's Bleek." Her voice was whisper soft, tinged by fear. "She's been hanging out with Tim Bleeker." A sharper note edged in. "Oh, I should have spoken to her. I should have —" Her dark eyes were searching the ground in front of her, and Finn reached a hand over to his girlfriend's knee to comfort her.

"Baby, it's not your fault. You know that. Neve has her own free will."

"You don't understand, Finn. It's not like that. Bleek is, is different. Powerful. He . . . he makes you *want* to."

Nix eased in, careful not to break his gaze from the dark-haired girl. He needed her to know they could trust him.

"It's okay. I know how Tim Bleeker works. And I can help Neve. I just need to find out where she is."

Evelyn looked up, startled, then focused her eyes on the fire-lit ground.

"Help her?"

"Yeah. I don't know, man. I'm not sure Neve Clowes wants to be helped," Finn said.

"No, she does, she does," Evelyn corrected him.

"Listen," Nix resumed, "you know he's going to take her wherever it was he took you. You know," he continued, "he's going to do to her whatever he tried to do to you. He's going to finish it. Evie," he said again when she still wouldn't answer him, "she's already been gone a whole day."

Evelyn suddenly looked up. "A day? That's more than enough time." She shook her head vigorously and there were the beginnings of tears in her eyes.

Finn took one of her freckled hands. "If you don't want to —"

But the girl seemed to have found her courage. "No. He's not going to do it again. Not to her. She's what, sixteen? Jesus." She swallowed and lifted her chin, looking directly at Nix. "He's in the tunnels. The Shanghai Tunnels? Under downtown? That's where they are. I know it. That's where he took me."

The tunnels, he thought. That's what Morgan said.

Evelyn's mouth was tight and there were standing tears in her eyes but she wasn't crying. Nix could see it. She was too angry. "There's an entrance down on First, right across from the river. It's in the men's room of a shit-hole bar down there. Some guy's name. Danny's, I think it was called. There's a door in the floor in the men's bathroom and that's the entrance we used. I know there are other ones, but that's the only one that I know of and there are so many drunks and junkies in there that no one cares whether you never come out of the bathroom."

Nix started to rise when Evelyn stopped him.

"You can't go down there now. It's not safe for you. It'll be crowded now and no one knows you down there. You have to wait till morning."

"We don't have time, Evie."

"You don't understand. You won't even get past the first room. You have to go only when there aren't people around. They'll think you're a narc or something." She leaned toward the boy, still grasping Finn's hand. He was looking down now, at his feet. "Look. This isn't like some squat you're happening upon. Really bad people are down there. They'll hurt you."

She turned to Finn and he looked up at her, his eyes sad. She returned to Nix.

"He's trying to make her OD. But for whatever reason . . . I don't understand it. I've never understood it, he needs us —" She caught herself. "He needs the girl to do it herself. It's some sick thing in him or something. He won't force it on her. He'll just keep her there until she does it to herself. And then . . . and then I don't know." Her eyes fell. "I got out before then."

Nix stopped and thought about what Evelyn was telling him. If it was true, that Bleek needed the girl to do it herself, was it because of Bleek's own history? His mother was kept in unwilling isolation, on dust, in the limina. Perhaps, he hypothesized, the cutter didn't want to do what had been done to him. Which would mean — Nix tentatively allowed himself the thought — Bleek had some kind of a conscience? Small, misshapen, but real? He wasn't sure how this would help him, but he tucked it away and again addressed Evelyn and Finn, who were both lost in the campfire's flames.

Nix couldn't stop himself from asking.

"How? How'd you get out? And where were you?"

Finn shook his head. "Too much, man. This is bringing up too much."

"No," Evelyn replied, her eyes fixed. "No. I want that asshole caught. I don't remember where it was. Somewhere farther, beyond that first room. No one was there. Except something . . . something woke me up. It wasn't Bleek. He had gone somewhere. Something else. When I woke up, all I remember is that there were all these tunnels leading off in different directions. Like in a star shape." She forked her hands out to indicate lines radiating. "Or something. It was really confusing. I didn't know which one to choose, so I just . . . walked. And eventually I was outside. I was so fucked up I don't even remember opening that last door. I just kept thinking: Follow the light, Evie, follow the light. I kept saying my own name. And the next thing I knew I was under the Burnside Bridge. I swear. It was like I just . . . appeared there. A couple of times I even went back there to try to get in" — she glanced away from Finn — "and there was this grate thing there, but it was locked."

"But didn't he try to stop you?" Nix asked. "Keep you from leaving?"

"Bleek?" Evie looked sad. "No." And that's when she started crying. "No, he didn't try to stop me. I mean, he tried to coerce me; he told me I didn't *really* want to leave him, but he never, like, grabbed me, or tied me up or anything, or even locked the door. It was like it wasn't interesting to him to just capture me. He wanted me to *want* to be there. And Neve is doing it, too. It's like he won't — can't — do anything unless we let him."

Finn was shaking his head and Nix noticed he was crying too.

"No, baby. No."

"Yes, Finn. It's true." She turned back to the dark-haired boy. "You have to wait until morning, and then if you go you have to be very, very careful. I don't know what Bleek would do to you. I don't even know what he wants with Neve, why we were there in the first place. And in the Shanghai Tunnels? No one but tourists and junkies go there. But you can't go now."

"No, dude. You need sleep," Finn said.

It was true. Whatever was heading his way, he needed to rest to endure. He — his body—was tired. "Yeah, okay," Nix agreed.

He sat while they made ready for bed, Evelyn spreading out a few blankets in the red tent to the left of the blue one they slept in. Nix sat in his chair, watching the fire.

"But the teeth. Evie, you said something once about the teeth —"

"Yeah, that was weird. I guess it was some kind of hallucination or something." She started to zip open the lining of the tent, motioning for him to climb in. "They weren't exactly sharp. More like pointy. Like yours." She tipped her head and Nix felt a clamp of panic in his gut. He ran his tongue over his teeth. He'd never thought of his teeth as pointy. But were they? Had the inhabitation already started to wear on him?

"You need to go to sleep now, Nix. We'll wake you up before dawn. Then you can go down. When the sun rises it will be better."

"C'mon, buddy." Finn helped his exhausted friend from his

seat and led him toward the red tent. Nix imagined soft blankets cupping him. He longed to sink into them, but he couldn't stop thinking about the tunnels, and that room Evie described.

"But how did you know? How did you know which way to pick?" He was just next to her now, nearly limp in Finn's wiry grasp. She looked stronger, less pained than before.

Her voice was a whisper. "I don't know, Nix. I just wasn't ready to go. I don't know how else to explain it." She stopped zipping. "Now go to bed. You have a long day ahead."

A hoarse "yeah," was all he could muster. He ducked into the darkness and heard a last zip behind him. Just how long was anyone's guess.

CHAPTER 21

MORGAN D'AMICI IS A TWAT. *Morgan D'Amici is a cold-blooded bitch. Morgan D'Amici is a frigid, neurotic Ice Queen. No. Ice Witch. Snow Sorceress. Popsicle-licking Princess of the Below Zero. Morgan D'Amici is a —*

Fairy.

The word made Morgan laugh and she grabbed her pillow and held it over her head to calm down. Everyone in Yvonne D'Amici's one-step-above-a-trailer home was still in bed. It wasn't yet dawn. Out of a thick, dreamless sleep, she had awoken, snug under her covers, cracking herself up.

Nix had said it best: *Flying fucking fairy.*

Shouldn't she have felt worse that her darling brother's darling girlfriend was lost somewhere under the sway of an evil cutter named Bleek, whom she herself had been tweaked by only a day before? (No. She rather liked it.) Shouldn't she have been upset that Nix hadn't called to tell her where to meet him in the morning? (No. She knew he would.) And Yvonne. Poor, dilapidated Yvonne, hanging on her children's successes like a kiddie-pageant mother, slugging Long Island Ice Teas at the Spaghetti Factory, picking the garlic off her breadsticks *so as not to ruin her breath for Todd,* hugging her children compulsively every time the waitress came by to ask if they wanted refills of their Cokes — shouldn't Yvonne have annoyed her, like she usually did? (No. Morgan *lurrved* Yvonne that day.) Even K.A. seemed to sense something was up, the light in his room still on when she woke up sometime in the early morning to pee. Shouldn't she have been worried about this, at least?

No. No. No. Everything was a mess. Yes, everything was a mess. And somehow, it felt —

Delicious. Thrilling. Sexy.

The day had come. How easily she had caught on, Morgan thought, staring into the warming darkness above the bed. *Of course* she hadn't told K.A. about Neve. Why would she have? She had called Neve's father — fat old man — after she got home from the park, told him K.A. wasn't home, and that she'd call him as soon as she heard anything. A lie. She'd have to make something up about where her brother had been, but that wouldn't be so hard.

You're a frigid bitch, a cow-eyed college boy she'd once rejected told her. She took it as a compliment.

She sat up and rolled the covers down from her T-shirt-warm shoulders. Dawn was breaking, and Morgan could make out lemony green streaks in the sky above the rosebushes. She hadn't gone into the forest the night before, she realized; she must no longer be under the sway of her subconscious. Good. It meant she had more control now.

A plan was in the making. Shadowy, long-term, but a plan nonetheless. So Nix was a ringer. Good. She would need one. And Moth — she'd show him. And not just for his stunt in the park. No. The boy needed to pay for messing with her that first night at Ondine's. He had promised a kiss. Morgan never forgot a promise.

Moth she would seduce, Nix, use. Bleek she would learn from; Viv she would conquer. Ondine she would destroy. Neve, well, it didn't much matter what happened to her.

She wouldn't be called a frigid bitch for nothing.

An hour passed; she watched the aqua lines of her digital clock morph into other lines. The only thing that mattered was Nix's call. She already had messages from Jacob on her phone. She ignored them.

At last her phone buzzed.

"Corner of First and Ash," he said. "Now."

She had no time to reply before he hung up, and he didn't have a cell so she tossed the phone on her bed and got dressed quickly in the half dark. Jeans, bra, dark long-sleeved T-shirt, hoodie. She smoothed her hair back and eased on her white baseball cap. Over her hoodie she put on a thin black ski vest.

She slipped her wallet into her pocket, grabbed her cell phone, and shook out her duvet cover and her sheets. Morgan D'Amici always made her bed.

She was ready to go. She crept down the hallway past K.A.'s room and started to edge open the kitchen door when she remembered that she should leave a note for Yvonne. There were Post-it notes by the phone. She'd just scribble something about needing to be at work early —

A hand on her shoulder made her jump, and she was about to scream when she felt broad fingers across her mouth. She was struggling to see who it was when she heard the familiar soft scratchiness.

"Calm down, Morgue. It's just me."

K.A. loosened his grip and she turned around in her brother's arms. She hadn't counted on him being awake, and here he was in front of her, fully dressed. Tousled blond hair poking out from under a trucker's hat, running shoes, jeans. Just like his sister.

She whispered, but her voice was stern. "Do you want to wake Mom?"

"What's going on?" He looked sad.

Morgan turned and shrugged. "I have to go to work. They need me to do some accounting before opening today."

Mom, Had to go to work early, she wrote in an even hand.

"Jesus Christ. Do you think I'm an idiot?" Morgan could hear the mounting anger in K.A.'s constricted whisper. "Jacob's been calling me all night, asking me whether I've heard from Neve." He leaned closer. "He said he saw you last night with Nix, up at the park, after we had lunch. He said he told you Neve hadn't come home and you said you were going to try to find out where she was. Why didn't you tell me, Morgan? What the hell is going on?"

She gripped her pen and looked up.

"I don't know what you're talking about."

She knew what her face must have looked like — cold and blank, the face of a liar — but she didn't care. Nix was waiting for her; she had to meet Bleek in the tunnels and nothing, not even her brother, was going to stop her.

"Look, they're expecting me at work, and I have to go. I don't know what Jacob Clowes is telling you about where he saw me, or whom he saw me with, but it can wait. He's upset. His daughter is a mess and I guess he doesn't know where she is, and he's trying to draw you into the drama."

Be back later! xxxx Morgan

She put down her pen and started to slide past her stunned brother when she realized he was trying to beat her to the door. Was he . . . was he trying to stop her?

"Are you kidding me?" Morgan stopped in front of the sink, her hands perched on the counter behind her. K.A. turned the toggle on the knob, locking it, and situated himself in front of the door. "You're going to stop me from going to work? That little bitch really has you wrapped around her coke pinkie, doesn't she, Kaka?"

She tipped her chin up but he didn't move.

"You need to tell me what's going on," he demanded.

She sighed, playing the concerned sister, though the gestures, she knew, were undermined by the amount of hatred she felt. She wanted K.A. out of her way. Now.

"You don't need this in your life and I certainly don't. It's really too crazy."

Her brother only stared.

"We can talk about it at work," she tried. He leaned farther into the door.

"You're not going anywhere until you tell me what you know about Neve."

The expression on her brother's face would have broken her heart, if at that moment she'd had a heart to break.

"I. Don't. Know. Anything." Morgan forced the words through tight teeth and felt a chilling inside of her. She was conscious of the room around her: the one she knew so well, the one she had spent many evenings in with K.A., washing dishes, joking, having soap fights. Now he had her cornered. Which is exactly how she felt: trapped, like an animal.

She barely heard the first knife slip off its magnetic strip before it went whizzing by.

K.A. jumped away from the door, his jaw open, staring. The

knife had lodged itself a few inches inside the door frame, right where his body had been a moment before. Morgan followed its trajectory.

"Did you —" He squinted and stared at her, now beside him. "Did you just throw a knife at me?"

"No," she replied, her hand now firmly on the doorknob. This time she wasn't lying.

She ran into the driveway, started her car, and accelerated. First and Ash. This was all that mattered now. She never noticed the black Mustang trailing behind her.

V

ONDINE

CHAPTER 22

REEN BEAN."

Ondine felt a soft hand on her shoulder. She rolled over but the hand stayed. *Off. Want it off.* She was sleeping. She registered that it was her mother's hand, which she was glad about, but Ondine didn't want to get up. She wanted to stay in bed and dream about — what was that she was dreaming about again? — Pollen — a hazy sky — coral pink petals — blue beyond.

"Green bean, honey. Time to wake up," her mother whispered again. Oozily Ondine started to remember. A plane. Spilled club soda. Her father picking her up. A dark drive. Lights on water. Then a house, not her own. She opened one eye and then another. Trish Mason was sitting on the edge of the unfamiliar bed Ondine lay in, her face smiling above a taupe silk sweater. She felt a swelling of love and sat up to hug her mother. Behind her the light coming through the white-curtained window was bright and there was a single pink rose in a vase on the desk next to the bed.

Tomorrow morning. Rose Garden. Grant Park.

"What time is it?"

Trish must have seen her daughter's eyes rolling around in her head because she put a hand on Ondine's forehead. First the palm, then the back of the hand.

"I'm not sure. Nine-thirty or so? Are you okay, honey? Do you have a fever?"

Ondine shook her head. "I'm fine . . . much better. I . . . I just need to know what time it is. I promised to call someone at . . . at ten. Is it ten?"

Trish sighed. "Hold on; I'll check the alarm in the bedroom." At the door she looked back. "Are you sure you're okay?"

"I just need to know what time it is, Mom."

Her mother walked out the door and down the hall. Ondine could hear Max bounding down the stairs, calling to their father, who must have been in the kitchen preparing breakfast.

"Nine twenty-three," Trish called from the other room, already walking back toward Ondine. She would sit on the edge of her daughter's bed then, like she often did. To see how the plane ride was, to spend time. To talk.

Ondine was already out of bed and yanking on the clothes that she had worn the night before. Underwear, bra, jeans, hoodie mini, RVCA jacket. She was slipping a foot into a tennis shoe when her mother walked back in.

"What's going on? Why are you putting your shoes on?"

"I . . . I have a . . ." What, what the hell did she have? Ondine scanned the small room for her other sock, which she located under the bed. "I have a school friend who's here for the summer . . . at Evanston. At Northwestern." She groped for a name, choosing a girl she vaguely knew from gym in eighth grade, who was good in kickball. "Lissa. Lissa Griffiths. She could see me only this morning, and I promised. I'll be back in a few hours."

"What?" Trish's hands were limp beside her in the doorway. "Why are you going now? And who is Lissa Griffiths? You've never mentioned her. What's going on, Ondine? You just got here." The woman stepped closer to her daughter, her voice gaining in intensity, her hands moving from her side to her hips. "We need to *talk*."

Ondine nodded and avoided her mother's eyes, working the other foot into its tennis shoe. "I know. I know. I want to. I want to talk. I just have to meet this girl. Lisa . . . *Lissa*. Lissa Griffiths. I must have mentioned her to you. She's a new friend of mine." God, she was terrible at lying. What kind of teenager was she?

"Supercool," she added pointlessly, avoiding eye contact. "Lissa's supercool. Helping me with physics. You know how hard physics is for me."

She knew she'd better stop before she started inventing an entire backstory for Lissa involving various science fair victories, favorite nonsuspicious extracurricular hobbies (amateur filmmaking, squash), and which college Lissa would be applying to for early admission after her summer spent taking sailing lessons at Northwestern. Ondine grabbed her wallet off the desk and was at her mother's side giving her a kiss before Trish could say another thing.

"Tell Dad, okay? I'll be home by one. . . . *And don't worry*," she added, in a voice that would make any mother suspicious.

Bewildered, Trish received her daughter's brief, tight hug and then it was just Ondine, bounding down the stairs toward what she dimly remembered from last night to be the front door. She was in Chicago. She'd have to remember to look at the house number as she left, and the street name. She hoped her mother wasn't following her, but really she didn't care. She had to go to the rose garden to meet whoever was supposed to be there. The dream she'd had about the sky, the pollen, the blue beyond — abstract and mystifying but insistent, too, like someone's name you've forgotten, or the particular bend of a tune — had told her to.

Ondine slid through the front door before her father came out of the kitchen.

"Bye, Max, bye, Dad, justgoingtomeetafriendbebackinan-hourortwo!"

She had no idea where the rose garden or Grant Park was,

but as she scanned the street — 727 Emerson — she saw a convenience store at the next corner, and figured she could get the information she needed there. Or call a cab. If someone were meeting her there, as the note had told her, they'd wait.

A wind blew off the lake. Ondine wasn't used to the cold. She rubbed her hands together and stuffed them into her jacket pockets.

Cell phone. She'd forgotten her cell phone. She decided against running home to fetch it, her fingers brushing the edge of the paper napkin she'd stuffed in her pocket the night before. She did not look at it. What if the writing had disappeared, made of lemon juice like in *Harriet the Spy*? What if she had imagined the whole thing?

Tomorrow morning, Ondine whispered. *At the rose garden.*

She checked her watch: 9:34. "Ready as I'll ever be," she said to herself, and broke into a jog.

ꙅ ꙅ ꙅ

CORNER OF FIRST AND ASH, NIX HAD SAID. *Now.* Well this was now, and Morgan was nowhere to be seen.

He stood on a curb a few yards from the planned meeting point, behind a tree so that he wasn't obvious, but clear enough so that he could see every shadowy figure that made his — or her — way out of a Portland dawn toward Danny's Bar. A few bums weaved past the place where he was supposed to meet her, but for the most part the movement was the other way around. Even drunks needed sleep, and every few minutes a hunched figure, usually lighting a cigarette, stepped shakily off the front steps of Danny's and turned right, back up to the buildings of downtown.

It had been forty minutes since he'd left the squat silently, so as not to wake Finn or Evelyn, though the curly-haired girl had met him on his way out, handing him a Clif Bar and a mini-flashlight and telling him to be careful. "I will," he'd said, dispensing with his usual sarcasm, and Evelyn had smiled softly and crept back into her tent.

Now Nix was taking what he had decided was going to be his last look down both streets and the greenway that lined the river: nothing except an early morning yuppie jogger from the Pearl. He was going in. Hell if he'd wait for Morgan, though something about the equation wasn't fair. He wasn't used to trusting people, let alone Morgan D'Amici. Those mineral eyes; those tight, thin lips — Nix quickened his pace, shaking his head. If she didn't make it, it wasn't his fault.

He was about to step up onto the curb in front of the bar when he heard the swishing of denim against denim and Morgan was beside him, outfitted in a white cap and jeans, dark vest, sneakers. Her face was cool. Nix wondered if that meant she was as scared as he was.

"Where were you? I've been here for ten minutes!"

Nix kept his eyes on the tavern and didn't slow down. "We shouldn't speak too much," he said, ignoring her question. The admonition against speaking had come out of his mouth before it had even entered his head, yet he knew it was the right thing to do. "We're going in there." He tipped his head at the bar in front of them.

Morgan snickered. "That shit hole? You should've warned me, I'd've worn boots —"

"I said *don't talk.*" Nix halted and she almost bumped into him. "Look. When we get into the bar, follow me toward the men's bathroom like we know where we're going, and for fuck's sake, *don't speak.*"

The dimples that gripped the girl's lips tightened. Nix noticed he was holding his breath. He tried to let it out but couldn't. Finally she nodded, and a sigh blew out of his mouth. "Good. In the men's bathroom there's a door that leads to the Shanghai Tunnels. You know what I'm talking about?"

Morgan proffered another mechanical nod, but turned her head away.

"If we get separated," he continued, "look for light. That's the way out. Daylight. Brightness." He shrugged. "I don't know what else to tell you. You're —"

"On my own?" Her voice was morning-husky. She smirked, raising an eyebrow. "We haven't even had sex yet, and already you're planning on leaving me before breakfast."

"Something like that."

"No worries," she continued smoothly. "You're not the only one who wants to find Neve."

Nix looked at her. The girl's eyes were trained on his, defiant yet weirdly calm. He'd somehow forgotten, or underestimated, that he wasn't the only . . . changeling. The word made him queasy. He wished Ondine were there. That she wasn't was his fault.

"No. No. That's right," he said.

"Damn straight it is."

As if they'd both heard the same starting gun, Morgan and he turned on their heels, skipping onto the curb and up the steps to Danny's.

ↄ ↄ ↄ

THE DOOR UNDER THE BRIDGE, Raphael had said. *Look for the door under the bridge.*

Use that one, not the one in Danny's. That one is too dangerous.

The cutters control that territory now.

That's not how it used to be.

It was that last sentence that played in Moth's mind like a sampled loop as he walked, hands in his pockets in the chilly morning air, toward the Burnside Bridge. *That's not how it used to be.* Raphael had used the phrase often with Moth and Bleek, when he was teaching them the lemma.

"Take dust," Moth remembered him saying once. "Dust was just something we used every so often to keep a pet happy. Now it's being manufactured by the kilo, sent all over the world. I know it's important for the exidis." Raphael shook his head and sighed. "I know we're supposed to increase our kind. But I don't like it. It was better when there were fewer of us. It was better . . ."

He would trail off there, ending each lesson with the mournful coda: "That's not how it used to be." Now Moth understood what his old guide had meant.

The whole story had come out the night before, over countless cups of coffee. "I never touch the stuff anymore," Raphael had said, into his fourth or fifth espresso. "Too much for me now. But I need it tonight. You sure you don't want any?" Moth shook his head and stayed silent. The shock of what Raphael was telling him was enough to keep him awake for a year.

"I was a scion," he had started, staring into his demitasse. "I had trained with Viv for years before you and Bleek went through the change. That's why I look close to the age I really am. Scia are careful to control their fay energy. It doesn't leak all over our corpa like it does you —" He laughed bitterly. "Or me, now."

"But I wasn't good at it," Raphael continued. "I was too distracted. I was an artist. I was successful. The scia gave me wide berth. At the councils they agreed, year after year, that it was important that I be able to deepen my practice. They thought it would be good for the exidis. They thought I might learn something about Novala that they could not discover using traditional scientific means. And I was. I was going places that no one, not even Viv, could have gone."

Raphael had looked up, and Moth had seen the guilt and fear in his hooded eyes.

"But the problem was that the more I worked, the farther away I got. I wasn't a good scion, and the council knew it. The pet I was given —" He'd stopped, clenched his jaw. "They did that then. Each of the scia was given a pet. We were encouraged to procreate, to make more corpa to inhabit. It was wrong. There are plenty of willing humans —" He'd stared at Moth. "I got one pregnant. She had a child. I didn't want him to stay in the tunnels. I fought them. I tried to steal him and his mother away. They caught us."

Raphael had stopped again and put his hands over his eyes, as if he couldn't bear his own memory. Moth could only watch, stunned, as he spoke into his palms.

"They eliminated her. And they kept the child. They were going to banish me then, demote me, send me somewhere horrible, but Viv intervened. She suggested I be named a guide. She thought the responsibility would be good for me. I didn't want to leave —"

Raphael — mighty, all-knowing Raphael, whom Moth had

looked up to for so many years — was crying drily, his voice a choked whisper.

"I didn't want to go through the exidis. I was scared. Viv helped me. She brought the child to me; she let me train him. My aim was to treat both of you equally. Not the same, but equally. You were both different and both important. I tried to do it well. . . ." He faltered.

And maybe you would have, Moth thought, if one of us wasn't your son.

"Tim . . . Tim was just confused —"

"I knew it," Moth said, unable to hide the bitterness in his voice. "I knew you favored him."

Raphael lowered his eyes. "I thought you — the two of you — would help me be braver. Would help me do it, go through it. I had seen it. In my work I had seen Novala. It was so . . . *beautiful*. But —"

"Never mind." Moth cut him off. "What else?"

Raphael took a moment to resume. He placed his hands together so that his palms met. He spoke softly, but he would not meet Moth's eyes. "So she watched over us. She was kind. She loved me, I guess. Or close to it. We started an affair."

"Who?" Moth asked.

"Viv."

Raphael had sighed then, and Moth had wondered what, in this labyrinth of a story, would come next.

413

"And that's when I found out about Ondine."

Ondine. Of course it all had something to do with her. It was why Viv had been so keen for Moth to watch over the girl. It was why the scion had known she'd be difficult. Moth felt a strange pulling in his chest. He only hoped she was somewhere safe.

Raphael looked at his hands. "Viv got a job at Xelix Labs. With Ralph Mason, Ondine's father."

Moth nodded.

"She knew she wanted to do something. She knew she didn't like the way the pets were treated, and she didn't think it was right anymore to simply take corpa, put them through the change, dope them up on dust, and then discard them at the ring. You already know how dangerous the exidis is." Moth assented. "It used to be worse. In the sixties and seventies, a few died every time. They were just getting the rings going then and couldn't control the reactions. Viv had been really scarred.

"She wanted to change it. She wanted to find a way to" — he gestured to Moth and back to himself — "to mix what we are. Fay mixed with actual human genetic material. Eggs, sperm. Whatever. She wanted to mutate the DNA. To conceive a new changeling — in flux, one wholly of this world, this human world, but part fay. In between, see? Betwixt. Really and truly. It would mean no more exidis. No more pets, no more corpa, no more dust. We could move in and out, then. I wanted that so

414

badly. I was behind her. Of course I was. After what had happened to the girl — Tim's mother — I couldn't stand what we do. How we get from here —"

Raphael waved a hand around his head and looked up. Moth followed him, almost surprised to find only Raphael's strange computer-generated images around them like walls of a virtual house, the Portland darkness quiet.

"— to wherever. To the cosmos. I believed in Viv. I still do. I believe in Ondine. That's why I stayed. That's why I agreed to be an outcast. I wanted to be near her. I came back here from New York. I was on the jury that gave her the prize to be in my class. I've been watching her, too, along with Viv, along with you. I have been helping, in my way."

He stared, still averting his eyes.

"Viv would be eliminated if anyone found out about this. What she's done is perfectly forbidden. She would be named a cutter. Immediately."

Moth had nodded then, as solemnly as he could muster, but privately he had bristled. Too little too late, wasn't it? But his former guide had continued before he could speak.

"I told Bleek about the whole thing. I don't know why. I wanted him to understand that we were part of a new generation. That what had happened to his mother wasn't ever going to happen again. Viv had accomplished something amazing. Miraculous. Part of where we were going — part of our human destiny — she had achieved it here, on earth. We had Ondine. Ondine would show us where to go. We just had to wait for her to gain adulthood. We just had to wait —"

"For now."

"Yes." Finally Raphael met his gaze. "We knew you were the right person to train her. You knew Bleek. You knew us. She could have been sent anywhere, but we wanted her here. Near her mother."

The wickling's last word left Moth cold. What did Viv know about being a mother?

"So why is Bleek hunting Neve? Shouldn't he be after Ondine?"

Raphael frowned. "He doesn't want to procreate with Ondine. He wants to *be* her. Or he wants to figure out a way to make one like her. A new creature, half fay, half mortal, all powerful and without the ticking time bomb that inhabits us common changelings. We're just cups, Moth. Just holders for something greater. Our time here is limited. Ondine is the thing itself. Think about the power that she has wrapped up inside of her."

He stopped. Moth studied him: older than he should have been, afraid and weak. A wickling. Yes, that was Raphael.

"Bleek certainly has. That's what he's doing with Neve. It must be. He's going to try to do what Viv did. At least that's what I think he must be doing. But he needs a ringer to accomplish it. No one can effect the change without a ringer."

Did Raphael know about Nix? For some reason Moth decided against telling him.

"After she has the baby he'll try . . . to get rid of her. I don't know. I thought I knew Tim. I don't."

That's where it ended. The whole sordid tale. With Neve in the tunnels, right where Moth was heading.

He had offered Moth a bed, to catch a few hours of sleep before the next day — it was four AM when Raphael sipped his last bit of coffee — but Moth had begged off, saying that he had to get to the tunnels. He had to stop whatever Bleek was doing. Raphael stood and showed him to the door.

"Do you know how to get in?" It was the last thing he had asked, and it seemed trifling to Moth after the early morning revelations.

"No."

"The door under the Burnside Bridge. Sometimes it's locked. Whether that's an impediment is up to you. It always was for me."

It always was for me.

Walking along the Willamette River in the half-light of dawn, Moth understood now what the older man had meant. Raphael hadn't had what it required to enter the limina. Not physically, but psychologically. He couldn't kill his own son, no matter how evil Bleek was. But Moth was different. He'd proven it to himself earlier, when he'd threatened to end Morgan's life — and his own — to prove to Nix the reality of the ring.

He scanned the dark underside of the bridge for the door, eking out of the shadows a handleless rectangle of solid metal. Below him, the diffuse light of dawn coated the misty river like an aura, and a phrase popped into his head: *Ignis fatuus.* Foolish light. The glow that led wanderers, seeking what they thought to be a lantern, to a quicksand death in swamps. Science said it was created by the spontaneous combustion of marsh gases, but superstition supposed the lights to have another cause: fay. Legend had it that they lit the lights — swamp gas, will-o'-the-wisp — to lure humans to their death.

Wasn't that what fay had always done? Lured humans to them for their own use, for their own needs? A few died, yes; but, otherwise, weren't they very careful? Moth looked above him at the lightening sapphire dome of the sky. Wasn't it all in service of something higher? Weren't they taking humans somewhere better? Wouldn't she lead them?

He let the girl's intelligent, searching face fill the spaces where the shadows deepened. Now that he understood what Ondine really was — a goddess of sorts, half human, half something else — a cover had been pulled back on a dark well Moth knew was his own soul. He wanted Ondine to topple into it. He wanted her under his control, under his wing. Viv must have wanted that with Raphael. Even, in his own screwed up way, Bleek must have wanted that, too, with Neve.

Matters of the heart. Viv had told him the emotions of humans were present in all fay. It was left over from before the change. It could not be helped. Was this tremor, this disturbance, something like love?

You must commit yourself to the exidis before you're allowed in. It is not enough merely to "want" to decide. You must actually make a decision. You must relinquish all possible futures save the one to which you commit yourself.

Moth stepped back from the door, disoriented. Was that Viv he'd heard or a memory of her speaking? Then Raphael's face, looking at him, and away.

The sun had almost risen.

Ondine. If she was what Raphael said she was, she would only help him.

He pulled a slender matchstick-sized pick Viv had given him to practice his mancing with and started to work on the lock. A few deft turns of the hand and darkness enveloped him. Moth reached an invisible hand out and felt stone mixed with earth at his side, and above him. He stomped the ground and a muffled echo sounded. He was on the other side of the door now, that he knew. In the tunnels. He could not see his own arm in front of him, but somewhere, far off, a yellow light flickered. He walked toward it. His journey had begun.

CHAPTER 23

HE BAR PART HAD BEEN A CINCH. Cake. Pie. Butter. Sunday morning coming down.

Morgan repeated as many synonyms for easy as she remembered from mornings at Krakatoa with Li'l Paul to keep her mind off of the darkness that was closing in around her. Even Nix, only a step ahead, was hard to see. Back in the bar all they'd had to contend with were the few customers still nursing the first of their morning beers and a nonchalant bartender who barely acknowledged the two as they made their way semi-uncertainly toward what looked to be the toilets. From under a neon Coors sign a man laughed and pointed at them, but Nix seemed not to notice so Morgan ignored him. Clearly the fine patrons of Danny's had seen this routine before and besides that, were drunk enough — or tired enough, in the case of the bartender — not to care. And negotiating the bathroom, while a skosh fragrant, was straightforward. Nix sidestepped a dozing man leaning against the wall, gave the all-clear sign to Morgan, and they both stepped inside. There was a hatch in the floor of the wheelchair stall; Nix unlatched it, and together, neither looking back, they descended a metal grate stairway. At first it was completely, utterly black, the densest black Morgan had ever seen, but a pale yellow glow burned somewhere farther down and they followed it.

Morgan was certain they were not alone. The darkness was crowded, it seemed, with sounds. Metallic clanging and the plashing of water, and then darker, lower, the scrape of something against stone, and a scratching wheeze she could only interpret as human breathing. *Mooooorgaaaana.* Had someone just called her name? Like in the forest? No. She was scared, she told herself. Despite her bravado that morning, she was scared. Though she had promised herself that she would be strong — what was Morgan D'Amici if not strong? — she reached forward, terrified, to make sure Nix was still there. She felt his slender back, and before her next step hit the earthen floor, his warm hand closed around hers.

Nix and she stayed linked, walking slowly through darkness, till they reached a brick-walled room, the shape and size of a small building's cellar. A single gas camping lamp sat in an alcove lined with rough-hewn wood, the source of the light that they had seen upon entering the tunnels. It had the uneasy feeling of a place that someone had just left.

"Nix?" she whispered. "I don't —"

She was about to utter something craven, something utterly

un-Morgan-like — she wasn't sure what — when Nix thankfully interrupted her, pointer finger pressed first to her lips, then to his own. She silenced. They weren't to speak. He looked at her, and then away, at a different door from the one they'd come through.

They were to go there. But how did he know? They were in the Shanghai Tunnels. Scary people came down here — looking for — looking for what? Morgan tried to telegraph her thoughts to Nix but the boy only stared at her again, obviously waiting for her to signal that she was ready to follow. She stopped, confused. Time had become loose, like a hangman's loop, and she felt light-headed and disoriented. She could feel the dead-endness of the place, its creepy history: shanghaied sailors and old hookers and doomed loggers and dead Indians and suffocating Chinese railroad workers. She felt a strong urge to run but quelled it. Humans were always wanting to do things they shouldn't, she told herself, go places they weren't supposed to be. It was just like during the change, when she was a child, in the forest. That's why she was scared.

She let go of Nix's hand.

Why did they have to be silent? It couldn't be for anything as simple as escaping detection. Was it something about those wheezing sounds? Weren't they just junkies looking to score? Weren't she and Nix more powerful than them? Why didn't they have flashlights? And where was Bleek?

Morgan had done her duty. She had gotten Nix into the tunnels. Now she wanted to go home. She stood up straight and nodded at him, but he only bobbed his head curtly and turned to walk on.

That little bitch Neve. She got us into this.

There were three low, primitive doors leading in three directions. The one they had come in by, which Morgan knew was behind her — she resisted the urge to turn around and run back toward it — and two in front of them, one on the right and one straight ahead. Neither were marked, or suggested any kind of different destination from the next, but Nix stared at each in turn, as if judging, weighing, walking down the length of the corridors beyond with his mind. He reached for the one on the right, and as he walked through it Morgan wondered what had made him choose. She was tempted to make him stop and explain his decision — to tell her why he knew in a way she didn't, couldn't — but just as quickly as they had entered the dully lit room, they exited, and darkness swallowed them whole.

She held back now, conscious that Nix must have sensed her cowardice. Only the day before she had jumped at the opportunity to follow him, thinking it would get her closer to Bleek, thinking that it would provide her with some opportunity for power. But the labyrinth of the tunnels and their stubborn, unplumbable darkness offered nothing — and terrified her. Who would find her if she died down here?

She felt a dull clotting in her throat. She should have at

least told K.A. where she was going. At least K.A. should have known.

When we get out of this, I'm going to — I'm going to neutralize that conniving little crack. No way is she dating K.A. and . . .

Morgan let the poisonous clouds fill her head, walking quietly and swiftly toward what she could see was the next light. Where Nix was taking her, who knew, but if Neve got out alive she was going to make that little strung-out whore pay.

Dumb cow. She probably wanted everyone to come looking for her. She'll probably be pissed that K.A. isn't here. But then, she's probably fucking Nix, too.

She entered through yet another low doorway on the right and stood alone. Nix must have taken a step beyond. She reached her head back out past the doorjamb, then chastised herself because she wouldn't have been able to see anything anyway. Hearing light steps, she called the boy's name. She had gotten farther behind than she intended.

"I'm back here," Morgan half whispered. "I'm back here, at the room."

More scuffling, closer. He was heading back and would be angry that she'd spoken. She was glad she'd called, though; she wanted to speak again but didn't dare. She looked behind her. A wooden table sat in the middle of the room, another lantern upon it. So these rooms — they were occupied. Morgan wondered what they had been used for in the old days. What unspeakable things had happened here?

Long chains lay on the shadowy floor, and were those . . . cuffs? And that thick, dark substance smearing the top of the table, was that —

Not down here. Not down here.

She couldn't help herself. "Nix," she called, and moved toward the door. No one answered. No hand covered hers.

Morgan picked the lantern up by its handle and once again approached the doorway, intending to hold the light out into the dusky passageway. Earthen walls were illuminated, still bearing the jagged scars of where they had been hacked out by picks and shovels and hands a hundred and fifty years before.

The steps ceased. She raised the lamp again, closer.

She saw the blood first, blooming raggedly across the girl's midriff, an apron of smudgy brown. Like a painter's smock, Morgan managed to think before she stepped through the doorway, pale and glassy-eyed and utterly silent, her skull shining through matted fine blond hair. The girl was dirty; the sundress she wore was smeared and splattered, and a strap hung like a broken petal off her shoulder. In the glare of Morgan's lamp, she stopped. She pulled her parched lips back. Her teeth glinted and a sticky pearl of saliva welled at the right corner. It was only when Neve lifted her frail, bruised arms and lunged toward her with a sudden violence that Morgan finally allowed herself to scream.

CHAPTER 24

ONDINE WAS THINKING OF RAPHAEL. "The last thing I make before I die will be a hole," he'd said in a lecture she and her mother had once gone to in New York, the first time she'd ever seen him. She'd tittered a little at first — it sounded pornographic — until she realized he was talking about a grave.

Raphael made things — holes, cairns, oceans, mountains — with computerized wood and water and mud and stones, and colored pigment, and shadows and frost, and then printed his creations with digital ink, on huge LED canvases, in tortuous linking combinations that Ondine could only imagine came from the machinations of a computer never put to sleep. Tiny things moved among the patterns, all interspersed with a tepid yellowish light. The result was a mirror to this world of despicable and eerie flatness. All Ondine could think was: I'm glad I don't live in there. And: I wonder what does.

He could make something here, Ondine thought, walking

past the vast, solid milky-blue canvas that was Lake Michigan. I could make something here.

She was heading toward the rose garden at the center of Grant Park — the taxi driver had told her where to go — and had seen a small silver fish, no bigger than the eucalyptus leaves they had back in Oregon, lying dead in the grass some distance from the lake. Too far for the fish to have gotten on its own. A bird must have dropped it from its beak. Its eyes had been eaten out by ants already, and a silent column of them was entering its body through the holes in its head. Immediately Ondine thought of Raphael, and envisioned a painting: the silver fish, the water behind, the column of ants, but far, too far, from the lake.

How we get from here to there; how it makes such delicate sense. How every story, even the one she was living, was an attempt to explain that improbable jump.

It was past season and only a few wilting petals hung on to their frizzle-topped hips. No benches beckoned, and Chicago's rose garden — unlike Portland's pride — was small enough to see entire. So Ondine just stood there, hands crossed over her chest, looking up at the skyscrapers or at the tops of distant trees, or the blue lake beyond, every so often scanning the level of the bushes for the brown woman who had served her a club soda at 30,000 feet the day before.

Surely the woman would approach her if she were here.

Surely she hadn't imagined the whole thing. She looked at her watch, then pulled the napkin out of her pocket, staring at its neat black letters, slightly fuzzy at the edges from where the ink had bled.

"I'm glad you came."

A shining voice reached her ears and Ondine looked up. It was she. Deb. Donna. Whatever her name was, who used to sell chemicals on the road. Her seatmate on the plane, wife of Mike, though she remembered a different voice. With the migraines. Who had offered her eyedrops, which Ondine refused. Still carrying that purse, black, shiny, which she was reaching into now with a pale, freckled, bony right hand. Ondine's heart skipped and something lower slipped. She turned on her heel to run.

She had been tricked. Manipulated. Again. If they had converts on planes, if they could single Ondine out, find her, track her down —

She started to panic but checked herself. She had almost reached the border of the park. If she could breach it she could run away. She could go to the police —

And there was Donna again. In front of her. Deb. Diane. How had she gotten here? From there? And it was not a gun or a knife in the woman's hand, but a small brown bottle with a black stopper. Eyedrops.

"Ondine."

When had she revealed her name? How did this woman know her? She was in Chicago now. It was a day later. She had stayed with her parents last night. Her mother had awoken her. She had eaten no breakfast.

The woman approached her and Ondine backed up into the pathways that cut through the roses like a small labyrinth. The woman, her dark hair pulled back today to reveal massive purple-gray eyes behind fuchsia middle-aged lady glasses, stepped toward her, still holding out the small glass bottle.

"Ondine, look at me. Look at me carefully. You know who I am. You came here because you know. We must not spend too much time or energy on this. There is a cutter after you. The stewardess —"

"Flight attendant —," she whispered. Was she stoned? What was happening to her?

"On the plane. She will kill you. She tried last night, with the club soda. That's why I tipped it over. She — or someone — is here at this park, right now, I am sure of it. She gave you that note to lure you here. I am lucky I intercepted it. I can stay only for a moment, or she will try to kill me, too."

What was she doing with her face, this woman? Was it her glasses? Was it the shadow of a building? How did she get it to look like that, her eyes getting bigger, the black hair pulled back, coiling into a ring of —

"We can change a little, most of us. Our appearance. Obviously we don't want to do that too often. Humans scare easily with things they don't understand."

Ondine stilled here, aware of nothing but this woman in front of her, the eyes, the light breeze ruffling the leaves around them. Everything was pixilated and very, very bright. From outside, she knew, the scene comprised nothing more than two women, one older, one younger, one brown, one pale pink, stopping in a park to say hello. But inside she was that little silver fish, in something's beak, about to be let go.

"His name is Tim Bleeker. You know him. He is dangerous. Right now he is planning something with your ring — to hurt your ring. He has sent another cutter to kill you. You must use these drops. They will help you see clearly. Just use them. Then fight. We don't have any time."

The woman straightened, reached into her purse once more, and handed Ondine a letter.

"Read this. I have to go now. She is coming; I can smell her, and I must go. You have to help them. They need you. The key is in your blood. Are you hearing me, Ondine? The key is in your blood, and you have to find a way to use it. You don't need to understand yet, but are you hearing me?"

Ondine could not do anything. She could only stand and stare.

Beyond the woman she could make out an old lady standing

by the edge of a bank of trees, her hand tethered to a leash, at the end of which was a small black dog.

"You have the power to fold the worlds. But perhaps you are still too young. Have you discovered who you are yet? Have you had the inkling?"

The woman moved closer now, her quartz-colored eyes wide and staring at Ondine's own. It was Viv, she realized. It was Viv. The woman whose egg —

The woman who had donated —

Ondine wanted very much to sit down and cry.

"No," she whispered. She had no idea why she'd just spoken.

"It's all right." The woman reached her hand out slowly and placed the small bottle in Ondine's palm. She felt herself grasp it. "If a changeling is given her gift too soon, she risks not feeling its full weight. The burden of her power." Viv paused, staring. "It's why they gave us wings in their pictures. It's why they make us prettier than them. Power is very heavy. But you're ready, Ondine. You're ready now. You must . . ."

She was already moving away, quickly now, looking around. "I have to go. Take this and use it." She looked at the girl one last time. "I'm sorry this is happening so soon. I'm sorry I could not clear your path."

Then she stopped. "I love you, Ondine. We all do."

By the time the words reached Ondine's ears, the woman was gone, faded into the space between the trees at the edge of the park. She felt the smooth bottle in her hand. The old woman with the dog lifted her head and walked away.

∽ ∽ ∽

WOULD IT ALWAYS GO BACK TO THIS?

This meaning alone, in a dark place, looking for something he wasn't even sure he could see.

It wasn't until Nix reached a dead end — his feet stubbing an earthen wall, hands searching damp dirt — that he knew he had lost Morgan. He had told her to be silent; now he regretted it. He could die — or at least, his body could. How foolhardy he'd been to come down to the tunnels, with no real sense of what he could or could not do. Nix didn't like being underground. Every hair on his body distended, sweat trickled down his clammy neck. He was afraid to move lest he touch something — someone? He didn't know what was around him because he couldn't see anything, and the whole reason he'd come down here, to find Neve, seemed distant as the sun. Something he read in high school came to him:

Abandon hope all ye who enter here. Dante.

He had to find her. He had to get close enough to take the light.

He traced his hands across slimy earth and found a corner, turning to face it. Despite the thudding in his chest, he willed himself to calm down. His throat constricted — what was that bitter smell? — but he made himself stand up straight, thereby knocking his head against the ceiling and feeling damp earth trickle inside his collar. When had the ceiling gotten so low?

With one hand on the wall he fumbled for the mini-flashlight he had tucked into his pocket before he'd left the squat. He hadn't wanted to use it, hadn't wanted to allow himself to be seen, but now . . .

A cold, white light illuminated a shoe, and Nix was almost surprised to realize it was his own. What he had thought was dirt was gray clay, scored with soft, round marks, as if hollowed out by dripping water. He bent to look at them. Overlapping ridged grooves were interrupted here and there by flatter, rounder, wider impressions — somewhat familiar. Surely he would have remembered going into a room. Was he that disoriented?

One of the impressions was separated from the others. He traced it with a trembling finger, inscribing a rude, squarish circle, hollow at the center. He laid his fingers against the wall.

The last creation before the grave.

Palm prints. They were palm prints. Someone desperate in the dark, trying to get out. Then the light was going, searching, darting everywhere around him in the small cavern. On every surface he could see, in every square inch, overlapping palm prints pushing against clay.

Nix dropped the flashlight and it rolled away from him. He

grabbed for it and the light skipped over something metallic. With one hand he held the flashlight, and with the other he pried the necklace from the clay and held it in front of him. It swayed and glinted in the light. Cheap, gold-plated.

Neve, it read, in cursive hand.

That's when Nix heard the screaming.

ဢ ဢ ဢ

THE FIRST THING MOTH SAW on the other side was the door behind him.

He walked toward it. Was it the door he had just come through? He took a step, reached out his hand to touch it, and found himself farther away than when he'd started, his hand nowhere to be seen. Another step. Farther again. He turned. It was an empty earth-lined tunnel Moth saw, but strangely, as if constructed from fading Christmas lights. One corner of his vision was illuminated and he wondered what it was that gave the tunnel its eerie, ultraviolet cast. Had he already entered the limina? Was this what it looked like? As if he were playing Xbox with night-vision goggles?

He reached a hand in front of him. His stomach seized when he didn't see it rise. He dropped it and once more lifted it. Nothing. All he saw was the light, seemingly brighter now, but a strange shade of cold blue. Everything else, the walls, the ceiling, he saw as if through a screen.

He turned once more and again there was the door, which he walked toward, reaching his hand out —

He was walking backward. He wasn't used to paying attention to his eyes, but as he rolled them around in their sockets he realized: something had happened to them. He swiveled his head. Right was left. Left, right. Even before he reached a trembling hand up to touch his face he sensed his eyeballs had moved, or grown. They seemed to be on the side of his head now, and larger—much larger. He reached his hand up, straining his peripheral vision. Finally he caught sight of his hand moving.

He had eyes on the back of his head.

No, that wasn't right. But he could *see* behind him. He touched his forehead, patting the now-puckered skin. Two eyeballs domed there, the lids pulled back in tight rings, almost half the size of his hands. Even the shapes had changed, growing ridges and bumps. He could not touch them without burning.

He felt farther up. Two warm stalks, soft and furry as feathers, sprouted out of his temples. Perhaps an inch high, they arced into the damp tunnel air, and when he released the one he had touched, Moth realized that he could control them. They responded to something in the air — not sound, but something else, something more chemical, like a taste.

Smell. He could smell it. Dying human corpa.

"*Moth,*" he whispered.

He'd morphed. This was it. What Viv had promised. He reached behind his shoulder blades for wings and felt nothing, just the smooth stickiness of his leather jacket.

Was this what she had meant about not using the full extent of his powers until he was ready? Until he'd committed to the exidis? But he didn't remember deciding. Had he missed something, some clue he'd given himself? All he remembered was being under the bridge, the moment before stepping into the darkness. Ondine's face had appeared to him and he had felt something — an odd pulling, a disturbance. He had felt for a door and found it, heavy and iron, unlocked it, and slipped in. It had been as easy as that.

Moth felt one of his antennae move minutely and involuntarily. His eyes shifted and again focused on the burning light in the distance. Something was there. He could smell it. He walked toward it, noting how the tunnels and the mold and lichen offered up new, strange patterns. Wings and bull's-eyes and seeping spots. This was so different, this feeling of certainty, even if it was limited to the realm of the senses. Something on the floor leaned against a brick wall: a human, Moth knew, not by its shape or color — his spectrum had been reduced, he realized, to whites and violets and blues and pinks — but by its chemical composition. Decaying flesh, nitrates. This one was no longer alive.

Tripping across a soft leg, he felt liquefying flesh squish, drying bone crunch. His heart squeezed but he continued.

Faster Moth crept, practicing his shifting gaze.

He didn't hear the voice until he was almost to the light. He wanted to move into it — no, not quite *into* it, but to the very edge of it, where the shadows were blackest. He paused at the edge of a low, dug-out door.

"If you think I'm going to help you get out of here, you little slut, you're dead wrong. Don't mean to be so blunt, but you're the one who got us into this."

The figure stopped near him and Moth heard an uncomprehending whimper, then another nervous laugh.

"You and your lizard-faced lover. *Bleek*. He doesn't even know what he has coming. What did you think, that he was *in love* with you? Or were you just high?"

Moth recognized the fierce whisper. He leaned past the edge of the door.

Neve was clamped to the edge of a low table with what looked like a woman's leather belt. Her head hung between her knees and she was swaying. With his altered vision he could make out a white dress, smeared with something darker, all across the front down to the hem. Whatever Bleek had intended to do, Moth realized, he'd already at least tried.

"You are never going to get out of here, darling Neve." A hand picked up the lantern on the table. "But I am."

Morgan was already turning when he spoke. She jerked and turned her eyes into the darkness, where he was still hidden.

"So it was you I smelled."

"Who is that?" Her voice raised to a tinny squeak.

"You know who it is."

Morgan lowered the lantern and stared. Moth smelled shampoo, sweat, and crumbling, terrified corpus. He felt his antennae strain, his eyes turn.

"Moth?"

"That is what I am. But what are you?"

It had just come to him. What he had been learning, studying for years, was now all available to him in an instant, without thinking. Her response was instantaneous, jumbled. One after another. She hadn't yet gotten control of her gift, but it was showing itself at Moth's command. First a long, forked black tongue licked toward the darkness, then the talons of a bird of prey scratched. The wings of a bat stretched out and were just as quickly replaced by a rat's hungry, nibbling snout. All predators of his kind, and all interspersed, bits of Morgan, screaming in frustration. Viv had been right. Morgan was an adept morpha — already. Far beyond what Moth had been capable of at her age. Adept, but untrained.

"I know what you are." He spoke calmly through his fear, noting that his voice seemed to have lowered, become stronger. He liked its new timbre. "And I knew what Bleek was, early on.

I just didn't want to admit it. Viv will be very happy with me when she knows what I've accomplished."

So this was what he had been meant to do. He'd failed early on with Bleek. He could redeem himself with Morgan.

She crouched in the shadows, her head shaking. "No — It's not what you think. I'm just here for K.A. I got lost. I'm just angry —"

Now he seemed to be upside down. His eyes rolled in their sockets so as to be still fixed on Morgan, who had crouched near the door and was now looking up at him with a stricken, terrified stare. He was quivering, yes, shaking inch by inch. But getting closer. He could smell her so clearly now. She was sweating, releasing herself. Still sweet, Moth thought. *I never did get that kiss.* And though he knew that this wasn't right — Morgan had the potential to be a cutter; he knew what cutters did — he also felt the deeper, almost sensual need to get closer to her. Taste the nectar she was now emitting freely, in clouds as soft as honeyed mist. He wanted . . . he wanted to suck at her. . . . He felt himself dropping . . . past the light. . . .

It was not Morgan's mouth that Moth found himself heading toward as he landed with a tongue that had suddenly grown to almost a foot, and turned rough and grayish black, but something hairless and foul-tasting, rotted from the earthen tunnels. Moth leaped off the body he had landed on almost as soon as he touched it.

"We were always close, brother, but not that close."

Bleek laughed and dusted his jacket with long, pale, and pointed fingers.

Ꙩ Ꙩ Ꙩ

K.A. HAD WAITED FOR A HALF HOUR OUTSIDE OF DANNY'S before he picked up his cell phone, not sure whom to call. He had spoken to Jacob before he'd gone to bed, promising him he'd spend the day looking for Neve, but it was too early to phone him now. He wanted to let the man rest. Though he knew the situation with Neve was serious — enough to merit Jacob's calling the cops — something also kept K.A. from panicking. Neve was with Tim Bleeker; that much seemed clear. He didn't allow himself to think the word "dust," let alone "sex," but he knew his sister had been right, and he'd not wanted to see it. Now he needed to find Neve, get her home, and get her help.

What confused him, what caused him to be sitting in his car outside of Danny's like a cheap detective, cell in his hand, hat pulled low, was what the hell his sister was doing with Nix Saint-Michael at a seedy bar in downtown Portland at sunrise. Nix Saint-Michael, whom he'd thought was his best friend.

"Morgue."

He spoke the word and the cell dialed her number. While he waited for the line to connect, he felt heat rise to his face, even sitting here alone in the car. K.A. had never messed with his sister's business; Morgan wouldn't have tolerated it. Even being there, spying on her, made him feel ashamed.

The call clicked into voice mail. "Hi, this is Morgan. Leave a message —"

K.A. hung up and tried again. "Hi, this is . . ."

"It's K.A. Call me as soon as you get this. I'm . . . I just want to talk to you. So call me."

Now what? Nix didn't have a phone. What would he say, anyway, besides asking the boy what he knew about Neve? He'd have to go inside. There'd be a scene. He hadn't seen Nix since he'd left for soccer camp, and now that he'd heard about him being with Neve, he'd have to confront him. K.A. didn't like scenes. They reminded him too much of his father, the last man he wanted to be.

His sister was in there — on dust, too? — and he knew he'd have to get her. He pulled his cap lower on his head, feeling self-conscious about his baggy jeans and new Stanford sweatshirt, a boy in a boy's costume. Nix and Morgan walking into a downtown Portland bar at dawn, while suspicious, didn't feel outlandish. Was he just too innocent, after all? Was that why Neve always kept her distance?

K.A. walked across the street, head down, hands in pockets. He might not be sophisticated like his older sister, but he knew one thing: Danny's at dawn was no place she should be.

Inside was dim and dank and sickly sour: his father on a Sunday afternoon. He tried to ignore the swelling nausea, surveying the room for Morgan and Nix. It was far past closing time, and the stragglers were asleep. The bartender had started to put chairs on tables. K.A. approached.

"I'm looking for a girl — seventeen, black hair, blue eyes. She came in here about a half hour ago with a friend of hers, a guy."

The bartender shrugged and shook his head.

"People come in here all the time."

"Hey, officer," the one drunk not asleep called from the other side of the room, "the doughnuts are down the block."

K.A. leaned over the bar, taking off his baseball cap. The bartender folded his arms in front of his chest.

"I'm no cop. I'm in high school. I just want to find my sister. She came in here with a . . ." He almost said friend, then amended himself. "With a guy, around my age, Indian. Native American. They never came out again. I'm sure you saw her. I'm just worried about her, man. She's my sister."

The bartender scratched the back of a hand with his stubbled beard. He narrowed his eyes but didn't say anything.

"Listen, man. I just want to find my sister."

"Feathers not dots," the heckler yelled. But K.A., fighting the desire to kick his teeth in, ignored him. The bartender picked up his rag and resumed wiping.

"The junkies like the women's room."

"My sister is not a junkie."

"The dustheads like the men's room."

"Dust and junk. Never touch the shit myself."

"Shut up, Ed," the bartender said to the drunk in the corner, though by then K.A. was halfway out of the room. Right before he opened the door to the men's bathroom, he remembered something. Maybe it was the laughter of the man in the corner, maybe it was the fleeting image of Nix's solemn face. But he realized there was one person who might know what the hell was happening with Nix, and he still had her number on his phone from before his trip to California. He just didn't know why he hadn't thought of it before.

CHAPTER 25

APHAEL INMAN HAD SAID TO HER, the time Ondine had attempted to draw a storm:

"The big things, they're not so literal, are they? Not so representable. Storms, eruptions, the tsunami, the earthquake. They are vast. They are unpaintable. Natural power masses and fractures into the elusive abstract. The gestalt, Ondine. How do you evoke the gestalt?"

She had run to Google and looked up the word that night.

"A unified symbolic configuration having properties that cannot be derived from its parts. . . . A German word that does not translate easily. . . . A complete pattern or configuration . . . elements so unified that it cannot be described merely as a sum of its parts."

Now here she was in Chicago, by a gigantic lake — itself a gestalt, Ondine thought, a giant hole, negative space filled — having just met with a horribly familiar stranger, *her biological mother* (the thought was enough to make her pass out), who had told her that her ring was in mortal danger.

Take them. Then fight.

Walking quickly across the park, Ondine looked down with jittery, unseeing eyes at the letter the woman had given her. She would not open it. Things were as they seemed.

She called her mother from a pay phone, asking hoarsely if there had been any calls. Trish sighed. "Your phone was ringing off the hook, honey. So I finally answered it. I thought it was you. It was K.A. D'Amici. He said he needed to talk to you, but that he was going to be out of cell reach for a while. I told him to leave a voice mail. Is everything okay? Where are you?"

She was at the lake, she said, with Lissa Griffiths. She would be home in an hour. There was nothing to worry about.

Her legs shook and her throat burned. Three times she'd had to dial her voice mail on a pay phone to get it right.

"Ondine, it's K.A.," the hurried message had said. The boy sounded like he was in a small room, and she thought she could hear the warbling strains of country music in the background. "Look, I don't know where you are but I need to talk to you. Neve is missing. And . . ." He cleared his throat. "I'm trying to find her. She's . . . she might be in the Shanghai Tunnels . . . under downtown. And Morgan, too. And Nix. I don't know why I'm telling you this, but in case something happens . . . in case something happens, call Jacob Clowes and tell him what I'm telling you." The phone pulled away and she heard the boy's voice again, this time closer. "I'm going down there. I'm in Danny's Bar. Danny's Bar," he repeated. "On First and Ash. I'll call you when I'm out."

He hung up. Ondine pressed five. The message was delivered at 9:28 AM, almost an hour ago. 7:28 AM Portland time. There were no other messages.

It took her a second to cradle the receiver.

She half jogged the few hundred yards over a busy highway to a dock at the edge of the lake. Boats creaked, but other than that it was quiet. She sat at the edge of the water and looked down, then stared dumbly at the horizon. Boulders and chunks of concrete sat submerged, the only movement the pulsing of the lake weed and the tiny wavelets that crested with regularity along the wooden and stone embankment she was perched on. She had to fight a monstrous urge to throw herself in.

Slowly, carefully, she opened the envelope. Though the words seemed to swim in front of her, she tried to take in as much as her eyes allowed her.

She is a cutter. She will eliminate you. She tried last night.

Despite herself, Ondine cast around for the black woman from the airplane the night before, the one she had felt so comforted by, the one who had given her the club soda. All she saw were tourists; a few businessmen strolling; a couple of teenagers skipping stones, one in a White Sox T-shirt. No one harmful. No one out to get her.

Farther down, on the highway median Ondine had crossed a moment before, a group of people shimmered. Distant traffic halted; a few horns bleated; everything sounded slow and wavy. Then a smaller thing, shaking, trotting toward her, out of a bright weave of moving cars. A dog. A little black dachsund, the one from the rose garden.

She stood up and walked up the granite blocks toward the highway. A car was lodged halfway across the median.

The old woman.

The sky was very blue; the sun shone. People stood around. She walked faster toward the crosswalk. Cars stopped, a few horns hung in the still summer air. Red lights flashed, a siren mounted, and she remembered:

The old woman from the park, she had seen her again, after she got off the phone. Something about the woman's voice — "Come on, Henry. Come now." — had scared her and she had run across the highway, not waiting for the light to change. The blocks of granite at the edge of the lake must have drowned out the sound of the car veering off the highway, headed for . . .

"Excuse me —" She stopped a couple coming from the median. "What just happened?"

They shook their heads and frowned.

"Some car skipped the median and almost hit an old lady.

447

The driver is in bad shape. The lady lost hold of her dog — a little dachsund. Have you seen it?"

Ondine nodded, staring. The driver was in bad shape.

"He went over there." She pointed.

"Tell the old lady that. She's frantic."

She arrived at the scene at the same time as the ambulance.

"Where's the old woman?" she asked a stranger. He shrugged. "I have to tell her her dog is okay." The man stared and she was conscious of the fact that she held only two things: the opened letter and the brown eyedrop bottle. She curled her hands into her sides.

"Ask the paramedics," he said. "They probably are getting her in the ambulance. She was okay. The driver — she wasn't so lucky. Are you related to her?"

"No." Ondine paused.

The man crinkled his mouth and looked down. "Oh. Just. Just that you're both black." He waved his hand. "Stupid assumption. The old lady. She's okay."

A stupid assumption that she was related to the driver of the car that had almost hit the old lady. A black woman. The one who was now in very bad shape.

Ondine looked around the dissipating crowd and saw an official-looking man in a red jacket standing near a car, mumbling into a walkie-talkie. He did not look up till she was there standing in front of him.

"Do you know where the old lady is?" He smiled distractedly and Ondine continued. "I — I saw her dog."

His ear to his walkie-talkie, he nodded. "She'll be very happy," he said loudly, as if he were talking over some other conversation. "That's great." He tipped his head toward the ambulance, whose lights were fluttering in the corner of Ondine's vision. Cars still honked, but people were starting to walk away.

"Over there. She's in the back."

Ondine nodded and started toward the ambulance. She turned, almost forgetting, and called back: "Is the driver okay?"

"Can't release that information, ma'am," — he waved Ondine on — "but the old lady, she's fine. She's just back there." She headed in the direction of his hand, rolling the brown bottle in her fingers, then rubbing her thumb against the glass. Was it the way he nodded? A certain flicker in his eyes?

No. She was imagining things. She was walking toward an ambulance to tell an old woman that her dog was fine. She was about to go home and talk to her mother. She'd throw the stupid letter away. Everything would go back to normal.

She undid the top of the bottle with a shaky hand and put one drop in each eye. Just a drop. What would a drop hurt? She blinked, still walking, toward the open doors of the back of the ambulance. They were thrown open, the universal sign of "this is being taken care of." She stepped toward them, still blinking from the silly thing she had done to her eyes.

"GOOD TO SEE YOU AGAIN, MOTH."

Morgan's delicate hands covered her head, and she was crouching near the end of the table Neve was belted to.

She could hear Bleek's voice. Whatever had just happened to her left her feeling pain, everywhere, as if each of her bones had been jammed. Her skin felt ill-fitting; her temples pounded. She was desperately thirsty. So this was what losing control felt like. This time she would not look up. She did not want to see the coiling slippery thing that had been trying to ram itself down her throat just a moment before. She nudged her tongue between her lips and could taste it there, under her nose, Moth's sticky leavings. She could not think about what to do next. Everything had gone awry. Nix was gone; Moth — whatever he was now — had overheard her threatening Neve; and Bleek, she didn't know what Bleek would do. They had stumbled into his private torture chamber, that much was clear, and as Morgan crouched there, terrified, Neve's broken crying began to seep into her, slowly and surely as the blood on the girl's sundress had bloomed over its center. "Nonononono," the girl moaned. "Nonono, not again. Bleek, I don't need any more."

Need more what? What the hell had Bleek been doing? Morgan willed herself to look up. Get a hold of yourself. Whatever it was that Moth had commanded her to do, whatever shapes he

450

had released inside her, she would not reveal any more. Not until she was ready.

Too soon, Moth had said at Ondine's party, and he was right. It was too soon and she had much more to learn.

Fingers scraping the ground, she felt cold earth and forced herself higher against the wall she had backed onto. Moth was straightening, too, his head turning back and forth, trying to locate Bleek's shape in the flickering darkness. She didn't want to look at the cutter yet, but she could hear him.

"You're looking . . . terrible as usual, old pal. No, really. Sticking around hasn't been so good on the old bod, huh, *James*? And you used to have such a manly one. Such a chick magnet. Really, it's sad, what happens to us. That's why I've got Neve here." Morgan edged her eyes over to Bleek, who smiled cruelly, hovering over the tied-up girl. She had recognized the fiend's voice and was now gasping for air, begging.

"Please, please. No more."

"She's helping me." Bleek looked up. Neve, on the ground and still belted to the table, followed his eyes.

"Please." Morgan saw tears forming. "Please someone help me."

He ignored her. "If you think you're gonna get the girl, Moth, you've got another think coming. Morgan, dear. Thanks. No, I mean it. *Thanks.*"

He turned, whispering, and Morgan started shaking and

could not stop. She backed against the wall farther; her palms felt cold, moist earth. Everything: the darkness; the dead human smell; the horrible, raw crying of Neve. Her blood-spattered sundress. Morgan's own guilt. They wormed into her head and twisted there, nibbled and oozed.

No, it was too soon.

Now it was Bleek's voice in her ear.

"Muchas gracias for aiding me with this little problem, *Morgue,* but you've failed in one crucial aspect." He was up against her, his face pinched. "Nix. Where is he?"

She was trying to coil herself tighter into the shadows, but could not go any farther. She moved her eyes to Moth, who stared at Neve, clearly wanting to help her. The girl had dropped her head and was weeping silently into her knees.

"I don't know where Nix is, Bleek," Morgan whispered. "But Neve's not well. You need to let her go."

"But you're the one who tied her up, Morgana dear." He laughed and turned back to the tied-up Neve. "So far she's been so easy. Easy-pleasy Neve. But now. Well, I suppose you know what happened." He grabbed a fistful of blond hair and jerked. "You ran away, didn't you, silly little girl? I guess I should have expected it. The cave is . . . Well, let's just say it gets a little *cozy* in there. Doesn't it, pet? But fortunately Morgana found you."

Bleek inched his stubbled muzzle into Neve's neck.

"We want you to stay awake after all. We have a long nine months. *Hm?*" He laughed again, and Neve wailed hoarsely.

"Let me go. Please, Tim, let me go. Please. I'll be good. I won't tell anyone. Please let me go —"

"Well —" Bleek aimed his eyes now at Morgan, who felt her fingers again grasp the wall and her gut loosen. "You'll have to ask your friend."

The light in the room had changed. Subtle, but altered. Morgan looked up, careful not to betray too sudden a movement. Ever so slowly, as Bleek prodded his runaway slave, Moth lifted the lantern that had been on the table. He was not staring at Neve anymore, but at the wheezing creature in front of him, with a look of hatred and determination so profound Morgan found herself shaking. Would he hurt her too? Just as the lantern was at its highest point, Moth flicked his eyes to her. Though she could not read them completely, she sensed what he wanted her to do.

"What about me," Morgan heard herself say. "I thought you liked me." And Bleek — hideous, vain Bleek — turned, a smile haunting his lips.

"What, my love?"

"I said I thought you liked —"

The lantern came down on Bleek's head in a sputtering crash.

"Me!" Morgan bellowed, and Moth lunged. For a moment, everything was chaos. Bleek, doused in fire, rolled onto the table. Morgan bent to free Neve's wrists, helping her up.

If she could just get Neve to the door, they could make their way out of the tunnels. Morgan would be the heroine. Moth wouldn't be able to accuse her. He would be the mistaken one. She would be right. Neve she could explain later — a sister's insane jealousy. Moth could take care of himself.

"Come on, Neve —"

While Bleek writhed, Morgan pulled the confused girl toward the hole in the wall that was blackest — beyond which she thought she could see the barest suggestion of daylight. Neve dragged.

"Morgan?" She whimpered. "Morgan, help me — I'm sorry — I —"

"Faster!"

"I'm scared —"

One last look over her shoulder at Bleek, who was starting to stand now, the fire having skipped from him to the kerosene-spattered table.

Just one more step.

"Neve!"

A shadow entered the frame. The last in the world Morgan had expected.

∽ ∽ ∽

HELL WAS DIFFERENT FROM HOW K.A. HAD PICTURED IT. He thought it would be hot, but it was cold. Cold and it smelled like death, despite the fire that was now raging in the center of it, lighting everyone a putrid shade of yellow-green. Devils, it turned out, had beautiful names. Like Timothy and James, Neve and Morgan.

Not his sister. Not her. She was saving Neve. She was there with her arms wrapped around the girl, heading out the door K.A. had just entered, her hands tangled in his girlfriend's hair. Yet how did she know Neve was down here, in the tunnels? And Neve, why was there blood all over her?

Innocent, perfect Neve. Lightest, whitest, purest snow, melted by the fire that licked the walls of the death chamber around her. Lovely Neve, scratched and bruised, and her big eyes hollow. And her white teeth bared. Running to him, her skinny arms flailing, *Help me K.A., help me,* and behind her his sister. *Toward the light, K.A. Run toward the light.* A turn, and a presence in the doorway, hands on his shoulders, cold.

Bloody Neve. Lovely Morgue. Then a blow, to his chin, from below. Bone against bone, flesh against flesh, hurling K.A. backward. Burning, enveloping pain. Swelling, magnificent pain. Blackness, and an even softer blackness, lit by tiny stars.

The avenging archangel: Saint Michael.

∾ ∾ ∾

IT WAS HER LIGHT THAT GUIDED HIM. At first Nix had followed a distant glow in the direction of the voice he had heard screaming, but that was extinguished and another emerged in its absence: hotter, more intense. When it started to move — away from him? — Nix panicked, thinking he'd lose it, and so he'd sped toward it in the darkness, and when he'd reached it he was so certain he'd have to confront Bleek that the reflected, altered visage of K.A. D'Amici shocked him, and he punched. Nix's closed fist hit the younger boy's jaw and K.A. went reeling backward, into the curved chest of the jerking body that Nix realized was Tim Bleeker.

What K.A. had been holding before became Nix's, and Nix was suddenly in possession of the glowing white thing he had been trying to find: Neve. Beautiful, bloodied Neve, the ring around her a ghostly white. He moved in front of her to shield her. To his left, Morgan D'Amici stared, shaking her head, mouthing, *No, no . . . K.A.* Past her, near the back wall, was Moth, eerily transformed, his bulbous head rudely lit by the fire in the middle of the cavern Nix had stumbled into.

Except for Ondine, the ring was all there.

Too late he realized that K.A. was trying to do the same thing he was: save Neve and escape. And too late he understood that the figure now holding K.A., pinning his arms behind his back, was none other than the one he had come to kill. Remnants of a small explosion were visible — glass on the floor, rivulets of flame running up the walls. Metal chains, at the end of which looped handcuffs, spiraled on the ground.

"K.A!" Morgan screamed.

"I couldn't have planned this better myself." Bleek smiled, his eyes skipping from Morgan to Moth to Nix and Neve and back again. "Oh, wait. I did! My old best friend and my new best friend. A stranger in my arms." Bleek tightened his forearm around K.A.'s neck, which he now held against his shoulder. "And my girl close by. Neve, honey. Come to Daddy."

Nix turned. Curling his hands more protectively around her soft upper arms, he sensed the girl was too scared to move, though he noticed that her eyes didn't leave the creature standing hunched, half-scowling, half-grinning, in front of them. What had Bleek done to her? For the halo of death around her was shining, pulsing now, starting to go through its changes.

"Run, Morgan!" Moth shouted from the back of the room. "Get out of here!"

"No . . . K.A.," Morgan cried. "I won't leave you, K.A. —"

"Go, Morgan," her brother said groggily. "Get out of here. They're all crazy. They'll hurt you —"

"Oh no, you're not going anywhere, bitch." Bleek drew a shining blade from his jacket and held it to the boy's throat. "You make one move and your little Kaka dies. This is the kind of party where everyone is invited."

All Nix could do was hold on to Neve. He tried not to breathe.

"Really, I couldn't have asked for a better situation. Of

457

course this one . . ." He traced the blade across K.A.'s throat and the boy closed his eyes. A spidery crimson thread trailed. ". . . isn't of use to us, but that's for later."

"Moth, do something!" Morgan yelled. Nix tried to meet the older boy's eyes — a sign of what to do — but Moth only stared, hatred stiffening his face.

"Cat got your tongue, old buddy? You were normally so chatty with the girls. For a while there I thought you were batting for the other team."

It was meant to distract. Inch by inch, Nix observed, Bleek was starting to move himself and his hostage toward the door where Nix stood in front of a trembling Neve.

"Do it!" Moth whipped his head around. "Do it now! Kill him!"

Nix was confused. Was Moth talking to him?

"Kill me?" The cutter spoke to Moth, but stared at Nix. "And how do you propose the lad do this, James? You are on my territory now. I rule here."

He was now within a few feet and advancing. Nix had started to back against the wall nearest the door, still clutching Neve, but there was nowhere to go. If he escaped with her, K.A. would die. If he stayed, they all would.

"I should have eliminated you when I had the chance, back in Eugene," Moth spat. "I should have done it. If I had only known you were Raphael's *bastard son —*"

Raphael Inman? Ondine's art teacher? Nix saw Morgan's eyes widen, but Bleek only snorted.

"Oh *boo hoo*. Saggy ass finally tell you his little sob story? Too bad for you, finding out so late. We were on Oprah last week. You know what, Moth?" He seethed, inching closer to Nix all the while. "You belong in Novala, with the fairies. Though," he paused and fake sighed. "It's going to be hard to explain how you lost the girl *and* the new changelings. And we both know you don't want to be eliminated. That's just devastating. Your body tortured; your consciousness synonymous with eternal pain. Your everlasting home a perpetual moat of despair." He sighed again. "Really shitty. *Literally.* Oh, what to do —"

Moth yelled this time.

"Do it, Nix! Do it!"

Neve's head followed Moth's and they were both staring at him, waiting. Neve, for the first time, seemed to recognize that it was Nix — her old friend Nix — standing in front of her, and the recognition made her whimper and her knees buckled so that he had to turn to catch her. He knew the shimmering too well now. Blood traced faded curlicues along the inside of her forearms and splattered onto her toes. Her hands were dirty. Dried clay caked her back. What had Bleek done?

Even K.A. was staring at him, waiting, though for what, he could not imagine. What did the boy think he was seeing? Bleek stepped forward again, more boldly now, still holding K.A. and the knife, as if he knew no one was going to stop him.

"You can do it, can't you?" Moth whispered loudly. "Can't you transfer the ring of fire?"

Nix seized. Could he? If what happened with Jacob was real, then he should be able to. Yet he knew there was something wrong with the equation. He couldn't just transfer Neve's fate. With Jacob it had been different. The old man punching him had made the girl choose a path that eventually led her here, to the tunnels. That was how the fire must have jumped. But this. This was different. Neve was still burning. He couldn't just transfer her fate without Bleek making a different decision, separately, inside himself that would eventually lead to his demise.

Yet Moth seemed convinced. There must have been something he knew that Nix didn't. What was Neve there for? Why did Bleek want her? And why had he . . . where was the blood from?

"I can't —" Nix whispered, staring. He was shaking his head, begging him with his eyes to reveal no more, but Moth, whether from fear or incomprehension, would not cease.

"But you have the gift," he continued, his voice screwed to a manic pitch. "You're the one. You're the ringer. Save her, Nix. Before it's too late —"

Bleek started laughing, his stiletto jogging against K.A.'s throat, his head thrown back in a sick imitation of delight. "Oh this is rich. Nix, the seer. The great oracle of his generation. And

I've got him by the balls." He turned and faced the ringer again. "Yes, please do. Please do engulf me in flames. That's what you see, right? A ring of light around someone doomed to die? Except, shit for brains —" He had taken the belt that had been used for Neve and tied K.A.'s wrists together. Just as quickly he was next to Nix, starting to unwrap the changeling's arms from his charge. Though Nix was clinging fiercely and Neve was struggling to get away, the fear of her ever-increasing fire sapped his will.

"You don't know the whole story. You don't know where it all started. Or when it might end. But I do. That's the whole reason I lured you down here in the first place. I don't want my little pumpkin to die . . . yet. That's why I need a ringer. For Nevie. And for what's inside her."

This time Bleek bent down to one of the chains and in one deft movement cuffed the confused, frozen Nix. Just as quickly, he grabbed Morgan's wrist beside him and did the same, though she managed to swipe a long-nailed hand across Bleek's face, drawing a few viscous pearls of what was left of his desiccated blood. He did not stop. Leaping across the wreckage to corner a caged Moth, Bleek continued to address Nix, his buzzing voice hovering in air around them as he bent down to pick up another chain.

"Everything's got to start somewhere. And thanks to Raphael," he sneered at Moth in the corner, still edging forward, "I know a little secret about Ondine. She's special, I hear. Has something the rest of us don't. I found out what it is and how to do it again. I'm going to do what every parent wants to do. Make myself, only better. I just need you, my friend, to get started. Neve isn't going to die. Well, not right now at least." He smiled evilly. "I *need* her. I think I almost *love* her." Bleek stopped at Neve and tipped the girl's chin up. She was sobbing. "She hasn't taken so well to being down here, but she needs to stay alive during this — *ahem* — procedure. And for a good while after. But I'm sure you can manage that, can't you? Huh, Neve?"

Morgan struggled against her shackles, whispering fiercely now. "He's making a ring. He's trying to inhabit Neve's baby. He's impregnated her. He'll kill her after he gets what he wants. That's why you see the fire. You have to stop him —"

"Shut up," Bleek hissed, and struck Morgan with the loose end of an iron. She moaned and fell, and K.A. lunged.

"Moth might have figured this whole thing out had he been an iota brighter." The cutter brandished the swinging weapon in front of him, and though Moth had been sidling toward him slowly all the while, Bleek spun the metal lasso and plucked him off the wall. In an instant he snapped Moth's cuff into place and pushed him back again. The changeling tripped and stumbled.

"But see, this was always the problem with us. He was just too stupid. But Nix . . ." Bleek paused and looked at Nix squarely. "Go ahead. Give it all you got. Just to let you know: she *is* going to die eventually, after I've gotten what I need from her. That's what happens to humans. Eventually they die. That's why we don't *really* love them."

"Neve!" K.A. yelled helplessly, and tried to pull his hands apart.

"Pick it up now, Neve. It's time."

It was the girl's face in response to Bleek's harangue that finally made up Nix's mind. Even in her state, she had understood something of what was happening to her, what she had been brought down there for. Her face crumpled and she swayed on her bandy legs. She was about to lose consciousness, he knew. She crumpled to the floor, exposing an already red-ringed wrist, as if accepting her fate. K.A. lurched toward her again.

Almost tenderly, Bleek lay her wrist in the last cuff and picked up the chain it was attached to, held it and tugged.

"That's a good girl. Nice and tight. We're not going anywhere till this is done."

Neve's light was exploding now in fervent sparkling bursts. Nix didn't have time to work out the implications of what Morgan had revealed to him, just that Neve had to stay alive no matter what. K.A. was still straining on his knees toward the girl, and Nix felt he had no other choice but to try to save her, even if it meant dying himself. He concentrated on Neve, on her sleepy dark brown eyes, closing now; and on Bleek, focusing every last bit of his energy on making the fire move . . . moving it to Bleek, who stood now, howling, his head thrown back in ecstasy, his knuckles white upon the chains now wielding the fire —

"Yes, yes! That's right. Open it up. Feed it. . . ."

Then Nix felt it: a current of burning, electric energy moving among them, along the metal chains all five of them were cuffed to, K.A. in the center, his eyes wide. His teeth rattled and his eyeballs felt as if they were about to burst. He smelled burnt hair and struggled to keep his eyes open, on Neve, who was a poisonous shade of white, her eyelids half open, teeth chattering, as the current entered her. She burned and then quelled, burned and quelled, as if fate itself couldn't decide which way to take her. The rest of them ignited in response. K.A., Morgan, Moth, Bleek — they all wore the ring now. Nix, too? He knew only one thing: they were all going to die. That's what the light meant. And Nix himself, his own power, had doomed them.

What had he released?

"Stop it, Nix!" Moth tried to pull away from the chains. "He's tricked us — it's what he wanted! The ring — I didn't know, Nix. . . . I didn't know. . . ."

"I've lost it. . . . It's beyond me. . . ." Nix was far away, as if in another room, hearing his own cries.

"Can't you . . ."

With the last coherent energy he had, Nix lunged at Neve through the violent stream that now linked all of them, through the chains, all of it channeling into her. Bleek stood laughing in the middle of the ring, his hands gripping the metal, unconcerned now with his captives.

"It's the ring!" Moth yelled. "He's inhabiting her! Stop him, Nix. Stop him!"

Nix's mind raced. *Inhabiting her. Nine months.* The exidis had to have an entrance, he realized. A beginning: a time when they were all changed. A moment when they ceased being simply human and became something more. Flesh and blood, electrified by the all-encompassing energy of the universe. Was that his gift, then? Not just to monitor the ring, but to complete it? Scenes from his own life flashed: Bettina's garden, silver water, a bird flying above. When did he himself go through the change? He remembered Daddy Saint-Michael, a boat, no land around for miles. *You are from the void,* his grandfather had said. *From nothingness.*

Could he still do something? Could he still try to swallow it? Trying to move the fire didn't work — it had only spread among them. But could he douse the fire? With himself? *Nix. From nothingness.* Could he do that?

He stepped through the ring to the other side and smelled burning hair and singed flesh: his own.

He lurched toward Morgan and Moth first, straining against his bonds and trying, with the force of his body, to dislodge them from their posts, free them from their chains and send them against the wall. He felt them burning under him, felt the melting of their lives into his: Morgan's memories, Moth's memories, his own. They were struggling underneath him, but they were still breathing. Was he?

"Give me your hand, Morgan."

Moth must have been unlocking her somehow. Nix heard Moth's garbled grunting. In his haze he could manage only a whisper:

"Go. Look for daylight."

He felt Bleek's heat against him, burning stronger now, and with an effort unlike any he'd ever expended, he willed the darkness in him to expand, just for a moment, just enough to protect the others. On the humming edge of reality he saw Moth weave toward K.A., and untie the boy's wrists.

"Neve!" Nix croaked. "You have to get her —"

He moved his head and saw Bleek's ecstatic, fiery glow. Then K.A., moving toward Neve, reaching for her hand. There was nothing Nix could do now. In trying to save Neve, he had lit the fuse for their collective energy. Nix was close to the edge. Death? Novala? He didn't know which.

It was what Bleek had wanted all along. To lure them here, use Nix's power — mysterious even to himself — then cast him aside. He wouldn't let him. Wherever he was going he would take Bleek with him. He only hoped the others could find their way out.

There was only one person who could help them now.

"Ondine," Nix whispered. "Cover us, Ondine."

It was all he remembered before collapsing.

CHAPTER 26

THEY HAD FELT LIKE HUMANS WHEN THEY GRABBED HER, but they were not. She could see that clearly now.

She had read the letter quickly before taking the drops, holding her breath as she had sat by the lake. Now the words burned in front of her eyes.

Dearest Ondine, I am your mother.

One sat in the front of the ambulance, driving. Three were in back with her: one monitoring the IV, another holding a knife pointed at the gurney she was strapped to. Out of the needle in her right arm curved a thin violet plastic tube, tinged with red, from the blood they were filling bag after bag with. The third just sat there and shook his knees, staring at her and laughing. Ondine closed her eyes and tried to remember.

You're different. In you runs both the pure cosmic energy of the fay and the blood of a human. You are alone of your kind.

"How much did he say he needed?" she heard the nervous

one ask. And another, an older-sounding one to her right, said, "As much as she's got."

She felt her body losing its strength. She tried to run through the details of what the leg-shaker had looked like when he had spoken to her outside the ambulance, before she had taken the eyedrops: wavy brownish-black graying hair, higher on the top than on the sides. Lean long arms. Red EMT jacket. Brown eyes. But she kept losing hold of the image in favor of what she had seen once he jumped in the ambulance after her, locking her in. Corkscrews of sinuous yellow-green radioactive light twisted near the surface of his sallow skin, turning him — and the rest of them — into not so much humans as skin sacs holding what looked like huge, muscular green glowworms. Their teeth were sharp and tiny, as if filed, and though Ondine had shut her eyes after they had first forced her, at knifepoint, to lie down on the gurney and accept the needle, she could smell their rotting flesh. They were going to suck her dry.

We are coherent structures of electrified plasma. Placeholders, basically. It has to do with the way structures are stacked in other dimensions. We ourselves are tesseracts. When the ring gets formed, "we" slowly disappear, leaving only the human shells behind. That's the exidis.

For a long time they had been parked. Now they were driving, and the potholes of whatever street or highway they were on made them jostle and bounce, and she could feel the needle jiggle sickeningly in her arm, and every so often Ondine winced as the jittery leg of the nervous one bumped against her. She willed herself not to respond. She was having a hard enough time maintaining consciousness, with all the blood they were taking, and quickly, too. This was bag number three. Or had she lost count?

The key is in your blood. Take the eyedrops and fight.

But she hadn't been able to fight, at least not yet. The creatures had gotten to her too quickly, and they were strong. She strained at the tethers on her ankles and wrists. She wondered if she'd even moved.

Think of a fish, as one of the humans' theoretical physicists has put it. You'd be dimly aware of a world "out there," but have no way to access it, no way even to think about it. Unless you were pulled from your medium, which of course is possible. But then you'd die. But you still wouldn't understand.

Ondine was trying to maintain hold but her mind kept skating out to the gray edges of consciousness, to the letter she had read too quickly, to her mother and father, to Viv and Nix, Morgan, Moth, Neve, K.A.

And Bleek, she remembered feverishly, who wanted to kill her.

Blood, she reminded herself. *The key is in my blood.* It was reddish violet, different from that of the creatures around her. When she had looked down at her skin, even after taking the eyedrops, her body had been different, too. Not glowing, more solid.

You're special. I got you early enough.

It had something to do with her blood, then. Was her power released when her blood was? But why did Bleek want it?

A butterfly flaps its wings. . . . Connected . . . Everything is connected.

She was . . . a changeling? The thought made her want to pass out, which she was close to doing. But here, now, in the back of a careening ambulance — how fast were they going? — Ondine did not want to lose consciousness. She could not take one more bag. She did not want to die.

She heard a voice. Dark, muffled, but present. In her bed, under the twisting green leaves of the Rousseau jungle so many weeks ago, she and a boy had become one. Fused. Now he was speaking to her, asking her for help.

Cover us, Ondine.

Cover us? Like in a game?

He carries a bit of Novala with him — everyone in his line does. He's there right now. Between the worlds. Can you meet him there? He can help you. It's called the breach, Ondine. Very few ringers survive the breach. . . .

"She's almost gone," the older one said. He tugged at the needle in her arm. "Should I disconnect her?"

"How many you got?"

"Three."

"Get one more. He said he wanted at least four."

470

What I've done is forbidden. They would eliminate both of us if they knew.

Ondine cracked an eye. Just a sliver — not enough for them to see the white. The older one, the gray-haired one, was extracting the needle from her forearm.

A butterfly flaps its wings.

She made a fist and squeezed.

"I can't get it out."

A hand on her jaw knocked at her chin.

"Let it go, little girl."

Ondine squeezed harder. She felt the cold terrible point of metal at her throat and in her arm and the stink of cutter breath on her face. She let her features sink into a stony stillness but kept her fists tight.

"I said let it go."

"I think she's going into shock." It was the brown-haired one, she deduced, who was leaning over her now, talking. Someone else must have held the knife. "I can't get the needle out with her fists like that."

"Take the straps off and jiggle it. She's not coming back."

"Aw, fuck. My coffee. You think the asshole could drive?"

For a moment the knife moved away from her neck while her captors rearranged themselves, starting to unbuckle the straps on her wrists. Ondine waited until she felt the last peg give on the left strap. She saw the brown-haired one bending over her.

The other with the knife was dealing with his coffee. Number three stood turned away by the IV.

She moved her left hand to her other arm, extracted the needle, and aimed for the brown-haired one's eye. Yellow fluid burst from the bulb, and just as he screamed, the other looked up from his spilled coffee and Ondine sat up, reached over herself with her left arm, and went again for the face. She missed his eye, but the hand holding the knife fumbled it and before the standing one had moved the IV aside and bent over the gurney to pin her down, Ondine had twisted out of the way and with her one free arm felt along the coffee-stained floor. She looped her fingers around the knife's handle, and just as the men pulled her back, she thrust it into a flaccid thigh. One screamed. The van lurched and screeched to a stop.

"What's going on back there?"

"I'll kill you," she breathed through tight lips, and dug the knife in a little more. "I'll sentence you to everlasting pain.

"Hold hands," she said. They hesitated. She pulled the knife out and lunged at the older one's shoulder, and he bent down in wincing pain.

"Hey!" again from the front, and the slamming of a door.

"I said hold hands. Don't fucking let go." And they did. "Now, you," Ondine said, wagging the knife recklessly at the third one, who had manned the IV. "Take the straps off." First the feet, then her right hand. Ondine was free.

She heard the driver knock along the side of the ambulance. For a moment everyone was silent, Ondine looking from face to face, the knife still held in front of her. In the split second their idiot attention skittered to the sound of the driver fumbling at the back door, Ondine was at the small window that separated front from back. She was the only one small enough to shimmy through, which she did with the wriggling speed of that little fish she'd seen in the park. But it was dead and she was . . .

Quickly she ducked into the front cab, locked the front doors, and put the car into drive, engaging the emergency brake. She was alive. Alive. Never before had she been so thankful she was petite. They were scrambling toward her. She could hear it. She scanned the dashboard and found what she was looking for. Just as a red-jacketed arm plunged through the small portal that separated front from back, the back door light illuminated and she stepped on the gas, hard, releasing the brake. The car bucked and lurched. She heard the gurney skid, something heavy fall, cries from behind.

She sliced her captor between his thickly webbed fingers straight to the bone and finally he let go.

Up a curb, she veered hard, right and left, till she heard the crunch of body against steel, and muffled cries.

Horns sounded. She tried to right herself, narrowly missing a car. She heard a last thud. The blood that still trickled from where she'd stabbed him had appeared fluorescent; now it was slowly darkening. Her vision was returning. The first wobbly sign she saw read LAKE FOREST, and she pulled off there, thinking the "lake" in the name sounded promising. She'd drive from there to Evanston, wherever that was.

The frothy tops of oaks and maples threw green lace reflections along the ambulance's windshield. She was weak, and getting dizzier by the minute. A vast shining openness greeted her and she took a right, hoping that this was the direction Evanston lay in. Her head was pounding and she was vaguely aware that she was weaving along the road as village after village coasted by. Highland Park, Glencoe, Kenilworth. *Cover us, Ondine.* She was surprised she'd been able to concentrate, with all the voices and sounds that were crowding her head: Morgan's raspy, insistent breathing. K.A.'s lumbering trudge. Running. Something else, a kind of high frequency hum. And under them all Nix, calling her. *Ondine,* he was saying over and over. *Cover me.*

"I'm here," she heard herself say aloud. She slowed the ambulance, transfixed by a bend in the boughs of a tree trailing the lake. A truck passed. Evanston Dodge, a nameplate read. What would they think, her parents? *I thought maybe I should finally give blood.* She rolled down the window. A light wind blew. *But no one has your blood, Ondine.* She sat still and looked at the breaking waves and the clear water and concentrated as hard as her spent body would allow.

I'm here.

She saw the lake as if from above: a giant hole in the earth puddled in glacial blue. It rocked, undulated, throwing up patterns as regular as a stone thrown in a pond. Then she saw all of them: caves, caverns, the holes in trees in the earth, graves, and closets, and trapdoors. Pockets and windows and all the places in the visible world that opened up, bordered the invisible one. The one she now knew she was a part of. Like latticework, ever-shifting, ever-moving, ever-opening. What was visible was just one thin sheet, pocked with holes, promising a gate, a thruway. Viv had told her she had the power to fold the worlds. But how? Could she tunnel through them, as Raphael had so long ago suggested? Could she meet Nix there, between the layers?

She shook one out and started folding.

"Nix," Ondine whispered, "show me what to do."

In her mind she flew to him. Over plains and mountains and patchworks of crops. Over the Rockies, violent in their strength, their sudden, jagged height. The vale of Eastern Oregon, its wheat-colored bulk, then green and blue, ringed in cones of fire. Explosive St. Helens, Hood, Rainier, Shasta, Denali, Cotopaxi, Popocatepetl, Kilauea, Fuji. Names that flooded back to her now, here, in the flattest landscape imaginable. All around the Pacific. Had she actually learned about them? In geography class? Or did she just know them, only now speaking them, like an incantation?

Hurry — hurry — hurry! — ring of fire —

Ring of fire! Spin round, ring of fire —

Leading straight to the burning center of the earth. The energy that kept the planet from dying. Her home. Portland. Her portal.

The tunnels.

Shake them open.

When Ondine reached 727 Emerson, she had nothing left. She lay down on the front porch, just a little after noon on a Friday in June. *The day after the solstice,* Ondine thought fuzzily as the world slipped away. How funny. She hoped her father would find her.

The End

HE COFFEE CUPS IN THE LIVING ROOM started rattling at 10:22 AM. Raphael Inman woke up at 10:21, confused. He had overslept. Had he had a bad dream? Dreams came so rarely to him these days. Even his imagination was starting to drain, like a reservoir with a hairline crack. When the shaking started — enough, even in Southeast, several miles from the epicenter, to move the alarm clock a few inches on the nightstand — he knew his old gift of seeing was still present, if dulled by the intervening years, like a language you learned as a child and never returned to. It almost made him happy, that something was left of his old self. So much had been lost.

The earthquake lasted a few seconds. For a moment Raphael panicked. Had he set the TiVo? He had. Before he got up to turn on the local news he lay in bed, feeling for aftershocks. There were none. The thing was finally at an end. He had been waiting for a sign and this was it.

He rose in his pajamas — now that his body was aging so

quickly, they almost suited him — and went to the living room, turning on Portland One and punching "record" out of habit. He was always using things he got on the news for his work.

His work. What a joke.

B.J. Rainer, the redheaded Internet porn actress who'd broken into newscasting, was reporting. When she'd first started, viewers had recognized the bubbly cub reporter as their favorite fetish model from sinpeaks.com, and a minor Portland scandal had ensued. It turned out to be good for ratings. Raphael caught her, in cargo pants and a faux military jacket, walking across the street from the television studios in the Pearl, the crew running behind her. The camera bounced, as did B.J.'s breasts.

"Why is it that disaster strikes on the sunniest days?"

She was staring into the camera, her yellow-flecked eyes surprisingly empathic.

"Thanks, Gil. I'm Bobbie Jeanne Rainer and I'm standing at the corner of First and Ash. An earthquake, six point five on the Richter scale, has struck downtown Portland, causing severe structural damage to several buildings."

The camera panned down First, along the Willamette. Raphael saw Danny's Bar. The pedestal-supported overhang crumbled onto the cobblestone street; the barred windows were broken.

The tunnels. Had Moth made it in?

Now Bobbie Jeanne walked backward, her bankable pout

and tousled just-got-out-of-bed auburn bob leading him straight toward an empty Burnside Bridge.

"The thing we're really worried about here is Portland's underground infrastructure. As we learned after the Spring Break Quake of ninety-three, the city of Portland is built on a drained riverbed. We're talking swamp. Do we have that graphic, Gil?"

A pseudoscientific picture of pale sand and wiggly arrows meant to suggest shaking, and the silhouette of a city, flashed on the screen.

"Which means that during an earthquake, the ground beneath downtown liquefies and turns to actual quicksand. As you can see behind me, the area is deserted. This report is uncorroborated, but people around here have told me that the legendary Shanghai Tunnels, the underground network of passageways that were this city's heritage from its rollicking nineteenth-century days of wine, women, and song, are gone. Collapsed, Gil. And we're waiting for information about whether there are any missing —"

"I've got a few names here." She unfolded a piece of paper she'd been holding and started to read from it. "Twenty-two-year-old Timothy Bleeker of Eugene; fifty-four-year-old David Prouty of Seattle; and eighteen-year-old Nicholas Saint-Michael, recently relocated to Portland from Sitka, Alaska. If anyone has any information on these three persons' whereabouts, please call the number listed at the bottom of your screen. Can we get pictures with that?"

Raphael sat down and held his head in his hands. Tim. His son Tim was dead. He had condemned him, led him to quicksand, just as the old stories foretold. And he had caused, indirectly, another to die, Nicholas Saint-Michael. And poor David Prouty, whomever that was.

But no mention of Ondine.

B.J. turned again to face the camera.

"Just to recap: There's been an earthquake in Portland, six point five on the Richter scale. No aftershocks have been reported, and we're coming to you live from downtown, on the river, the epicenter of this temblor —"

He turned and clicked mute.

They'd be gone. The Shanghai Tunnels would be gone. Which meant that one vital avenue for the cutters to steal humans and deliver dust would be destroyed. At least she had accomplished that.

And here is where he stopped. Rewound. Stopped again.

There. Just there.

A scene he thought he'd caught out of the corner of his eye a moment earlier, just as the shot was switching to Gil Farnsworth. Danny's Bar, all bulging glass and concrete, the bridge in the distance. And someone, a lone shadowy figure, just small enough to be unrecognizable, head turned, walking away. The figure was hunched; he could not tell the color of the hair. It was nothing more than a scribble at the edge of the screen.

He could not help but hope it was his son.

Raphael could see it, yes, but he'd never be able to make what he saw real. Never again be able to transform the imaginative into the actual. He'd had a chance to do that and had turned it down. He'd been too much of a coward. What they had done — its power was so awesome, its effects so massive. It both awed and silenced him.

One by one he started to transfer the files he'd recorded from the earthquake. They took a while to download, though that was fine. He needed them to gestate, sink in.

Work that. There. Go deeper.

With that he resumed his attention to his latest masterpiece.

෨ ෨ ෨

It was Viv, after all, who finally met Moth, though he chose a river, not a wood.

They met at Astoria, where the Columbia empties into the Pacific. The sand is wide there, and the mouth of the river thick with forest. On an afternoon in late summer, the sun is close to the horizon already, and everything looks as if it has been dunked in honey.

They walked a pace or two apart, Viv on the side of the sea.

"I want to stay a little longer. I want to stay with Ondine."

At these last words the black-haired woman stopped and

looked out to the ocean. Moth, earnest, his green eyes intent, stared after her. Perhaps he should have been more humble. Perhaps, he thought, he should have hidden his desire more. But he couldn't. He wasn't that person anymore.

"I know it's . . . unusual. But if she's training to take your place, shouldn't she have a protector? Shouldn't someone be here to help her?" He took a deep breath. He'd thought it out beforehand, prepared it even, but only now did he feel he had to use it — something so personal.

"*He* did it," Moth whispered. "Had you not been here, he wouldn't have chosen to stay. Maybe he would have returned."

The allusion to Raphael must have pained her, but she did not show it, only blinked once. Moth silenced. He had said too much. Yet he had to stay. He had committed himself, yes, but differently. He wanted to continue his training here, near Ondine. Now that he knew what he was capable of, there was nothing that they couldn't accomplish, together. Especially now. Now that Nix was —

Moth didn't quite know where Nix was.

"Nix has disappeared. He is either dead or in the —"

Viv turned her head and eyed the changeling narrowly.

"Watch yourself, young Moth. Nix is more powerful than you will ever be — than you can even imagine. If, indeed, the ringer's corpus has perished, we will soon know. And —" The look on her face was colder than he had ever seen it. He immediately

482

regretted his words. "If he is in the breach, he must find his way out. A changeling cannot stay there long. You know that. You speak as if you wouldn't be sorry if you lost the greatest gift your generation has. You stupid creature. Do you think another one will just appear for you? Or perhaps that you yourself might learn the secrets of the ring? You cannot. The ringer is different from us. The ringer is more precious than any."

"Except Ondine," Moth whispered and looked at the sand beneath his feet. And at the waves a little farther out, rushing in, pulling out. Rushing in —

"You do not know what you are saying."

After a certain length of time, Viv pulled her eyes from the ocean and trained them on Moth's. She did not smile, but her expression was not without empathy. Wisdom shone from the stern opacity.

"Raphael made his choice just as we all have had to. Just as you have to." She looked hard at the boy. "As you have already. You have begun your journey, Moth. It started in the tunnels, just as you told me. You must undertake the exidis soon. You must not overstay in your corpus."

She opened her palm. "Let me see your sign."

Moth remembered the first time he'd seen one: the sign of the uninhabited. The tattoos they got when they were initiated would change then, just as their fay energy was leaving the body. Their tiny blue X, tattooed with special ink, would be circled and crossed, and colored in. It signaled fission had occurred; the body was no longer inhabited. He had seen one only once, in passing, in Seattle. He was forbidden to speak to the man, well into his fifties, but he looked at him for signs of knowing. Nothing. He was in a business suit — crisp, pressed shirt and slicked-back hair. They were not allowed to look at them too long, much less speak to them or in any way show them their sign. To them it was a relic of a wild forgotten youth, a different time. Seeing another's could trigger a memory, Viv had explained. So Moth had glanced once and walked on.

She frowned when he rolled back the cuff of his long-sleeved T-shirt. His had been half activated by the ringing in the tunnels, smudged now, as if the X were spinning. He knew as much but had not wanted to tell her.

"You must return," she said.

He nodded, but kept his eyes down.

"There won't be a ring till fall. You have the rest of the summer if you want it."

He nodded again.

He needed the time.

∽ ∽ ∽

THEY MET ONCE MORE AT THE TUNNELS TO SEAL THEM OFF. This time it was just Moth and Morgan, though Ondine had called.

She was coming back, but not till September. Moth said he would wait. They worked slowly, at night, Morgan passing Moth buckets of water in which to mix the cement and Moth paving cinder block after cinder block, checking the level by flashlight, just like he was taught to do the summer he worked construction out on Lopez Island. They couldn't get very far past the Burnside Bridge door — the earthquake had taken care of mostly everything — but Moth wanted to make sure the tunnels were gone for good, and though they had never found the cutter's body — or Nix's — whatever leaked out of Bleek he wanted to shut in forever. Morgan, too.

They'd bought fluorescent orange paint to keep out whoever might be poking around, but when Morgan dipped her brush in, she stopped and looked up, the flashlight's reflection lighting up Moth's clean-shaven face.

"Do we just write 'Keep Out' or what?"

Moth looked at her hard. He had just gotten used to trusting the girl again. He walked over and dipped his own brush in the can.

"No, that won't be enough. We need something that will last. Something everyone can understand — even if they don't speak English. A symbol."

"An X?" Morgan shrugged. She wanted to get out. She remembered too much.

"Something like that," he whispered, and once more stepped

over to the concrete wall. He traced a large X, a mirror of what Morgan would soon wear on her wrist, dipping his brush again in the canister to encircle it. Then he drew a line through the X's center so that the lines formed six pieces of pie. He daubed a slash in the wedge on the right and the left, and one on the bottom, till it became a more defined sketch of the universal symbol of Don't go in there, Don't touch this, Stay the hell away.

Morgan held her brush up as if to start but stopped, the bristles curving against the wall. A drop of orange began its slow descent and her eyes followed it.

"Where do you think he is?" she said softly.

"He'll come back," Moth replied, though his voice did not sound certain.

"Just fill those in," he said, kindlier this time, and Morgan did, working carefully, as she always did, to not go over the lines.

∽ ∽ ∽

Everywhere he looked, the only thing he could see was water. Ocean blue-gray and misty at its brim, or slick as oil, or coming at him in dark swells twenty, thirty feet high. They crashed over the edge of the boat he was on; if it was a boat, though the creaking black hull and the clanking made it sound like one, and the weaving and bobbing on the skin of the sea made it feel like one, and in the salt tang of the wind he could smell one. There did not seem to be a captain, and Nix himself was the boat's only crew. He did not know where he was heading, only that it was somewhere, for the boat was moving, and he on it. What felt like days passed . . . or were those months? Or years? Sometimes the sun came out and turned everything a brilliant, jewel-like blue. He did not eat; he drank the rainwater that collected in tiny puddles on the deck, reflecting the sky. He looked at the stars at night and they seemed to look back at him. He waited for he knew not what. Every day he woke to the line of the horizon encircling him and looked for land.

∽ ∽ ∽

How do you end a fairy tale that has no ending?

In a house at the edge of a forest in Southeast, a girl eats pancakes with her brother. She doesn't sleepwalk anymore, and they don't talk about what happened in the tunnels, though some late summer nights, when the moon is out and the sky is black, she hears a whispering. *Morgana.*

Another girl plays Scrabble with her father and mother and brother on a firefly-lit front porch, just outside of Chicago. She loves the fireflies, though their color reminds her of them. She knows she will go back once fall arrives, but for now, everything can wait.

A father and his daughter sit on their terrace in the Portland hills at noon: she in a string bikini, he in tattered cargo shorts. They listen to music and sip ice teas. The daughter reads a magazine and doesn't speak about the fluttering inside of her. Her father doesn't ask.

A man who used to be called James waits.

And somewhere on a sea, a sea like none he's ever seen, on a boat with no captain at the edge of the world, a young man is sailing north, home.

To Cindy Eagan (wow!) and your contagiously energetic team at Little, Brown Books for Young Readers — Phoebe Sorkin, Kate Sullivan, Connie Hsu, Kerry Johnson, Christine Cuccio, Tracy Shaw, Gail Doobinin, and Elizabeth Eulberg — sincerest thanks. I am proud to be in your company. To Richard Abate, Kate Lee, Dale Peck, Calvin Baker, and James Gregorio, gratitude going on three years. Ausgeseichnet! to Raphael Hartmann for being my first reader, and tausend danke to Jana Fay Ragsdale for her PDX knowledge and intrinsically cool ways. For my sisters, especially Lauren, who spun out the mystery, and to K.B.M., who inspired its contours. Thank you, Danny and Elizabeth, for your Buffy-derived wisdom, Susan Muñoz for title wizardry, and grazie Davie G., for all those French fries at Westville . . . Thomas, for your suspension of disbelief, muscular optimism (!), and for making breakfast.

This book is dedicated to my father, Kirk Brayton Smith, who introduced me to Oz.

BETWIXT

INTERVIEW WITH
TARA BRAY SMITH

How did you first come up with the idea for *Betwixt*?

My favorite books when I was a kid took place not really in this world, and not in a total fantasy world, as in Harry Potter or the Lord of the Rings, but in a place that is somewhere in between—like Narnia or Oz. *The Lion, the Witch, and the Wardrobe* told the story of real children, transported to a magical place that was just on the other side of that strange closet. In Oz, Dorothy really lives in Kansas. I liked the idea of there being an alternate current that hums and crackles just at the edge of our visible world. Now I realize it is a metaphor for the sometimes confused and ill-at-ease way we feel in our (often humdrum) lives, but as a child I thought of it more realistically: if you enter that forest, you'll go somewhere else. Somewhere exciting. I liked that. Perhaps immediately transported back in time, as was the case in a book by one of my favorite authors, Zilpha Keatley Snyder, who wrote about ESP, a possessed cat named Worm, and, in a book I remember vaguely, a

holler somewhere in Appalachia, where children would immediately be taken to a Native American village of long ago. I can't remember the plot exactly, but I remember the tone: eerie. Not scary exactly, but definitely strange. *Witch of Blackbird Pond* had that feeling too.

So we have a place, a not-here, not-there world somewhere in between, and the kinds of characters who would most easily move in and out of that world were changelings, another fascination of mine held over from childhood. Changelings were fairy creatures traded at birth with real children, with odd powers and a seeming lack of human empathy. So in one of these tales you'd have a friend who was sort of strange, had weird eyes, and talked differently than your other friends, and you could imagine she or he was a changeling. I thought this was an interesting character problem: what if you were one of these creatures? And how could the mythology be adapted to explore and understand some of the concerns of our contemporary world?

BETWIXT

What inspired you to write the complex interwoven realities of the humans and the fay in the novel?

I started writing about a group of real kids in a place I like, Portland, Oregon, and realized that I couldn't just replay old fairy mythology in a contemporary setting—that has been done so many times, and I am more drawn to stories that are somewhat far out: if you've read the Oz books, that's what I mean. Tik-Tok? That was a weird character, straight from the particular imagination of Frank L. Baum. So as the story started getting more and more complex, and the reasons and realities of these kids began showing themselves independently from any standard "fairy tale" plot structures, the more I started plunging into the mysteries of what I actually wonder about. I grew up in a place where I was surrounded by the natural world: stars, ocean, forests, plants. I think about these things—what is out there? Are we it? What is body . . . what is mind? And I know I've been thinking of these things since I was a kid, so other kids must be thinking about them too.

Betwixt combines elements of suspense, fantasy, and romance. Did you begin the novel with all of these overlapping themes in mind, or did one element start out stronger than others?

I started the book with the premise that I was writing about a group of kids—friends, enemies, lovers—who "feel different." It's a classic adolescent and young adult trope, because you are different then: a creature neither adult nor child, with all the freedom of being older but with a different level of responsibility. It is a chilling, beautiful, important time, and it gets lumped in with this whole idea of being "a teenager," which I always found to be a lifeless and enforced category. Alexander the Great died when he was in his twenties; most of human history, our romances and our tragedies, are about people who aren't much older, and sometimes younger (as in the case of Romeo and Juliet) than the characters in this book. So Ondine, Morgan, Nix, and Moth were people who were trying to understand who they were, and what the world was, not a very different task from any person who is growing up. The difference is that they are on an edge: they are straddling worlds. So all the genres: fantasy, romance, suspense, come out of this teetering position—the place from which most drama springs.

The narrative jumps back and forth between several characters. Was it difficult to keep track of everything as you were writing, or did you always have a clear idea of the plot's progression?

I decided to write from several limited third-person points of view because this is a group tale: no one character dominates. Somehow I felt this was in keeping with the tone of the book; this is not a traditional hero's journey, where one person stands in as Everyman. Betwixt is more the story of a group: each character has his or her own path, and those paths I hope delineate some of the various experiences young people have today. If I had a clear idea of the plot's progression I would probably stop writing. How boring! I had an outline, but you also want to surprise yourself, as a writer. Ondine and Nix, Morgan, Moth, K.A.—I had characters, and some of the problems of the book I pulled in because I wanted to wrestle with a few of the structures of old-fashioned fairy tales and fay mythology. But their questions, and their quests, come from them, from people I know, from history, and imagination, and from me, all mixed together to create something new.

Did the developments of the plot/characters in *Betwixt* take you by surprise, or did you know where the story was going as soon as you started writing?

They most definitely took me by surprise. I knew I wanted some standard mythological structure to the book: so the names of the characters and some of the character arcs are based on fay lore. But as I wrote, and as the world started to unfold with its own complications and desires, the lineaments of the plot had to deepen and expand also. That's where some of the science fiction elements of the story come in.

Why did you choose Portland as the setting? The story has such a strong sense of place that it seems you must know the city very well.

I lived in Portland fifteen years ago, when I first graduated from college. I was really in love with the city. I was young and curious and so my boyfriend at the time and I roamed a lot: hiking and driving and camping and walking. We were poor, we were "youths." I took buses everywhere; I explored. The light in that place is very peculiar—almost green in the summer. It's a beautiful place, the Pacific Northwest. Part of me wishes I could have stayed there; that's probably why I revisited it in fiction.

You were born and raised in Hawaii and currently live in Germany. How did these experiences in different cultures/locations influence your writing?

The difference between where I was born and where I've lived since has been so acute that it provides an interesting problem for my writing. People immigrate all over the globe, as they've done in the past, but now it can be done at speeds that bring with them a sense of immediate displacement. On Friday this week, I woke up in Düsseldorf. On Saturday, I was in Honolulu. We take these kinds of movements for granted, but it does mess with your head, and tends to make physical reality seem somehow less solid, more "virtual," to use an overused word. I'm exploring those emotions—of displacement, of location, of movement in and out—in *Betwixt*.

BETWIXT
DISCUSSION QUESTIONS

What do you think is the significance of the characters' names?

Ondine, Morgan, and Nix seem to have unique abilities related to their fay nature. What is the relationship between each character's supernatural powers and their personalities?

The three main characters have very different reactions to the revelation of their true identity. What would your reaction be if you were in their place?

The drug "dust" features heavily in the story. If dust were really available, what do you think its affect would be on society?

How did your opinion of Moth change as you learned more about his character?

Morgan says that she is not capable of loving someone—do you agree?

What do you think is the significance of the word "ring" given how it is used to describe different things in the story?

From all that the story reveals about the fay and changelings, do you think they are beneficial at all to humans, or is their relationship only damaging?

Which path do you think Morgan will choose? Or do you think she is already on her way to being good or evil?

What do you think Bleek's ultimate goal was? Did he achieve this goal by the book's end?

Get ready to
obsessorize
over the next
POSEUR
novel.

Keep your eye out for
the third book in this
juicy new series,
Petty in Pink,
coming July 2009.

POSEUR

The Good, the Fab
and the Ugly

Available now

Being a celebrity princess isn't always a fairy tale.

SECRETS OF MY HOLLYWOOD LIFE
FAMILY AFFAIRS

After ten seasons of filming the hit TV show *Family Affair*, Kaitlin thought that she could see any curveball coming. But with a plotting new actress on set, all bets are off. Can Kaitlin keep her sane boyfriend, her insane job, and her composure in the face of this new star power?

And don't miss
SECRETS OF MY HOLLYWOOD LIFE

and

SECRETS OF MY HOLLYWOOD LIFE
on location

available in paperback!

FOUR BEST FRIENDS. FOUR DIFFERENT PATHS.
ONE YEAR DESTINED TO CHANGE EVERYTHING.

FOOTFREE AND FANCYLOOSE

A novel by Elizabeth Craft and Sarah Fain

Becca, Kate, Harper, and Sophie all have dreams just within their reach in the funny and compelling sequel to the acclaimed *Bass Ackwards and Belly Up*.

And don't miss
BASS ACKWARDS AND BELLY UP
now available in paperback!

Welcome to Poppy.

A poppy is a beautiful blooming red flower
(like the one on the spine of this book). It is also
the name of the new home of your favorite series.

Poppy takes the real world and makes it
a little funnier, a little more fabulous.

Poppy novels are wild, witty, and inspiring.
They were written just for you.

So sit back, get comfy, and pick a Poppy.

poppy

www.pickapoppy.com